PRAISE

"Spencer's fiction debut . . . features a straightforward detective plot that's enriched and deepened by touching on issues of class, race, and gender. An engaging police procedural with a little something extra."

—*Kirkus Reviews*

"Dark, gritty, tense, atmospheric. I loved *Black River*."

—Candice Fox, #1 *New York Times* bestselling author

"Sharply plotted and relentlessly paced, it kept me guessing until the last page."

—Michael Robotham, *New York Times* bestselling author of *When You Are Mine*

"A meticulous thriller with a cast of stand-out characters and an intriguing setting. I could not stop reading it."

—Sarah Bailey, author of *The Dark Lake*

"Propulsive and intricate. A crime thriller that is absolutely not to be missed."

—Hayley Scrivenor, author of *Dirt Town*

"*Black River* hooked me and wouldn't let me go. You're going to want to read this one with all the lights on."

—Tim Ayliffe, author of *The Enemy Within*

BROKE ROAD

OTHER TITLES BY MATTHEW SPENCER

Black River

BROKE ROAD

MATTHEW SPENCER

THOMAS & MERCER

Text copyright © 2025 by Matthew Spencer
All rights reserved.

Published by Thomas & Mercer, Seattle

www.apub.com

Amazon, the Amazon logo, and Thomas & Mercer are trademarks of Amazon.com, Inc., or its affiliates.

EU product safety contact:
Amazon Media EU S. à r.l.
38, avenue John F. Kennedy, L-1855 Luxembourg
amazonpublishing-gpsr@amazon.com

ISBN-13: 9781662512537 (paperback)
ISBN-13: 9781662512544 (digital)

Cover design by Jarrod Taylor
Cover image: © Nico Herma / plainpicture

Printed in the United States of America

To Brenda

1

The thrum of the phone woke Rose Riley in her bed, and she clocked the time as she answered: 11:09 p.m.

The mobile allowed O'Neil through on Do Not Disturb. "Sorry, we're sending one out." His voice tight, a herald of disorder. "Better pack a bag."

Riley swallowed, mouth gluey, white wine, and swung her feet to the floor. Her fingers, cupped on her brow, nursed solid pain—a hot arc of resentment, insomniac self-pity. Fucking duty roster, taking years off her life. Yep, Homicide was killing her.

O'Neil gave her a moment to surface. Three days into a week of on call, and Riley had guessed she wouldn't get away free. It was a big state, from Goodooga to Moruya, and somewhere, someone was going to get killed. And O'Neil would send her out to look.

She went to clear her throat, a reflex that escalated, sending her hawking and hacking for the glass of water on the bedside table.

"Tourist trap in the Hunter," O'Neil said phlegmatically as the racket died down. "Female, twenty-seven. Half-naked on the floor. Husband called it at triple zero. He's there with an alibi."

Riley dug grit from an eye and put him on speaker as she walked to the kitchen.

"It's snaked through the channels," he was saying. "The uniform inspector at Muswellbrook, the Super at Cessnock—half the district's awake."

Riley picked up her pen by her notebook on the counter.

"Place called Red Creek," O'Neil said. "Flyspeck, round Pokolbin. You know it?"

She knew it. Maybe fifteen kays out of Cessnock. It wasn't even a village, just a few buildings on a back road in the vineyards. She hadn't been through it for years. She traced the route in her head.

"Close to home?" O'Neil said.

"Yeah." Sort of. Her family was from a little north, just up the valley. They'd sold and moved when Riley was eleven. She found a fresh page in her book. O'Neil had said *tourist trap*. "Victim in a house, or what?"

"Town house, I'm hearing. In a row of six, just been built. Airbnbs, mostly. But the victim owns, with the husband." O'Neil read out an address and Riley wrote it down.

"So she's in her own home?" she said.

"Mm. It's preliminary. Local detectives are there."

"Crime Scene?"

"Cessnock. Beth Gatjens."

Riley pressed buttons on her red Nespresso and slotted in a pod.

"The doc's en route," O'Neil said. "Newcastle, Cranky Frank Powell. You get going. I'll wake Priya."

"Wait." Riley went to the fridge. The dead woman could be anything—aneurysm, accident, addict. Triple A. Sleep was precious, there was no need to wake Priya.

O'Neil was reading her mind—a simple task as her brain waited for caffeine. "Cessnock's a shit show, and you know it," he said. "I don't want you up there on your own."

"I'm not on my own. You just said half the district's awake. I can be there in ninety, take a look—if it's ours, I'll call Priya."

O'Neil grunted, an equivocal noise she knew well. Yeah, nah. He was going to wake Priya. "Go," he said.

Riley hung up. She ejected the pod and inserted another, watching the second shot hiss into the glass. She topped it off with cold milk and gulped it on her way to the bathroom. She'd showered two hours ago, before bed. She splashed her face and brushed her teeth, eyes staring over black smudges as she rubbed in moisturizer, rolled on deodorant, and tied back her hair.

The coffee kicked in and she moved with composure. Gatjens would maintain the scene. Riley took two Panadol for lack of sleep and drank water, swept toiletries into her wash bag, and dressed. Stretch black trousers, a long-sleeve gray T-shirt, dark fleece. Frank Powell was a good pathologist if you knew how to play him. She pulled out her small suitcase and packed for four days. *Make it five.* Laptop, chargers, notebook. She trod into her sneakers, clipped on her Glock, and opened the door. She had put the garbage out earlier. Milk in the fridge . . . Fuck it.

She went down the communal stairwell and over to the car. It was clear out and cold: late winter, late August. Late Monday—the streets were quiet as she went around the block and made an illegal right onto Victoria Road. The western edge of the city glowed, a tall slab, as she crossed the bridges. There was no traffic, and she needed a servo, so she took the ramp at Artarmon and flashed her lights up the highway, pulling in at Turramurra for fuel and supplies: iced coffee, Chokito, water, gum.

On the M1, she pressed shuffle on her playlist and sat at 160, blasting past the Highway Patrol tucked in at the dip on the river at Mooney Mooney. The Pnau remix came on and Riley turned it up loud. Something in the chorus summoned her mother, and the hairs on Riley's arm stood on end.

At Ourimbah, the music cut out as the phone rang. Priya Patel. Riley thumbed the button on the wheel.

"Hi," Patel said in a tone that said, *Bugger it.*

"Yeah." Riley checked her blind spot and moved out to take a line of three semis. "I'll look, if you want. Might be a long trip for an overdose."

Patel yawned. "That's what O'Neil said you'd say."

"But?"

"He thinks we might be there awhile."

Riley felt the wind blast from the trucks. Something was up. O'Neil had worked the phone before waking them, speaking to the detectives on scene and the State Crime Command.

"He wanted to come," Patel said. "That ain't gonna happen."

O'Neil wasn't coming to the Hunter Valley, whatever his instincts. He'd inherited a mess in Killara that had been botched from the start. The Chatswood cops had taken three weeks to call Homicide, and now it was O'Neil's to clean up.

"Where are you?" Patel said.

Riley merged. "Kangy Angy."

"I'm getting going. See you there."

The music came back as Patel hung up. Riley cracked the iced coffee, sipped, arched her spine. Adam Bowman had given her the red Nespresso machine to wean her off the sweetened service-station caffeine—but it hadn't worked, she just double-dipped and drank both.

Bowman had appeared at her door with a box, and she'd watched as he assembled the coffee maker in her kitchen. He'd stood back and admired the gift. "You'll think of me every morning," he'd said.

He'd been pretty right. And a hopeful lament in the way he'd said it had struck a chord with her too. She'd felt it before he said it—his fitting the little black plastic trays to the machine and plugging it into the wall had sent a charge deep through her as well.

You couldn't take your eyes off Bowman for a second—well, not off his words.

Riley had been slow to learn this. How long had she known him? Two and a half years, give or take—she'd met him the day after she'd first seen Patel. Riley and O'Neil had been working a triple murder, and O'Neil had seconded Patel into the investigation from Parramatta. She'd never gone back, she was Homicide now. Bowman was a reporter, covering the case for his newspaper, and Riley had brought him into the tent and used him to her advantage. He'd done well out of the arrangement—he had written a bestselling book on the case and was driving an Audi.

That was another gift he'd given her, unannounced, at her door: a signed copy of his book, inscribed with kind words and with a letter in an envelope between the hard covers. After he'd gone, Riley read the letter, a lump rising in her throat, and had to rinse her face at the sink. She soon read the letter three more times, but for a while she left the book on her shelf. She knew the story, she'd lived it and given it to Bowman, complete access to the police file.

The book caused a media stir and put a target on her back at work—envy at her public profile was twisted into disapproval and spat back at her by her superiors. Riley rode it out, with O'Neil's support. But she detected other currents around the book too: quieter, more considered comments from junior officers, colleagues in the squad, old friends, one of her two sisters-in-law. Her mother.

One afternoon, bored at the start of four days off after a week of on call, Riley had opened the book to have a skim. She'd finished it twenty hours later, rolling over in bed to digest it. The next day, she had read it again.

South of Newcastle, Riley cut left off the motorway, into the sticks. She swerved to avoid roadkill, a big roo and a few crows. She was on the fringes now, thin armies of eucalypts in the headlights, the odd clapboard settlement scattered on either side of the road.

Cessnock was sleeping in tendrils of valley fog. She came in on streets lined with weatherboards—coal miners' cottages: three kids to a room, one bath, black swans sculpted from car tires in the yard. V8s in driveways, truck cabs on curbs, utes on the grass. A proud building filled a corner, Cessnock High. Under the sulfur glow of a streetlight, two youths in hoodies on push-bikes watched her go past. 12:49 a.m. Right onto Vincent Street, and it felt battened down. She took the dogleg on

Wollombi and knew the police station was behind her. In the shadow of Maitland and Newcastle, Cessnock was unevenly resourced—there was no major hospital, but the prison had an exclusive wing for sex offenders, and the cop shop was state of the art.

A car wash, a pizza place, Macca's, Oporto, auto parts. She cleared the town and followed the road north, past the airfield, crossing into wine country. The first marker was the Rydges, a four-hundred-room resort with a golf course. Riley went left on Broke Road, and her headlights picked up the signs: cellar doors, restaurants, wedding venues, a fudge factory, breweries, function centers, Teas & Jams, a petting farm. She went through the big roundabouts at the heart of the tourist area and headed west.

After a few kilometers, she saw a patrol car backed into a side road. Riley made the turn, pulled up, and lowered her window. A constable in the driver's seat pointed over his shoulder with his thumb. "First right, then right and right again," he said. "You'll see it."

"You taking plates?" Riley said.

The constable nodded. He was a kid, maybe twenty-one, with a wide-open country face. Riley held his eye a moment: a sentry, her first taste of his tribe. There was a dynamic with local cops. Homicide was housed at Parramatta, so on a murder, in the regions, Riley was a city detective who'd been sent out.

"Go easy," he said. "There's unsealed road."

She drove on, flicked to high beam. The constable's directions matched the map on the dash. After the first turn she was on dirt, then back on narrow bitumen, her lights strafing grassland interspersed with sections planted to vine. She slowed at a sign that said Red Creek, and rolled up to a couple of buildings on a crossroad. Riley had a memory of an old sandstone pub close by, but she couldn't see it as she idled. There was a takeaway on the left corner of the intersection as Riley turned right past a café and drove fifty meters down the road and right again onto a gravel drive filled with vehicles flashing red and blue lights.

She took it in as she parked. A strip of six town houses alone in the scree. The uniforms had it taped off, a couple of neighbors in dressing gowns on the sidelines, already a reporter—print, no TV. No command post established. An ambulance, a police minibus, a black Land Cruiser, four patrol cars, unmarked Sorentos, two Crime Scene vans, a Mercedes-AMG Coupé. Shoe and Tire officers in white Tyvek were hunched on the shoulder.

1:11 a.m. Riley unwrapped the gum and took a piece as she reached for the glove box. Things ran better with a name badge, especially out here.

She closed the door of the Holden and walked slowly. The entrance to each property was privacy-fenced. A local detective stood at the second gate, on his phone. Cessnock, Riley guessed, maybe Singleton. He watched her approach.

His eyes scanned her light-blue sergeant's badge, and he hung up. "Rodrigues," he said. "That was fast."

Riley looked down the path. Modern, stone and dark wood, two stories, a neat little yard. An open front door. "Who's been in?"

"Uniforms, ambos, then us," Rodrigues said. "Now only forensics. The doc just turned up."

Good. Riley chewed.

Rodrigues tossed his head with black parted hair. "We've been door to door. Only one other's occupied. Plus the pub." He pointed forty-five degrees from the crossroad. "Through there. And the café." His arm swept back over her shoulder. "Café owners live upstairs."

The café was a wooden terrace with a veranda at the crossroad. Riley had seen lights on the second floor.

"The pub was closed when we got there," Rodrigues said. "A staff member was cleaning up. Branxton girl, nineteen. My guys are speaking to her, find out who was in. There's CCTV at the bar."

"Thanks," Riley said. "The car park too—at the pub. Check for cameras. We want regos. I saw your perimeter."

He made a note. In the cordon, the rear of the ambulance was open, with a man sitting on a stretcher, talking to a uniformed liaison standing at the doors.

"That the husband?" Riley said.

Rodrigues didn't look up. "Yeah."

"You got his version?"

"Worked late with his boss, at the office in Maitland." He turned pages. "Some sort of mining geologist. Got home about ten thirty."

"Name?"

Rodrigues leafed. "Nigel Armytage. Victim is Penelope."

"Armytage?"

"What?"

"The wife—has the same surname?"

"Oh." Rodrigues squinted at the page. "Yeah."

Riley surveyed the row of town houses. A new build—the turfing and landscaping and the gravel drive had not yet settled into place. "They local?"

"Nah. Came up after the pandemic, rented a place out towards Broke. Usual story. Decided to stay. They bought this off the plan. Moved in in June."

Riley went back and popped the trunk of the Calais. Rodrigues followed and waited as she shrugged into a bunny suit. There were a lot of deadshit detectives, but this one . . . maybe not.

They walked back to the gate. June: the couple had lived there two months. Riley tucked her notebook under an arm to put on gloves and booties. "Keep the husband here while I go in," she said.

Rodrigues nodded and she walked up the path. A uniformed constable logged her on to the scene.

The town house was silent. There were rooms on either side of the front door. A home office to the left, tidy. Flowers in a vase on the desk, colored glass bowls in a row. A big framed black-and-white photograph on the wall, a woman in the nude, soft focus . . . try-hard avant-garde. Riley pulled up the blinds. The windows were locked open an inch and intact.

She crossed to the second room. A double bed covered in a damask quilt, built-in wardrobes, a chair, a wicker basket with scented soaps. It didn't feel lived in—a spare room for guests. The windows were closed and secure.

In the hall, a staircase ran up to a second floor and down to a space belowground. She went down. A laundry with a fridge and a toilet. She opened the fridge—beer, white wine, soft drinks, an unopened liter of Lite milk. Next door was a carpeted room with couches and a big TV on the wall. That was it. No external exit.

Riley climbed back to the ground floor and went down the hall. An open-plan living room and kitchen spanned the width of the house. At the end, glass doors led to a rear deck and into the night.

Two forensic investigators and a fingerprint tech worked the room. A kitchen counter cut the space in half, and on the far side a police light on a tripod shone down.

Riley trod carefully. Behind the counter, two figures in Tyvek squatted over the body of a woman lying on her front on the floor.

The forensic pathologist, Frank Powell, sensed Riley and peered up. "Look what the cat dragged in."

She ignored him and nodded at the second person. "Beth," she said.

Crime Scene Sergeant Beth Gatjens rocked back on her heels. "Hey, Rose. Been a while."

Riley's eyes moved over the body. Long, thin tanned legs, pink knickers on inside out with the tag showing, a disheveled white T-shirt, no bra, a mane of blond hair out loose, arms at right angles like she was getting ready to push up.

Her face was in profile, with one cheek to the floor. An almond eye open. Young, taut, pretty. "Jesus," Riley said.

"Mm." Powell stood.

"You think drugs?" Riley said.

The pathologist's mask creased in what Riley guessed was a frown. "I think sex."

"Smothered?" Riley crouched. "Rape?"

"Or consensual—gone wrong," he said. "We need to roll her."

"Look at the undies." Gatjens thrust her chin. "On inside out. A woman who is alert and sober wouldn't do that."

"Maybe she wasn't," Riley said. "Sober."

"It's a thing guys do," Powell said. "They try and re-dress a body but get it wrong."

Riley looked at the wrists and hands and then crab-walked down to the ankles. No marks, no chafing.

Powell knelt across from Gatjens. "Let's flip her," he said.

Riley gave them room and watched as they rolled her with care. Brown eyes open, features beginning to discolor. Her T-shirt had been sliced up the front.

"She's still warm." Powell pointed to the purple pooling in the face. "Lividity just starting." He felt her hand. "Rigor not well developed, but it's here—in the fingers."

"You want to do a rectal temp?" Gatjens said.

Powell scowled. "Not if we think intercourse. Lawyers'll fuck us for it later."

"Time of death?" Riley said.

"I'd say four, five hours ago." Powell looked at his watch. "Around nine p.m." He got his face in close to the neck and stared. Slowly he moved his gaze up to the dead woman's eyes. He looked up and blinked. "It's subtle, but it's there."

Now Gatjens leaned in, and Powell pointed to the front of the neck. "Asymmetric bruising," he said. "The lividity makes it confusing."

Gatjens grunted and looked over the face.

Powell pulled down an eyelid.

Gatjens sat back.

Powell made eyes at Riley.

"Spit it out," she said.

"See for yourself." He pointed again, and she took a knee and bent in. He pulled down a lower eyelid, and she saw tiny dots of blood.

"Eye bleed," Riley said. "Petechiae. She's straining . . ."

"Not bad, Detective. Petechial hemorrhages form in cases of neck compression. It interrupts blood from the brain going back to the heart. Builds up pressure in the venous return."

"She suffocated?"

"No. An external force to the neck." Powell lowered his mask. "She was strangled to death."

2

Riley went out the front door and around the side of the block to the rear. A strip of lawn had been laid parallel to the development, and she walked along it. There was more timber fencing to screen the back decks. She stood behind the Armytage property and looked out. The land sloped away into scraggly country under stars, with no structures or lights in view. She finished an anticlockwise lap of the row and went back to the kitchen and watched forensics photograph the body.

"Her phone was on the lounge," Gatjens told Riley. "Husband might have the code. Save some time."

Riley changed gloves.

"We bagged a wineglass off the counter," Gatjens said. "Only one. Big as a fishbowl."

Riley opened the fridge. A bottle of white, half-empty. A bowl of pasta covered with Glad Wrap. Milk, cheese, eggs, juice, condiments, fruit, and vegetables. She closed the door and turned to the sink. Two saucepans drying on a rack. Everything shipshape. Jars of nuts, flour, sugar, salt, and rice were lined up in the pantry. A row of spices. Tins, bottles, boxes.

Six chairs sat up straight under a dining table, and toward the rear deck, sofas and an armchair were sprawled around a gas fire and another television on the wall. Bright cushions and a cashmere throw dressed up the lounges. Double income, no kids. A coffee table carried large hardcover books on art, wine, architecture, photography, design. There were wedding pictures in frames on a shelf. The husband was handsome, trim, smiling, and the wife glowed—liquid brown eyes and a button nose, a cute rebuke to a flawless face.

Riley went from picture to picture, drawn to the victim. Beauty wasn't a myth. It was a magnet—it sucked shit toward it.

A forensic investigator was working at the glass back doors.

"Point of entry?" Riley said.

The constable's head dipped: negative. "It's locked solid. Nothing jemmied." Both side walls were shared with the neighbors. The constable watched Riley looking. "No access either side," he said. "No doors, not even a hatch or a flap. It's the same in the basement and the top floor."

"Check the ceilings." She made a note in her book: *floor plans*. "See if you can get in the roof."

Gatjens gestured from the kitchen. A black leather handbag sat on a stool. They knelt on the floor, and Gatjens emptied it on plastic. Purse, sunglasses, tampons, Panadol, a makeup pouch, tissues, mints, keys, a pen . . . Gatjens bagged it all.

"Did he use her keys and put them back?" Riley asked.

"The place is still new," Gatjens said. "Does the developer have keys?"

Powell had his mask around his neck and was preparing to leave. Riley walked with him to the front door and saw Patel out in the cordon, suiting up at her Camry.

Standing beside Powell, Riley nodded out at the drive. "Constable Priya Patel," she said. "Have you met?"

Powell looked across. "I don't believe so."

They watched Patel walk up and log in, and Riley introduced them.

"I was in Gujarat only last year," Powell said. "Fascinating."

Patel's mouth twitched at the corners. "Take your word for it."

"Frank thinks detectives know fuck-all about dead bodies and fuck-all about homicides," Riley said. "Isn't that right, Frank?"

Powell frowned in agreement. "To be brutally honest, quite *frankly*, yes. But they do investigate them."

Riley crossed her arms. "You said *consensual?*"

"She wasn't bound," the pathologist said. "Or at least, no ligature marks on her hands or feet. No abrasions, no defensive wounds. She didn't fight."

"Maybe he drugged her?" Riley said.

"We'll know soon enough." Powell looked at Patel. "Something else: She didn't suffocate, she wasn't smothered. And there's no imprint of a gag."

"Okay," Patel said.

"She's not bound, she's not gagged. But she was strangled and found in a state of undress. She didn't fight." Powell made an O shape with his lips. "There's a question for the neighbors—did she scream?"

Outside, across the yard, the ambulance was still backed up with its doors open and the husband sitting on the stretcher.

"Look," Powell said, "we have trouble when a woman dies and the male partner says it happened during sex. It's often difficult for us to work out whether it was truly an accidental death during consensual sex—whether something had gone wrong during . . . *play.*"

"The husband's not saying that," Riley said. "He says he came home to find her."

"Mm." Powell nodded to Patel and went to log out with the uniform on the path. At the gate, he turned and called, "See you at the morgue. Probably Wednesday. I'll let you know."

Patel followed Riley, and they stood at the stairs. "You see the duty officer?" Riley asked. "Rodrigues?"

"Yeah."

"Seems smart. We can call for more bodies if we need them."

Patel was looking down the hall. No sign of a struggle.

"Did she open the door to someone she knew?" Riley said. "More than one person?"

"Play." Patel frowned at where Powell had been standing. "He means bondage?"

"S'pose." Riley poked her chin up the stairs. "Check for whips, chains, handcuffs. Rope or straps—anchor points on the bed to tie down. Dildos—you'd know what they look like."

"Sounds like your place," Patel said. "Down to the gimp mask."

Riley left her and went out into the cordon. She came up to the ambulance slowly, O'Neil's voice in her head: *Ground zero—from here, you work out. Be delicate, keep him close, get as much as you can. If he's done it, he's at his most vulnerable now while it's all blowing up . . .*

"Mr. Armytage?" she said.

His face was ashen, slightly moist.

The floor of the load space was at waist level, and she put down her notebook. "I'm Detective Sergeant Riley. From Homicide. I'm very sorry for your loss."

His larynx bobbed.

"We have to find who did this—to Penelope. To your wife. Can I call her Penny?"

"Yes. Pen."

"Thank you. You can help us. Can you tell me what happened this evening?"

Soupy eyes blinked. She had to lead him, or she wouldn't get anything.

He said he'd been at the office in Maitland. He was a geologist, worked in coal, moved around.

"Like fly-in-fly-out?" Riley said.

He sighed. "Not quite. There are field trips. And I do a lot here." He stared at the town house.

"But you were in Maitland today?"

He'd worked from home in the morning and driven to the office after lunch to work with his boss and a colleague. They had a project due Friday.

Riley took down the office address. Nigel Armytage's boss was male, and his colleague was female. Riley wrote down their names and asked for their numbers, and Armytage read them out from his phone.

"Before the triple zero and after you left work, did you make any other calls?"

He stared at his mobile. "I called Pen."

"I see." Riley paused. "Would you mind if I looked? It could be critical."

He met her eye for the first time and held out the phone.

"Thank you." Riley took it and scrolled. The triple zero at 10:41 went on for four minutes and thirty-nine seconds. They'd kept him on the line while they dispatched. A call to Pen at 7:44: two minutes and three seconds. Riley scanned down the list of recent calls, scribbling names: *Mum, Kate, Simon, Dad, Rock, Maria.*

"What time did you leave the office?" she said.

He was vague on time, on when he left work.

"Did you leave with your colleagues?"

"I got home at ten thirty-seven," he said.

Riley smiled. "Thank you. That's very precise."

He'd come in the front door and gone straight to the kitchen. The lights were on. He'd rounded the counter, and Penny was face down on the floor.

"Did you touch the—" Riley broke off. "Did you call to her? Did you touch Penny?"

He'd called out. He'd shouted. He'd put a hand under her forehead, blown in her ear, hugged her head, felt for her pulse in her neck, then her wrist.

"Did you move her?"

"I half rolled her at the shoulders. Before I called the ambulance." Then the operator had kept him searching for a pulse.

On the stretcher, he glistened as his gray face drained to pale green. Riley gave a short whistle, and a paramedic climbed through from the front of the ambulance and pulled open a drawer.

Riley pumped the husband twice more: his wife's phone passcode and the name of her best friend. He slurred out a number and a name, and she wrote them down and backed off as he bent toward the ambo and threw up in the sick bag.

3

Riley leaned on the Calais beside Rodrigues. It was 2:02 a.m.

"We're going to need a room," she said.

"I had a liaison book you," he said. "Motel down the road."

"An incident room."

He rippled at his gaffe. "We got the new station at Cessnock," he said. "Plenty of space."

Riley chipped gravel with a heel. It was fifteen kays into town—too many cops at the station, too much gossip, too much resentment. It was better to run lean. And the Armytages weren't Cessnock people. "Nothing round here?"

His mouth anchored down. "There's the old post office. Bit up from the crossroad."

"Let's have a look."

Riley pushed off and was behind the wheel, pressing the ignition, while Rodrigues blinked at her over the hood. He walked around and climbed in beside her. She backed up and was edging out of the cordon when a woman walked into the headlights and waved. Riley blew air and braked, and the woman came up to Rodrigues's window. Riley slid down the glass.

The woman bent in, hard jawed, and then smiled—her crooked mouth, not her eyes.

Rodrigues sat back in case he'd get bitten.

"Laura Nolan," the woman said. "*The Mirror*."

"You're a long way from home," Riley said.

"Not really. I'm the bureau in Newcastle." She held up a notebook. "So, a woman in her twenties. Name's Penny Armytage. With a *y*."

"The *Penny* or the *Armytage*?" Riley said.

"What?"

"You been through her mailbox?"

Nolan's head twisted at a coy angle. "I would, but you got it taped off." She jiggled her eyebrows at Rodrigues. "I *did* have a cup of tea with the neighbors."

Riley stared out the windshield. "Female. Twenty-seven. Cause of death unknown. We're waiting on the autopsy. Don't quote me. That's it."

Nolan scribbled in a notebook. "You're Homicide. And you're looking at the husband."

"The husband is distraught and helping police with inquiries."

"He found her?"

"No comment."

"He's given a statement."

"No."

"I could see you—at the ambulance."

"I had a chat. He'll give a formal statement when he's feeling better. Nighty-night."

"I'm going to name her."

"I hope you're right. Didn't come from us."

"Fuck." The reporter's face scrunched. "Can't you just confirm it?"

"Next of kin."

"Her husband's right there."

Riley had seen an extended family photo in the wedding shots. "She's got parents. People who love her." She pulled the button for the window. "I understand, for a journo, that might be hard to believe."

The reporter straightened and Riley drove off, Rodrigues still pinned to the headrest.

"You know her?" Riley said.

"Nup, never seen her. Cessnock's got its own rag, but they must be in bed." He pointed left out the drive. "Then right at the crossroad, and it's on the left, fifty meters."

Riley crawled up and sat at the intersection, leaning forward to hug the wheel and look around. The takeaway, ahead of her, faced diagonally across to the café, still with a light on, to her right. There was one other building—dark, with no sign. "What's that?"

"It was a hippie shop. Incense and candles and crap. It's a woman in Cessnock, but she's closed up."

"Hippies in Cessnock," Riley said. "Times change."

"You know the town?"

"Bit. I went to primary school in Branxton. We had a place, south of Belford."

"No shit." Rodrigues looked over, the balance between them in sway.

"My dad's family's land. He grew up there. I was just a kid when we sold. Moved down to Sydney."

"That where your mum's from?"

"No. God—she was Muswellbrook."

"Far out." He scratched his nose. "Couple more generations, you'd almost be local."

"Not to Cessnock. We'd be blow-ins." Riley smiled. As a kid, the joke had been to hold your nose and say it. She held her nose. "Cessnock."

Rodrigues nodded: Cesspit, Methnock—he'd know all the Nock-nock jokes. In the glow of the dash, she eyed him. A green tie neatly knotted with a white shirt, black suit, and fine dark wool overcoat. He wasn't from Cessnock, not born and bred.

"What about you?" she said.

"Grew up in Sydney. Now here I am."

"How long?"

"Three years."

"Mr. Local."

"Yeah right. I'm not even a blow-in. You know what some woman called me the other day?"

"I hate to think."

"A New Australian. Like, fuck—I hadn't heard that for a while."

Riley laughed. "You think this is Cessnock?" She tilted her head back at the scene. "Someone from town?"

"Could be. There's a transient element, with the prison." He stretched a black-suited leg in the footwell. "It's a jail town. Crims washing through. Families move here because Dad's doing time. Dad gets out and they hang round."

She indicated and turned right. After fifty meters, Rodrigues pointed at a squat sandstone building behind a low wire fence. She pulled in and put it in park.

"It's one room, like a little hall," he said. "It's maintained—council hire it out to tourists for parties."

Riley left the headlights on, took the heavy flashlight from the door pocket, got out, and walked up to the building. There were no windows in the facade, and the door was hard timber, locked tight. She walked over to the corner and shined the flashlight down the side wall. There were bars on a small window up high. She walked down the path, past a mounted gas water heater, and ran the light along the back wall. It was the same setup: a locked door and no windows.

Rodrigues had followed her. "It's secure," he said. "And we'll change the locks."

She played the beam around. There was some outdoor furniture, a teak table and chairs, on a patch of grass. Beyond, she felt open space, dark and cold. She went and looked down the other side of the building. No windows, no access, a paling fence. "Red Creek," she said. "Fill me in."

"It's an old pit stop. That's what it was—a pub and a post office, a place to pull in and tie up your horse. The route's changed over time, so the pub's a little off the road, over there." He pointed. "Now it's all about wine. There's cellar doors in every direction. More than a hundred. They're open to the public, and they draw a lot of tourists. People drive around, stay for the weekend, taste wine, go to lunch. They stop here for a coffee or a pie. Or a schooner."

"A tourist stop?"

"Yeah. It's quiet now—Monday and Tuesday. But it builds through the week. The Hunter might get seventy weddings on a Saturday. They stay in the big resorts—or at vineyards or Airbnbs—and move around. Lots of traffic passes here."

"The big resorts. You've got the Rydges . . ."

"There's three more. Cypress Lakes." He swung his arm. "Couple of hundred rooms and a golf course. Families like it, little kids can ride round on bikes. And the conference trade. Two hundred sales reps on chardonnay."

There was a corrugated-metal bin by the back door, and Riley flicked out her gum. Wine country was a magnet too—it drew shit toward it. A lot of people moving through.

"We'll need guest lists," Riley said. "All the hotels."

Rodrigues nodded. "Because it's Monday—or it was—occupancy rates will be well down."

"What about locals?"

His hand found the nape of his neck. "They'll come when it's quiet. Grab a coffee. Or drink at the pub."

"From Cessnock?"

"Oh Christ no. No one from Cessnock would ever come here."

"Why not?"

"Too far—you know, metaphorically. Wine country, that's for top-shelf dickheads. That's for Sydney."

"Who, then?"

"Locals?" He shrugged. "Grape growers, vineyard workers. The odd miner, or their wives."

Riley walked back past the gas heater toward the headlights. "I thought miners lived in Cessnock?"

"Yeah, well, that changes, back and forth. They earn good money. Some live out round here now, on the residential estates. Others give it a try, don't like it, move back to town. That's what the town houses are, the start of a development. You come back in a few years, it'll be a gated enclave. Lot of big utes driven by Filipina brides."

Riley turned in the lights to scan his face for resentment. "New Australians?" she said.

He took it on the chin. "Got me there."

"You said the Armytages were around for a while, before they bought?"

"More than a year."

"You know them?"

"Nah. Just asked around."

Riley stepped out of the headlights and nodded at the old post office. "What do you think?"

"Telstra's got coverage. There's a bathroom, a small kitchen. I can get it mopped out."

"Will it piss 'em off in Cessnock, if we set up out here?"

"Doubt it." He pondered. "I'll keep an ear to the ground."

They went back and got in the car. "The husband," Riley said. "When you took his version—he said he worked late in Maitland, with his boss?"

"Yeah." Rodrigues reached for his seat belt.

"Did he mention anyone else? A female colleague?"

"No. Just the boss."

Riley backed out. "With the canvass, capture everything," she said. "Red light, speed cameras in a radius—say, what, thirty kay? Harvesting regos. All the CCTV you can find. Shops. Servos. In the morning, we want overalls, SES, to walk in lines at the scene. Up to the crossroad, out to the pub, down the paddock behind the house. Map it out in grids."

"I'll get a prison list too," he said. "Who's just out. Sex offenders on bail."

"Yeah. But not only who just got released." Riley went left at the crossroad. "There might be a dirtbag inside with something to say."

He made a note.

She went into the cordon and parked. The ambulance with Nigel Armytage was gone. She pressed the cabin light and opened her notebook on her lap and dismissed Rodrigues with a nod. He got out and she watched him cross to the town house. He was compact, neat, a slight limp, but he walked like an athlete—poised, contained.

Her notebook was a leather-bound A4. She wrote lists in dot points under eight headings: *Timeline, Autopsy, Canvass, Victimology, Scene, Husband, Links, Jail.*

Her phone rang, and she looked at it and bit her pen. Trevor Toohey. Penelope Armytage had got the Homicide Super out of bed.

"Sir."

"Woke up for a leak and saw a heads-up from Command," Toohey said. "Media's asking about this girl in the Hunter . . ."

"Manual strangulation. Married. No bindings, no forced entry, nothing knocked around in the house."

"So, the husband?"

"He's got an alibi with witnesses. There'll be an electronic trail."

"How's he look?"

"Shot to pieces. Just had a spew."

"But?"

"Dunno. There might be a gap in the timing. He's vague on most of it, then very precise at the crunch. Local detective got his version, then I locked him in. Might be discrepancies around who he was with."

"Who was he with?"

"Female colleague. Male boss. At the office in Maitland."

"You start with the boss?"

"Yeah."

"What's with the press?"

"*The Mirror's* got her name. Penelope Armytage. They'll've googled."

"And?"

Penelope Armytage was leverage. Riley wasn't going to waste it. "She's young, white, professional, gorgeous. Nice house, nice couple. Swanky wine-tourist spot. Husband's a geologist, she was in marketing. *Mirror*'s camped out drinking tea with the neighbors. It's going to blow up—deluxe."

Wheels turned in the silence. She knew he was googling.

"Army-tage," she said. "With a *y*."

A dyspeptic grunt as he found her. "What d'you need?"

She let him chew on it. Media glare was painful, but it brought some advantage.

He sighed. "One analyst."

"One analyst—if it's Wendy. Plus, a local detective. Rodrigues. He was first here."

"All right." Toohey sniffed. "But that's it. No fuckin' whinging. Where you gonna be? Cessnock?"

"At the scene. Red Creek. There's an empty, old post office. Can you put in a word?"

He grunted again and hung up, and Riley went back to her lists. *Beauty* was one of a dozen points under *Victimology*, and she circled it now. If it was stranger murder, someone Penelope Armytage didn't know, then he'd seen her somewhere and chosen her. Looks like hers sucked the oxygen from coincidence.

Riley got out. The dressing-gowned neighbors and the reporter Laura Nolan were nowhere to be seen. Patel was at the gate with Rodrigues.

"Nigel's parents are at Wangi Wangi," Patel said. "Liaison drove him over."

"Penny's parents?" Riley said.

"Gray nomads," Rodrigues said. "In a van, in the Tanami."

Riley looked at the block. "It's just the one set of neighbors?"

"The first place is empty, unsold." Rodrigues held up his notebook. "These three are sold, all to investors. Two are on Airbnb, one's up for lease. There were four people—two couples from Sydney—in number five on Friday and Saturday night. We'll talk to them. There were cleaners in there on Sunday." He leafed a page and looked down the row. "Then you have Julie and Rod Clark. Owner-occupiers, both sixty-eight, both retired. Sold the family home in Strathfield and bought in. They're told this is stage one of a new gated estate—pharmacist, café, spa, grocer, hundred and forty homes, option for assisted living. Golf courses nearby. They love golf, wine, and cheese. Paradise on a stick."

"The Clarks know the Armytages, but only to wave or a chat on the drive," Patel said. "Julie's asked them in for a drink, but it hasn't happened. They're young, they're busy, they don't play golf. They're friendly, normal, there was nothing that stood out. No fights, no arguments."

"And the Clarks heard and saw nothing yesterday," Rodrigues said. "No strange vehicles. No screams, no visitors. Julie saw Penelope leave the house for a jog around five. That was the last sighting. She didn't see her come home."

It was now 3:00 a.m. Forensics had packed up. The undertakers had been and gone.

Riley turned to Rodrigues. "Where's this motel?"

Patel swung in behind Riley, following Rodrigues's taillights out of the cordon. They went right, away from the Red Creek crossroad. Riley saw a sign for the pub—THE PACKHORSE INN—and a driveway entrance as she passed, but the building wasn't visible from her vehicle in the dark.

The motel was close, a kilometer down the road. Rodrigues braked and indicated, and Riley followed him in. Patel parked beside her, and they popped the boots for their bags.

It was an elongated single-story building in timber and stone with a metal roof. Night-lights in bollards glowed at intervals. It looked new, a modern rendering of a classic country highway motel. The car park ran parallel to the row of rooms, and there was one other vehicle, a white Volvo 60, in a bay farther down.

Rodrigues nodded at the Volvo. "My guys rang the motel manager and door-knocked the place before midnight." He pulled out his notebook. "There are eighteen rooms, only one occupied—two adult guests, a male, fifty-three, and a female, thirty-eight. He's married, but not to her. They're up from Sydney for a long weekend. We got their movements. They were out in the vineyards from about four till ten— two wineries, a bar, and a restaurant. We'll confirm their version with the venues today. We ran them both and the rego. All clean."

He slipped the notebook into an inner pocket of his suit jacket, and Patel and Riley followed him across the bitumen. There was a key drop on the wall at the entrance, and Rodrigues read a number off his phone and pressed in the code. He took the two room cards from the box and used one to activate the glass door.

A sensor triggered lights in the empty reception, and Riley paused to take in the lobby. The use of stone and wood outside had been replicated in here. It was muted, tasteful—beige, caramel, tan, ochre— and a dead ringer for the Armytage place.

Rodrigues watched her, his hands in the pockets of his overcoat. "Same developer as the town houses. This is the southwest boundary of the title."

Riley's eyes brushed Patel's. *Developer.* Beth Gatjens had said it, too, asking about keys.

Patel shifted her grip on her suitcase. "The land from here to the town houses, that's the new estate?"

"Correct," Rodrigues said.

The guest rooms were down a corridor. He walked with Riley and Patel, then handed over the cards.

"The manager's Karen," he said. "You're booked for a week, but she can take you for longer." He started back toward reception. "See you in the morning."

Their rooms faced each other across the corridor. Patel went into hers and turned to close the door. "Try and sleep," she said.

Riley keyed in and lugged her suitcase onto a built-in counter that ran the length of the wall. She unclipped her Glock and wrote *developer* in her notes next to *floor plans*. She kicked off her sneakers and undressed and took a hot shower.

Sleep was tricky, but with three fingers of minibar bourbon, she found it.

4

Morning light was leaking around the edges of the blinds when Riley woke. Raising her head, she cracked an eye for the time: twelve past nine. Back on the pillow, eyes shut, she did her sleep arithmetic. All up, including in her own bed before O'Neil's call, she'd nudged seven hours. Not bad. She swung her legs, her feet found carpet, and she padded through to the bathroom.

Toxicology would be a week. Was that it? Drugs or alcohol—was that why there'd been no struggle? Or more than one person to constrain her? Or someone Penelope knew?

Riley flushed and, thinking about coffee, went out and stopped to stare . . . a red Nespresso in a corner on the counter. She shook her head, where bloody Bowman was reclining rent-free, and slotted in a pod. The machine was the exact model as hers, so she knew how it worked. She pressed the button for a short black, opened the bar fridge under the counter, and found a single-serve box of UHT milk with a straw.

Her phone pinged with a message from O'Neil. No words, just a link to an article in *The Mirror*. Riley clicked through. The headline, Young Woman Dead In Pokolbin, sat over a photo of Riley talking to Nigel Armytage at the back of the ambulance. The image quality wasn't great, Nolan must have taken it with her phone. Embedded in the piece was a second picture—Penelope Armytage in a bikini at the beach.

Riley read the story. Laura Nolan had named Penelope Armytage but hadn't attributed it to the police. The article said Homicide Squad detectives from Sydney were on scene, but it didn't name Riley or Patel. That wasn't a professional courtesy, Nolan just didn't know their names and, in the middle of the night, had been unable to find them.

Riley clawed at the UHT straw, inserting it to squeeze milk into the coffee—Nolan felt shameless, a quiver of mayhem in the brittle jut of her jaw. Riley sipped and pinched at her phone to zoom in on the image: Penelope Armytage at the beach, laughing, arms out to the camera in mock remonstration. Nolan must have scraped it from Instagram. Riley typed *Penelope Armytage* into Google and did a News search. *The Daily Mail* had already written through *The Mirror* copy and was running a piece with a series of five pictures hoovered from Penelope's socials: at the beach, at a bar, in bed with a book, at a vineyard drinking wine. They even had her on her wedding day, with Nigel.

Nolan would see the rival coverage and be encouraged by it. For a regional reporter on a big-city tabloid, Penelope Armytage was a ticket to ride.

Riley drank the coffee, knowing she had Bowman if she needed to hit back at Nolan in the press. Bowman was a friend, and they worked well together, combat bonded, and she could trust him in the same way she trusted Patel.

She showered and was half-dressed when Patel knocked on the door. Riley opened it in a flurry, and Patel stood watching as she roamed the room, getting ready. She rummaged in her suitcase, went through to the bathroom, came out with her toothbrush clenched in her teeth, buttoning her trousers.

"Multitasking," Patel said.

Riley looked up and blinked. She had worked several regional cases with Patel, the two of them shacked up together in country pubs or hotels for weeks at a time. It was always a retinal shock to view the constable first thing in the morning, glossy as a goddess from a milk bath—and it wasn't UHT. Patel was twenty-eight and looked about fifteen.

Tucking in her shirt, Riley spoke through her toothbrush. "What're you schtaring at?"

"Not sure." Patel closed one eye. "Sleep well?"

Patel looked like she'd slept in goose down at a health farm. Riley, starting to dribble, brushed past her and spat in the sink. "Yeah, well"— she rinsed her mouth—"so asks the Queen of Sheba."

Patel was studying her nails. "You actually think the Queen of Sheba was from India, don't you?"

Riley came out of the bathroom and grabbed Patel's hand. The nails were painted a lacquered pale pink. "Are you seeing someone?"

"Wouldn't you like to know." Patel left her hand sitting in Riley's as her eyes wandered to the 375 of bourbon half-drained on the counter.

Riley uncoupled, hoisted her fleece from a chair, and they went out and walked down the corridor in silence and identical clothes. For Riley, the outfit was a habit: On a major investigation, she kept to sneakers, stretch black trousers, T-shirts, and, if needed, a fleece. The dress code had started from convenience and deepened into a talisman, a contract with her victims—Riley was there to serve, always on, good to go. Patel had noted the uniform early on and copied it.

At reception there was a woman on the desk, thin and prim, pale, with an exclamation mark of close-cropped red hair. A name tag on her tan cotton sweater said KAREN. She saw them coming and started nodding to herself. "Officers." Her glances, low, met their chins, their noses. "It's terrible, I'm in shock. I'm sorry, I wanted to stay up to greet you . . ."

"It's no problem," Patel said. "It got late."

Karen was still nodding.

Riley looked around. "Is there, ah, breakfast?"

"Yes, sorry. Of course." Karen's head stilled. "We have a continental breakfast. Gluten-free granola, sourdough toast."

Riley swallowed. Which continent, Antarctica?

Karen motioned across the lobby. There was a bulbous alcove with an island counter, tables, and chairs. "We have a communal pantry. Three cooktops, two ovens, microwaves. It's a flexible catering model"—she took a breath—"which we have designed."

Riley stared at the setup. "What, like cook yourself?"

Karen's mouth tightened another notch. "Yes. It isn't going to suit you, I can see." She gave a nod to her own shrewdness. "It's for the wine tourists. Almost exclusively, they're our clientele."

Patel cleared her throat: *Let's go.*

Karen, oblivious, was explaining her exclusive clientele. "They visit the providores in the valley and pick things up. Some duck from Branxton, perhaps. Some goat's cheese. The idea is, they bring it back here and prepare it."

"Nice," Patel said. "But—"

"But that's not why you're here." Karen eyed the alcove. "There are things there for breakfast."

Patel went across the lobby to investigate.

Karen watched her departing back. "We do have quick meals you can purchase with your room card and heat up at any time. Shepherd's pie, lasagna, pizzas."

"Okay," Riley said.

Karen rolled into her welcome spiel. There was no room service, there was no daily clean. "Please stack the dishwashers in the communal pantry." There was no one on reception after 6:00 p.m. "Your room card will get you in the front door." She pointed with her nose. "There's an after-hours number if you need us."

"The guests that were in last night," Riley said, "have they gone?"

Karen's voice lowered. "They checked out early."

Riley rubbed her fingers on the raised reception counter, an artisan admiring the joinery. "Nice place. Is it new?"

"Coming up to two years." Pride set her neck and shoulders. "We built from scratch."

Rodrigues had described Karen as the manager. "You're the owner?" Riley said.

"Oh yes."

Riley arranged an expression of deference. "I might have this wrong, but I was led to believe the town houses and your motel are part of the same development."

"No, that's correct, in a manner of speaking. It's an Oakeshott development."

Riley opened her notebook on the raised desk. "Oakeshott?"

"They're a property group from Newcastle. We had to stand up to them, hold our ground. It went sour. But here we are."

Riley waited for Karen to go on, and made notes. Oakeshott Construction was a one-stop shop: developer, architect, builder. They were buying up parcels of land across the valley and throwing up low-rise, midsize residential enclaves. The Armytage block was phase one of their third project, zoned to stretch from the town houses to a boundary at the motel. It had been a departure from the company formula— Oakeshott Construction had designed and built the motel despite having no capital in the site. Karen and her husband owned the land.

"What's your husband's name?" Riley said.

A moment on the lips. "Jayson."

Riley paused, pen poised.

"Cassidy," Karen said, and watched as Riley wrote it down.

"Do you take the same surname?" Riley said.

"Yes."

Patel came back from the communal kitchen with a shake of her head. "That all looks a bit complicated."

Karen frowned in agreement. "It's there if you need it. I recommend the café, the takeaway, and the pub. That's breakfast, lunch, and dinner."

Riley closed her notebook.

"Such a beautiful girl," Karen said. "They stayed here, you know."

Riley put the cap on her pen. "When was that?"

"Last year. When they first came over to the valley for a break."

The name of the motel was stenciled onto the glass entry doors: THEQUIRK@REDCREEK. Riley hadn't noticed the branding when Rodrigues brought them in at 3:00 a.m., but she read it now as she followed Patel out.

A damp morning, a weak sun in a pale sky. Riley gathered her bearings in the daylight. The country stretched in shades of gray-green, purple, white. No vines in view. To the west, the slopes of the range were dark with bush. The valley floor had been cleared to the escarpments. On the flats, pockets of gums stood in grassland, dense from two years of rain. She was close to home. She breathed it in, wet earth pungent with her ghosts.

The motel was in a hollow with no other structure in sight. At the north end of the car park, a secondary gravel drive snuck behind the building and ran seventy meters or so down into a ring of foliage. Riley guessed it hid a storage shed or even a house for the Cassidys. If they could be summoned after hours, they had to be close. She had assumed they lived on-site.

Patel rode with Riley in the Calais. The road rose and then leveled off, and after a kilometer the town houses appeared on the left and Riley slowed. There were emergency vehicles and a police bus on the drive. At the rear, a line of SES and officers in overalls was moving down a fenced paddock.

Patel looked the other way, across Riley to the right. "Pub."

Riley pulled over by the PACKHORSE INN sign she had seen in the dark, and they got out. There was a sealed drive, but even in daylight the pub was obscured from the road by a fall and curve of the land. They walked on the bitumen, and after forty meters the building began to reveal itself, square shouldered and cream yellow.

It was the real deal, a colonial coach house—sandstone blocks, two-stories tall, a cast-iron balcony, a corrugated roof. The sealed drive ended in a car park at the front, and a gravel road led out of that and along to the back of the compound. A timber extension ran at a right angle off one side of the original building and joined a cluster of outbuildings at the rear—former stables and kitchens around a paved courtyard, Riley guessed.

There were no vehicles and no one around. Smoke from a chimney. Riley checked the time—10:28 a.m.—and googled. It opened at eleven. There was a sign by the door: 1852. MEALS. ACCOMMODATION. FINE WINES.

"Guest rooms," Patel said.

"It's bigger than it looks," Riley said. "Rabbit warren out the back."

The pub was almost directly opposite the town houses, but with tree cover and gradient, there was no line of sight. It was about eighty meters, as the crow flew, to the Armytage place. To walk, without bush-bashing, it was longer—up the drive, along the main road, down the gravel to the town house. About one hundred and fifty meters.

They trudged back to the Calais, hands in fleeces, the smell of woodsmoke. Riley drove, measuring distance. From the sign for the pub on the main road, it was fifty meters to the left turn onto the gravel for the town houses. She didn't take it—staying on the road, it was another hundred and fifty meters to the crossroads. She pulled up at a stop sign. The takeaway and the café were open, and half a dozen cars were parked.

Patel got out and looked in at Riley. "So, duck with goat's cheese, toasted?"

Riley pointed. "Old post office is there. You can walk."

Over the road, on the footpath outside the café, two women stopped their conversation to stare as Patel crossed to the takeaway. They were middle-aged, in jeans and sweaters, with blond bobs.

Riley turned right, drove the fifty meters to the post office, and parked beside an unmarked dark-blue Passat. Two vans sat farther down, a black Iveco alongside a white Hyundai.

The door to the stone building was ajar, and Riley went in. It was one large, open room, about eight meters by twelve. Technicians were installing cables on trestle desks, and a whiteboard and a big monitor had been hung on a wall. Two cleaners were mopping and wiping.

Rodrigues was sitting off to the side with a laptop, in his clothes from last night.

He glanced up as Riley picked her way past empty boxes. "Fast work," she said.

His tie was askew from his loose collar, and there were smudged crescents under his eyes. "Your Super spoke to my Super."

Media glare. The bosses were dancing. Rodrigues sat back to stretch. He'd gotten the incident room established and organized the overalls for the walk-through at the scene like she'd asked. That was good: not having to ask twice.

He looked about thirty and had a ring on his finger. "Married?" she said.

He made a fist. "Yeah."

"Cop?"

"No. Schoolteacher."

"You got kids?"

"Pregnant."

Riley sucked her lips. "There's something not right," she said, "with the scene."

His body gathered, preparing to be stripped down.

"It looks pear shaped," Riley said. "You need to decide."

"Decide what?"

"Do you want to jump aboard? It'll be long hours, hard driving. I don't have a pregnant wife at home."

There was molten gold in his eyes as they flashed. "I haven't been home."

She nodded at the room. "You've got us set up. You should go now, get some sleep."

He made no move to leave. "You think the husband?" he said.

"I think that's where we start. We need a download of his phone. Names, numbers, texts, emails, photos, socials. WhatsApp. Recently deleted. What's the correspondence with his accountant? His bank? Life insurance? Make a file for the analyst. Look for any salacious crumbs—a girlfriend, or mates playing up."

"You think there's a window?"

"The pathologist can't be specific—time of death. It's give or take an hour."

"From Maitland, it's a thirty-minute drive. There are two main routes, unless he's been tricky. We can track him."

"Say we rub him out," Riley said. "His alibi holds."

"Yeah."

"That's where it stops adding up. The scene says someone she knows."

Rodrigues shrugged. "A lover?"

"Nice lover. Pops around and strangles her to death. Appears not to panic."

Patel came in with white takeaway bags and surveyed the space. "Cozy."

"I'd show you around," Rodrigues said, "but this is it." He pointed to an internal door on a side wall. "Kitchen, and a toilet. Through there."

Patel held up the food. "I got extra. If you like bacon."

They ate at a trestle desk. Riley swiped at her phone and saw a missed call from Bowman. He'd have seen the Armytage story in *The Mirror* and the picture of Riley at the scene, and now he was sniffing.

"What're you smiling at?" Patel said.

Riley met her amused eyes. Caught. Patel knew the answer—she was close with Bowman, too, and she could read all Riley's smiles.

Riley went back to her phone. There was an email from Toohey saying Homicide analyst Wendy Yang had been assigned to work the case from Parramatta, as Riley had requested. For grunt work, Toohey wrote, lean on the locals. Cessnock will loan you the detective you asked for.

Rodrigues was stripping rind and fat from his roll.

"That pub is close," Riley said, "and they've got guest rooms?"

He stopped chewing and swallowed. "I thought you'd be better at the motel. More private."

"Yeah, no, that's good. I meant last night, with the canvass. Were there guests booked at the pub?"

"No. Like I said, Monday."

"And the canvass, you said they spoke to a girl on the staff?"

He reached for his notebook and turned pages. "A server. Rachel Evans, nineteen. We'll be back there this morning, talk to the publican."

Riley wiped her mouth with a napkin and scrunched up the greasy rubbish from her roll. "What's your name, by the way?"

"Christian."

"I'm Rose. That's Priya. She calls me *boss*."

Christian Rodrigues nodded. "I know who you are."

5

Adam Bowman drove through Cessnock, on the lookout for a certain pie shop and thinking about Truman Capote.

Capote's idea for *In Cold Blood* had come from a newspaper story about a family killed in rural Kansas. Bowman's own idea was percolating—and it had come from a news report. His ideas came from reading the news: a snippet in a story on a Monday morning or a Tuesday afternoon. This morning—a Tuesday—Bowman had been scrolling *The Mirror* and clicked on a piece about a dead woman in Pokolbin, and there was a picture of Riley at the back of the ambulance.

Good Christ. Standing at his kitchen counter, Bowman had needed to sit down. He read the story and called Riley . . . No answer.

At home, he'd tried to go about his morning's work, making calls, but was restless with thoughts of Riley on a killing in wine country. He kept checking his phone, but nothing from her. He looked in the fridge for perishables. Not much: cheese, milk, a sagging peach. Did he dare eat a peach? It was 11:15 a.m. He was on the road around noon.

He packed for a week and didn't tell his news editor he was going. He didn't have to. His true crime book had sold well and kept selling, and the royalties had bought him autonomy, a different kind of life. He'd quit his job as a staff reporter at *The National* and gone freelance. He did what he wanted and got paid by the word. But it meant he had to come up with ideas.

In Cessnock, he cruised the main drag. The city council, a Lowes Menswear, cafés, solicitors, a tobacco station. Yellow letters on a window that said TAX ACCOUNTANT. Country Charm knickknacks, a HAIR & NAILS sign, a barber doing good trade. Billy the Squid Fish N Chips.

Bowman knew there had been a famous pie shop in this town, and now he remembered it had burned down. That's why he knew about it—the bloody thing had burned to a crisp. He'd read about it in a newspaper. He saw in his rearview mirror that his quest for the bakery was annoying the bloke in the Ford Ranger behind him. Bowman sped up. He could get something to eat in the vineyards.

In Cold Blood was a book about the real murder of a real family, but in it the author had embellished. Capote had tried to exonerate himself from this treachery with claims he'd invented a new genre, the "nonfiction novel"—but there was no wriggling out of it. *In Cold Blood* was true crime and Capote had made stuff up, treating the living and the dead with contempt.

Bowman's own true crime book had treated no one with contempt, except for all the fuckers who deserved it.

He passed the old beehive brick kilns at Nulkaba and saw signs for places and brands he knew from a life spent peeling labels: Lovedale, Capercaillie, De Bortoli. He went left and passed the Hungerford Hill estate with a big dish on the roof that looked like a telescope pinging Pine Gap. Tourist country. Broke Road was the spine, running east–west, from which it all splayed—cellar doors and providores sat between rows of vines or fronting scrubby plain. Bowman was familiar with the Hunter in a Sydneysider way—weddings, parties, anything. The roads were quiet early in the week.

It was almost 3:00 p.m. when he stopped at a yield sign at a crossroads and peered around. Red Creek. He didn't know it, had never even been through it. A couple of cars were parked outside a takeaway, and across the intersection a white station wagon idled with its passenger door open in front of a café. A woman came out with a tray of cups and got into the car, and Bowman watched it drive away. Media.

He indicated and followed, slowing as the station wagon went right onto a gravel driveway. He pulled in and stopped. The gravel ran about fifty meters to a row of town houses, bald and bare on the edge of a paddock. Police had taped off the block and a good chunk of the drive. Vehicles sat inside the perimeter, and Bowman studied them . . . patrol cars and vans. Uniforms to hold the scene, and forensics. No Riley, he saw. No Patel.

Outside the cordon, the station wagon had pulled up beside an Outlander. The woman with the tray got out and passed coffees to a cameraman and a photographer. Local press. Sydney newsrooms would be taking wires and packages, but none had so far sent a team.

Bowman picked up his phone and searched. Laura Nolan had updated her story for *The Mirror*. There was no picture of Riley this time, just images of the dead woman and her husband, grabbed from their social feeds. He read the piece. Nothing was attributed, but on background someone was gunning for the husband. Bowman wondered if the drop had come from the police—if a Cessnock cop, or even Riley, was feeding the reporter.

Laura Nolan was based in Newcastle, tabloid-trained to hunt and kill. Bowman didn't know her, but he'd seen her byline often enough.

Behind him, a BMW went past on the main road and braked left at what looked like a sign for a pub. Bowman backed out from the gravel and followed . . . The Packhorse Inn. He made the turn onto a tree-screened lane. There were half a dozen vehicles in the car park of the old pub, and he killed the engine as a couple alighted from the BMW and headed for the door. Tourists, well heeled, retired.

Bowman locked the car and walked. At the entrance, he saw the pub offered accommodation. There had been no sign of Riley's Calais, but it would be hard to get closer to the scene, and he hoped she was staying here.

He stepped into a warm wood-paneled saloon, with the bar on the right and a dining area to the left. Five men in work clothes stood around a raised table, drinking.

Bowman waited by the beer taps as the barman served the couple from the BMW. It was taking a while. The wife ran a finger down a wine list while the husband rocked gently on the balls of his feet, hands in trousers, staring ahead at a shelf of spirits. Bowman scanned a food menu on the bar. The woman turned a page on the list, and the husband was now humming along with her perusal. "We had a nice wine yesterday," she mused, "at a lovely tasting."

The barman was a big dude, fortysomething, in a black polo with PACKHORSE INN stitched on the breast. He leaned across to the woman's list and pointed. "You want the local drop, sémillon?"

Her husband stopped humming and went still. The woman's nose wrinkled. "But do you have a white?"

The barman's eyes, hooded, betrayed no response to the blatant tourist ignorance. He bent again over the list, and his moist brow caught the light. "That one's not bad. Thirty bucks."

As the woman considered this, an internal door behind the bar opened, and a second staff member walked out and up to Bowman. "What'll it be?" she asked.

"Ah, Stone & Wood," he said. "And the Guinness pie."

She reached for a glass and pulled the beer. She was older than her colleague, late fifties, no polo uniform, no nonsense. "You here about the dead girl?" she said.

"What makes you say that?"

"You don't look like you play golf."

This might have been a compliment, he wasn't sure. "Can I book a room?"

The woman closed the tap and placed the beer down. "How many nights?"

"Four?"

She frowned. "Should be right. I'll get my book." She went out the door she'd come through.

Bowman sipped. The retirees had chosen their wine and were paying. Down the bar, one of the workers from the raised round table was waiting to be served, his eyes skimming Bowman.

The woman came back with a thick blue diary. "So, till Saturday?" She turned pages on the counter. "Two-ten a night, that includes a cooked breakfast."

"There's cops up from Sydney," Bowman said. "Are they staying here?"

Her pen stopped, and she looked at him. "What are you—newspaperman?"

He nodded.

"Who with?"

"Freelance."

Her lip curled. "I'll need your license and a credit card."

He dug for his wallet and put the cards on the bar, then pulled out a stool and sat. "What have you heard?"

She copied the details from his license. "Not much. Police knocked on the door late. I'd gone to bed. They spoke to Rachel."

"You the boss?"

She handed back his ID. "That's me."

Bowman slotted the license into his wallet. The woman had an edge, practical rather than callous. Someone had just been killed across the road, but she wasn't buying into the drama—no histrionics or displays of grief. Straight talkers were useful, you could straight talk straight back. "The dead woman," he said. "Did you know her?"

"Bit. I'd seen her once or twice. I knew of her."

"How's that?"

"Pub talk. I knew they'd bought one of them places"—she thrust her chin—"over there. And that she was doing work for Bob."

"Bob?"

"Bob Bruce." She glanced across to the men drinking at the table. "Not in today."

43

Bowman looked over too. "Who are they?"

"My regulars," she said. "You leave them alone."

The men ranged in age from maybe forty to perhaps sixty. A knitted sweater, a hi-vis vest, a faded windbreaker . . . each of them weathered from working outside. The group saw Bowman watching and put down their glasses in perfect male murmuration.

"I'm serious," the woman said. "You can stay, but I don't want no journo making trouble."

Bowman felt no hostility from the men—they viewed him as an exotic, just escaped from a zoo. They resumed synchronized sipping. "What do they do?" he said.

"Cellar hands, vineyard workers, growers."

"So this Bob Bruce—he works in wine?"

She eyed him like he might be a bit slow, a two-toed sloth on the lam. Then she laughed. "Hey, Red," she shouted out to the men at the table. "This bloke wants to know if Brucie works in wine."

All the men paused with their schooners near their lips. One put his glass down. "Dunno if 'work' is the word I'd use," he called back. "But he don't mind drinkin' the stuff."

The woman smiled and looked at Bowman. "That's not quite right," she said. "Bruce is a winemaker. So he likes drinking beer."

6

Riley drove on back roads through a patchwork of paddocks interspersed with vineyards. Rows and rows of bare vines, hard pruned for winter, gnarled crosses in a weird burial ground. She skirted Cessnock and picked up the Maitland Road.

Midday on Tuesday, and the traffic was light. She'd left wine country and slowed through clapboard satellites, car wrecks on blocks, unweeded gardens. On the system, Rodrigues had shown her who they had residing, from the sex offenders and the wife bashers to the break-and-enters on bail. From here, Riley could take the Rapist Highway all the way to the beach, where it deviated. There were 137 men listed on the Child Protection Register for the Mid North Coast, where families with young kids congregated on holiday. Pedophiles loved a sea change.

Maitland huddled in its bend of the river. Nigel Armytage's office was in a redbrick stand-alone down on the levee. She pressed a bell and waited.

A white-bearded man, belted in beige, opened the door. "Detective." He held out his hand. "Howard Johns."

They shook and he stood with his arms at his sides.

"Thank you for seeing me," she said. "Is there somewhere we might talk?"

He turned into the corridor and looked back at her, and she encouraged him to lead. They went upstairs to an open-plan office with desktop computers around a long central workstation. The place was empty. Johns gestured to a smaller table near the windows. Riley sat across from him and opened her notebook. She put him at sixty, soft-spoken, educated. The look in his eye, she knew from experience: bewildered, professional, absorbing the news.

"You said on the phone that you worked back with Nigel last night," she said. "That was here?"

"Yes." Johns cleared his throat. "With Maria."

"Maria?"

"Maria Voulgaris. Another geologist."

"She's not working today?"

"I spoke with her after you called. I told her not to come in. She's very upset."

"Did you often work late, the three of you?"

"Regularly. Mining projects are time critical. Delays are expensive."

"What were you working on?"

"A model. Of a coal seam."

Riley's pen hovered. "What is that, exactly?"

"The model? Or the seam?"

"Both."

"It's a 3D geological picture of a layer of rock, fifty-two meters deep, southwest of Singleton. We drilled holes to define it, and now we're building a computer model. We superimpose the topography. We interpolate data points to define faults, depth, thickness, properties, qualities . . ."

"A layer of rock?" Riley said.

"Coal. Several million tons' worth. When they dig it up, you'll see the scar from space." Firm ground—his knowledge made him comfortable.

"Did you know Penelope Armytage?"

"I'd met her a couple of times, in here."

"You didn't socialize?"

"Not with Penny, no."

"With Nigel?"

46

He turned a hand on the table. "We'll have a beer if we're on-site at the mines overnight. Share a meal."

"Did he speak about Penelope, their relationship?"

"He would mention her. But nothing significant." Johns rubbed his nose. "He didn't confide in me, if that's what you're asking."

"You think he had something to confide?"

"I don't know." Johns paused. "I didn't say that."

"Nothing *significant*?"

He turned his palm again. "There is one thing. But it's common in the industry. And I don't want to gossip."

"I'm just drilling holes." Riley held his eye. "I need all the data."

His jaw clenched in his beard. "Look, I'm a bit green. So is Nigel. But we work in the fossil fuel industry. So we're compromised."

Riley waited.

"We take their money, the coal miners'—we keep the lights on, but we know we're not saving the world."

"You mean bribes?" she said.

"No, no." He almost laughed. "Nothing like that. It's more . . . middle class. Ah, a question of hypocrisy—not corruption . . . You understand?"

"Not really."

"Yes, sorry. Look, I'm a geologist, so is Nigel. We're geologists who find coal. When you burn coal, you burn carbon. Right?"

Riley shrugged.

"That's what's making the world hotter. That, and the farting of cows."

"Okay," she said. "Is this the gossip?"

"No. Well, almost. The gossip is, we're torn. We're in favor of phasing out fossil fuels, but we're paid to help dig them up. It becomes a moral question—one that can cause friction at home."

"Penelope didn't like Nigel's job?"

"Yes. And it can become intractable, quasi-religious. Right and wrong. She was having trouble seeing past it. She wanted Nigel out."

"Of the house?"

"Of the industry."

"They were fighting?"

"He was under pressure. I don't know how bad it got."

"Was he looking to leave?"

"The coal industry, yes. He's looking at copper and gold. Copper will be massively in demand to make the renewable industry work. The problem is, it's all boom and bust. Right now, despite what you might hear, there's money in coal. In the first twenty years of this century, global consumption of fossil fuels *increased* forty-five percent. It's not what the media tells you, it's just the truth. The world needs it, *our* society needs it. And working in it pays for nice things—like a new town house in the vineyards."

His tone honed to an edge of disapproval. But not for the husband—for the dead wife.

"Last night," Riley said, "were you here when Nigel left?"

"Yes. I locked up. We all left together."

"What time, exactly?"

"It's hard to be precise. A little before ten."

"Think about what you did on the way home. You drove?"

"Yes."

"Did you listen to the radio? Did you stop?"

"No. It's a six-minute drive. Actually . . ." He went to a workstation. "If I boot up, it will tell me when we shut down." He tapped at a keyboard, and Riley went over. Stepping back, he pointed at a software program with a *last altered* message and a time and a date.

"Do you mind if I photograph that?" she said.

"Not at all. I logged out at nine forty-two. A bit of chat as we tidied." He swiveled his arms. "We were all in our cars by . . . nine fifty?"

"Where does Maria live?"

"Newcastle."

"How old is she?"

He frowned. "Late thirties?"

"Married?"

"Yes. To Sophia. After the plebiscite. Lots of plates broken."

Riley kept her face blank.

"She wasn't rooting Nigel on the side," Johns said. "I can assure you of that."

7

Bowman's pie came with mashed potatoes, which he used to mop up the gravy. After draining his beer, he left the empty plate and glass on the bar and went out to the car for his bags. Back inside, the boss with the blue diary was waiting to show him his room. Her name was Sandra Hogg, and she owned the place.

"Ale in the blood," she said, leading him through the saloon. "Four generations, we've had it." She opened a door and they went into a dank internal passage that wound through the stone heart of the original inn. Sandra slowed to show him the way . . . right, right, left . . . past closed-off nooks. "Coal closet"—she pointed—"scullery, cellar . . ."

They came out into a rear foyer and went up a cedar staircase to the second floor and the guest accommodations—six rooms along a carpeted hall. Bowman's was first on the right. Sandra unlocked the door, and parking his suitcase, he draped his garment bag on an upholstered armchair. The room was clean, modern, spacious, with a desk he could work at. He walked past the bed and looked in on an ensuite.

"Never seen a country pub where I didn't share a bathroom," he said.

Sandra was in the doorway. "We renovated a couple of years back for the wine tourists. There are things they expect."

He gave silent thanks for the wine tourists.

"You've got the run of the place." She nodded down the hall. "No other guests till Friday."

His mouth stretched in lost hope. "No cops?"

"No cops." She shook her head. "Or not yet. Breakfast is from seven, in the saloon. Lunch, dinner, drinks—I had Michael start you a tab in the bar."

She left him to it, and he unpacked, hanging his jacket and shirts, then plugged in his laptop, checked his phone. Nothing from Riley. He took his notebook, locked up, and retraced the route down the stairs and through the flagstone passage to the saloon.

There was a family of four, the two kids very small, having an early dinner, and a smattering of drinkers through the rest of the room. The bunch of grape growers had shot through, their round table empty, and there was no sign of Sandra. Bowman took his same stool at the counter, and the big barman approached, languidly unracking a schooner and holding it to the Stone & Wood tap in a fluid movement. "The usual?"

Bowman smiled at the nonchalance—he'd ordered one drink, from Sandra, yet the barman had him pegged. "Sprezzatura," he said.

The barman hesitated, unsure if Bowman was changing his order. "Eh?"

"It means you're a Renaissance man—good at your job."

"Know what a bloke drinks. That's me job." The barman poured and plucked a coaster from a pile and put the beer down. "Started you a tab."

"Thanks"—Bowman raised his glass to him—"Michael."

The man nodded. There was no one waiting to be served and he loitered. "Them Sydney cops," he said. "They're staying at the Quirk. Two of 'em. You were askin'."

Bowman swallowed, beer and disappointment, a familiar brew. "Where's that?"

"Down the road." Michael's head jerked. "Close."

To his left, in the dining area, Bowman watched a young server clear the plates from the table with the little kids.

"That's Rachel," Michael said.

Rachel smoothly shouldered through a swing door to what must be the kitchen. Bowman touched his notebook on the bar . . . Sandra had said it was Rachel who had spoken to the cops last night.

He sipped, blinking over the rim at Michael, and kept his voice light. "You here last night?"

"Nup. Get Mondays off."

Michael's eyes went to the entrance, and Bowman turned to see a man and woman walking in. A journo and her snapper. They cruised, cynical. She was late twenties, jeans and navy blazer. The photographer was older, pushing fifty, salt-preserved and sun-damaged. Newcastle, half his life in the surf. He headed with his camera to a table in the corner, and the reporter came to the bar, three meters down from Bowman. Michael was there to meet her.

Bowman turned away, scooped his notebook into his lap, propped his elbow, held his chin, listened as she ordered. Glass of pinot gris, a Resch's, bowl of nachos. Michael moved around the bar, and Bowman kept his back to the woman until he heard her pay.

With a surreptitious sip to swivel, he saw her strutting to the table. He picked up his phone and googled *Laura Nolan* in Images. It was her, he could see it in the chin. Until recently, Bowman could move around anonymously, unrecognized—invisible, even, to a woman like Laura Nolan. Maybe not anymore. His book had put him in the public eye, and he'd done the rounds to promote it, including the morning shows on the networks. Nolan would watch that crap, Bowman knew, because that's where she'd see herself: on camera doing breakfast TV. And if Nolan did recognize him, she'd be awake to his history with Riley.

She put down the drinks and walked back across the room—heading for the toilets. The photographer, buried in his phone, hadn't registered the arrival of his Resch's. There were booths on either side of their corner table. Michael was loading a glasswasher. Bowman took his schooner and weaved through to the booth beside Nolan's table. The photographer didn't look up, and Bowman slid in and along a leather banquette to a shady corner. The high back of the booth would screen him from Nolan arriving from the bathroom.

He drank and waited, his notebook tucked beside him. Nolan came back . . . He couldn't see her, but she'd sat at the table and was talking on the phone. "Mm. One sec, I gotta write it down." Bowman opened his notebook too. "Okay, so with a *y*. Spell it all again. Mm. And the charges? Wait, conspiracy to defraud. Fifty-seven. Failure to lodge."

Bowman scribbled, but the details trailed off to a series of monosyllables, a final "I get it," and the call ended.

It went quiet at the table, Nolan and the photographer didn't talk. After a few minutes, the young server Rachel swung past with their food order, and Bowman was left to eavesdrop on the precise crunching of media snouts in the trough, eating corn chips.

The police station in Cessnock was a windowless bunker, clad in gray and light brown, with sections of black steel-mesh fence. It took up a corner block, with vehicles sliding into the compound through a security gate off a side street. An old weatherboard cottage, the original cop shop, had been preserved in the redevelopment and now sat ensconced in a Besser-block boundary wall.

The cottage's yellow paling fence marked a second entrance to the upgraded facility along a concrete drive. The whole thing looked over a vista of car dealers: Nissan, Kia, Toyota, Jeep, Mahindra, a "prestige" yard, Hyundai. There was a tire store for blowouts, and an auto parts and accessories shop. Cessnock was vehicle-proud.

Riley drove around the station and parked on a back street, under the gloom of a huge, dilapidated brick church, St. Joseph's. Next to it sat two other enormous brown-brick buildings—a rectory with a rusting roof and a Catholic hall. Three in a line, eerie, forlorn, utterly quiet. They were still in use, Riley guessed, but only just. Christ had evacuated Cessnock, run out of town on a donkey led by the pedophile priest Vincent Ryan.

The public entrance to the police station was tiled in bright blue, and in the foyer a uniformed senior sergeant waited at the desk to take Riley through. His badge said HARRIS. "Sarge," he said.

Riley gave half a nod. "Sarge."

The door clicked, and he held it for her. He was fortyish, solid, maybe six three. Riley came through and the door closed behind her. "Nice pad," she said.

"They poured seventeen million into it. Shoulda seen it before."

"I remember." The little weatherboard, next to the brick courthouse.

"Court's as is." Harris motioned. "Except now we're connected, internal. We used to do outside wanders. That was never good."

Riley nodded. She'd seen it in other towns, the cops walking suspects in the open air between the station and courthouse, exposed in full view.

Harris was broad across the shoulders, lantern jawed, some football in his posture, rugby league. He wasn't a desk jockey. He'd run a general duties pack, out on patrol.

Rodrigues had orchestrated this meet and greet, Riley knew. She'd chosen to isolate in a room at Red Creek, but Rodrigues wanted her to hear from a cop on the ground, someone who knew the locals and the lay of the land.

"You been here awhile?" she said.

"Coming up fifteen years."

They walked in step down a corridor. The place hummed, officers in and out of doors met Riley's eye. Word had got around: They knew she was here, and they knew who she was. Some of them might even have read Bowman's book.

She looked in as they passed the detectives' room. Command would use a facility like this to house special units operating all through the region and the Mid North Coast.

"Who've you got here?" she said.

"Sixty cops. Highway Patrol, Child Abuse, Sex Crimes, Raptor," Harris said. "Gangs. Hence your mate Rodrigues."

A piece of puzzle clicked for Riley: Rodrigues had come out of Gangs. Sydney, probably southwest. Hence his demeanor. The Lebs and the Albanians had been recruiting seventeen-year-old Islanders to pull the trigger—750K for a hit.

Harris stopped and opened a door. Inside, Patel and Rodrigues were on their laptops at a rectangular conference table. There was a one-way glass viewing window into an adjoining, empty interview room. Riley pulled out a chair and put down her bag. Rodrigues motioned for Harris to stay. The senior sergeant stood in the doorway.

Rodrigues had showered and shaved and changed clothes—black suit, white shirt, orange tie. Dark circles. "You get some sleep?" Riley asked.

"Couple of hours."

She checked the time: 4:22. Nigel Armytage had agreed to come in at 4:30. She looked from Harris to Rodrigues. "Thoughts?"

"We could give you a list," said Rodrigues. "Recent releases, who's residing, who's come up from Gosford to stay at Grandma's. Twenty names."

"Mm," Riley said.

Rodrigues threw to Harris, leaning in the door. "We've got a good understanding of who's around," he said. "Rape, battery, domestic violence. We've got plenty who are capable, but it wouldn't look like this."

"Go on," Riley said.

"If it's one of ours, you would expect them to act as they normally do. That means grog, it means meth. Lots of noise, big fuckin' mess. It means shouting and fighting, and the neighbors calling us round."

Patel sat back from her laptop. "If they're under pressure, they might act differently."

Harris looked pained. "Even if it's spontaneous—one of ours roaming through Red Creek and seeing the victim and grabbing her or breaking in—it wouldn't look like this."

"And if it's not spontaneous?" Patel said. "If it's planned?"

"We've never discerned that pattern with a local," Harris said. "That's an outsider."

"What do you know about the husband?" Riley said.

"He's clean, so . . ." Harris swayed his chin at Rodrigues.

"So we're working him up," Rodrigues said, and looked at his screen. "Nigel William Armytage, thirty-two. Born, Newcastle. Parents both doctors, retired. Nigel was sent to boarding school in Sydney and stayed there for university. Then he was back in Newcastle but moved around for work. WA and Queensland. Then back to Newcastle when he landed the Maitland job. He met Penelope. That was four years ago. They moved in together in Newcastle and then got married. The wedding was at a Hunter vineyard two years ago. They started spending time out there. Penelope had a digital marketing company and was picking up some winery contracts. Hence the move. For Nigel, he was closer to the mines, and the commute to Maitland was easy."

Riley looked back to Harris in the doorway. "What do you think?" she said.

"No priors, no form." He crossed his arms. "Pure domestic. Start with their friends. His former girlfriends. Does he have a temper? Is he controlling?"

"Yes," Riley said. "But also, he's an outsider—to you. He's a local, he's residing, but he's a cleanskin, not known to police."

"Understood," Harris said.

"I don't want him getting a rail's run because he's a nice middle-class scientist with a university degree and a good job. He's not hardcore Methnock, but that's not what we're looking for." She turned to Rodrigues. "The town house—is under mortgage?"

"Correct. They had some money to pour into it. But there's an eight-hundred-grand facility with NAB."

"Right," Riley said. "He's got a new mortgage, and perhaps an unhappy wife."

"We can put eyes on him," Harris said. "Down with his folks on the lake."

"Maybe." She gestured at the glass. "Let's see how this goes."

Through the viewing window, the door to the interview room had opened. A uniformed constable brought Nigel Armytage in and sat him at the desk. He stared at his hands, linked on the surface. He looked blank, in shock, very tired.

"What are we looking at?" Riley said.

"A zombie," Harris said from the doorway.

"A scientist," Rodrigues said. "Educated, smart."

"Beautiful wife, beautiful town house in beautiful wine country," Riley said. "Scientists might call it a pattern. What car does he drive?"

"Defender—the new one," Patel said. "Real wanker truck. Maybe a hundred and thirty grand."

"There you go," Riley said. "Beautiful. Everything's lovely and shiny and new. But lovely Penelope doesn't like his job. He's digging up coal. That's not beautiful, that's what knuckle draggers do."

"So he's a vain little prick," Harris said.

Nigel Armytage was facing them, oblivious, through the window.

"Let's say he's intent on appearances," Rodrigues said. "The appearances are funded by the job, and the job's under threat? Is that the theory?"

"Or maybe that's Penelope?" Patel said. "She's high maintenance, social climbing with wine, demanding. She wants it all, he gives it to her. But then she turns on him. She wants it all, but not from coal."

"A few too many sauv blancs," Rodrigues said. "The argument escalates to slaps—"

"And then he's got his hands round her throat," Harris said. "Now he sounds like a local."

Through the looking glass, Nigel Armytage hadn't moved. Again, Riley heard O'Neil's voice in her head: *The formal statement from a husband the day after the murder of his spouse creates conditions that can never be replicated.*

I.e., *Don't waste it.*

Switch, manipulate, misinform, lull, rattle, exploit—those were the rules. The spitballing around the table about Nigel Armytage wasn't really a theory, it was just a way for the team to warm up before stepping into the room.

Patel closed her laptop. "How do you want to play it?"

Rodrigues sat beside Patel, both sleek and lean—they were the same age, and Riley realized they'd bonded. If Patel had been unhappy with Rodrigues, Riley would have sensed it. She looked through at Nigel Armytage, and back at Rodrigues and Patel in their radiance. Beautiful.

Manipulate, exploit.

"You two go in and start things off," she said. "I'll watch from here."

Patel and Rodrigues sat across the desk from Nigel Armytage, and Patel went through the preliminaries for the tape.

It was Tuesday, August 26, 4:43 p.m.

In the viewing room, the uniformed senior sergeant, Harris, sat at the table with Riley, watching as Patel took the lead with the husband. It was the third time Nigel Armytage had given the police his movements, and Patel was probing for inconsistencies by building rapport.

Armytage's story was lining up with the version of events he'd given twice at the scene, with what his boss, Howard Johns, had told Riley, and with the electronic timeline Rodrigues was constructing. Armytage had driven the most direct route home from Maitland, traversing Cessnock to the north. He was still not exact on timing, which was normal, but RTA cameras and phone data from Telstra corroborated the trip.

"You left Maitland at 'about ten' and arrived home at what time?" Patel said.

"Ten thirty-seven," Armytage said.

She smiled encouragement, her head bobbing. He'd made the 10:37 claim twice now.

"Hear the precision?" Riley muttered to Harris. "It stands out in the vagueness."

"Even with the data, there's wriggle room," Harris said. "There's nothing to say he wasn't home at ten twenty. All we know is the triple zero at ten forty-one."

"Pathologist says she was killed at nine."

"Yeah," Harris said. "Give or take an hour."

"That's an hour and a half," Riley said.

In profile, Harris made a face. "The docs have been out before. For me, a woman killed like this, strangled or smothered in her house—that's the partner. Always the partner."

Through the glass, Nigel Armytage drank water.

"This bloke's got witnesses," Harris said. "But look at the alibi. Almost watertight, but dribbling. Want me to give him a touch-up?"

It had gone quiet next door. Patel was waiting for Riley to come in and replace Rodrigues. Riley stood, stretched her neck, gathered her notebook. "Keep watching." In the hall, she knocked on the next door and went in. "Mr. Armytage," she said. "I'm sorry I'm late."

He acknowledged her and watched as Rodrigues stood and left the room. Riley sat in his chair.

"For the tape," Patel said. "Detective Sergeant Riley replaces Detective Senior Constable Rodrigues at"—she looked at her phone—"eight past five p.m."

Riley opened her notebook. "Eight past five. Ten thirty-seven. Around ten. Can you pick the odd one out, Mr. Armytage?"

He scratched at the back of his head. "Pardon?"

"You left home at 'about two,' you arrived at the office 'around two thirty.' Takeaway food was delivered at . . . ?" Riley looked to Patel.

"'Seven-ish,'" she said.

"You left work at 'around ten' and you arrived home at 'ten thirty-seven,'" Riley said.

Armytage was blinking at the roll call. "Yes."

"Scientists would call it a pattern. Can you pick the odd one out?"

He looked confused. "You're concerned that I remember the exact time I got home?"

There was a quizzical touch to his raised eyebrow, which interested Riley, and she smiled. "How were things at home?"

Consternation flared, incinerating his bemusement. "Not very good. My wife was lying dead on the floor."

"Before that."

"Could you be more . . ." He paused for effect. "Specific?"

"Last week, last month. On the weekend. Was there some yelling? Trouble at home?"

"There was no yelling."

"But there was trouble," Riley said. "Because Penelope wasn't happy."

He sighed, looked down to his left. "You've spoken to Howard. Or Zoe?"

"Who's Zoe?" Riley said.

"Her friend. I gave you her number."

Riley nodded.

Armytage clasped his hands on the table. "It's no secret. Pen didn't like my work. She wanted me to change jobs. I spoke with Howard, and my folks. Pen did the same. And we talked about it together. It was a discussion—an argument, not a fight."

"What did you say?" Riley said.

"In the coal debate, there's hypocrisy everywhere. But I said I'd move out of the sector."

"You called her a hypocrite?" Riley said.

His eyes came up, rheumy. "Yeah. Probably. Everyone's a hypocrite with climate change. With their dogs and their iPhones and their holiday homes. The limousine liberals driving between their mansions and their farms and their coast houses, gaslighting the gas industry." He blinked. "Jesus, how did we get on to this?"

"You told Penny you'd get out of coal," Riley said. "And that resolved things?"

"What?" Disgust thinned his lips. "Wait. You think this is relevant to her murder?"

"If you were in a domestic dispute, then yes, I think it's relevant." He looked to Patel. "You think I killed my wife over fracking?"

"No one said you killed your wife," Patel said.

"Did you?" Riley said.

He shook his head in stunned disbelief.

"Did you kill Penny?" Riley said.

He met her eye. Wounded, resolved. "I did not kill my wife."

"What's fracking?" Riley said.

His mouth came open. "Are you serious?"

"Fracking?" Patel pinched her chin. "Mr. Armytage, what is that?"

There were tears in his eyes. He took a breath. "No." He shook his head. "I'm not going to do this. It's too stupid for words."

"It's a simple question," Riley said.

Armytage wiped at his face with a sleeve. "It's a process of extracting gas from a seam. A relatively clean way to generate energy from coal."

"And Penny didn't like it?" Patel said.

"No one likes it, especially round here."

"Here?" Riley said.

"Grape growers—farmers. Everyone watched *Gasland*. Now fracking's the bogeyman."

"Is it something you're involved with?" Patel said.

"No."

"Then why bring it up?" Riley said.

He raised a hand. "Sorry. It's confusing. It's just shorthand for the whole argument. Pen worries the mining companies will unleash coal-seam gas in the Hunter. We couldn't be associated with that and live where we do."

"Ten thirty-seven," Riley said.

Armytage wiped at his cheek again. "What?"

61

"The time you got home. Ten thirty-seven. How come you're so sure?"

"I don't know." He stared at the table. "I looked at the clock on the dash when I parked. Ten thirty-seven. It stuck with me for some reason, I just remember it." He swallowed. "You know how that happens sometimes? Like an omen."

8

Riley followed Patel out of the police station entrance, onto the back street, below the three dark Catholic piles, relics now to loss and squalor.

Across the road, by the Calais, two male youths vaped on the stairs leading up to the church. One was in a Newcastle Knights flannel, stained gray tracksuit pants, and ankle-high purple Reeboks. The other wore a dark pin-striped suit and UGG boots. They stared at Patel as she went to the car. Riley walked on the footpath to the driver's-side door.

The youths hung on the steps above her, two meters away, rodent-faced under mousy-brown mullets. "Sweet ride, eh," the suited one said.

Riley pressed the fob to unlock the Holden and looked him over. The suit was from the Salvos, or maybe his absent father's grandpa. Under the pinstripes and greased lapels, he wore a white T-shirt with a thin black tie printed on it. He noted Riley's gaze and opened the jacket wide. "Me lawyer, yeah," he said. "Cunt tells me, like wear a fuckin' tie to court."

His mate coughed on his vape. "Worked heaps, but eh. Got . . . what's it?"

"Bail," Suit and Tie said. "Got me like bail, eh."

They looked eighteen. "What did you do?" Riley said.

Suit and Tie made a face. "As if. Fuckin' nothin', eh."

His mate sniggered. "Stole a sausage. Fuckin' ALDI."

Suit and Tie kicked out at him with an UGG boot. "You can talk, ya fuckin' dog, can't ya."

The vaper blew sweet, rancid air. Riley got in the car beside Patel and pressed the ignition, drove around the bunkered station, and went left past the columned courthouse.

"What d'you think?" Riley said.

"Little things," Patel said. "When he talked about Penny, he used the present tense."

Riley took the road north out of town, past the prison and the nursing home and the cemetery. "People stare at you here. Have you noticed?"

Patel scoffed. "Nice of *you* to notice."

"What, because of color?"

"Yeah. You don't see it. This place, it's all white."

They were passing a flat row of brick shops with a restaurant sign— BILLU'S CURRIES—and Riley lifted a finger off the wheel to point.

Patel looked out the window. "They're pioneers. Here to wean people off Macca's four nights a week."

Riley liked Macca's for breakfast. Cessnock had been a peripheral presence in her childhood, and she viewed it now like a cop. Hard town. No airs and graces, but there was civic pride.

Patel was on a roll. "Why choose to be insular? There's this whole tourist-wine industry on the doorstep—money for jam, literally—and Cessnock just says, 'Nup, we're not playing that game.' It's like putting Boggabri in Bordeaux."

"They're miners," Riley said. "That's the way it's always been. It's a more honest dollar than flogging plonk."

"You respect that?"

"Yeah. Why not? Fuck the goat's cheese set."

"It's more than that—it's a refusal to experience the world. Most people here would never have been to Sydney."

"Most people here would never have been to Kurri." Riley had been to Kurri Kurri this very day, returning from Maitland. It was Cessnock's neighbor, ten minutes east.

"Hence the ability to stare at Asians."

Flat country was going past. "Back to Nigel," Riley said. "What did I miss?"

"Respect," Patel said.

Riley slowed and turned left, into Broke Road and the vineyards. "Respect for Nigel?" she said. "That can be your job."

"Okay." Patel shrugged. "But it's what you missed. *Treat with respect.*" She was quoting O'Neil. "If Nigel's in a position of privilege, then assume he's earned it. He's a geologist because he's clever and he's worked hard."

"It's not about privilege," Riley said.

There was a fudge shop and then a Tuscan-pink cellar door with curved walls and a little tower. "You see him as smug, condescending," Patel said. "You think he thinks he's the smartest person in the room."

Riley ran her tongue over her teeth.

"I think he's bewildered, in shock," Patel said. "I think you took a shortcut. You want to misread his frustration for arrogance."

"Because . . . ?" Riley said.

"Because arrogance is useful to us. An arrogant man can do terrible things."

True.

"He's a scientist trying to come to terms with something incomprehensible," Patel said. "It's not condescension he's showing, it's confusion. I know he might be our guy. But don't twist what we saw. Remember, the poor bastard just lost his wife."

"There's a high probability the poor bastard just strangled her to death on the floor," Riley said. "You heard Powell, the pathologist?"

"Mm."

"Female victims of homicide are often smothered or strangled, and the partner kicks up dust. Even Harris just said it. The partner—always the partner."

Patel didn't answer, and rightly so: Riley was just falling back on the obvious, stating things they both knew.

Through the windshield, ridges rose on the range. Riley's father had taught her the names of the mounts, she could orient herself instantly in the valley. Her father had run motley livestock and trapped feral goats—never once milked for cheese. He'd fixed machinery on the side. He'd thought about grapes, and paid a man, an agronomist, to run his eye over the place. The scientist had come and gone for a week and then told Bill Riley, *No, the soil's no good.* A year later the land was sold and the Rileys were living in Campbelltown. Bill Riley leased a garage. Rose was eleven.

If Riley went back now to the old place, she knew what she'd see: the soil planted to vine.

Her father had seldom spoken of the farm, but she saw how living in the city changed him, had subtly diminished him—he'd stayed steadfast, kind, and true, and he'd worked hard, but he'd done it with a broken heart.

He'd been dead five years, and for a long time Riley's mother had never mentioned the farm. Then, six months ago, she had called Riley and talked about Bowman's book. "It's a funny thing, you know, Rose," her mother said. "But I'll die now with one regret."

Riley at that point hadn't read the book yet and felt frustration stir, wondering what liberties Bowman had taken and written down.

"It's not losing the farm," her mother said. "I'm over that. It's in the past. I don't regret it."

"Wait, what?" Riley said. "He wrote about the farm?"

"No, no. But your father—" Her mother's voice caught. "He will never get to read the book. That's my regret."

Bill Riley had never read a book in his life.

"He would have read this one, by God," her mother said. "He would have read it twice."

Patel shifted beside her because there was an oncoming vehicle. Riley corrected a fraction left into her lane.

"You right?" Patel said.

"Yeah, sorry." She shook her head. "*Memory* lane."

Patel dug in the console and passed her a piece of gum. Riley unwrapped it as her phone pinged, and she slowed to look. A text from Bowman—no words, just a link to a *Mirror* article. She handed it to Patel to read.

Patel swiped down the story. It was quiet in the car. "We might have a problem," she said.

In his room at the Packhorse, Bowman sent the *Mirror* link to Riley and then read the top of the story again. Cops Haul In Husband In Hunter Slaying, the headline read. The byline was Laura Nolan.

> Homicide detectives this afternoon interrogated the husband of murdered Red Creek woman Penelope Armytage, 27.
>
> Nigel Armytage, 32, was questioned at Cessnock over the killing of his wife, who was found dead late last night in the couple's new town house in wine country at Red Creek.
>
> There are no other suspects, sources said.

Bowman could see Riley had read his message, but she hadn't responded. He took his fleece vest and his notebook, locked up, and went down the stairs and through the pub, out to his car. Nolan and the photographer were long gone. Earlier in the booths, the munching of corn chips at the next table had given way to sounds of typing, and Bowman now guessed he'd been listening to Nolan write the Armytage story.

It was dark, after seven. He drove left down the road, and in less than a kilometer his lights found a motel sign: THEQUIRK@REDCREEK. He turned in and saw Patel's Camry in the car park, with one other vehicle, a green MG. The glass sliding reception doors were locked, and the lobby was empty under low light.

Bowman left the Audi and followed a gravel path between the car park and the long building, trying to see into rooms. Each had a neat timber deck, accessed by heavy glass doors, but blinds were down and no light crept around any edges. There was no one in any room down the row. If the MG belonged to a guest, he realized, they must be in a room on the other side. Riley and Patel weren't here, he could feel it—they were out with Riley's Calais.

He wondered again if the police were feeding Nolan angles, using the reporter to rattle the husband. Surely that was what he had overheard earlier, Nolan speaking with a cop on the phone. It made sense, there'd been talk of charges. Conspiracy to defraud—Nolan hadn't published that.

Nolan's story was a beat-up: Of course the cops had brought the husband in, they needed to take his formal statement. Nolan could have got wind of that and extrapolated. Or Riley had a leak on her team, some local cop who'd called Nolan and tipped her off. A leak would be good, for Bowman. Because Riley could use him to hit back, and then the game would be afoot, dueling banjos.

Bowman, ruminating, had crossed the bitumen away from the building, into the full dark. Trees loomed, and he felt eyes on him, nocturnal. From close above, a bird called—three notes, laconic, all-knowing. Not a crow, a raven.

Turning back, he saw a bright light come on at the motel entrance. A man came out the glass doors, checking around as he walked to Bowman's Audi. He peered in the driver's-side window and circled the car. Bowman headed over, calling out on approach, "Evening."

The man's eyes narrowed in query as Bowman emerged from the night.

"You after a room?"

"No, I'm . . ." Bowman motioned at Patel's car. "Here to see a guest."

The man's eyes flicked to the Camry. "You police too?"

Bowman took a slow, official breath. "This your place?"

He nodded. They stood in silence for a moment, in the glow from a night bollard. "I saw her, you know. In the afternoon."

Bowman felt cold in his arms in his vest. "Saw her?"

"The dead girl. Up the crossroad." His head swayed. "Yesterday."

"Okay," Bowman said. "What was she doing?"

"Running."

"Running? From whom?"

The man eyed him. "Not like that. Jogging. Like I said when they came knocking last night."

Bowman rubbed at his cheeks. The man thought he was police. Bowman could milk it before coming clean. He moved to the Audi and bent for his notebook. "Do you have a minute"—he looked toward the motel entrance—"for a chat?"

The man shucked a shoulder. They walked, and he keyed through the glass doors with a card. Lights clicked on in the lobby, and he led Bowman across to a guest area with tables and chairs. A sign on a wall said THE PANTRY, and the space was fitted out as a full kitchen, with appliances in pairs: sinks, ovens, commercial fridges, three cooktops.

The man was a symphony in tan, from wind jacket, to sweater, to trousers . . . even his shoes. Pale skin, marked by weather. His face mottled and blasted, with small blotches and a thin scar on a lip where a freckle or cancer had been cut out. His straw hair was sandy, thinning and swept back. He looked late forties, average height, average build—but trim, not running to fat.

Bowman waited until they were seated. "My name's Adam Bowman. I'm a freelance reporter, but I'm filing for *The National*."

"Oh." The man went still. "I thought you were the police."

Bowman simulated surprise and took the lid off his pen. "Can you tell me again about yesterday? The whole day—start from when you got up."

The man looked blankly at Bowman's blank page.

Bowman waited but nothing came, and he started over. "Sorry, what did you say your name was?"

"I didn't."

"Pardon?"

"I didn't," the man said, "say my name."

Bowman made a shape with his lips.

The man's face slid open, showing his teeth as he smiled. He was on his feet suddenly, walking away. "Can I get you a drink?" he asked over his shoulder. He put a card on a wall reader, opened a fridge, and looked in. "Coke? Water?"

"No." Bowman blinked. "Thanks."

The man closed the fridge and ambled back, empty-handed. "I don't think I want my name in the paper," he said, resuming his seat. "With my business and all."

"I can—"

"Not this." He tossed his head at the lobby. "Karen runs the show. But I've got clients. I'm a consultant." He grinned. "An entrepreneur."

Bowman was finding he did need a drink.

"That's hard to spell." The man pointed at the notebook. "How about you say"—he made quote marks—"*A local businessman saw the girl jogging around the crossroad at five*? Will that work?"

Bowman's pen tapped the table.

"Good. All this is a self-catering model we developed, to run off a guest card." He held up his card. "Fully integrated, low cost. No staff. It's my intellectual property."

"Wow," Bowman said.

"We're rolling it out to other owner-operators. Motels." He pushed back his chair. "Look, sorry, I gotta go."

Bowman took his notebook and they stood.

"Now, you're sure you don't need a room?" the man said.

Bowman shook his head.

At the entrance, the man keyed open the door. "You should come back, another time. I'll show you the setup." He ushered Bowman out. "You could do a story on that."

Riley drove through the wide roundabouts at the center of the tourist district and out past a Mercure resort and an alpaca barn and Ye Olde General Store. Patel read out the Nolan story that Bowman had sent, then put down Riley's phone.

"Nigel will think it came from us," Patel said. "Especially after the interview."

Riley pulled in at a lay-by and picked up the phone to scroll the *Mirror* story. Nolan might have a source at the station. It was better to discuss it here rather than in the incident room with Rodrigues.

Patel flicked on the interior light. "Could be she's got a cop talking. Or it could be nothing. Nolan saw Nigel coming in and joined the dots."

The story would put pressure on Nigel Armytage, if he had something to hide. But if he was guilty—or an innocent man, mourning his wife—and he believed Riley was using the media to attack him, then it was a problem. Respect wasn't just about decency, it was also strategic.

Whether a suspect or a victim, the husband was a vital asset, and Riley needed to keep him close. To challenge him point-blank in the interview room was one thing, to feed him to the press quite another. "We explain to Nigel that we didn't brief *The Mirror* and that we'll freeze Nolan out," she said. "Whatever she writes—it didn't come from us."

Patel motioned at the phone. "We can undercut Nolan with Bowman. He's ready to get in on it."

"Yeah, but for what? All we'd get is a media circus. And we'd be bringing in the clown."

Patel laughed. "In his clown car."

Riley shook her head. Bowman's Audi was a whiny little two-liter piece of shit. He might as well have bought a lawn mower.

"It's an Audi, mate," Patel said. "He's showing his status."

"Status? He looks like a television chef from Double Bay."

"I did see him on the telly," Patel said. "In quite the shirt— peacock blue."

Riley had started to note that as well, Bowman's new clothes. "How often do you see him?"

"What, without you?"

Riley nodded. Three or four times a year, the three of them would meet for a meal.

"I dunno." Patel frowned. "Maybe every six weeks. Why?" She looked over. "Are you jealous?"

"No. Or I don't think so." Bowman was good at maintaining their friendship—once a month he'd call Riley and they'd go for a drink.

"Did you read the book, in the end?" Patel said.

Riley grunted. She'd read the book three times, in the end.

"And . . . ?"

"Yeah," she said. "Interesting."

Patel made wide eyes.

Riley looked out the windshield. "It wasn't what I thought it would be, at all."

"Maybe that's because you've never actually read a book."

Riley nodded.

Patel laughed again. "No, I'm joking. You're right, it is different."

"In what way?"

Patel hesitated, gauging the barometer to check if Riley was serious. "It's a murder story, with this plot that we all know, but somehow he meshes that with this character, this real person that, I mean, we know too." Patel lifted a finger at Riley. "That would be you. And he uses you, all these *details* that he sees, good and bad, but, you know, true. I mean, I know you, too, and I watch you, but when I'm reading it, I'm just nodding, at the"—she made an O shape with her lips—"perception, I guess. The depth. He just dives way down deep, and tells the story"—she scratched below her nose—"through you . . ."

"Isn't that what books do?" Riley asked.

"Some, maybe. But I think what he has—what he *found*—is clarity. Pure air. I mean, as you're reading it, you don't realize, it seems so simple, but you're gliding along, and you can't stop. You can't stop reading—literally, you can't put it down."

Riley nodded.

"Well, that's craft," Patel said. "That's Bowman. It feels simple, but I don't think it's easy. I mean, fuck, talk about respect—you have to respect what he did."

"I respect Bowman," Riley said.

"I know you do."

"But . . . ?"

"But nothing. Well, except, I mean we interact with him in an established way—it's not a rut, it's loose, it's banter. If we want to work with him, we shouldn't change that. Because it's a dynamic, it's tested. We know it gets results."

"Why would we change it?"

"You don't think of him differently? I mean, after the book?"

"He didn't insult me."

"No. God, I mean the opposite."

"Yeah, but it's not sickly. He didn't praise me as some hero."

"No."

"You're in there too. So's O'Neil."

"Yeah." Patel smiled. "We're in there too. But he tells it through you, and that must be weird for you to read. Doesn't that alter how you view him?"

"I suppose. I know I've got to watch him, there's more than meets the eye. But I've probably always realized that about Adam. And . . . I mean, I watch him in a good way, it's not about trust. I trust him, completely." Riley looked at her phone. "You know, even my mum likes it. The book."

Patel breathed through her nose. "See, that's what I mean. You saying that, that's a change."

"I talk about Mum. I call her every week."

"Not that. You're fishing for a compliment. You've *never* done that."

"Really?" Riley shifted. "Well, do tell."

"Are you serious? Your mother, reading that book? I mean, it's like a gift."

"Her daughter's in a book." Riley straightened. "It happens—cops are in books. O'Neil's in about seven."

"Fuck me drunk." Patel shook her head. "You can't actually be that dumb, so you're being cute. You said you read it, yes?"

"Yes."

"Like actually read it, not looked at the pictures?"

Riley shrugged.

"How many times?"

"Once. I mean, I might have read some bits twice."

Patel's head shied back at the lie. "You really want me to spell it out?"

"I didn't go to uni. So yeah, spell it out."

"You're right—he didn't paint you as a legend, some cartoon. That would be all the shit books O'Neil's in. What he did is much . . . quieter.

He saw you. He watched you while we worked the case, and then for months after, all those times when he called you, or visited, and you gibbered away."

"He asked questions," Riley said, "and I answered."

"Yeah, and he listened—very close. He studied you. Your foibles, your courage, your fears—what's good about you, plus why you can really suck. And somehow he found this essence, and he rolled it into this story. Your mother, reading that? I mean, fucking come on. He knows you like she does. And then he wrote it all down."

Riley sniffed.

"Phew, it's getting hot in here." Patel pressed the button to crack her window. In the light of the cabin, Riley caught a flash of a pink-painted nail.

At Red Creek, Rodrigues was moving around the incident room, printing out the relevant visuals and pinning them on the felt boards that now lined the walls. Patel started helping: maps of the region, crime scene photos of the town house, timelines, a victimology list, pictures of Penelope Armytage . . . It was 8:00 p.m., twenty-four hours since her death.

Riley sat stretched out, with her hands behind her head. "Where are we weak?"

"Victimology," Rodrigues said. "Her movements. Even on the day."

Riley unlinked her fingers, reached for a Texta, and stood. "Draw it."

Rodrigues took the Texta and went to a big map. "The town house." He made a red dot. "She works from home in the morning. Nigel is there. At two p.m. she has an on-site meeting with a client, Gully Breeze Estate, a winery, here." Rodrigues traced the route. "It's not far—three kilometers on back roads. There are no cameras, we don't clock her, but we've confirmed she was there. She met with the owner, a certain Bob Bruce."

"What do we know about him?"

"Fifth-generation winemaker, big rooster in the district."

"Clean?"

"Just traffic stuff."

"And?"

"Gossip. Known as a world-class pisshead. Which is saying something, round here. He can get a bit cuddly with, ah, females in his employ."

"Age?"

"Fifty-eight."

"Married?"

Rodrigues nodded and stepped over to his desk for his iPad. "Yeah." He swiped. "To Diana, same surname. There are three adult kids."

"We been out to see him?"

"Not yet."

Riley studied the map. "Then what?"

"Penny drives into Cessnock." Rodrigues came back and drew. "She pays at Woolworths at three thirty-eight. Then goes home. The male neighbor down the row saw her car after four. She's a regular runner. The female neighbor saw her leaving for a jog about five. The café owner saw her here. Motel owner saw her here." Rodrigues marked two dots around the Red Creek crossroads. "Four sightings. Timings line up."

"Does she lock the door when she runs?"

"There's a question."

"The motel owner—that's Karen Cassidy?"

Rodrigues put the pen in his mouth and swiped again at his iPad. "No. Her husband, Jayson Cassidy. That's Jayson with a *y*."

Riley thought back. Karen had watched her write *Jason* in her notebook and hadn't corrected her. A small thing, but the woman could have pointed out the error. "Who did the Cassidy canvass?"

Rodrigues read again from the screen. Two Cessnock junior constables had door knocked the Cassidys at midnight and spoken to them. Karen had then opened the motel, and the constables had spoken to the only two guests—the philanderers from Sydney with the Volvo. Their movements had now been verified with the venues they had visited in the valley on Monday afternoon and evening.

"Where do the Cassidys live?" Riley said.

"In a house behind the motel."

She pointed at the iPad. "Can I see that?"

Rodrigues handed it over, and Riley skimmed the witness statements. Jayson Cassidy said he had been driving through the Red Creek crossroad to the motel and seen Penelope Armytage jogging on the road "around five."

Riley handed the screen to Patel and waited while she read.

Rodrigues watched them. "You want to look at Jayson?"

"It's more the links," Riley said. "The Cassidys and the Armytages. The motel, the developer, the town house. We give that to the analyst."

Patel passed him back the iPad. "What else?" she said.

"I spoke to Penny Armytage's best friend," Rodrigues said. "She's coming up from Sydney tomorrow to walk through the scene."

"She say anything?" Riley said.

"Loves Penny. Loves Nigel. Oh my God."

"Any talk of marital fighting?" Patel said.

"No. She spoke with Penny every few days. Penny moaned sometimes about Nigel's work with the mines. But she was very loyal to him. She worshipped him."

"Anything on Nigel?" Patel said.

"The friend likes him. She said all Penny's friends like him. He's caring. Respectful. He wanted kids with her."

"Did we get to Penny's parents?" Riley asked.

"Yeah. They're flying in from Alice. Might be twelve hours."

Riley looked at her watch: 8:07 p.m. Karen had said something about lasagna.

Patel nodded at Rodrigues. "You should go," she said. "See your wife."

They packed up and he turned out the lights. It was cold on the porch as he pulled the door closed and handed them each a key. "I had a guy out," he said. "Changed the locks."

"Thanks." Riley walked down the path. The thought of Penelope Armytage's parents made her feel very tired.

9

The Newcastle Department of Forensic Medicine was at the bottom of a scrubby slope behind the hospital. Frank Powell took Riley and Patel through from the main entrance and briefed them as they walked the morgue's corridors.

It was Wednesday morning. There had been the standard full CT scan of the body in its bag on arrival very early yesterday. "Radiology shows no injuries, no breaks, no fractures." Powell held the door to his autopsy suite. "No damage to the neck."

He handed them masks, gloves, gowns. Beth Gatjens and one of her constables were ready in scrubs. The body bag was on a slab, and a technician waited for the detectives before he cut the police seal.

Powell started with sexual assault swabs for DNA. The hands, face, neck, breasts—anywhere the attacker might have touched. The pathologist went carefully, Gatjens assisting.

They paused at the right arm. Gatjens held up the limb, and her constable took photos.

Powell waved Riley over. "See the bruising?" The pathologist pointed at the inner part between the elbow and shoulder. "Now the other."

Gatjens picked up the left hand and held the arm aloft.

Powell examined the upper limb. "The same here." He made room for the constable's camera and turned to Riley. "She's been grabbed with two hands from behind. Hard. The bruises are finger marks squeezing the fleshy parts of both arms."

After studying the wrists, Gatjens moved to the ankles. "Nothing," she said.

Powell was at the neck, and he beckoned Riley again. "It's as we said at the scene. Asymmetric bruising, either side of the voice box." He pointed. "A thumb and four fingers. Manual strangulation—he's using his hands."

"No scratch marks," Gatjens said. "He's kept his nails short."

The crime scene constable took an overview photograph of the mouth with the lips closed, and then Powell used forceps to pry open the jaw and swab the tongue and around the cavity for semen. Gatjens bagged the sample, and Powell went back in with forceps and a dental mirror, pulling the upper lip and then the lower, studying the gums and the teeth. He hummed, concentrating on the close work, then grunted. "Tweezers."

The technician handed him the instrument.

He dug around and swore and changed his position. "Come here, you little bastard."

More humming, then he pulled the tweezers from the mouth, held them out over Gatjens's open bag, and deposited the object he'd extracted. She put the clear plastic up to the light. A piece of yellow material, five millimeters long.

"Foam?" She handed the bag to Riley, who looked and passed it on to Patel.

"When did she last see the dentist?" Patel said.

Powell turned to continue with the autopsy. He moved down the torso and performed the intimate swabs for semen. "He wore gloves. It's likely he wore a condom as well."

Gatjens bagged the samples.

"Was she raped?" Riley asked.

"No injuries," Powell said. "She's a woman having regular sex. That's all I can say."

The constable took more photos.

Powell spoke over the body to the technician. "Full neck dissection." The technician began assembling tools on a trolley.

Powell walked toward a trough of stainless-steel sinks and beckoned Riley. "We have to shave her, the back of her head," he said. "I'm sorry, the family won't like it." He was going to cut through her neck from the back, and then a mortician would stitch her up neatly. The missing patch of her beautiful blond hair would distress the people who loved her.

There was nothing Riley could say. The evidence had to be gathered.

"Pop out for a bit," he said, nodding to her and Patel. "We'll talk in half an hour."

She was thankful for the pathologist's etiquette—she hated the smell of an autopsy suite, and she didn't need to hear the grind of the saw.

At a coffee machine in a corridor, she pressed buttons and passed a plastic cup to Patel. Black, with a dash of formaldehyde.

They sat on a bench. "Foam in the mouth?" Patel said.

"Let's rule out the dentist. We might need a court order."

Patel texted Rodrigues to track down Penny Armytage's dentist.

Riley pulled out her notebook and wrote *Foam*. Under it, she wrote *Pillows, cushions, mattresses, sofas, soft toys*. She sipped her coffee. Time passed and she let her mind drift. Crime Scene had collected the Armytage rubbish and gone through the drains. She made another note: *Check waste for foam*.

Powell texted and they went back in. A mortician was sewing up.

"Neck dissection shows no pattern of a ligature," the pathologist said. "It confirms manual strangulation. It's subtle, with very few injuries, but they are nonetheless there."

Riley picked up the evidence bag with the material taken from the mouth. She agreed with Gatjens: yellow foam. "Let's call it foam while we wait on the lab," Riley said. "Like the filler used to stuff a cushion."

"She wasn't smothered," Powell said.

"No." Riley set the bag down. "But he grabs her from behind and has to keep her quiet. He pushes her straight down on the lounge and presses her face into a cushion. He holds her there until she begins to asphyxiate. The fight goes out of her."

"In the struggle, she bites the cushion," Patel said.

"But he doesn't keep going and smother her," Gatjens said. "He turns her and strangles her. Why?"

Powell was scrubbing at a sink. "He fucks up. He thinks she's dead. He turns her and she regains consciousness, so he has to finish her."

"But why *strangle?*" Gatjens pressed. "Even if he has turned her, he'd be more likely to continue as he started—grab the cushion back and smother her."

"Maybe there's no time," Powell said. "She wakes up fighting, trying to scream. The cushion falls on the floor."

"No scratch marks," Gatjens said. "And nothing under her fingernails."

"Agreed," he said. "There's no sign she's fought him. So, scenario two. He chooses to turn her and strangle her manually." He looked at Patel. "Why?"

"He wants to use his hands," she said.

Powell pulled off his gloves. "And?"

"He wants to see her face," Patel said.

"Mm. All right—he wants to watch, he wants to use his hands." Powell toweled off his forearms. "And with the hands, what else?"

"Premeditation," Gatjens said. "He's wearing gloves. Keeps his nails short."

"Okay. He came prepared." Powell threw his towel in the sink. "And?"

"Manual strangulation," Patel said. "He wants to feel."

"He was enjoying it. But it's more than that." Powell widened his eyes at Riley.

She looked at the body on the slab. He was enjoying it, organized, prepared . . .

"He's good at it," she said, "because he's done it before."

10

Riley sat in the Calais on the gravel outside the Armytage town house. Penelope's parents and best friend had been walked through the scene. Riley had met them but hung back, leaving Rodrigues and Patel to chaperone them in the property and then escort them to Cessnock to be interviewed.

A small group of camera crew and reporters, camped outside the cordon, had been busy documenting the activity. Riley watched them put their gear away. Laura Nolan wasn't in the pack.

Riley pulled out, went left to the crossroads, and drove the route Rodrigues had traced in Texta on the map last night. She was on back roads, narrow bitumen, some dirt. Bare vines ran in rows on either side.

There was a sign for GULLY BREEZE ESTATE. Riley turned in over a cattle grid, through a white paling fence, and up a manicured drive lined with magnolias and agapanthus. The cellar door was hidden behind sculpted Murraya, with cars in a visitor parking area to the left. Riley went right, following a sign pointing to the office, and came out at the rear of the main building in front of a big shed. There were two utes—a white Hilux and an old green Navara—and farm equipment on the apron.

Riley parked to the side, scribbled down the regos of the vehicles, and got out. There was a chance Bob Bruce wasn't home. When she'd visited Nigel Armytage's boss yesterday in Maitland, she'd arranged it in advance. But today, with Penelope's client, it was different—Riley hadn't let the winemaker know she was coming.

A sign at a back door of the building said OFFICE and another on the shed said DELIVERIES. There was no one around. A lone blue gum stood watch.

The high roller doors to the shed were up, and Riley stepped into the entrance. It was cavernous, a thousand square meters, she guessed. The space was cold and dim and smelled medicinal, like Band-Aids. Four stainless-steel tanks sat against one wall, and racked rows of wooden barrels ran along another. Hoses, presses, a pyramid-shaped concrete vat with taps and gauges, pallets of packaging, and a forklift. She heard a clank deep inside, metal on metal, and she stood for a moment to let her eyes adjust to the gloom.

She took a breath and called out, "Hello?"

There was no answer, but a strange stillness settled, and she knew someone was in there and had heard her.

She waited under the roller doors. A gust went through the tree and the leaves rustled. She was about to call again when she saw a figure coming from the shadows: a man in a cap. He walked without making a sound and held a long wrench by his side.

Riley's weight shifted a fraction as her body started to ping messages: Her back was exposed to the open courtyard.

The man had stopped about six meters from her and was staring. Dirty work clothes, grime on a cheek, a thin arm lugging his wrench. His face was hollowed out, bitten by drugs, but Riley put him at forty—too young to be Bruce.

"I was looking for Bob Bruce," she said.

He stood motionless, the dangling wrench forgotten, and didn't answer.

Behind Riley, a screen door banged across the courtyard, and she half turned. A man had come out from the office and was crossing the apron toward her. He stopped, his eyes roaming her over. "Can I help you?"

"Mr. Bruce?" she said.

"Yeah." He was tall, hefty, a slight bulge of belly.

"Detective Sergeant Riley," she said. "New South Wales Homicide."

Bruce acknowledged her. "Been waiting for you to call." He stared at the ground. "She was here," he said. "Monday. Just a beautiful kid."

The worker with the wrench hadn't moved.

Bruce's mouth anchored down. "They say Nigel," he said. "You're talking to Nigel."

Riley swayed her head half an inch. "We're talking to lots of people."

Bruce caught the inference—*We're talking to you*—and swallowed.

"Somewhere we can talk, Mr. Bruce?" she said.

He started to turn to the office and must have thought better of it. He looked over at the worker. "You wanna fill that sprayer?"

The man put down his wrench and walked out past Riley. In the daylight, she could see his postcode tattooed on the back of his neck.

Bruce gestured to a trestle table just inside the shed, and Riley took a seat on a green plastic chair. He sat across from her and she opened her notebook.

"You employed Penelope Armytage?" she said.

"Not quite. We contract her services."

"To do what, exactly?"

"Digital marketing. Social media. Spruce up the website."

"How long has she been on the books?"

"Three months? Maybe four."

"When you met with her on Monday—how was she?"

"Normal. The same."

"Try to picture her. Was there anything that struck you at all? Was she distracted? A change in her tone? Her body language?"

He frowned as he thought. "No. She was her usual self. Bubbly, organized. She bosses me a bit. Says I'm a Luddite."

Riley wrote it down. "Did she mention her husband?"

He scratched near an ear. "No."

"Has she talked to you, previously, about Nigel?"

"Not really." Bruce ran a thumbnail on the table. "Don't mention the war."

Riley blinked at him, pen poised.

"Coal," Bruce said. "Nigel's in coal."

"She spoke about that?"

"A little, occasionally. She'd mentioned he wanted to get out of mining. I wasn't sure she was genuine."

"You thought she was lying?"

"No." His head went back. "I thought she might be telling me what I wanted to hear."

"In what way?"

"We've just had an eight-year fight to stop a coal-seam project in the vineyards. Gas wells, infrastructure . . ." He waved out the door. "We're talking an industrial landscape. Lines were drawn, it ripped the community apart. To my mind, Nigel is on the wrong side. We can't coexist, and we were here first. Penny had to walk that line. She said Nigel was thinking of moving into grapes."

"In what way?"

"Wine is about geology, and he's a geologist. The valley, we're sitting on a Permian swamp. That's why there's coal measures. All the groundwater is saline. But there's little patches of magnificent soil. Weathered. Volcanic. He'd know where to look."

Riley watched as Bruce spoke. Weathered but strong. Long-limbed. Right-handed. "You got some of that soil?" she said.

Eyes narrowed, defiant. "My grandfather's grandfather's grandad carved out the choice blocks. Dark chocolate, conglomerate. Generally east facing. Morning sun, afternoon shade."

His size was in his frame. Big-boned, it was in the genes. Probably bred with Riley's people. And the people before that, the old people, although his graying strawberry hair seemed not to say so.

"I saw your visitor parking," she said. "How many do you get?"

"Hundreds, on a busy day. Tasting."

"Was Penelope part of that?"

"Cellar door? Nah. I wanted her to."

"You wanted her to work at the cellar door?"

"Yeah. Pour wine for the punters."

"Why?"

Broken capillaries tracked across his face. Riley traced them with her gaze, like Rodrigues's map. "She's a natural." He shrugged again. "Funny, good with people—"

"You said she was bossy."

His head swerved. "No—that was just with me. She was teasing."

He'd liked being teased by Penelope Armytage. "She was attractive," Riley said. "It's best if you speak freely. Tell me what you know—and what you think."

He took a breath. "All right. She had it all going on. I mean, personality too. The full package."

Riley nodded.

"She's a pleaser, talk to anyone. Bubbly. Someone like that—she'd sell a lot of wine."

"Did she work with your customers at all?"

"No. If she was here, we'd meet in the office. But she wasn't here much. We'd email and speak on the phone. Really, she worked from home."

"Anyone else here, on staff, who she was close with?"

"I don't think so. Not close. She wasn't here enough."

"What about with your wife?"

"No. Diana hadn't even met her. Still, she's upset."

"Does she work here, your wife?"

"She works on-site but not in the business." He adjusted on his chair. "She's a potter. Ceramics. She's got a studio down the side." He pointed. "We sell her work in the shop."

"Where were you on Monday night?"

He held her eye. "Here. With my wife."

"Was anybody else here?"

"No. Kids are all at uni. Two in Adelaide. One's in Wagga."

Riley took him through his evening: He'd cooked pasta and eaten with his wife. She was in bed early—to read and then sleep by nine. She was a morning person, up by five. Bruce had cleaned up in the kitchen, done some paperwork, watched TV. He'd gone to bed around 11:00 p.m.

"Do any workers live on-site?" Riley asked.

"No."

She hoisted a thumb in the direction the man with the wrench had gone. "Who's that?"

Bruce's eyes flicked over her shoulder. "Dew."

Riley went to write it down. "How do you spell it?"

"D-E-W. As in moist." Bruce folded his arms. "He's one of my growers' boys. I've known him from day dot. We're trying to get him set up."

"In the business?"

"In a house with no drugs. In a job where he shows up."

"He done time?"

"Just remand. Or so his father says."

"You didn't check?"

Bruce's face hardened with disdain, as though Riley was from the council, inspecting health and safety. "It's not like I've hired him to run the place. It's a favor for a mate."

"Where's he live?"

"Broke."

"With his father?"

"No. Red's out round Rothbury. With the missus."

This rang a bell for Riley: Rothbury was close to home. "Dew lives alone?"

"As far as I know."

"Was he here Monday, working?"

Bruce had a think. "No. He's two days a week with me. Tuesday, Wednesday, usually. Monday he was with Red. They've got plots through Rothbury, up to Belford."

"You got other men working here?"

"Yeah. Two. In the vineyards. Bud burst in a week."

"Are they on-site now?"

He shook his head and checked his watch. Riley did the same: 4:13 p.m. "They're gone by three," Bruce said.

"I'll need full names, numbers, addresses of the staff. Cellar door, office, vineyard—everyone who's worked here in the past six months."

He nodded.

She stood. "Mind if I take a look?"

He gave a wave. "Be my guest."

The shed was deep and wide. Bruce went to the entrance and hit a switch, and lights came on. Riley walked along the concrete slab. Everything was neat, ordered, industrial. There were more vat-shaped tanks toward the back, very large and made from heavy plastic. They were labeled *GW* and numbered one to four.

Bruce was beside her. "Great Wall." He pointed at the labels. "Forty-two thousand liters all up. We're back shipping it to China."

There was a door ajar along the nearest wall, and Riley crossed to it and looked in. It was an alcove room, part office, part laboratory. There was a desk, reference books, and a lot of glassware on counters— test tubes, beakers, funnels, cylinders. Wineglasses, some half-full, were lined up on another counter with a testing apparatus. A small centrifuge sat in a corner.

Riley stepped in. There was open shelving with tubs and bags of chemicals. Dynastart, potassium bicarbonate, citric acid. She went to a sink and pointed at the doors of a cupboard. "May I?"

Bruce was in the doorway. "Of course."

There were more bottles on shelves under the sink. Riley read labels, some homemade: *Orthophosphoric Acid, Sodium Hydroxide, Buffer Solution, Copper Sulphate*. She pulled out her phone and took pictures. Bruce didn't object.

She walked back over to him at the door. "Thanks."

He moved to let her pass. "You think he used chemicals?" he said.

Riley didn't answer. If it surfaced in the press, she'd know he was talking.

She walked deeper into the shed. There were more pallets, these ones stacked with empty wine bottles wrapped in plastic and bundles of flat-packed cardboard.

A complicated row of stainless-steel machinery was laid out in sections along the floor. There was a lamp switched on over a trolley. "Bottling line," Bruce said. "We do it all here. Fill, seal, pack."

At the end of the contraption, there were more pallets, loaded with taped and labeled boxes of wine. Riley went over. "Just cardboard?" she said.

Bruce frowned, puzzled. "What do you mean?"

"To pack the wine. You just use cardboard?"

"Yeah." He picked up a flat box, opened it, and inserted a cardboard divider from a pile. "That's it. Twelve bottles."

"Nice." She scanned for foam. "No other wrapping?"

He peered at her. "You never bought a case of wine?"

"Not lately." She walked back toward the roller doors. On the wall, down from the light switch at the entrance, there was a white cabinet screwed up at chest height with FIRST AID written in green. Health and Safety . . . Riley resisted the urge to go over and open it.

Bruce followed her out. The worker, Dew, was on the concourse, standing beside a spray rig on a trailer. He had his cap off and was rolling a smoke. His fingers kept moving as he watched Riley cross to the Calais. She moved slowly and stared right back, took a long look at his ravaged face.

11

The police tape was still hanging around the row of town houses, although the press bivouacked on the drive had packed up and gone. Riley had taken the Armytage door key from the incident room and let herself in. The place was empty.

From the back deck, she watched roos graze in the twilight, her trigger finger curling on the balustrade. There were no vines in the view. Northwest facing, monochrome—the gray mob on white winter grasses. A land of leached grandeur. She understood why leaving here had withered her father.

She heard a car out front, crunching on the gravel drive, and thought it might be the retired couple. They were allowed access to their residence, and their vehicle hadn't been there when Riley parked ten minutes ago.

She was bent on the deck, looking out, her forearms resting on the rail, when Bowman came around the corner of the row, to her right. Their eyes met and they both looked away as he walked up.

"That police tape, out front," she said. "It means *Do not cross.*"

He stood on the strip of turf the landscaper had laid. "Saw your car." He was wearing a vivid blue turtleneck sweater encircled at the shoulders with rings of silver and red.

"What's with the sweater?" she said.

"I bought it online," he said. "Reminds me of my dad."

This sounded like a stretch, a Bowman contrivance. "Your dad was a tugboat captain in Norway? That, I did not know."

Riley did know things about Bowman's mother, and his dead brother—facts Bowman didn't know.

"How long you been here?" she said.

"A day. Saw your picture in an ambulance. Thought you might need a hand."

"Oh, good. You're here to help."

Patel was right, they had a settled mode of interaction. It came easy, felt natural, like they were very old friends—or siblings . . . Bowman's younger brother had drowned after witnessing their mother cheating on their father with another man. The brother was eleven, Bowman fifteen. Bowman knew his brother had drowned, and that his mother had found the body, but he didn't know of her infidelity or its role in the accident.

Riley had heard the truth two and a half years ago, while investigating the case at Bowman's old school, but she'd never told him. She didn't see it as her story to tell.

He glanced past her into the town house. "So, what is it? The husband, cut and dried?"

Riley straightened off the rail. "Don't believe everything you read in the press."

"Yeah. I was gonna ask you about that."

She peered out over the valley, and he turned to look too.

"Your place is close?" he asked.

He'd touched on her childhood, in the book. Things she'd told him.

The sun had bled away behind the range. She inched her chin to the north.

"My ancestors are from near Muswellbrook," he said. "Came out on the good ship *China*, in 1841."

"We might be cousins," she said.

He gave his wheezed laugh and looked along the rear facade of the row. "It doesn't exactly blend in, does it?"

Architecture now . . . Bowman had a way of talking in tangents, and Riley often had to stop and think to follow his logic. But yes, she agreed—the town houses were a scar on the landscape. Following his logic further, she realized he was angling to look inside.

"You here on your own?" he said.

Crime Scene had finished processing the house, and Beth Gatjens would formally hand it back to Nigel Armytage tomorrow. Riley considered Bowman's shoes on the damp grass.

He raised a foot. "I can take them off."

She knew she could trust him. "All right," she said. "Shoes off. And no touching."

He came up the three stairs onto the deck, trod out of his laceless blue leather numbers, and padded after Riley in rainbow socks. The rules between them were well established and well tested. She was granting him access, and he knew it was off the record, not even deep background—he simply couldn't use any of it without her explicit consent. There was no chance of deceit.

She crossed to the rear glass door and slid it back and forth a few times, Bowman's bright-colored toes wriggling by the track as she watched the door run . . . His book had altered him slightly, his response to success was a burgeoning self-regard. It was another thing to have an eye on—keeping old Twinkle Toes on the ground.

They stepped inside. Riley focused on the sliding door to clear her mind. It had been locked when Crime Scene arrived on Monday night, and Nigel said the key lived in the lock. It was there now. If the door had been unlocked, the killer could have come in from outside, locked up behind him, and left through the front door without needing a key.

She worked in silence, and Bowman didn't interrupt her. She went through the open-plan living room and kitchen and down the entry hall. If the front door was closed, it was automatically locked on the outside. Nigel said Penny would never go out and leave it open, and even if she had, it was hung to swing shut. Riley opened the door and watched it fall closed. They didn't leave a key hidden outside. The real estate agent, the builder, and tradies had all denied withholding spare keys. Rodrigues had shaken them down—names, numbers, regos, all fed into the data pile for the analyst to create layers. Riley made a note in her book: *locksmiths, key cutters.* It occurred to her that Rodrigues had called someone out to change the lock on the incident room yesterday.

Bowman loitered in the open-plan living space, peering at photographs and books. He had his notebook out, too, but no camera. When Riley went up the stairs, he followed. "No pictures," she said, and he nodded.

Nigel Armytage had indicated he would remain living with his parents for the time being, and Riley wondered if he would sell the town house—and what it would mean if he didn't.

On the second floor was the master bedroom with ensuite, another bathroom, and Nigel's office. It was Riley's first time up there, and she could find no tie-down points around the bed or anything else to suggest bondage. She poked around in the bathroom cabinets: toiletries, makeup, medicines, cotton wool—but no foam. She took a picture with her phone, then did the same with the drawers under the basins. In the ensuite, Bowman came in and peered over her shoulder. There were extras of everything: razor blades, shaving cream, toothpaste, shampoo, conditioner, deodorant, soap, tampons, mouthwash, pump packs of moisturizer.

"Laying in supplies?" Riley said.

"Or just a thrifty disposition," Bowman said. "They stock up when products are on special at the supermarket."

Riley squatted at an open drawer. The lab had come back with a preliminary read on the material in the mouth—a common foam used for all manner of things, including to stuff soft furnishings, and impossible to trace.

Rodrigues had tracked down Penelope Armytage's dentist in Newcastle—it had been more than nine months since Penny had been in.

Riley went through to Nigel's study and looked at the spines of textbooks and technical journals on the shelves. Her phone rang. Gatjens. "Beth," Riley said.

"I'm with Frank at the morgue," she said. "You're on speaker."

"Frank," Riley said. The pathologist didn't answer. Bowman was on the landing, and Riley waved the phone and shut the door on him.

"Okay, so hair and fibers, collected at the scene," Gatjens said. "There's hair everywhere. Mostly Penny, some Nigel, nothing pings. Unless it's Nigel, we don't think the killer shed."

Riley looked at the carpet on Nigel's office floor.

"But there's something else," Gatjens said. "We didn't see it. But we collected it when we vacuumed where her head had lain. A batch of fibers, cotton mixed with polyurethane."

"Polyurethane?"

"Spandex," Gatjens said. "With woven cotton."

Riley chewed her cheek.

"Crepe," Gatjens said. "Under the microscope, it's clear the fibers have been sliced. With scissors."

"Crepe?" Riley said.

"Bandage. We think he brought it with him. A roll of compression bandage. And scissors. He used a length he needed, then cut it. When he sheared it, it dropped tiny fragments on the floor."

Gatjens stopped and the line went quiet.

A crepe bandage and foam in the mouth. "He *did* gag her," Riley said. "You think he gagged her."

"I'll let Frank answer that," Gatjens said.

The forensic pathologist cleared his throat. "We have foam and a crepe bandage. Broad, soft materials. He grabs from behind, holds a block of foam to the mouth, and winds a gauze bandage over the top to keep it in place. He could do it in a fast, fluid movement. He's strong, probably tall. The materials are pliable but firm. It wouldn't leave a mark."

Gatjens again. "The force is distributed over too broad an area."

"It's possible he gagged her to keep her quiet," Powell said. "Perhaps to rape her, before he strangled her."

Riley stared at Nigel's desk. The scene had suggested the husband or someone else Penny knew, because he hadn't restrained her. No imprint of a gag, no binding marks . . .

"He gags her to keep her quiet," Riley said. "Hence the neighbors hearing no screams."

There was silence.

"But she could still fight," Riley said. "But there's no sign of a struggle. See?"

"Jesus," Gatjens said.

"He wants her alive, he wants her quiet, he wants her restrained," Riley said. "He wants control, he wants to take his time."

"He binds the wrists with the same materials," Powell said. "And the ankles. Soft and broad, no bruising."

Riley sat at Nigel's desk. The killer had been in the house and had come from behind. Penelope hadn't let him in. "He's gagging and binding," Riley said.

12

Riley was still seated in Nigel Armytage's study, night fallen and the room growing cold, when Bowman knocked and entered.

There were three big screens on the desk and chunks of rock lined up on a shelf. Riley picked up a piece and studied it. Shell fossils from Bob Bruce's Permian swamp. She thought about Bruce and his wine-man entitlement. *We were here first.* Yeah, except the coal was laid down a hundred million years before Noah discovered Beaujolais.

Bowman held his phone screen toward her. "This you?"

She saw a headline, Cops Mine Coal Case, Laura Nolan's byline, and reached out for the phone. *The Mirror* had snapped a picture of Nigel Armytage through a window in his parents' house. Riley read: Murdered Red Creek woman Penelope Armytage had allegedly been fighting with her geologist husband over his coal-mining job, police believe.

"Fuck," Riley spat.

"So it's not coming from you."

She swallowed, trying to think. Nolan's source could be anyone—from Nigel's boss, Howard Johns, to the winemaker Bob Bruce, to any one of sixty cops at the station in Cessnock. Rodrigues? *Fuck*—her gut said no, and Patel backed him too.

Bowman read the room and kept quiet, perching on a sofa along the wall.

She scrolled the story. It was cleverly worded, and in that sense it was true—Penelope and Nigel had argued over his job, and Penny was dead. Of course, the report didn't come out and say her husband had killed her. It was insinuating rather than defamatory. It went on to detail where the couple worked, making the distinction between wine and mines, but no one was quoted. There was nothing specific that could have come only from inside the investigation.

Riley tossed Bowman his phone. "It says *police believe*," she said. "That's weasel words, right?"

"In that . . . ?"

"It might not have come from police. A third party claims to have police knowledge—Nolan reports that."

"Did you have a third party in mind?"

Riley shook her head in admiration and tried not to smile—always on the take. "This Laura Nolan, do you know her?" she said.

"I asked you first."

She leaned back in Nigel's desk chair. "A third party could be Penelope's client, or Nigel's boss."

"Have you ever spoken to Laura Nolan—on the phone?"

"No. Why?"

"I overheard her talking to someone yesterday. About the husband. The claim was, he had charges."

Riley sniffed. That wasn't right. "Tell me exactly what she said."

Bowman leafed through his notebook. "This is a direct quote: *OK, so with a* y. *Spell it all again. And the charges? Wait, conspiracy to defraud. Fifty-seven. Failure to lodge.*"

Riley sat forward with her hand out. "Can I see?"

He passed her the notebook. "It's in shorthand."

She couldn't decipher it. "She didn't actually say *Nigel*?"

"No. But with a *y. Army-tage.*"

Riley passed the notebook back. Nolan didn't need to be told how to spell *Armytage*. She'd been writing it for two days. She'd even been through it with Riley at the scene on the night. "The charges," Riley said. "That's tax stuff?"

"S'pose."

"Can you transcribe, word for word, what she said? And send it to me?"

He shrugged.

"So, Nolan," she said. "You know her?"

"Nup. But she's latched on—and she's gonna work it. It's a big story now."

"Now?"

He looked at his phone. "It was always quite good—a dead, lovely young woman. But now you've got dirty scum coal-geologist kills photogenic wife over climate change. That's something for everyone. I mean, that sound you hear, that's the ABC wetting its pants."

"Except it's wrong."

"Wrong? Impossible. We're talking about a narrative, not about facts."

She knew his next question, and shook her head.

He asked anyway, without actually asking, couching it as an offer because he was here to help. "I can change the narrative if you give me the facts."

"Can't," she said. "Not yet. Can you do me a favor?"

He gave her a look she knew well: *What's in it for me?*

"Can you take a peek at Nolan?" she said. "Go through her stuff, say the last year. See who she talks to, who she quotes? Any cops? Bring me a list?"

"Yeah. Maybe. Why?"

"Small town," she said. "Crosscurrents, agendas. We don't have a handle on it."

"You've got a leak."

She raised her eyebrows, and he gave her another look: *Tell me more.*

She opened her hands at the room, at the access he was being granted. "Names," she said, "and we'll talk."

He pinched his throat under the roll-neck of the sweater. Their rules were well established, but she still had to watch him, a journalist at heart. She'd allowed him onto the scene knowing he would never

100

write anything about it without her permission, or use it against her to bargain or bribe. But if, independent of her, he found information she didn't want published, he might do it anyway. He would fuck her over in a story if it suited him, but he'd do it to her face and tell her why. Respect.

He saw it was time to leave. "Beer?" he said.

"Maybe. Later."

She flushed him down the stairs and he retrieved his shoes, and they went out the front, the door swinging locked behind her without the need for the key.

"Where are you staying?" she said.

"Pub." He pointed. "I looked for you last night, at the motel. Met the owner."

"Male or female?"

"Male, dressed all in tan. Wouldn't give me his name—said he had clients, that he was an entrepreneur. Said he'd seen the victim out jogging."

She nodded. Jayson Cassidy, Karen's husband. Riley hadn't met him. Jayson—with a *y*.

Riley watched Bowman drive away and checked the time: 6:09. By now, on Monday, the killer was in the town house, or close in the winter dark, preparing to enter. He'd come from behind—an ambush, he was inside . . . She turned to stare for a moment down the path at the front door. How was access gained?

In the Calais, she went left at the Red Creek crossroad and parked and got out. There were two vehicles and three customers at the takeaway. Wednesday evening. Tomorrow, she guessed, the tourist numbers would begin to build into the weekend. She walked in a square around the intersection. The café was closed. The traffic was light but constant, headlights every few minutes from any direction.

Doors slammed and the cars drove off from the takeaway. Riley went in and ordered two schnitzels and chips. Patel was in the incident room, Rodrigues had gone home to his wife. The shop was empty of customers, and she watched the chips fry. The Homicide diet.

A man and a woman, mid-fifties, were behind the counter—owner-operators, married, Riley saw. She got two bottles of water from the fridge and put them on the counter. The woman bagged them, and Riley flashed her badge. "The cops talk to you about Monday?"

"Yeah," the woman said. "They were here yesterday. In the morning."

The Mirror was on the counter with Penny Armytage's face on it. "Do you know them—the couple?" Riley asked.

"By face." The woman eyed the tabloid and looked away. "Not by name."

The husband turned from the fryer with a basket and knocked chips onto white paper.

"One or other of them would come in every few weeks," the woman said. "Maybe seen them three or four times, all up. Polite. Not much to say."

"Chicken salt?" the husband said.

"Ta," Riley said.

"We close early Monday, six p.m.," the woman told her. "We gave them a printout, the police. All the credit, debit cards used in the past month."

"She was seen here, jogging"—Riley gestured outside—"between five, five thirty."

The woman nodded. "Cops said the same. I told them I've seen her out doing her running, but not Monday. We didn't see that."

Her husband pointed at a door ajar to a room behind the fryer. "We were in the back, probably, cleaning up."

Riley took the food and the water and slid her business card over. "I'm at the old post office."

"Saw that." The woman picked up the card.

Riley felt their eyes as she walked to the car. There was no one around. Four streetlights in a square and, beyond that, the night, black with no moon. She drove the fifty meters to the incident room, and her phone rang as she parked. "Beth."

"I did a search," Gatjens said. "Unsolved female strangulation. There's three in the region, twelve in the state, thirty-one across the country."

Riley killed the engine.

"You search on 'foam in the mouth'—nothing. You search on just 'foam'? Nothing."

"Mm."

"But crepe-bandage fibers," Gatjens said. "That narrows it down."

"To?"

"One. In Canberra, nine months ago. I just read the file."

Riley's hand stopped on the door handle.

"Jennifer Morrow, married, twenty-nine. Husband was in Singapore for four days for work. No forced entry. Bruises to the upper arms consistent with being grabbed from behind. Found lying on her front. Semi-clad. Not bound, not gagged. Neighbors heard nothing. Asymmetric bruising to the throat. Petechial hemorrhages. Toxicology clean. Nothing in her mouth. Fibers from a crepe bandage found on floorboards at her head."

Mouth fallen open, Riley stared through the windshield. "Holy Jesus, fuck," she said.

13

Beth Gatjens spoke with the ACT Crime Scene sergeant from the Canberra case, and Frank Powell reviewed the autopsy findings with the performing forensic pathologist. Patel eliminated Nigel Armytage: He'd been digging holes in Central Queensland on the date Jennifer Morrow had been strangled.

Riley flew Qantas from Cessnock to Canberra and took a cab from the airport.

It was 10:00 a.m. Thursday, August 28. Trees with no leaves lined Belconnen Way like cold bureaucrats. The police station was low-rise in brown brick.

Detective Sergeant Richard Laver met her at the front desk. He was ACT Homicide—which made him a Fed. "Dick." He held out his hand. "Come on through."

His gray hair matched his suit. He led her across an open-plan floor, with cops working at desks, to a glassed-off meeting room. There were five cardboard boxes on a counter.

"I pulled it for you." He closed the door after her. "That's everything."

Riley put her bag down. "Where are you at?"

"Cold—but not closed."

"You read our file?"

His jaw clenched as he nodded. Riley had no issue with the Federal Police, but their territory was small, middle class, educated, and the murder rate was low—there was no frequency of homicide, so they lacked experience.

"And?" she said.

Laver put his jacket on the back of a chair and sat. "A woman dies like this every week."

"Not here they don't."

"Nationally"—he steepled his fingers—"a woman is killed by her partner or former partner, on average, every week."

Riley wanted cooperation, not a fight. Laver looked close to retirement, quoting statistics to pave his way out the door. "You still think it's the husband?" she asked.

He angled his head. "That's the problem. We've got no one. Andrew Morrow ruled himself out. He was in the air at the time, coming home from Singapore."

Riley had read the Morrow file twice last night and again on the plane. She looked at the boxes. "Can you take me through it?"

He took a lid off and folded his sleeves. Riley studied the crime scene photos, then turned the physical exhibits in their bags. The T-shirt Jennifer Morrow was found in had been sliced up the front like Penny Armytage's. Not similar—identical.

"He was using scissors," Laver said. "Not a knife."

"He's bringing things with him," Riley said. "Might have a backpack."

"We looked at that—CCTV in the area."

Riley made a note.

"He's organized," Laver said. "The scissors are practical but a mistake. The way they cut, shearing the crepe bandage—it left fibers."

Riley bit her lip. The killer was still making this same mistake. She looked through the glass wall at the floor of detectives. "There can be no word we've made this connection," she said. "I'm not here, right?"

"Right."

"Why does he cut the bandages on-site?" Riley said. "He's organized. He could pre-cut strips to length and bring them in."

"He's bringing scissors anyway, to cut clothes. A roll of bandage is neater, easier to work with, less handling of the material. It spools out"—Laver made a winding gesture—"it doesn't bunch up. And it's more flexible, with length."

Riley watched his arm go around.

He stood, trim. "Try to visualize it," he said. "What do you see?"

"Both times it's the same. He's in the house, hidden, when she comes home. He comes from behind, in an open living space. Room to swing a cat."

"Right." He loosened his limbs like he was about to play squash. "He grabs her from behind, pulls her in to him." Laver was physical, acting it out. "He has to keep her quiet, so a hand to her mouth straightaway, probably with a wedge of foam. Then"—his arm whipped around—"with the other hand, he's wrapping her head with bandage to hold the foam in place." He stopped and put his hands on the back of his chair. "That how you see it?"

Riley held his eye.

"It's a lot," he said. "She'll want to bite, kick, fight, scream."

"It's an ambush," Riley said. "Complete surprise. She has to take a breath to scream. That takes a second. That's all he needs. He grabs her hard, then pulls her to him. An arm around her chest knocks the wind out of her. Foam in his other hand to her mouth, and he's wrapping the bandage with his hand from her chest. She's gagged before she can breathe."

Laver rubbed his chin. "He's tall, he's fast, he's strong."

Riley had misread Laver's grayness: He had energy. He sighed and she felt for him. He was a good cop, facing facts.

"He's smart," she said.

Laver looked away and Riley let him process. The killer's use of soft materials was a tactic designed to mislead. No ligature marks, no forced entry, no struggle . . . it told a story, and Laver had read the scene as a domestic. Riley had done the same. But Laver had never corrected and got the Morrow investigation on track.

"We had the crepe but not the link," he said.

"Correct. We had you, but you didn't have us. Don't beat yourself up."

He closed his eyes.

From the table, Riley picked up a bag with the jewelry Jennifer Morrow had been found in. Two silver hoop earrings and a matching necklace, a silver ring with an orb of hot-pink resin.

"The husband kept the wedding band," Laver said.

The file said nothing was missing from the house.

"Taking trophies?" Riley said.

"Not that we can tell." Laver pointed to another evidence bag. "She was found in underpants. And the T-shirt. No bra."

"You think he re-dressed her?"

"Maybe." He nodded. "We hadn't thought of that, but I read your briefing note."

The timing had been different. Laver took her through it. Jennifer Morrow had been killed in the daytime—best guess, early afternoon. The husband had been in the air from Singapore, changed planes in Sydney, and got home to find her after 9:00 p.m.

Laver outlined his own methodology from when he first arrived on scene. Riley had just run the same case. She couldn't fault him. At the time, Laver didn't have a suspect, so he dug deep where he could—into Jennifer Morrow. The victimology was exhaustive, every lead tracked down. It had led nowhere, but it was now a treasure trove for Riley. She didn't have a suspect, either, but she had exponential growth: two victims.

Two women strangled 420 kilometers and nine months apart. The analysts would overlay it. Something somewhere had to chime.

She looked through the crime scene photos. The bathroom cabinets gave her pause. They weren't full of bulk buys from the supermarket, like the Armytage drawers, but there were vanity kits taken from airlines and mini lotions and wrapped soaps lifted from hotel rooms. *"Thrifty disposition,"* Riley muttered, quoting Bowman to herself.

"Pardon?" Laver said.

"Both houses, there's an excess of toiletries, like they're laying in supplies. But in a different way." She pulled up a picture of the Armytage drawers. "That's all presumably been bought from shops, perhaps on special. We'll ask the husband. Your guys are taking free stuff on their travels."

"Probably normal." Laver studied the photos. "I do the same. So does my wife."

"The buying or the taking?"

"Both."

On her phone, Riley took a photo of the crime scene picture of the purloined supplies. "What else?" she said.

Laver had fixated on point of entry. The Morrows hadn't hidden a key or left one with the neighbors. "Jennifer was very organized too," he said. "An actuary, risk averse, touch of OCD. She'd been mugged a few years back—not the type to leave the house open. The husband said the place was locked up when he arrived."

How was access gained? Laver couldn't figure it, so he did what Riley had done—lined up the husband.

"You thought he had her killed?" Riley said.

His face creased. "We had to look at it."

The theory was, Andrew Morrow had handed over a key to a paid killer and gone to Singapore. Laver had run a three-month covert op, tracking Morrow's car and bugging his phone, but got nothing. There was no lover on the side. The Morrows were young—they had looked at income protection and life insurance, but no policies were in place. They didn't even have a will. Jennifer had two siblings, and her parents were retired public servants—her inheritance would have been modest.

There was a portrait photo of Jennifer Morrow in a plastic sleeve, and Riley had an A4 image of Penelope Armytage in her bag. She put them side by side on the table and stood back. Laver stared for a long moment and looked up.

"Thoughts?" Riley said.

He didn't answer. He didn't have to. The women weren't identical. In fact, all they shared was blond hair. But looking at them together, Riley felt the bristle of connection. "Do you have video of Jennifer, showing the way she stood, the way she moved?"

He frowned. "I don't think we looked at that."

"We haven't either." Riley tapped her chin. "It just occurred to me."

"You think he saw them, chose them, staked them out?"

"They're a very similar age, physically attractive, a type. I think it's more than just blond hair. I think he's watched them—their posture, vibe, how they speak."

"Okay, he's selecting," Laver said. "But where?"

"Your analyst who worked on this"—Riley pointed at the evidence—"and you. You want to jump on board?"

His head tilted: *Maybe.*

"Just run everything you've got through the prism of Penelope and Nigel Armytage. We'll do the same, in reverse."

He gave a nod. "All right."

"And Andrew Morrow," Riley said. "Where is he?"

Laver looked blank.

"You might want to track him down," she said. "Check he wasn't anywhere near the Hunter Valley on Monday night."

Andrew Morrow was in Melbourne for work, and had been there since Sunday evening. He still lived in Canberra but had sold the house his wife was killed in. The new owners had rented the place out, and Laver called the real estate agent and drove Riley to the street in Ngunnawal.

It was freestanding, three-bedroom, white brick—a suburban 1970s bungalow, not a new build. A young woman with a baby on her shoulder opened the door, and Laver introduced himself and Riley, flashed his badge, and apologized. The mother was in a cardigan and gray trackies, no makeup, hair like she'd been napping in a windy hedge.

The real estate agent had warned her they were coming, but Riley saw that was all she knew. No one had told her she was nursing her infant in a murder house.

"I need to feed her," the woman said, indicating a darkened room off the hall. "I'll be in there."

Riley followed Laver into the kitchen. Baby paraphernalia dried in a rack by the sink. Bottles, nipples, pacifiers.

"Side windows were locked and screened." Laver spoke low. "Shoe and Tire got nothing in the yard. We figured he had to come through a door. Front or back. Nothing was forced."

Riley looked at the ceiling. "What about the roof?"

"No access, unless he cut in. And he didn't cut in." Laver tapped a foot. "Same with the crawl space."

Riley left him and walked down the room, studied the back door, and went out. In the little paved yard, thin garden beds ran on either side, under the windows. It was too meager to need a gardener. There was an air-conditioning unit and a gas hot-water system framed on the wall. She made a note: *Installation, repair*. But it wasn't the houses. He'd chosen the women, not the properties. Did he know them? Riley didn't think so. It wasn't personal, but it was sexual. She knew what a forensic psychologist would say: *Behaviorally rich*. She made another note: *Criminal history? Escalation*.

Laver was waiting in the kitchen, arms folded, his backside to the counter. "So the house was either open, or she let him in," he said. "Or he had a key."

"He keeps everything the same, except the timing," Riley said. "That's where he adapts. It's down to the husbands."

"He knows their movements," Laver said. "The pattern of life. He can gain access to the houses when the husbands are out."

The husbands. The houses. But it wasn't about them. They could have been anyone, anywhere—collateral damage. It was the women he was choosing.

Riley looked around the kitchen. There was a big book on the counter: *Baby Love*. She'd seen it before. Her sisters-in-law had swapped it back and forth when their kids were very young, like a manual.

Laver uncrossed his arms, ready to leave. Riley agreed. There was nothing here.

They went down the hall, and she peeked in on the mother, sitting in dim light with headphones on and the baby at her breast. Riley mouthed a goodbye, and the woman blinked and nodded.

Laver pulled the front door closed behind them, and they sat in his Kluger with the heater running. Riley opened her laptop and scrolled the Morrow file. Jennifer's underpants had yielded her fingerprints from the waist and heavy saturation of her DNA. But no semen—or anything else—from the perpetrator.

Laver watched as she read. "The bandage is our best bet," he said. "But even that's generic."

Riley clicked through to the lab report on the Morrow crepe. The chemical analysis had not identified a brand for the material. She knew Laver was right—the lab would determine if the fibers from the two scenes were the same material and color, but that was all they'd get. There would be nothing on class or type or brand, no link to point where the crepe had been made or purchased.

Laver put the Kluger in gear and started for the airport. The streets were dead, the universities on semester break, the parliament in the final days of winter recess.

Riley skimmed through the Morrow canvass and then the work done on tracking down services at the house. A woman had come to clean once every two weeks. A Telstra technician had been in a month before the murder. Taxis, Uber, deliveries.

"The Armytage house," she said. "It's a new build."

"Men at work." Laver pulled up at the terminal. "I'll go back to Morrow."

"Thanks." She unclipped her belt. "Any tradies—going back, say, two years."

He made a note.

There was an AFP sticker on the dash, and a thought occurred to Riley. The Federal Police . . . Laver would work with the Australian Taxation Office. She pulled out her phone and read out the charges Bowman had transcribed from his eavesdropping.

"Conspiracy to defraud is a federal charge," Laver said. "The fifty-seven—failure to lodge—is state. But tax, obviously. So yes, with both, the ATO would be involved."

"Can you look with the ATO?"

"Yeah. What name?"

"Nigel and Penelope Armytage, just to rule them out."

"And?"

"Jayson and Karen Cassidy." Riley wrote the names down for him. "*Jayson* with a *y*."

14

Bowman woke, cracked an eye, saw it was daylight but couldn't move, as though he was pinned to the bed. It was a familiar feeling. Every morning, he had it, it was how he greeted the day. The grogginess would begin to lift when he got up—he'd started taking a tablet to deal with insomnia, just ten milligrams of Phenergan. It was nothing, the stuff they gave kids to wipe them out on planes.

But boy, did it club him in the mornings. Any more sleep now would be exhausting, shallow dreams on a loop.

He fell back asleep.

At night, getting to sleep in the Packhorse wasn't easy. There was a presence in the inn that crept up on him in the dark and kept his head turning on the pillow.

He woke again, opened both eyes, hauled himself upright, and drank from a glass of water. Thursday. He'd been on the Armytage story for three days and hadn't written a word. He'd taken the room for another week, and *The National* had agreed to reimburse his expenses at $150 a day for two weeks—but only if he came up with a story. They didn't want him filing daily updates, stuff they could take for free off the wires: They wanted exclusive news, the definitive account of what was going on.

After the bathroom, he fell into another one of his morning pub routines—gazing around for something suitable to wear to breakfast. He needed coffee. A sarong wasn't going to cut it, and neither was the guest robe. He pulled on trousers, a T-shirt, and the complimentary slippers, then headed out with his notebook.

The flagstones on the ground floor were cold through the slippers as he negotiated the dank passage through the bowels of the inn. Doors hung closed on empty nooks. He was the only guest in the dining area and took his usual table.

The young waitress Rachel was on, her frizzy hair tied back. "Any news?" she said.

"You tell me."

Her features were supple, elastic with irony, and she made a face: *Whatever.* "So, coffee and . . . ?"

Bowman ordered an omelet, and Rachel disappeared through the swing door into the kitchen. There was the noise of a vehicle outside—air brakes, big wheels chewing gravel, clanking. From deeper in the inn, the barman Michael came into the dining area in a tracksuit and slippers, like he was just out of bed, too, and crossed the saloon, unlocked the main doors, and went out. There were male voices and more clanking. Keg truck. Bowman got up and went to look out a side window—great flap doors in the ground had been hauled open, and two men on the bed of a truck were rolling fresh kegs down a ramp into the cellar. Michael must have been under there to receive them.

Bowman went back to his table as Rachel brought his coffee. He thanked her and asked, "Does Michael live on-site?"

"Yeah, out back."

"What, with Sandra?"

Rachel balked in alarm. "Not *with* Sandra. *Ew.*"

Bowman sipped. "But Sandra's out there too?"

"Yeah, she's got like a flat." Rachel pointed. "Michael's on the other side of the courtyard, in a room."

"What about you?"

"What *about* me?"

"Where do you live?"

"Not here, that's for sure."

"But on Monday night, when the police turned up, they only spoke to you?"

"Yeah. It was late. Chef had gone home. I'd closed and was about to go too. Then they knocked on the door."

"What did they say?"

"Investigating an incident. They wanted to know who'd been in? Anything out of the ordinary? Were there guests staying?"

"And what did you say?"

"Just that. There'd been a few locals in, so I told them names. Said there were no guests overnight. There'd been a couple of tables in for dinner—I dunno, tourists. We take a name and number with bookings, so the cops took the details."

"You didn't say Sandra and Michael live on-site?"

"They didn't ask."

Bowman took another sip of coffee and looked at the girl.

"What?" she said.

"I just think it's strange. The cops come knocking about a murdered woman over the road and ask you who's in the building—and you don't tell them."

Color flushed her neck. "No, that's not right."

"What, then?"

"The cops . . ." Her lithe face was now brittle. "All they said was, they were investigating an incident down the road. I thought like, someone had burgled the café. They wanted to know who'd been in that evening and were there guests staying. So I told them. That was it. They didn't say anything about murder. Then I'm driving home, I see all the vehicles at the town houses, and I think, *So it's not a burglary.* Then there's a cop car on Hermitage Road, just sitting, and he flags me down, takes my details, and I ask, 'What's going on?' He tells me someone died at Red Creek. So that's like, when I knew."

"All right." Bowman bobbed his head. "Sorry."

She retreated to the kitchen.

Michael came back in the front door and locked it. Dusting his hands like a butcher, he gave Bowman a hooded glance on approach. "Morning," Michael said. "Any news?"

Bowman was saved from answering by Rachel shouldering through the swing door, delivering his omelet.

She deposited the plate and turned to Michael, who had stopped and was standing. She cupped her fingers and tapped him on the chest. "You want some eggs?"

Bowman watched. Michael blinked assent, pleased by the girl's playful touch but trying not to show it. She left, and he took a seat at the next table—facing Bowman. "You find them cops?" he said.

"Yeah." Bowman cut into his omelet. "The motel. Where you said."

Michael sat up straight with his arms crossed. "I know the owner, see."

Bowman forked in some egg.

"I done some work for him"—Michael thrust his chin—"down there. Just with the air-conditioning, 'cos the builder walked off. Yeah. I had to run the ducting, eh."

Rachel came out with a coffee for Michael. "Let me guess," she said to Bowman. "He's telling you about Oakeshott?"

Bowman had a mouthful.

"Nope," Michael said.

Bowman swallowed. "Who's Oakeshott?"

"Developer, buying up the valley." Rachel headed back to the kitchen. "You tell him, Mikey."

Michael scooped three sugars into his coffee and stirred. He licked the teaspoon and used it to trace an arc. "From the town houses to the motel, that's his land."

Bowman found his pen. Rachel brought out Michael's breakfast and lingered, her eyes on Bowman's notebook, and he asked them questions. It was pub talk, probably worthless, but he assured them they were off the record, that he would never quote them or use their names, and tried to hammer out what they knew. Oakeshott was a property developer, and a couple, Jayson and Karen Cassidy, owned the motel. Oakeshott had built the Quirk and then tried to pressure the Cassidys to sell, but they'd refused, and it had turned nasty, with bad-mouthing in the district and contracts not fulfilled—hence Michael being dragged in to fix the air-conditioning.

Bowman scribbled it down and then sat back. Michael had finished his eggs and rose to leave.

Rachel watched him depart. "He's a sweetie, right?" she said.

Bowman twirled his pen. He could tell Michael was pleased to have been asked questions and to have given answers.

"He's good to have around," Rachel said. "Sorts out the drunks."

"Yeah?"

She cleared Michael's empty table. "The army kicked him out."

"Why?"

"He won't say. So I'm not really sure . . ."

"But?"

"I think he beat the crap out of some soldier. With a pool cue."

15

Riley had slept in her flat in Rozelle. There had been no flight to Cessnock from Canberra late yesterday, so she'd come into Sydney and taken a taxi home. The stopover suited her: She needed more clothes for Red Creek. Patel had wanted to come down to her own apartment for the same reason, so she'd driven to Harris Park last night and would take Riley back to the Hunter this morning.

Riley smelled the milk in the fridge and checked the use-by date: It'd do. She pressed buttons on the Nespresso, and her mind flashed to the Morrow kitchen in Ngunnawal and the baby bottles on the counter. She rinsed out the sour-milk carton, wondering if Bowman had published an article.

She made the coffee and searched up news of Penelope Armytage. Bowman hadn't written anything, and there was nothing fresh from Laura Nolan. But he was right. The story had legs, and the *Herald* was getting into the action—they'd door-stopped Nigel's boss, Howard Johns, and were running pictures of a coal mine near Singleton where Nigel had worked. Riley read the piece through. It was tendentious stuff, almost absurd, and at the heart of it sat the tabloid lie that Nolan had planted: Nigel Armytage was guilty.

That was the narrative. Bowman had seen it—geologist kills pretty wife after she objects to his coal job.

Riley's boss Toohey had Police Media in Sydney handling inquiries on the investigation, and Riley was glad—it kept her out of it. She sipped. There was blood in the water, and she needed to protect Nigel. The parable around him was too strong. The media wouldn't slow down and test it, they'd skin him alive.

She showered, dressed, jammed clothes into her orange canvas duffel, and waited for Patel. There was an email from Toohey. The Super had inked a memorandum with the Federal Police to allow the flow of information between the Morrow and Armytage investigations. Laver and an ACT analyst were back on the Morrow case full-time for six weeks to ensure everything was re-examined in the light of Red Creek and to chase down possible new links.

Patel texted. Here.

Riley went out and down, slung her duffel into the popped boot of the Camry, and climbed into the passenger seat. Patel handed her a warm brown paper bag.

"Samosa?" Riley said.

"Aloo paratha."

Riley opened the bag and looked in. "What's in it?"

"Potato. You'll like it."

"Samosa's got potato. I like that."

Patel reversed. "Samosa's not breakfast."

Riley took a bite. There were two takeaway cups in the holders. "What's that?"

Patel put it in drive and went right. "Masala chai."

"You get me a Coke?"

"No."

Riley chewed. "Why not?"

"It'll kill you dead. Especially for breakfast." Patel indicated the cup. "Try that. It's sweet. You'll like it."

Riley slurped and raised an eyebrow. Not bad—it was good. "Resources are pushing up," she said. "Just had a note from Toohey."

Patel went right and right again on the narrow back streets.

"How's Rodrigues?" Riley said.

"You mean, is he our leak?"

"Yeah."

"Don't reckon. I think he's solid. Hundred percent."

"What about the station sergeant, Harris?"

"Haven't dealt with him, except when you were there, too, so I don't know."

Riley took another chug of chai.

"What's been reported, it's low-grade stuff," Patel said. "It could be gossip from the station. Or just gossip from the forest, not even from police."

Riley wiped her mouth on a serviette.

"On Canberra . . ." Patel pulled up at a light. "Your briefing note. There's one thing I thought. On tendency."

"Time of day?" Riley said.

"No."

"He hits Jennifer Morrow in the afternoon," Riley said, "then he changes. He kills Penny in the evening. That's pattern of life. He knows the movements of the husband."

"I get that," Patel said. "What else?"

Riley ticked off tendency evidence on her fingers. "Married females, roughly the same age. Killed in their homes while their husbands are out. Manual strangulation, no forced entry. T-shirts sheared with scissors. Crepe fiber left at the scenes. That's pretty tight."

"Yeah, but Canberra's a city. Red Creek's a dot, not even a village. That's the difference."

"He's moving around. And?"

"You asked Laver to examine tradies," Patel said. "Made me think, an itinerant worker."

"Okay."

"I was looking at industry links between the ACT and the Hunter, thinking perhaps mining expertise. You know, the CSIRO or the universities. So there's training, but no mining in Canberra. And then, what jumps out is wine." She pointed at the phone in Riley's lap. "Canberra. Wine. Take a look."

Riley googled and clicked on the first result: *Canberra Wine Region
. . . 140 vineyards, 40 wineries.* She scrolled through and pulled up a
map. The wineries spread north of the city, toward Yass and Collector.
It was a big area, eight thousand square kilometers.

"Can't fuckers just run sheep anymore?" Riley said.

"We could go for employment records," Patel said. "Is there a name
that turns up in both regions?"

Riley studied the map pockmarked with cellar doors. Every worker
at every wine operation in the Canberra district and the Hunter going
back four years? There'd be holes everywhere—operators that had gone
to the wall, casuals being paid cash. "If we start asking for that data,
from both regions, the word will get out pretty quick."

"The grapevine," Patel said.

"And then we've tipped our guy. Even if we get nothing, if he's
nothing to do with wine. People start talking, it hits the press that we're
out asking questions in Canberra. That's it. He knows we've made him
for Morrow."

"We can disguise it in Canberra," Patel said. "Laver can set
something up through the Feds. Pretend it's a fraud probe, or the ATO."

"We're already doing that—for real."

"Yeah, that's four names, on the quiet. We get that done first."

It might work. Riley finished her chai. They could run it by Laver.

Patel took the M2 west past Cheltenham. "That's wine," she said.
"Back to mines."

They talked it through as Patel drove, swinging north into the
tunnel off Pennant Hills Road. Mines didn't just employ miners: truck
drivers, cooks, diesel mechanics, engineers, hydrologists, geologists
. . . There were no mines in Canberra, but hundreds of jobs were
transferrable between the regions, skilled or unskilled.

After an hour, they turned off the motorway. Riley cracked her
window for a blast of air. Trees ran along creek lines. The country,
fenced into horse paddocks, was heavy after a year of good rain.

"There has to be a crossing point," she said. "A place where they meet. Not the victims—they don't need to meet."

"Somewhere he sees them," Patel said.

"Right. And it might be two years apart. But he sees them somewhere—or somehow."

"Somehow?"

"Doesn't have to be a place. It could be a job. An Uber driver, he drops them both home."

They passed the burnt-out wreck of a hatchback, slapped with a fluoro sticker from council. "Not many Uber drivers out here," Patel said.

"It's an example. There's a crossing point. Not necessarily a physical place."

They hit traffic south of Cessnock. "Friday," Patel said. "Here come the tourists."

They followed a tour bus and a string of cars through Pokolbin and headed for the motel to drop their bags. There was a row of half a dozen vehicles in the car park, all European SUVs. Patel pulled in beside Riley's Calais, and they got out and shouldered their luggage from the boot.

It was late morning, 11:11. Karen Cassidy was at reception, attending to two women with matching bright-blue ribbed suitcases and oversize totes that said CHRISTIAN DIOR. A young family sat around a table in the communal pantry, the two kids crumbling muffins while the parents drank coffee and read their phones.

Riley went down the corridor and keyed into her room, leaving the door open and dropping her duffel. The bed was unmade and there was a towel on the back of a chair, and clothes in a pile on the floor. Riley didn't mind, she didn't need someone cleaning up after her.

She put her laptop bag on the counter and glanced up to find Karen in the hall. "Good morning, Detective."

"Hi."

"A woman from the police station called." Karen squinted at the duffel at her feet. "I understand you and Detective Patel will be with us for some time?"

A Cessnock liaison was handling logistics. "Right," Riley said.

"I've blocked off the rooms, so they're yours." Karen's eyes went to the clothes on the floor. "I thought it might be time for a clean."

"No hurry." Riley, hands in her back pockets, studied the mess. "Maybe Monday?"

Karen pecked out a nod under cropped rosella-red hair. "There's a laundry at the end of the corridor." She flapped a wing. "Through the green door. It's not for guests, but you're both free to use it. I'll let the staff know."

"How many staff are there?"

"Just the three. A girl a couple of days on reception and two more for housekeeping."

"Tight ship."

Karen frowned, false modesty. "It's our model. Less service than a hotel but more than an Airbnb. We had a traditional hotel, with a manager, but we sold it to build this."

They'd innovated backward—their model was a caravan park without wheels. "You run it with your husband?" Riley said.

"That's the whole idea. He does the back room, I do the front desk. It's designed to be run by a couple, along with housekeeping—no room service, no night shifts, no breakfast chefs or servers. Just cleaning. The girl on the desk is part-time, to allow us to consult."

"Consult?"

"We have an association, Invent Motels Australia. There's a brochure at reception. New members join to implement the model."

"Can I get a list of your staff? Names, numbers, addresses? It's routine. We're talking to everyone."

Karen consented, turned on her heel, and was gone.

Riley went to the door, hauled the duffel in past the bed, and put it on a low table near a sofa. On the rear wall, caramel curtains were closed over floor-to-ceiling caramel blinds, the color of Karen's slacks and cotton sweater. Bowman had noted it with Jayson, dressed all in tan. It must be a theme for the model—Brown Motels Australia.

Riley pulled the chain to raise the blinds and reveal a glass door. She unlocked it and stepped out onto a small, screened wooden deck with a round metal table and two chairs and a view of the car park. The patio was edged in grass, then gravel, and she crossed over them onto the bitumen and looked back at the building. Each room in the row was identical—a door opening onto a square of outside deck. It was a scaled-down commercial facsimile of the setup at the Armytage block. Riley counted: There were nine rooms along this front-facing strip.

A black Mercedes swung into the drive, and Riley went back inside, locked up, and lowered the blinds. She stepped into the corridor, pulled her door closed, and knocked at Patel's room. The green door to the laundry was at the end of the hall. Riley counted again while she waited. There were nine rooms on Patel's side. That was it: nine rooms on each side of a long corridor, eighteen cabins on Karen's tight ship.

Patel came out tying back her hair, and they went past reception to the Camry. There was tourist traffic on the road. Patel slowed as a Tesla indicated left and turned into the Armytage drive. At least one of the places on the block was listed on Airbnb. The police tape was gone, and Crime Scene had formally handed the town house back to Nigel.

"He's going to sell up," Patel said. "Rent a place in Maitland."

Riley nodded. Good cop, bad cop—Patel was a good cop and had kept a line open to the husband. His wife had been murdered by an unknown serial offender, and the press had pinned the crime on him. Riley needed to go and visit, to pay some respect.

There were cars parked at the crossroad and customers at the café. Patel drove through and pulled up at the incident room.

Rodrigues was at his desk and looked over as they walked in. "Shoe and Tire sent a photo," he said, poking an elbow at a big screen on the wall. "I'll bring it up."

Riley slid her bag down and stood in the middle of the room. The screen flickered as Rodrigues tapped and a picture appeared. Riley moved closer and studied the image. It was a partial shoeprint in white powder on floorboards.

"The Armytage hall," Rodrigues said. "To the right of the internal doorway into the kitchen and living room."

Riley pictured it: To the right of the door was dead space created by the stairwell. "Is that builders' dust?"

"Sanding from the plaster." He was reading off his laptop. "The place was cleaned after construction. They missed bits around the skirting."

Patel stepped up to the screen. "They think a tradie?"

"Maybe. The shoe pattern is unusual. The small triangle shape at the top and then the swirl at the heel. It's not a common tread . . ."

Patel stared at the image. "And?"

"The techs like the print. It's not the toe, someone working front-on to the wall, sanding or painting or plastering."

Riley's fingers were pinching her lip.

"It's the top-right edge," Rodrigues said, "and then the edge of the heel. It's someone standing side-on to the wall." He stood up and turned in the position. "Like they're listening at the door."

16

In navy cords, a new shirt of popping blues, and his checkered cornflower jacket, Bowman cruised Pokolbin in the Audi. Friday morning, and something was up. He'd been hoping to run into Riley, but her Calais hadn't moved from the motel car park in twenty-four hours, and Patel's Camry was nowhere to be seen. Riley had been away overnight, somewhere, and now Patel had gone too.

The police tape had been removed from the scene at the town houses, and the media had broken camp—they were digging dirt on the husband, a job they could do from the office.

The Guardian had just had a crack at Nigel Armytage. They'd discovered Penelope's father had worked high up at Optus, making millions as an exec, but had come over all post-material when he'd retired and had taken to driving around the Central Desert with Penelope's mother in a van. At the last federal election, he'd tipped funding toward the Teals and been on the record about the need to "phase out coal."

The father wasn't on the record today, in the article about his murdered daughter, but *The Guardian* had quoted "sources close to the family" and got the point across: Nigel Armytage's morally unacceptable work had put a strain on Penelope, who had a "sacred" love of the landscape. There was a line toward the end, from the anonymous source, that had actually, literally, nearly killed Bowman: Penny feared that with her marriage to a coal geologist, she had put herself on the wrong side of history. Reading at breakfast, Bowman had almost choked on his bacon.

He drove back to the Packhorse and went up to his room. Four days on the story now, and still he hadn't written a word. It was quite a dry spell, even for him, and he felt the stirrings of frustration. It was warm in the room, and he stripped out of his good clothes and into his writing gear—a sarong and T-shirt. It was time to knuckle down, or at least make some calls.

Bowman had been waiting for Riley to give him a break on the story, but all she'd given him was a job—to sift through Laura Nolan's byline in *The Mirror*. It wasn't difficult, and he'd spent some time at it on Wednesday night and on Thursday. He'd worked at *The National* for more than twenty years, and, despite going freelance, he still had his log-on for the newspaper's publishing system. The broadsheet *National* and the tabloid *Mirror* were siblings—same owner, same stable, same building in Surry Hills. Same operating system: Bowman had complete access to everything Laura Nolan had ever filed.

Nolan appeared to run the Newcastle bureau of the Sydney tabloid on her own, and she'd been busy: courts, cops, and local government issues through Newcastle, Singleton, Muswellbrook, Maitland. And Cessnock.

After Bowman's conversation with Rachel and Michael at breakfast yesterday, he'd refined his search for Nolan's stories. She'd written nothing about the Cassidys or the Quirk motel, but the name Oakeshott paid out: nine stories. Bowman had gone through them last night. Half were reports on development applications, but a series of four articles about a local government imbroglio caught his eye. A Cessnock councillor had resigned for reasons not made clear, but Nolan had ridden it hard. Although Oakeshott's company was on the periphery of the story, the name kept coming up.

Retying his sarong, Bowman took a seat at the small table in his room and phoned his former colleague Forrest West, a property reporter on the Business desk of *The National*. Bowman had known Forrest a long time, since they'd been cadets together two decades ago, and Bowman regarded him as the best type of journalist: socially awkward, smart, dowdy, and a true specialist on a deeply unfashionable round. There was no self-justifying, right-side-of-history, speaking-truth-to-power bullshit. There was no self-regard—but in the commercial real estate sector, Forrest knew all the holes in the ground.

Forrest answered and Bowman greeted him. Forrest always sounded nervous, spoke very fast and often talked over people, although he wasn't meaning to be rude. And Forrest didn't do small talk, it baffled him.

Bowman said, "Tell me—"

"Yes," Forrest said.

"There's a company, Oakeshott Construction. What do you know?"

"Oh. Midsize, sixty staff, not taken public. Neville Oakeshott's the founder and CEO. He started as a real estate agent in Cronulla, then began buying greenfield sites south and west. You know, build a sewer, sell vacant blocks to builders, then charge the household to connect. I mean, development—really, ask anybody, it's all about the poo. He made a lot of money, then went to Newcastle, got in up there. He'd be worth . . . sixty mil. That's his personal wealth, not the company's. Now he's in the Lower Hunter."

"Doing what?"

"Same as before, buying up plots. I think he's got three sites. They're building maybe two thousand apartments, gated residential communities. He bought a wine estate for himself last year—you know, to live in, I think."

"What's it called?"

"Mm, one sec." Bowman heard keys clacking and Forrest humming. "Cockatoo Hill. It's an old Hunter family compound. Vineyard, winery, cellar door, restaurant, residence. I hear he operates from a table in the restaurant—that's his office."

"Nice."

"Mm. He just flew a bunch of journos in by helicopter. They all wrote it up."

"Wrote it up how?"

"Oh, well, you know—it was the foodies. The-pimped-leaves-of-radicchio-danced-on-my-palate."

"So, just a junket?"

"Yeah. Oakeshott's gone all in on the Hunter. He's trying to use the restaurant to lure investors. Got some hatted chef. Destination dining. Here, have a cutlet of coelacanth, and would you like to buy a condo?"

"You reckon he'll talk to me?"

"If you ask the right way. Why?"

"There was a woman murdered in Pokolbin this week," Bowman said.

"Saw that."

"Yeah, in a new town house. There's a row of six out in the scrub at a place called Red Creek. The name *Oakeshott* has been whispered."

"That'll be his build for sure, but want me to check?"

"If you don't mind."

"Give me five. I'll call you back."

Bowman did his own News search while he waited. Armytage–Oakeshott. The connection hadn't been made in the press.

Forrest called back. Oakeshott Construction had bought seventy hectares at Red Creek four years ago and won approval to build 150 apartments and a small commercial strip for offices or shops.

"I'll text you Neville's number, but it didn't come from me," Forrest said. "If you want him to talk, just say you're working on a piece about city folk moving to the regions for the lifestyle. That'll get you through the door quick smart. It'll probably get you lunch."

Bowman thanked him and hung up, and when the number came through, he called it.

A male voice answered. "Hello?"

"Ah, Mr. Oakeshott, my name's Adam Bowman. I'm a journalist—with *The National*."

There was a pause. "Yeah."

"I'm writing a piece on people moving to the country, for the, um, lifestyle . . . ? I was thinking about Mudgee, but I was thinking—I thought, the Hunter. You know, bit closer to Sydney, and that."

"And it invented wine tourism."

"Yeah." Bowman made a face at himself in a mirror on the wall.

"It's the second most visited tourism destination in the country. After Sydney."

"Right."

"Did you say *The National*?" Oakeshott said.

"Yes. I'm actually in the Hunter now." Bowman winced at the mirror. "You know, having a look around. Everyone tells me to speak to you and see your cellar door."

"Yeah. What time?"

Bowman looked at his watch. It was 10:40 a.m. "I could do twelve thirty . . . if that suits."

"Make it twelve forty-five, at the restaurant. I'll be here."

Cockatoo Hill Estate was on a hillock on its own, surrounded by rows of bare vines and with a view over the patchwork of the valley. Bowman was early, so he walked around the buildings, watching rain clouds on the range.

There were a dozen cars in the visitor parking. The winery and a private residence were down a slope, set apart from each other and well removed from a modern rectangular building in timber and glass and polished concrete that housed the cellar door and the restaurant. Bowman followed an ENTRANCE sign into a whitewashed vestibule strung with three large black-and-white aerial photos of the Hunter landscape. Each had a wall label, and Bowman paused to read one. POKOLBIN #2. LUXURY LIVING AMONG THE VINES. TWO-, THREE-, FOUR-BEDROOM APARTMENTS. SPA, GP, GROCER. There was a website, a mobile number, an Instagram URL. Brochures stamped VINEYARD LIVING sat in tasteful piles on a zebra veneer shelf.

Bowman went through an arch into the cellar door—high ceilings, spacious, with polished gray concrete floors, five pale-timber communal tables, a fifteen-meter-long serving counter in chocolate stone. He saw a wall of glass-fronted refrigeration stocked with rows of white wine, the bottles arranged in blocks by label. Above the fridges, TASTING ROOM was stenciled in foot-high Barbie pink.

A few couples stood at the counter with glasses of wine, sniffing, swirling, sipping, murmuring. Two young women in white collared shirts and brown aprons were on the pour. Bowman tugged at his jacket and walked along the counter, and one of the servers greeted him. "Here to taste, sir?"

"No. I'm after Neville Oakeshott . . . ?"

"Of course." She held an arm out. "The restaurant's through there."

He walked under another arch, through another whitewashed hall with aerial photos and brochures, and into the restaurant. There was soft carpet underfoot now, dark brown.

Another young woman in an apron and white shirt was stationed at a lectern with a laptop. "Good afternoon, sir. Did you have a reservation?"

"Uh, no. I'm here to see Neville Oakeshott."

"Of course." She looked down at her screen. "From *The National*?"

He nodded. She didn't have his name, so Oakeshott mustn't have caught it—the developer had just heard the name of the masthead, and that had got Bowman through the door. That was lucky. It meant Oakeshott wouldn't have had the chance to google him.

The woman led him to a table with a view of grapevines running down a slope to a square dam. She pulled out his chair, pushed it in underneath him, poured him a glass of water from a silver jug, and retreated.

Bowman placed his notebook on the white damask and glanced at the tables on either side. There was a woman on his left drinking champagne. She was dining alone, just the bottle beside her in an ice bucket—actual French bubbles, not Hunter sparkling. She was dressed in a green silk blouse under a tight gold jacket and looked about twenty. Plates of morsels were arrayed around her, but she wasn't eating them, she was photographing them with her phone.

Bowman looked farther afield: Eight more tables were occupied . . . couples, a subdued trio, two more solo diners taking pictures. A flotilla of brown-aproned servers cruised the thick carpet. There was a hush on the room, the clink of cutlery on crockery, a discordant score to the absurd theater.

He went back to eyeing the woman next door. Her blouse stirred a memory. After his book came out, Bowman had taken Riley to dinner at a swish place in Barangaroo to thank her and celebrate. The restaurant was called Cirrus, but they'd drunk a lot and Riley labeled it Cirrhosis. She had been between investigations, completely relaxed, and had worn her hair out, and velvet pants, gold heels, a silky blouse in basil green. Bowman had a photo of her from the night on his phone.

Down the room, a man swept in past the lectern without a glance at the door girl. Pale-lemon shirt open at the collar under a powder-blue suit with brown shoes lighter than the carpet. A full head of silver hair was whisked back, fondling his collar. Bowman stood.

They shook. "Neville Oakeshott."

"Adam."

His suntan said summering in Europe on a yacht—or naps in the solarium. "You'll have a glass of wine?" he said when they were seated.

"Sure."

A young server shook out linen napkins on their laps, Oakeshott acknowledging the gesture with a practiced rub on the back of the girl's hand. "Bring the ILR," he said with a moist smile. "The '05."

The server nodded and scarpered.

"It's not one of ours," Oakeshott said. "But it's the region's finest aged sémillon. Very special. It's drinking nicely, for lunch."

Bowman had an interest in wine, because he drank a lot of it, but no actual knowledge. He cleared his throat. "What do you make here?"

"Sémillon, of course. Chardonnay, Shiraz. That's it. This site"—Oakeshott waved out the glass wall at the view—"that's the way it's always been. I bought the whole operation—lock, stock, all the barrels—and kept the winemaker on. Let him run his own show."

"Who did you buy it from?"

"Old Hunter family. It was emotional, for them. But money—it's a salve."

The server came back holding two enormous glasses, upside down by the stalks, and a bottle of wine. She trickled a tipple into Oakeshott's glass to taste, and again he found her hand and rubbed. "Just pour it," he said with another wet smile.

The server kept her eye on the table as she poured for Bowman.

"Do you eat everything?" Oakeshott said, and Bowman nodded. Oakeshott curled his index finger at the server. "Just bring the roe, the oysters, the scallop, and the kingfish." He paused and glanced at Bowman. "Duck or beef?"

"Ah—"

"Duck," Oakeshott said to the server. "And the fioretto. And a bowl of chips."

She retreated. Bowman sipped his wine.

Oakeshott surveyed the room. "Tonight to Sunday, we're booked solid. Lunch and dinner."

"It's new?" Bowman said. "The restaurant?"

"Yeah. We built it from scratch. And incorporated the cellar door."

"I saw the photographs in the hall. You're building golf course resorts, is it?"

"No." Oakeshott scowled. "A golf course costs a million bucks a hole. And then you have to maintain it."

A second server brought bread and pots of butter.

"What we're doing," Oakeshott said, "is residential enclaves, with shopping precincts, small employment zones."

Bowman took some bread. "For offices?"

"Yeah, but even for little factories. Mechanics. So people can work on cars. More V8 Holdens in Cessnock than in any other postcode." He looked at Bowman's notebook. "That's a fact."

"Is that the target market?"

"Part of it. The miners. The other part is city people, who like all this." Oakeshott gestured at the table.

The butter was fluffy and had some flavor in it. Bowman chewed and drank, polished the smeared rim of his glass with his napkin.

Oakeshott was talking about walkways and pathways and bike paths.

Food began to arrive. "Whipped cod roe and Espelette pepper," the server said. Then some oysters. "Kumquat mignonette."

Oakeshott picked at the food and outlined his plans to build recycling plants for sewage, while Bowman ate and the server refilled his wineglass.

More small plates arrived: scallops, a thinly sliced white fish, sculptured piles of shaved roots and leaves. The scallops were surrounded by an algal bloom that looked like it had been scraped off a pier down at Newcastle.

Oakeshott wasn't really drinking, but the server was prompt at refilling Bowman. The vase-size vessel was deceptive—a fair splash from the server looked like the merest dribble in the glass. But just as he was starting to appreciate the flavor, the bottle ran out. Oakeshott was still talking, and Bowman pulled a pen from his pocket and pretended to take notes. The duck arrived, with a vegetable side, a bowl of chips, and a bottle of the estate Shiraz. The server changed Bowman's glass for an even larger balloon.

"The Hunter was the dominant wine region in the country fifty years ago," Oakeshott was saying. "It invented wine tourism. Now we reinvent it and extend it."

"How do you do that?"

"Quality restaurants, quality accommodation, quality table wines. Close to Sydney. But you don't come to stay, you come to live."

Bowman half listened as he ate. He limited himself to one glass of the red—and one top-up. When the last of the dishes were cleared, he brought his notebook in to where he could write properly, and said, "Are you concerned the murder of Penelope Armytage will affect your plans?"

Oakeshott had been running his tongue around his teeth, but now his face went still. "What?"

"Have the police discussed the murder with you?" Bowman said.

Oakeshott stared at him across the table. "With me personally? No."

Bowman wiggled his Biro in his fingers.

Oakeshott had a glow on, under his tan. "Why do you ask?"

"The Armytage house—is it part of one of your developments?"

"Maybe. And?"

"Maybe?"

The businessman sat back and linked his fingers on the table. "Okay. Yes. So what? It's a domestic. What's that got to do with us?"

"I just wondered if the police were talking to you."

"With me? No."

"With your company?"

He watched Bowman's pen. "A detective has spoken with our construction manager. On the phone."

"What did the detective want?"

"Our employment records regarding the town house build— subcontractors, everyone we used."

"And you provided those records?"

"Of course. We regarded it as routine."

"Routine?"

"A routine part of a murder investigation. It's a very new building. We believe the police are inquiring about everyone who has been . . . in the vicinity."

"So there you are," Bowman said. "That's what it's got to do with you."

135

Oakeshott wiped his mouth with his napkin and stood. "It's been a pleasure, Mr. . . . ?"

"Bowman."

"I hope you enjoyed your meal." Oakeshott touched the table near Bowman's glass. "Be careful on the road. You can see yourself out."

17

Riley worked through Friday afternoon in the incident room with Patel and Rodrigues. Patel brought coffees and salad rolls from the café on the crossroad, and they ate at their desks.

Since Wednesday, under the oversight of Rodrigues, two young Cessnock detectives had been compiling a list of everyone contracted by the developer Oakeshott Construction to work on the Armytage build—from the project manager to the kid shoveling sand for the landscaper.

The obvious move was to go to the court in Cessnock and apply for search warrants for all the tradies, executed simultaneously at 4:00 a.m. on a weekday before anyone went to work. Go through every house and every wardrobe and bag every pair of shoes. But it was a long list to target—forty-seven names—and a wide net. A dozen of the workers were no longer in the region, seven were interstate, and four had left the country.

Riley felt it was too unwieldy to take to court. "Too many names, too speculative," she said. "It's our first time to the magistrate. We don't want to piss him off."

"Her," Rodrigues said.

Riley popped some gum. "You know her?"

"Amanda Patton," Rodrigues said. "She's a single mum, raised two daughters. She's tough. But she likes me."

"Likes you how?" Riley said.

"Her eldest ran into strife with a boyfriend last year. I was in court one day, and Patton took me aside and told me about it. She asked if I might have a chat with the bloke."

"What was happening?" Patel asked.

"All the coercive stuff. It started out, he'd question everything she did. *Why'd you buy those apples? Why'd you put your keys there? Why're you wearing that top?* He was trying to control who she saw, cutting her off from her sister and her mum. By the time we got called in, it was physical."

"'We'?" Riley said.

"I took Harris with me. The sergeant from the station. Sorted it out old-school."

"Where's the boyfriend now?" Patel said.

Rodrigues shrugged. "Last I heard, living in his dad's basement. Harris swings by from time to time."

Riley looked at the long list of tradies. "You think Patton'll sign off on this?"

Rodrigues sat back. "We could narrow the search down—just the contractors who had been on-site from the start of plastering."

"That's good," Patel said.

Riley agreed.

At his desk, Rodrigues called the junior detectives who had collated the original list and instructed them to whittle it down to the tradies on-site toward the end of the build: Drywallers, plasterers, painters, and the sparkies who had to return and finish off after the decorators. But six town houses was a big project, and there was a long list of defects picked up after completion, so glaziers, roofers, and plumbers had been called back. Architects, certifiers, locksmiths, the cleaners themselves, real estate agents—they had all been through at the end. And then there were the workers not contracted by the developer: removalists, white goods and furniture deliveries, telcos.

It was tedious work, but it had to be done right: If they missed one person in the sweep, the whole thing was a waste of time.

It was after 6:00 p.m. when Rodrigues stood, stretching his shoulders. "Friday-night cop drinks, wanna come?"

Riley considered for a moment, but she was tired and declined.

"Where?" Patel asked.

"In town, good little group. Just for an hour. You should come."

She stared at her desk, and Riley encouraged her: "Go." The alternative was another Friday night bouncing off the walls in a country motel.

Patel closed her laptop and went with Rodrigues, and Riley was glad. It was useful to have Patel mingling with police from the station.

She locked up and drove to the takeaway, stood in line behind a young male in hi-vis and an older tourist. The married couple were behind the counter. Riley ordered dim sims and a Greek salad.

At the motel, the car park was almost full, and guest rooms were lit up behind curtains and blinds. Riley keyed through the glass entrance. Across the lobby, in the pantry, a couple sat drinking wine at a table with a plate of cheese between them. Riley walked down the corridor, unlocked her door and pushed it open, and stood where Karen had stood in the morning, viewing the room.

After closing the door, Riley sat at a counter over the minibar and ate a couple of dim sims. Then she stood and stripped and threw her clothes on the mound of washing on the floor and went into the bathroom and took a hot shower. She found a fresh towel and wrapped it around her chest and looked at herself in the mirror. Dark hollows under her eyes. She rubbed in face cream and rolled on deodorant and went and found her pajama bottoms and T-shirt under the pillow where she'd stuffed them.

The minibar hadn't been restocked. There was an inch left in the 375 of bourbon, there were bottles of wine, whisky. She poured a glass of white, finished the dim sims, and pecked at the salad. She refilled her wine and got into bed, staring at the black TV screen on the wall. She couldn't be bothered to turn it on. She texted Patel to say she was going to sleep, put her glass on the bedside table, hit the lights, and settled into her pillow.

At 3:00 a.m. she came up out of a dream and lay very still, listening. A noise had woken her. She reached for the reading light and got out of bed, went to the bathroom, and filled a glass of water and drank while she sat on the loo.

She came out, turned on more lights, and stood at the door again, staring into the room and recalling Karen. *It might be time for a clean . . . There's a laundry through the green door.* Riley walked back toward the bed and stopped at the pile of washing on the floor. She crouched and considered the clothes, how they had fallen and how they sat, the things she had worn on Monday night and Tuesday and Wednesday. She saw Karen's eyes scoping the room, seeming to look for something, settling on the dirty clothes.

Riley poked at the pile. The long-sleeve gray T-shirt she'd worn on the first night was near the top of the heap, under her things from today. But she'd thrown the gray shirt on the floor days ago and then chucked more things on the stack as she'd worn them. She was a slob, but she was a slob with habits—she always built a mound. On Monday, the first night, when O'Neil had woken her, she'd packed for five days: She hadn't rummaged in the dirty clothes, she hadn't double-dipped.

She sat back on her haunches. Housekeeping hadn't been in, and the minibar hadn't been restocked—but while she'd been away in Canberra and Sydney, someone had been in her room. Someone had gone through her clothes.

18

The motel's communal pantry was busy with guests at Saturday breakfast. To avoid the hubbub, Patel brought pastries and a cup of fresh milk to Riley's room, and they ate sitting at the built-in counter. Riley made coffee from the Nespresso and relayed her suspicion that someone had gone through her things.

Patel stood and toed the heap of clothes. "You sure?"

Riley felt sure but couldn't be certain.

Patel's face made it plain she had no desire to interrogate Riley's dirty laundry over breakfast. "And anyway, so what?"

Riley chewed her Danish. She had thought the same: They were in a motel. It was part of the deal. Staff would enter the room for myriad reasons.

Patel shook her head as she glanced around. "There's no hard copy?"

Riley knew better than that. Her case files were digital, her notebook was always with her, and she stored any paperwork in the incident room.

They drained their coffees and went out to the Calais and headed to their desks at Red Creek.

At noon, Riley left Patel working with Rodrigues and drove down to see Nigel Armytage at his parents' place on the lake at Wangi Wangi. Penelope's parents had severed contact with Nigel and his family—in grief, they were lashing out, looking for someone to blame, and the press reporting had led them straight to their son-in-law. They believed he had murdered their daughter.

Riley sat with Nigel on a bench on the back porch overlooking the water, and they talked for an hour. She apologized for her line of questioning, listened to his grievances, and swore to him that she had nothing to do with the attacks in the media. She soaked up his anger and then steered him back toward Penny, to his memories, and they both smiled as he told her stories.

Then she turned to face him on the bench. "There's some pictures I want to show you. But I need you to promise to keep this between us. It's very important that you discuss it with no one, not even your parents. Not yet."

He nodded, and Riley pulled out three pictures: portraits of Andrew and Jennifer Morrow, and a shot of the bungalow in Ngunnawal. Nigel stared at them for a long time and shook his head. "Who are they?"

Riley said their names, occupations, ages, address.

None of it meant anything to Nigel. But he was no fool. He held the picture of Jennifer. "She's dead."

It wasn't a question, but Riley answered. "Yes."

He put the pictures between them on the bench. "That's why you stopped questioning me. The same thing happened to her. You think the same person killed her."

"It's a line of inquiry, yes."

He pulled a red handkerchief from his fleece pocket and wiped away tears. "You can't put it out there in the media, to clear my name?"

"The killer can't know we've made the link. It's our best chance of catching him."

"What about Pen's folks? Can you talk to them, at least?"

Riley had known the question would come, and she'd weighed it. She didn't want to promise Nigel that she'd talk to his in-laws but then delay, and she didn't want to lie. Everything now with Nigel was black and white. Too many people had let him down already. "Let me think about it," she said. "If they're talking to reporters, we might need to leave them out of it for a while."

The handkerchief was balled in his fist. "Soon?" he said.

"Yes. But probably not yet."

Nigel closed his eyes to accept this, and Riley admired him for it. It took courage, and decency, to withstand the catastrophe he was enduring.

He picked at the handkerchief. "You know, I didn't even own one of these." It was red silk, and he held it up. "My dad gave it to me yesterday. He came up to me in the kitchen and handed it to me. He didn't say a word. I remember he used to carry them around when I was a kid."

"Your father's proud," Riley said. "He's raised a good man."

They sat for a time, looking out over the lake.

"Our analysts are comparing data, with Penny and Jennifer," Riley said. "It means Detective Patel will have to speak to you regarding Penny's movements. Questions like where did Penny travel for work, and where did you go on holiday? It's best if you speak with the same officer each time, so details don't get missed."

Riley took her leave, and he stayed on the bench.

Inside, she shook hands with his father, hugged his mother, and gave them her card. "Look after him," she said. "Call me anytime. I can't say all the things you need to hear—not yet. Just that . . . please try to ignore the press." She left the parents in their living room, her victims. She would meet them again in weeks, in months, down through the years.

On the way back, she took local roads to avoid the Saturday tourist traffic. Past Cessnock, in a paddock, two hot-air balloons were laid out, deflated, following their morning flight. Purple and orange, yellow and blue. Riley's stomach burned and her face hurt from the physical toll of the visit—all the chemicals and clenching unleashed with the effort to be with Nigel and his parents and respect their trauma.

In Red Creek, vehicles lined up at the crossroads—city SUVs, coaches, a stretch limousine. Cars were parked at the café, with customers in a line out the door. She saw Rodrigues walking with two takeaway cups, and lowered her window to holler, "Want a ride?"

It was fifty meters to the incident room, but he grinned and came around to the passenger-side door and climbed in.

"Far out." Riley drove at a crawl. "Busy."

"Weddings," Rodrigues said. "You should see it when there's a concert *in the vines*. It's like Glastonbury—in chinos." He held the coffee cups on his knees. "Sorry, didn't get you one."

She reached over and took the nearest cup from his hand. "This Priya's?"

He frowned at the remaining coffee on his knee. "S'pose."

Riley took a good sip. "Never mind."

His phone pinged, and he dug it from his jacket and looked at it . . . then cast a side-eye at Riley.

She knew she didn't want to hear it. "Mm?"

"Your reporter mate, Adam Bowman . . . ?"

Riley indicated to park. "Yeah?"

"Highway Patrol pulled him over for a breath test yesterday, out on Broke Road after lunch. Took him to Cessnock, license suspended. Midrange DUI."

Saturday night, bouncing off the walls in a small country town . . . Except Red Creek wasn't a town, and on Saturday evening it was busy, with party buses shuttling drunks around.

It was 6:00 p.m., and Rodrigues had gone home. Riley locked the incident room, drove with Patel to the Packhorse Inn, and turned down the drive. There were fifteen vehicles out front: a tourist minibus, SUVs, utes, a collection of vans.

A group of adult males, early twenties, spilled from the main entrance and swayed in a circle in the car park. "Uh-oh," Patel said.

Riley let the Calais idle. Uni students. "Might be a bucks party. You could get lucky."

An older male appeared from the shadows, slid open the side door of the minibus, and waited while the group piled in. He hauled the door closed and got in the driver's seat, someone turned the music up, "Khe Sanh." The vehicle moved off.

Riley did a circuit of the lot. With no sign of Bowman's Audi, she knew it must be sitting on Broke Road where the Highway Patrol had flagged him down. Riley parked. They hadn't told Bowman they were coming, but they guessed they'd find him here.

The hum of the pub hit them as they entered—woodsmoke, yeast, the low din of voices loosened by truth serum. It was busy but not heaving. Riley walked over to the bar, Patel beside her, and felt a ripple on the air at their presence. Couples and small groups—wine tourists—were clustered through the pub, oblivious to the detectives. But to Riley's right, a posse of drinkers at a round table were watching her. She saw the winemaker Bob Bruce among them, and he greeted her with a half-raised glass.

The barman, serving a trio in chinos, had noted the police presence as well. He was mid-forties, heavyset, perspiring.

Behind the counter, his female colleague came up to Riley. "What'll it be?"

She pointed at the beer taps. "Two Stone & Woods."

The woman unracked a schooner and started to pour. "You the Sydney cops?"

Riley acknowledged it. The woman, late fifties, clearly ran the show. "You Sandra Hogg?"

"That'd be me." She'd given a statement to Rodrigues's local detectives on Tuesday, and Riley had read it. Sandra put the beer in front of Patel and started on another. "You staying down the Quirk?"

"Yeah," Riley said.

"Bit quieter down there."

Riley handed over her Amex. Bowman was nowhere to be seen. "You got a guest here, Adam Bowman?"

The woman gave a damp chuckle and pointed with her forehead. "The resident sage."

Riley and Patel turned. In a corner, dimly lit, Bowman was sitting at a table on his own. He held up his near-empty glass.

Riley looked back at Sandra. "Better make it three."

They carried the beers over. Bowman was perched in the middle of a U-shaped booth, and they took a seat on either side. "You two need to work on your tradecraft," he said. "Stick out like a pair of parrots in here."

"While you blend in nicely," Patel said. "Another nearly dead white male."

He took his fresh beer.

"Didn't see your car out front," Riley said.

"News travels," he said.

"How are you traveling?" Riley said.

He opened his palms at the table. "Confined to barracks."

Riley shook her head. At least he hadn't called her and pleaded special treatment when the cops pulled him over. "What happened?"

"Drank some wine at lunch. With Neville Oakeshott."

"Why did you go see him?" Riley said.

"Protestant work ethic."

Sipping, Patel nearly choked. "After four days sitting in a pub, your work ethic drove you to go get pissed at lunch?"

"It didn't drive him home," Riley said.

"I wish I was Protestant," Patel said. "What do you do when you're relaxing?"

"Different stuff." Bowman turned his glass. "It's a broad church."

In the booth, the three of them were sitting in a row along the back wall, with a view of the room.

Bowman dipped his beer toward Bob Bruce's table. "You got your locals there," he said. "That's Red, Vat, Stalk, and Bore Drain. And I hear you know Bruce."

"What'd you hear?" Riley asked.

"You paid him a visit. You met Red's son."

Riley paused to remember the name of the man in the wine shed. "Dew," she said.

"Dunno. I just heard you ran into Red's son, and that Red's son doesn't like cops."

"What led you to Oakeshott?" she said.

Bowman made a *danger is approaching* humming sound . . . Sandra had come out from behind the bar and was drawing closer. She swept in and cleared his empty glass. "This is Sandra," he said. "Our host."

"We met," Sandra said, her eyes skipping from Riley to Patel. "Did you want to eat?"

Patel answered, "Sure."

Sandra went to get menus. "Oakeshott's name came up in here," Bowman said, with a nod at the bar. "Plus, he's pals with the reporter Laura Nolan. He uses her."

Riley held her glass near her lips. "Uses her how?"

"There was a blowup in local council eighteen months back. I don't know what happened, but a councillor walked. Nolan was in the thick of it, getting the drops. Oakeshott was mentioned in dispatches."

"Mentioned how?" Riley said.

"Anodyne stuff. But Nolan's young, and she was younger then. It's a way green reporters reveal their sources—unwittingly. Quote the source elsewhere, alongside the main game—it's a way of saying thanks, a pat on the back. Oakeshott's a player, so he'd like that. He wants his name in the press."

"You think Oakeshott speared this councillor, using Nolan?" Patel said.

"I'll keep looking." He squinted. "But yeah."

"What else?" Riley asked.

"You tell me."

She sipped.

"You said get a name and we'd talk," Bowman said. "The name's Neville Oakeshott. You knew it already. He built the victim's town house, he wants to build a lot more. He built the motel where you're staying. He doesn't like the owners, the Cassidys. I'm guessing you knew that too."

"He said that?" Riley said.

"No, that's pub talk." Bowman tipped his glass at the room.

"From the locals?"

"The barman and the server." Bowman looked across to the dining area, where a girl in a white polo was clearing a table.

Riley watched the big man behind the bar. "What's he got to say?"

"He's got a soft spot for Cassidy, doesn't like Oakeshott."

"And?"

"Socially, a little awkward. But self-contained, not shy. Practical. Good on the tools—in the cellar. Pours nice clean beer. Ex-army. Trouble around his discharge, rumor is aggravated assault. But I didn't hear that from him. With the rest of his life story, I'm familiar."

"From him?" Riley said.

"Yes. Grew up in Singleton. Same with Jayson Cassidy. Both from military families, they've known each other since they were kids. Cassidy's helped him find work, before this, and put in a word for him here."

"Name?" Patel said.

"Michael . . ."

Patel scrolled on her phone. "Sharp," she said. "Barman's Michael Sharp. Not rostered on Monday. There was a chef working, a Kenneth Nguyen. He clocked off at nine p.m. Monday and was gone by the time of canvass. Officers followed up, spoke to him Tuesday. Along with the owner, Sandra Hogg. A server, Rachel Evans, gave a statement on the night."

Bowman started to say something but stopped as Sandra arrived with the menus. He waited till she'd gone. "The media have pulled up stumps at the scene."

"And?" Patel said.

"It helps you to have the press think it's a domestic," Bowman said. "It keeps the story simple."

"Did we say it's not a domestic?" Riley said.

"You said the focus on the husband was wrong."

"I said the narrative was wrong and that we'd talk. I'll say it again—not yet."

"You've got a grieving husband who, let's say, didn't kill his wife, being *eviscerated* by the media," Bowman said. "And you're going to leave him dangling?"

Leather squeaked as Patel shifted on the banquette.

"I hope you know what you're doing," Bowman said, his shoulder nudging Riley's. "For your sake."

"Was that a threat?" Patel looked across Bowman at Riley. "Did I just hear a threat?"

Riley ignored it. Bowman was goading, using the dangling husband to pressure her for an angle. Sandra reappeared carrying two bottles of wine. "Compliments of Bob Bruce." She placed them on the table. "He didn't know if you preferred red or white."

"I actually like both," Bowman said.

Riley looked up to find Bruce coming over. "Detective," he said.

"Mr. Bruce."

"Sorry to interrupt." He glanced around the booth and nodded at the table. "That's a couple of drops we make. I thought you might be interested to have a look. As a thank-you—for your work." He cleared his throat. "For Penny."

A silence descended. Riley let him swing in it. Bowman and Patel had gone still beside her. If Bruce wanted to make a gesture—fine, she'd drink his plonk. But it bought him nothing except her scrutiny. Was the wine really a mark of respect, for Penny? Riley thought not. It was another form of goading, a power play, a loaded gift. He wasn't a suspect, but he could become one.

"Well." Bruce's mouth straightened. "It's Saturday night." He buried his hands in his pockets. "I'll leave you in peace, to have your dinner."

The young server brought an ice bucket and glasses, and Sandra cracked a bottle and held it up. "Who's having white?"

They each raised a hand, and she poured.

Patel picked up a menu, and Sandra left the server to take their orders. Bowman introduced them all. Rachel was eighteen, maybe nineteen, athletic—tall and strong.

"It was you here Monday, who spoke to the police?" Riley said. "I read your statement."

The girl's lips twitched. "They just wanted to know who was in, and that."

Riley stretched her lips too. It was who wasn't in that might be more interesting. But now wasn't the time to ask—the pub was busy, Rachel was working, people were watching. At the bar, Michael Sharp was leaning over the counter in close conversation with Bob Bruce, their heads almost touching.

Patel and Bowman ordered steak and, on Rachel's recommendation, Riley went for rendang. They drank white wine as Bowman talked a bit about the old inn. "Nooks, chinks, crannies," he said. "It's haunted, of course."

"Of course," Patel said.

The food came and they drank red wine. Riley read the label on the bottle: ROBERT THE BRUCE SHIRAZ.

"Just back with this reporter, Laura Nolan," Bowman said. "You thought you had a leak, you asked me if she was quoting cops."

"Was she?" Riley said.

"No. But it got me thinking."

The rendang had a kick hotter than a solar flare. Riley doused her mouth with wine.

"This Neville Oakeshott," Bowman said. "I pissed him off at lunch, and he threatened me . . . about drink driving. And then, fifteen minutes later, I got pulled over."

"A winery tips off the cops about a customer drinking too much and getting on the road," Patel said. "Wouldn't be the first time."

"They were a Cessnock patrol. They came out here from town."

"Where else are they going to come from?" Riley said. "Oakeshott warned you, and then he called the cops."

"He didn't warn me—it was a little coded threat. And then, bang." Bowman clicked his fingers. "He made it happen, fast."

"It was by the book," Patel said. "You were DUI."

"You mentioned Nolan to me, and you mentioned cops," Bowman said. "Nolan links to Oakeshott, and Oakeshott's got what, the Highway Patrol on speed dial?"

Riley swilled more wine.

"Dunno about your leak," Bowman said. "But Oakeshott's got a cop in his pocket."

19

Sunday morning, 5:05 . . . Riley woke, rolled over, and tried to go back to sleep, but after a few minutes she knew it was hopeless, her mind was grinding in tight circles. She swung her legs to the floor and headed to the bathroom.

She came out, drank some water, and stooped to scoop up the pile of washing on the floor. With the bundle under an arm, she stepped into her slippers and grabbed her room key and went out and down to the far end of the corridor, away from reception. She was a trespasser on the silence, the motel coiled in on itself in the predawn.

The green door at the end was unlocked, and she went through into a Besser-block chamber with four doors: STAFF, HOUSEKEEPING, STORE, LAUNDRY. She tried the handle of the laundry and went in, keeping the door open with her foot while her eyes adjusted, and she pressed the light switch.

It was a white room with white counters running along each wall. Four big washing machines, two on each side, sat under the counters, and in line above them four dryers hung on the wall. Two large tubs for dirty linen sat on the floor at the back wall. The machines were empty, but there was the hum of an extractor fan. There were laundry baskets and boxes of powder on each counter. Riley put her clothes in a machine, spooned in powder, closed the door, and pressed buttons.

She leaned with her backside to the counter and watched as the drum filled.

Leaving the light on, she went back out into the anteroom. The doors marked STORE and HOUSEKEEPING were locked. The STAFF door led to a changing room with a toilet, a shower, and lockers.

Riley went out and back through the green door to the guest corridor and her room, trod out of her slippers, and got back into bed. Her thoughts slowed. Getting up and doing something had eased her mind from its groove, and she fell back asleep.

It felt like hours later when she woke to a knocking on the door. She stumbled out and opened it, and Patel's arm came through holding an oily paper bag.

"What's the time?" Riley said.

"Nearly ten," Patel said. "You had a Sunday lie-in, you look great, let's go."

Riley took the bag and contemplated, dry mouthed, a flabby ham-and-cheese croissant.

"I'll be in the lobby," Patel said.

Riley made a double coffee, showered, dressed, clipped on her Glock, and ate a wedge of croissant as she went into the corridor.

There was a short line at reception, weekenders checking out, and no sign of Karen. A younger female was behind the desk, mid-twenties.

Riley followed Patel to the Calais. "What time did Karen say reception was open?"

"Nine till six," Patel said.

In the incident room Rodrigues was at his desk, finishing the warrant for the tradies. "The magistrate, Patton, got back to me," he said. "No promises, but she said she'd look if I bring it round to her place at five."

Riley put her bag down. Magistrates often looked at warrants at home after hours, but it was a good sign.

"What do you think of Bob Bruce?" she asked.

"Person of interest," Rodrigues said. "Penny's client. No criminal history. An alibi—"

"From his spouse."

"True."

"With the warrant, can we tack on a request to search Bruce's wine shed? There's a first aid kit. I'd like a look."

"Can do," Rodrigues said.

They settled to work. Patel hadn't briefed Rodrigues on Bowman's hunch about Neville Oakeshott having a cop on the take, and Riley didn't mention it either. Bowman could dig around and see what he could find.

Riley had a video call with her analyst in Parramatta, Dick Laver in Canberra, and the ACT analyst on the Morrow case. The analysts had been trawling the victims' social media accounts, scouring their daily and digital lives for any link between the couples, even if they'd visited the same place months apart.

"Nothing?" Riley said.

On the screen, the analysts shook their heads.

"I think we have to work from the idea he has no personal connection to the victims," Laver said. "And they have no personal connection to each other."

"Agreed," Riley said.

"It could be anything," Laver said. "They were at the same café two years apart, or a service station—someone out on the highway watched them pump fuel."

The best hope was that the two victims or their husbands had used credit cards, and that by layering the information, the analysts could make something chime. Laver was checking with Andrew Morrow about holiday or work trips Jennifer had made. Patel would do the same with Nigel Armytage.

After Riley briefed them on the shoeprint in the Armytage house and the warrants, the analysts left the call, and she stayed on with Laver.

"How'd you go with the ATO?" she said.

"Your victims are clear."

"Mm." She raised her eyebrows.

Laver held a palm out parallel and wobbled it. "Don't get too excited."

"But?"

"Your man Jayson Cassidy has got no convictions for fraud or tax evasion, no historic charges—or any pending."

"But?"

"Allegations. Someone doesn't like Cassidy, that's for sure. Whoever it is, they aren't coming forward. All we've got is anonymous tips—detailed, informed, but anonymous. Around conspiracy to defraud, so a criminal charge. But it didn't stack up for the ATO. There was enough for Audit to take a serious look. They reamed it up him sideways, but nothing stuck."

"Can you take another swing re: the informant, if there's any way to identify?"

"Will do," Laver said, and the call ended.

At 4:30, Patel went with Rodrigues to meet the magistrate. At 5:50, Riley locked up and walked out to the car in the twilight. She drove to the Quirk and sat in the Calais with a view of the motel entrance. Just after 6:00 p.m., the young woman from reception came out and crossed the darkening car park to a Yaris. She went right out of the drive, in the opposite direction of the Red Creek crossroad. Riley let her go, then followed her taillights at a distance.

They headed past cellar doors, signs for function centers, B and Bs, an alpaca barn. The Yaris went left on Broke Road, the tourist venues thinning out until there was only bush, the heavy foliage of state forest. The girl knew the road and drove fast. After several minutes, the Yaris slowed as it came up to Broke. Riley knew the village as a grid, seven or eight streets, maybe fifty dwellings, rimmed by the escarpment on the edge of the plain.

Riley had visited Broke often as a child, with her father. *Flat Stony*, he'd called it, but he was no geologist. Bill Riley had punted with miners here. Broke in Broke, flat stony in Flat Stony.

The Yaris went right and left, and parked outside a dark house. Riley pulled up behind her and got out. The woman's eyes flicked to the Calais and then back at Riley. "You following me?"

Riley took a slow step toward her and pulled out her badge. "Detective Sergeant Rose Riley," she said. "Homicide."

The woman swallowed. Still a girl, really. "I know youse," she said. "Staying at the Quirk."

"This your place?"

"Me mum's."

Riley looked at the cottage, a pale hint of weatherboard in the night. The girl's father had worked in the mines—or her grandpa. Or both. "What's your name?"

"Belinda."

"How old are you?"

"Twenty-one."

No lights were on in the house. "Is your mum home?"

"Not yet." She glanced at her watch. "She works till eight."

"Can we have a chat, maybe inside?"

The girl hesitated a moment and then pulled a shoulder bag from the Yaris, and they went up the path. Riley stood back while Belinda unlocked the door and hit a switch for a bare bulb. "Come in."

They went down a short hall, Belinda flicking on lights, into a small kitchen of pale-yellow cabinets with a Formica table and lino on the floor. To trendsetters in Marrickville, the kitchen would be an affectation, a retro joke, but to Riley it felt like home. It was no joke to Belinda either.

"I saw you at the Quirk," Riley said. "This morning."

She kept her eyes down, dropping her bag.

"Penelope Armytage. Did you know her?"

Belinda moved to the sink. "No."

Riley took a seat at the table with her notebook and motioned for Belinda to join her. "Penelope stayed at the Quirk with her husband, Nigel. Is that right?"

Belinda was in the motel's colors: camel slacks and sweater over a white shirt. Too much makeup, big hazel eyes with long lashes. Her hair, pulled back tight, needed a wash. "Yeah," she said. "That's what Karen said."

"You didn't see them? The Armytages?"

She shook her head. "It was a while ago. I've only been there like five months."

Riley took the lid off her pen. "What else did Karen say?"

"Just that. She tells everyone. Like, you know, she's connected. Bit of drama."

"Penelope worked for a winemaker, Bob Bruce. You know him?"

"Know who he is. But, like, I've never spoken to him."

"There's a man who works for Bruce. He lives here in Broke, I think."

"Wait, Dew," she said. "Yeah?"

"Yeah. You know Dew?"

She shrugged. "Bit. Since he moved back. But he's like forty. The girls know him, at work."

"The girls?"

"Deidre and Bec. Housekeeping."

Riley made a note.

"Deidre's like forty, knows Dew pretty well from when he ran off the rails, ya know? Bec's her daughter. Like twenty-three."

Riley inched her head at the window. "Do they live here too?"

"Nah. Cessnock. Deidre might have lived with Dew for a bit, when he was dealin'."

"He's not dealing now?"

"Wait, what?" Her mouth turned down as her eyes found the notebook. "I dunno. Don't think so. That's why he's back here, like going clean. Deidre says he ran off when he was twelve. ''Cos the old man's a cunt and a half.' Scuse the French."

"Where's his place?"

Belinda tossed her chin. "End of the road, left, first left, halfway down on the right."

Riley shifted. "At the Quirk, Karen's husband, Jayson—what does he say?"

A cloud crossed the girl's face. "About what?"

It wasn't fear, Riley thought. "About Penelope Armytage," she said.

"Not much. Like nothin'. But, you know, he doesn't talk with us anyway."

"To you and Bec"—Riley looked at her book—"and Deidre?"

"Right. Except maybe, he's in the mood, he might say hi. But me and the girls, we're not important, you know? So he doesn't bother. Which is fine."

Riley nodded.

"Wait . . . he talks, like, on the phone, to, I dunno—not guests, but for work? Should hear it—real big man, make this money, do this. He turns it on, but it sounds, just false."

"Okay, but then with you—and Bec and Deidre—he doesn't . . . interact so much? Is he the same with all of you?"

"Yeah." She swayed. "He's good at ignoring us, right? We get it, we're just the staff."

"But?"

She paused, pouted, rubbed at the table.

"It's all right, you can talk to me." Riley ducked her head to meet the girl's eye. "It's confidential. That's why I followed you, so no one knows."

Belinda frowned, nodding. "It's just weird, like, the way he blanks us," she said, "'cos we know he's watching."

"Watching?"

"Yeah, like you can feel it. On the screens."

Riley's scalp crawled. "The screens?"

"In the office, behind reception. He sits in there."

Riley had noted a camera at the motel entrance and another at reception. "He's watching you on CCTV?"

"Yeah, heaps. With the cameras."

"Where are the cameras?"

"The lobby, the pantry, like, the corridor. The car park . . . Deidre reckons he's got them in all the rooms, perving." She gave a laugh. "But that's a joke."

Hairs stood on the nape of Riley's neck.

"He ignores you," Belinda said. "Like he never looks at you. Except . . ."

"Except?"

"Except when you're not looking. Then he looks at you. Like, you know, on the bus, you catch men staring and that?"

Riley nodded.

"Like that, I've caught him. And staring at Bec. He won't bother to say hi. But he'll have a good stare."

It was a clear night, the cold biting Riley in the lower back as she walked the path from Belinda's cottage to the car. She had swapped numbers and a reassuring smile with the girl on the way out the door.

In the village, Riley went left and left, and kept her eyes out on the right of the street. Headlights strafed her, people coming home. She slowed. There was a Commodore parked on the road next to a ute in a drive. She lowered her window and shined her flashlight from the door pocket at the ute—the beaten-up green Navara she'd seen on the apron outside Bob Bruce's wine shed. She reached for her notebook and flicked through the pages, checking that the Navara plate she had taken down on Wednesday at the shed was the vehicle she was looking at now. Tick. She took down the street address and pulled out.

Dew the dealer with the neck tattoo, who Bruce was helping rehabilitate. Dew's father, Red, was a grape grower, a friend of Bob Bruce, and had been drinking with Bruce in the Packhorse last night. *Red's son doesn't like cops,* Bowman had said. Red lived out around Rothbury on the family place, and he grew more grapes on plots he owned between Rothbury and Belford. Riley had an inkling where that might be, and she thought she'd pay a visit tomorrow.

She turned left on the main road and cleared the village, into the forest, her high beam eating up the white lines of the blacktop. She concentrated on driving, alert for roos.

Patel's Camry was at the Quirk. Along the building, exterior lights lit the facade, but it was Sunday night and the motel had emptied out. Riley counted three guest vehicles and noted the camera in the car park near the foyer entrance. There was no one in the lobby or the pantry, and the door behind reception was closed.

On a whim, she slipped behind the desk and knocked. She wasn't expecting an answer, and was about to try the handle when the door opened.

Karen was out of uniform, in a sweatshirt and jeans. "Detective."

Riley found a smile. "The staff list?" she said. "I was hoping I could get it."

Annoyance flared. Karen's slow blink was practiced, unfurled on choice morons. "Of course."

It was a large office. Two long tables ran width-ways in the middle of the room, one behind the other, a good six meters of desk. Karen went to the first table and bent over a computer. Riley wandered down the room and along the back desk, to a bank of monitors showing the live CCTV feed. Car park, lobby, pantry, corridor. Karen clicked on a keyboard, and beside her a printer whirred.

On a monitor, Riley saw a man enter the lobby and pause to look in the pantry. She tensed, thinking he might enter the office, but he walked on, down the corridor. She watched him as he passed all the rooms and went through the green door at the end.

Karen straightened and turned and held out a piece of paper from the printer.

"Thanks." Riley took it and walked around the desk to the door. "Sorry to disturb you."

Karen nodded, and Riley went out, closed the door behind her, and crossed the lobby into the corridor. She knocked on Room 8, and Patel opened her door.

"Come," Riley said.

Patel didn't ask questions. Riley put her foot in the door while Patel ducked back into the room for her key.

They walked down the corridor, and Riley noted the camera high in the corner over the green door. "A man just went through," she murmured. "Must be Jayson. We're just here to get my washing."

They went into the concrete anteroom. The four doors were closed, and there was no camera on the ceiling or walls—and Riley hadn't noted vision of the space on the monitors. The door marked STORE was unlocked, and Riley went in. There was a light on but no one inside, just rows of shelving and dry goods for the pantry and a commercial refrigerator humming against the back wall. She went out and into the staff changing room, swung the doors on the cubicles. No one.

Patel tried the door marked HOUSEKEEPING. "Locked," she said.

Riley went into the laundry and flicked on the light. No one. The door to the washing machine she'd used was open under the counter and the drum was empty. She straightened. Her clothes, still damp, were in a basket on the counter. She looked around the room. The other machines weren't in use.

Patel called from next door. "In here."

Riley went out. The door marked STORE was open, and Patel was at the rear of the room. Riley went over and Patel pointed behind the fridge. There were a couple of square meters of space and a red door in the back wall. "Locked," Patel said. "Must be a way out."

They stood for a moment in silence. Then Riley went back to the laundry and stuffed her clothes in the dryer and turned the dial. The machine started to spin.

They stared at each other, and Patel shrugged. "Might put a load on myself."

In the corridor, they separated and went to their rooms, and Riley poured a glass of white wine and sat in a chair. She sent a message to Rodrigues in the WhatsApp group chat they shared with Patel.

CR you got a good tech? For cameras and bugs?

He came straight back. Yeah, there's a bloke—worked with me in Gangs a bit.

Could you get him over to our motel? In the morning?

I can ask.

OK. Tell him urgent. And not install. Sweep.

Sweep what?

Riley raised her eyes to scan the ceiling, as though in thought. She sent a response: Some rooms at Quirk.

A pause lengthened. Rodrigues was there, Riley could see he was reading, but he didn't respond. She rose and walked around the room, stopping herself from searching for cameras. She felt it again, the prickle at the base of her neck as her hairs stood on end.

20

On Monday morning Bowman waited in the pub car park, his woolly Patagonia vest zipped against the gelid air. Patel had agreed to take him out to retrieve his Audi, but with his license suspended, he couldn't drive it back, so Riley had been dragooned into the mission as well—against her wishes, it would be fair to say.

Patel's Camry came down the drive, and she rolled to a stop beside him with her window down.

"Morning. You look like my Uber driver," Bowman said.

"Don't fucking start." The window went up, and Patel killed the engine and got out.

Bowman put his hand on her arm and pecked her on the cheek. "It's good to see you, by the way," he said. "I didn't get to say that the other night."

Patel drew her head back to meet his eye, and then their cheeks touched as she gave him a hug. They came apart and she rubbed his vest. "Nice," she said. "Are you a sheep or a Sherpa?"

Riley's Calais did a loop of the car park and pulled up, and Patel got in beside her.

Bowman climbed in the back and sat up straight in the middle seat. "Home, James."

Riley adjusted her mirror to glare. "Don't fucking start."

They went up the drive and eased out onto the road, left, cresting a gentle rise and down the dip, past the Quirk. The weekenders were gone, the traffic was light . . .

"Nice day for a drive," Bowman said.

"Yeah"—Riley propped an elbow on the door sash—"perfect use of police resources."

Bowman directed from the map on his phone. They picked up a dirt road and went through vineyards, rows of bare vines on either side of the car. He leaned forward between them and pointed out the windshield. "See, the vines appear dormant," he said. "But if you look closely, you can spot tiny shoots of green . . . ?"

Up front, neither answered.

"That's bud burst," Bowman said. "It's literally today, September one. So that's the first growth. This year's vintage."

"Some people call it spring," Riley said.

"Yeah." He sat back. "Rachel told me. The server."

"What's her story?" Patel asked.

"Saving to go to uni in Bathurst next year. Family lives in Branxton. Dad's a winemaker."

Riley stopped at an intersection, and Bowman re-centered his map. "Left," he said.

"You should hire Rachel as your driver," Patel said. "If she's looking for cash."

Not a bad idea. He had to get to Cessnock for an interview that afternoon, and these two weren't going to chauffeur him. "Yeah, but Sandra," he said.

"What about her?" Patel said.

Sandra was tough, and Bowman hadn't cracked her. Naturally, in the pub, he'd been trying to duchess her because she was where the power lay. He'd given her his full attention, asked her questions and even listened while she answered. He'd spent up big in the bar. And yet Sandra, the termagant, was impervious to his charms.

"She warned me off harassing her locals," he said. "Christ knows what she'd do if she caught me employing her staff."

Riley slowed. Ahead, Bowman saw his car on the side of the road. The Audi was listing in a drainage ditch beside a fence edging a paddock of vines.

Riley pulled over and Patel got out. Bowman hauled himself out, too, and handed her the key as Riley bent in her seat and called through the open passenger-side door, "Oi. You ride with me."

"See ya." Patel jiggled her eyebrows at Bowman. "I'll leave it at the pub. Key on the front driver's wheel." The Audi flashed as she pressed the fob.

Bowman hesitated, aware he was being railroaded, then got back in the Calais beside Riley. She checked her mirrors and drove on.

"Thanks for this," he said, "by the way."

Her mouth tugged down. "No worries."

With Patel gone, a change in the air between them. "Sorry, this is tedious," he said.

"It's all right." Her tone was amicable. "I mean," she said, injecting a note of concern, "drink driving—you need to watch it."

"Yeah."

"I know you don't do it in Sydney." She peered out her window. "And it's harder out here."

He stared out, too, at fire-scarred forest, and they drove for a moment in silence. "Drinking in the landscape," he said.

She widened her eyes. "So here we are. You think there's another book in this?"

He hadn't thought that—he was just here for a story, a woman murdered in tourist country. "No," he said. "Should I?"

Her lips stretched, an ambivalent line he couldn't decipher. Was there more to the story, or something else on her mind? There was a sign for Broke, and she touched the brakes as they neared the village. They weren't heading back to Red Creek.

"I read your book," she said.

"Oh," he said. "Ah."

Something else was on her mind. She kept her eyes on the road, and he snuck a glance at her profile, her lissome neck as she swallowed.

He was proud of the book. He'd worked hard, taken care, poured the best parts of himself into it. He'd wanted her to read it but had given up hoping, thinking reading wasn't her thing and she would just let it slide. Now that it had happened, he tried to think what it might mean to her.

"You *really* did listen to me," she said.

"Yeah," he said. "That's sort of how it works."

"It's all right," she said again. "You did your job." She was nodding. "You did it well. We can talk about it. But the book's interesting, I liked it. And you were fair."

They skirted the village, past a bushfire brigade and a caravan park, and she picked up speed again on the open road, heading north. Were they going for a drive to talk about it?

"I don't mean we need to talk about it now," she said.

Bowman shifted a leg in the footwell. They were going to talk about it now.

"After the case—at the school—you said you were going to get out," she said, "leave journalism. But you didn't. You wrote the book, and you stayed in." She opened her hands on the wheel. "And for that, well, I'm glad."

"So I can write another book about you?"

"No." She pinged him a look, and saw he was joking.

"I'd miss the people," he said, "if I stopped."

"You hate the media. All the glass jaws."

"I'd miss the people I work with."

This gave her pause.

"I'm working with Priya," he said. "I like her."

"She likes you too. You're like her drunk uncle."

He gripped the grab handle at his shoulder. "So, you like the book, for which I'm glad, and you're glad I'm here. Anything else?"

"No. Just don't go changing. What is it you say about journalists?"

"A conceited journalist is a tautology?"

"Yeah. Fuck that. You got to walk the line."

"The line being . . . ?"

"Stay in but don't become a dick. Because if you get out, I know what'll happen."

"I'll drink my way through relevance deprivation while posting sanctimoniously on whatever the fuck they call Twitter?"

"Exactly. And I won't want to watch that—and neither will your mate Priya."

On the left, the scrub was giving way to ordered mounds of industry, and Bowman saw they were passing an enormous open-cut coal mine. "Jesus," he said.

Riley craned to look, her chin over the wheel.

He watched piles of glossy-black coal flick past. He'd never seen anything like it. "I didn't know it was just here."

"To me, that's the Hunter," Riley said.

Chunky yellow haul trucks were lined up stationary against a fence. In the distance, great hills of flinty overburden sat as high as the range. "Is this where the husband works?"

"No. Further north."

"Is that where we're going?"

Riley shook her head.

They left the mine behind, and after a few minutes, she took a right onto a back road heading east. The country was grassland, and then they came into another patch of vineyard. The area was fenced, and Riley pulled up at an open gate and idled, staring out. From the gate, a track led through a paddock of vines.

Eventually, Riley drove in, across a cattle grid and along the dirt. She put her window down. There were vehicles ahead, two utes, and a spray rig on a trailer, parked at a derelict cottage. She pulled up, killed the engine, and watched. The little house was abandoned, serving now as just a shed.

Riley got out and walked slowly toward it. Bowman followed, coming up behind her as she stood in the open front door. There was no one inside, and no one had lived there for years. Broken windows, broken floorboards, some bags of chemicals stored in a corner. Riley crossed the room and went through a second door. Bowman waited.

After a few minutes, she hadn't emerged, and he went in. On the left, through the internal door, was a kitchen—sagging counters, cobwebs, and a stained, old porcelain sink. He went down a skeleton hall, looking in two more doors until he found her in a room at the rear. She was standing stock still.

Phantom fingers of realization climbed his spine.

Riley came out of her trance and stepped over to him, holding his eye. Solemn knowledge flashed between them—the case at the school, his dead brother, Riley standing in Bowman's childhood house.

"This is it," he said.

"Because of the book. I wanted to show you."

Her farm. She'd brought him home.

Riley walked away from her old bedroom and out of the house. It was as she'd known, there was nothing for her here. The place had been bought, the land planted to vine, the house left to ruin. With breaths of cold air, she stood on the dirt and looked at the two utes by the spray rig. A red Isuzu she didn't know and the green Navara she recognized—she'd seen it parked in Broke last night and at Bob Bruce's wine shed. Dew's vehicle. The Isuzu was probably his father's, the grape grower Red. Riley had seen the spray rig, too, on the apron outside Bruce's shed.

Bruce had told Riley that Red owned plots between Rothbury and Belford, and her hunch had proved correct—it was on her family's old farm. Red must have bought it knowing the soil was right to grow vines. He'd maybe bribed the agronomist, who'd lied to her father.

Dew worked with Bob Bruce on Tuesday and Wednesday, and Bruce had said that on the other days, Dew worked with his father on Red's land. Riley had planned to come out here this morning to chase her hunch, but also, undeniably, to see the farm. Her decision to bring Bowman along for the drive had been spontaneous, even subconscious, and tied up with his book and her mother's talk of her father—and all of it mingled with Riley's knowledge of Bowman's mother and the loss of his brother. Those terrible things he didn't know and she'd never told him.

He had come out of the house and was beside her. "Incoming," he said.

She looked up and around. Two males in work clothes were stomping toward them between rows of vines.

"On the left is the grape grower Red, from the pub," Bowman muttered.

The men were thirty meters away, with Red leading the charge. Lagging a little was Dew. Father and son. Still a way off, Red shouted, "You can't do this"—a finger stabbing the air—"it's not right." A bucket hat on his head, his round face hot and lined.

"Do what?" Riley said.

Red stopped a couple of meters from them, legs bowed, arms out, back crooked, a gunslinger loaded up with arthritis. "Don't be fuckin' cute, I know who you are."

Dew had stopped, too, and stood a few steps behind.

"This your place?" Riley said.

"Yeah." Red gave her a leer. "As though you don't know."

"Why would I know?"

"What, you just drop in on strangers?" He jerked his chin. "Out for a drive."

"Maybe," Riley said. "Why not?"

"'Maybe' my fuckin' arse. You done your homework." Red's eyes flicked to Bowman. "And you bring the press on me land?"

Bowman coughed.

"Homework?" Riley said.

Red's lip curled. "Fuck off, we knew you'd come callin'." His head veered toward his son. "He was with me and his mother, Monday. So you leave him alone."

"Why would I come calling on your son?"

The old man wiped his mouth with his sleeve. "You pigs are all the same."

She looked past him to Dew, taller than his father, skinny and sallow. An oily cap on his head and his eyes in shadow. "How about you, Dew? You got something to say?"

He didn't answer.

"I heard you had a record," Riley said. "If I look it up, what do I find?"

"He's done his time," Red said. "That's what you'll find."

"Time? What I heard is, there'd been a spell on remand."

A vein pulsed in Red's neck.

Bowman shifted his weight.

"Tell me it's not rape, is it?" Riley said. "Or . . . little girls? Because then I am interested. And that would be bad."

"You show me a warrant," Red said, "or get off me land."

Riley threw Bowman a considered frown. "I might do that. Come back and have a look around."

Dew hadn't moved, but now he stepped forward and bent to whisper in his father's ear. Red's face went still and then flooded with surprise. He blinked, looked Riley over, then shooed her with the back of his hand. "Go on," he said, "get."

21

Riley dropped Bowman back at the Packhorse and read her phone in the car. The three-way WhatsApp chat was buzzing. Rodrigues had sent a message that his tech guy would be at the motel at 11:45 a.m. Riley checked the time: thirty minutes.

Patel had responded. She would meet Riley at the Quirk, and they could give the tech their room cards: But what's his cover story?

Trouble with your software, Rodrigues had written. Sydney system not connecting to Cessnock.

Patel had sent a thumbs-up.

Riley sat in the driver's seat, trying to weigh risk. If Jayson Cassidy had cameras in the rooms, he would see the tech sweep. What would that mean? She sent a message: If he makes us?

Rodrigues came back. If he bolts, we can be ready. One road out of the property. I'll put cars either side of his drive.

Riley sucked her lips. If they flushed Cassidy and he ran, that would be good, an admission of guilt, at least to the fact he was illegally recording his guests. They could then tear his life apart, and if he was responsible for the murders of Penelope Armytage and Jennifer Morrow, Riley believed the evidence would be there and they'd find it.

And if the sweep found hidden cameras and Cassidy didn't respond? Riley had two ways of thinking about that: He didn't know the sweep had occurred, or he knew and laid low. Which would make him a very cool cat. She texted: Unintended consequences?

Patel must have been thinking through the scenarios and messaged back: Benefits outweigh risk.

Riley agreed. They had to do the sweep. Apart from anything else, they couldn't stay in the rooms if Cassidy was watching them. Even if he was just a pervert.

Tech's name is Brian, Rodrigues wrote. But he answers to Projects. He's briefed.

Riley told Rodrigues to send Projects her number, then put the phone down and drove to the Quirk. There was a couple checking out at reception with Karen. With time to kill, she went down the guest corridor through the green door and into the laundry. The dryer she'd used last night was closed, and her clothes were still in there, unmolested. She bundled them under an arm. The door marked HOUSEKEEPING was ajar, and she looked in. All four walls were racked with shelving, stacked with guest supplies: linen, toiletries, bottled water. She did a quick lap of the space, but there was no second exit. The store door was locked.

In her room, she dumped her clothes in her suitcase. She went back out and through the lobby, nodding at Karen at the desk, to the car park. She pulled out her phone and pretended to talk as she ambled down the outside of the motel, parallel to the guest corridor inside. If Jayson Cassidy was in the office, watching on the screens, she would appear to be heading nowhere in particular, strolling to help her think as she spoke on the phone.

The building was rectangular. Toward the end of the long car park–facing frontage, she came to the last room in the row, with its neat timber deck. She stopped, her hand on her brow, the phone at her ear. Behind the deck, the balcony door into the room was closed and the blinds were down. Room 17: the last room on the left of the corridor, before the wall with the green door cut across the width of the building. Room 18 faced Room 17 across the corridor. That was how they were numbered—odd numbers 1 to 17 on the left of the corridor if you walked from reception, evens 2 to 18 on the right. Riley was Room 7, Patel was Room 8.

Riley strolled a tight circle, kicked some gravel, gesticulated with her free hand. She faced the motel again. To the left, after the last deck, there were several meters of Besser-block wall with no windows or doors before it turned in a right angle to the short western side of the rectangle. This end section housed the four rooms with their marked doors: STAFF, HOUSEKEEPING, STORE, LAUNDRY.

Riley went around the corner and down the shorter wall. Halfway, she stopped and walked away from the building and onto the grass. After several meters she turned and scanned the end facade. There were vents but no windows—and no door. She walked to the far corner and started up the other side. It was a mirror image of the frontage facing the car park—a short Besser-block section with no windows or doors, and then the even-numbered guest rooms started, complete with north-facing decks. There was no car park on this side. A gravel path ran parallel to the building, edged by a manicured lawn and then a view over paddocks of lightly wooded grassland. A hundred meters to the northeast, there was a stand of gums which, Riley guessed, hid the Cassidys' house.

She spoke short phrases into her phone as she circumnavigated the building. There was no second exit or fire door, just the entrance foyer and the eighteen balcony doors of the guest rooms. At the reception end, the dirt drive she'd noticed a few days ago ran off the car park to the stand of trees. She was back where she'd started.

Where did the red door Patel had found at the back of the store lead? The red door had no label: It didn't say FIRE, it didn't say EXIT. She stared down the building. There had to be a space behind the locked red door, and Jayson Cassidy had entered it last night. Utilities?

Patel's Camry was parked beside the Calais. Riley went in and saw Patel at a table in the pantry, an apple in front of her, reading on her phone. Riley hadn't had breakfast before the trip to find Bowman's car, and she used her room card in the self-service pantry to get herself a plastic-wrapped muffin and a coffee from a communal Nespresso.

There was a camera high in a corner. Patel had her back to it. Riley sat beside her, took out her phone, and sent a message to the group chat. The red door behind the fridge doesn't lead outside.

Patel bit into her apple.

Rodrigues replied: Where does it lead?

Dunno, Riley typed. He went into the store, left it unlocked, then went through the red door and locked it. Must have a room at the back.

Patel, turned away from Riley, held her apple in her mouth, and used her thumbs on her phone. Is this real, with Jayson? Or are we just casting around?

He's a witness, Rodrigues wrote. Among the last to see the victim alive.

Riley followed: He lives down the road. She stayed at his motel. His female staff feel he watches them. Equals person of interest.

Patel muttered into her apple. "We haven't even clapped eyes on him."

That was interesting, too, Riley thought. Jayson Cassidy had spoken to officers in the canvass on Monday night and to Bowman on Wednesday. But he hadn't shown his face to Riley or Patel. He might have been watching them—and, when they were away, he might have gone through their stuff. But Riley had no evidence for that, and Patel's instinct had been to rationalize the idea a member of the motel staff had been in Riley's room. Riley could follow that logic, and didn't want to overact. Still, she was intrigued that Cassidy had remained hidden.

Patel's apple core was on the table. She slumped in her chair and was typing. If you're serious, we need him on warrant. House, plus motel.

Riley drank coffee. Everyone worth looking at needed to be on the warrant. After the raids, the news would be everywhere that the investigation was targeting shoes. If they got nothing, they still sent a telegram to the killer: *Lose your footwear.*

A man came into the foyer, wheeling a hard-shelled black suitcase. Patel saw him, too, and sat up.

He had cop written all over him. Mid-fifties, beard and hair unkempt, black Hush Puppies, black jeans, and a knitted brown sweater. Riley waved him over and stood. "Projects," she said.

He scratched his scalp. "You're Riley?"

"Have a seat." She gestured. "Coffee, or tea?"

His gaze slid to her crumbling muffin. "Coffee, thanks. Black."

Riley went to the pantry and came back with coffee and a muffin.

Projects had parked his suitcase and was sitting across from Patel. "Nice digs," he said.

Karen wasn't at the desk at reception. Patel propped an elbow on the table and spoke into her hand. "There's a camera behind us."

Projects held his cup near his mouth. "Neat little system. There's more in the car park, a couple concealed."

Riley sipped. "Audio?"

He put his coffee down and rubbed his nose. "Can't say. But crisp vision. Be aware of the lip read."

Riley put her room card on the table and Patel did the same. Projects slipped them into his jeans pocket and drank his coffee.

"We'll stay here," Riley said. "How long?"

"Thirty minutes." Projects took his muffin, still in its packet, and stood. He grabbed his suitcase and wheeled it off across the lobby into the corridor.

Patel went to find a bin for her apple core as Riley's phone hummed. Gatjens.

"Beth," Riley said.

"I'm coming out to you, at the incident room." Gatjens spoke fast. "It's easier if I walk you through it."

There was a pause. She was in a vehicle.

"Walk me through what?" Riley said.

"The shoeprint. We got a match."

◆ ◆ ◆

With Gatjens still on the line, Riley went out of the motel and through the car park into the trees beside the drive, where she could speak without fear of surveillance.

"If this is Jayson Cassidy, tell me now," she said.

"Cassidy? That, I don't know," Gatjens said. "It's not that type of match."

Riley looked over her shoulder. She'd indicated for Patel to stay inside as cover for Projects if Cassidy reacted. There was a pair of Cessnock patrol cars on the road, stationed one hundred meters on either side of the turn into the Quirk. Rodrigues was out there, too, in his Passat.

"Can you brief me here?" Riley said. "We've got a tech guy in the Quirk. I don't want to leave him."

"Right. Well, wait. I need to pull over. I'll send you an image."

Riley started walking to her car. "I'll call you back in one minute." She hung up and sent a message to the group chat: CR come to Priya in reception. I'm in Calais.

Rodrigues confirmed with a thumbs-up, and Riley got into the Holden and grabbed her laptop from the passenger seat. She opened it and called Gatjens.

"Okay," Gatjens said. "So, Shoe and Tire got nowhere matching our sole impression with a brand or type or style of shoe. In the end, that was helpful because it means our pattern, the scalene triangle with the crescent mark at the heel, is distinctive."

Riley saw Rodrigues cruise in and park.

"We treat the markings, because we've not seen them before, as we would a randomly acquired characteristic," Gatjens said. "Something

177

that makes the shoe uniquely identifiable. It's as if he'd trodden on hot coals."

"Mm," Riley said.

"With no national database, all this was interesting but not helpful," Gatjens said. "All we could do was run manual comparisons of our print with shoe impressions from crime scenes, of which there are several hundred thousand."

"You narrowed it down," Riley said. "Unsolved female strangulation."

"Correct. Just as we did with the crepe. Three in the region, twelve in the state, thirty-one across the country."

Rodrigues strolled into reception.

"We started local, with Forster, Dungog, Newcastle," Gatjens said, "and then tried concentric circles pushing out—Sydney, Wollongong, the whole state, the ACT. Nothing."

"National?" Riley said.

"Queensland was a blank, so was Victoria." Gatjens stopped and waited for Riley.

"Not fucking Adelaide," she said. It was a proverb in the squad: If you were on a weird trail and it led interstate, you'd end up in Adelaide.

Gatjens made a clicking noise. "Sent you an email."

Riley opened it on the laptop. A street map appeared, with a house circled in red.

"This is from a case file," Gatjens said. "Fisher Street, Norwood. Adelaide."

"When?" Riley said.

"Seventeen months ago."

Riley stared at the map.

"It's just east of the CBD," Gatjens said. "The house was leased to a young couple, professionals, mid-twenties, no kids."

Another email dropped in from Gatjens, and Riley clicked. It was an image of a small bluestone cottage, set back from the road, with a red gate and a neat front yard.

There was a second file attached, and she opened it. A crime scene picture of a blond woman on her front in a kitchen, partially clad.

"Gina Watson," Gatjens said. "Twenty-five. Found by her husband, strangled at home. No sign of a struggle, no forced entry. Postmortem said no ligature, no bindings, no gag, no defensive wounds." Gatjens was reading. "Petechial hemorrhages."

Riley had gone very still. Seventeen months . . . eight months before Canberra.

"I just sent another image," Gatjens said.

Riley opened it.

"They got this," Gatjens said, "in some soil on the side of the front path in the yard."

It was a shoeprint, better than the partial sole from the Armytage hall. The same triangle at the top right and crescent at the heel.

"There's actually a tiny indent in a ridge midway down the sole," Gatjens said. "You can't see it here. But it's a characteristic shared with our impression. You can bag that and take it to court. Hundred percent. A definite match."

Riley blew air. "What did they do?"

"The investigators?" Gatjens sighed too. "They fucked it right up."

Staring at the image, Riley knew what was coming.

"They ran dead on the shoeprint. Wrote it off as a visitor, deliveryman, neighbor."

"They pinned it on the husband," Riley said.

"I spoke to one of their analysts," Gatjens said. "She sent me the file. It's not pretty."

Riley stared out the windshield as Gatjens went through it. The victim's husband, John Watson, had been an executive in the Coles supermarket group, visiting Melbourne on business before flying home to find his dead wife.

"There was wiggle room in the husband's alibi," Gatjens said, "due to the time-of-death window." Over time, the cops had fixated on John Watson: covert surveillance, showing up at his work unannounced, digging into his past, turning over his life. "They fed stuff from a phone tap to Gina's mother and her brothers—that John had called an old girlfriend, that he was close with a woman in his office." He and Gina had started dating at university. "They broke up for a few months after he made an arse of himself and put the word on another girl at a party. The cops tracked her down. She said John had been *insistent*. Not aggressive, not violent, but annoying and full-on. The cops leaked it all to the media."

Riley put her head back. "Jesus fucking Christ."

"It gets worse," Gatjens said. "They arrested him and charged him with murder. They had nothing, but they used it for pressure—he was inside for three months before the magistrate threw it all out at committal."

"Where is he now?" Patel said.

"Sydney. Gina's family still believe he killed her. His own mother died while he was on remand, his sister won't speak to him. He lost his job with the arrest. His friends dried up on him . . ."

Run out of town. "This Adelaide analyst," Riley said. "You like her?"

"She's smart," Gatjens said, "and still fuming—with the way it went south."

"All right, ask her for the uncensored version on the detectives who ran it," Riley said. "We'll keep it confidential. We need to know who's best to talk to when we fly down."

Gatjens hung up. Riley sat stunned. She opened her notebook and tried to start making notes. They would have to eliminate the Canberra husband Andrew Morrow and Nigel Armytage for the Adelaide date.

Her phone buzzed, an unknown number. "Rose speaking."

"Projects. You're all clear."

She blinked and peered out at the motel. "Nothing?"

"Clean as a whistle. Bathrooms, lights, pot plants, TVs, phones, minibar bottles, mirrors, upholstery, curtain rails, bedhead. Unless they're NSA, there's nothing."

"Both rooms?"

"Both rooms," Projects said. "No one's watching you, Detective."

22

Riding shotgun in his Audi, Bowman watched the fenced valley go past. Heavy grassland, shades of olive, was giving way to ordered rows of vines.

Behind the wheel, Rachel glanced down at the route he'd plugged into the GPS. "What's in Cessnock?" she said.

"A local councillor. Well, a former local councillor. Name of Matthew Drummond?"

Away from Sandra and the Packhorse saloon, Rachel had her hair out, and she shook her curly mane. "Dunno. What's he want?"

"He ran into strife on the council. Now he's off the council, and he might want to talk." Bowman had emailed Drummond asking for a chat, and last night he had emailed back with an address, saying 1:00 p.m. today.

Rachel was on a split shift, breakfast and then back for the evening until last drinks. It was Monday, her night to close the pub—as she'd done last week, when, out of nowhere, the police had turned up at the door. Bowman, when he talked to Rachel in the dining area or the bar, kept coming back to that Monday, trying to get the rhythm of the night. Sandra had worked, too, in the bar until Rachel finished serving meals, then she'd taken advantage of the quiet evening and gone to bed. For Sandra, it had been a normal Monday night.

Last week, between breakfast and her later shift, Rachel had driven home to Branxton, as she had done every Monday while working at the pub. Today, instead, she had agreed to act as Bowman's chauffeur—for fifty bucks an hour. Sandra didn't know that he was subcontracting her staff.

Spring had come. Rachel had grown up in the valley and was pointing out native plants as they passed: paper daisies, waratah, bottlebrush, grevilleas—"Flowering gums putting on a show."

"Did your dad teach you this?" Bowman said.

"My mum, actually. She's a botanist."

"But you want to be a winemaker, like your father?"

"That's the plan."

"So for a grape grower like Red, say, what's the go? He sells to someone like your dad?"

"Yeah. Red's got plots and blocks round Rothbury. He'll grow, harvest, sell by the ton."

"Does your dad buy from Red?"

"Nah. Don't think so. Red's a Lucas. With those blokes, it's old family ties. The Lucases have always sold to the Bruces. Like, you know, we're going back a hundred and forty years. The Bruces stand by their growers, through all types of strife. I mean frost, hail, drought. Twenty years ago, Red was getting ravaged by mildew, lost whole crops."

"Mildew?"

"Downey mildew. Nearly wiped Red out. He blamed his son, for not spraying. Hence Dew."

"So, Red's son—"

"Is called Dew. That's a nickname." She spelled it out. "For *mil*dew. Thanks, Dad."

"What's Dew's story?"

"Mm. Drugs. Red's a prick. Dew would take off as a kid, I think. I mean, that was thirty years ago. Then he'd come back, fuck up with the old man by like, not spraying. Take off again. Trouble in Gosford, washed up back in Cessnock. Now he's on the straight and narrow. Sort of. Like, Sandra's still got him banned."

"Banned?"

"From the Packhorse. He came in and tore the place up a while back, looking for his dad. On meth. It was bad."

"Were you there?"

"God no, I was at school. Michael was there, so Sandra was lucky, because Mikey put Dew down—with a baseball bat they keep behind the bar. It's folklore in the district."

They were coming into town.

"This councillor, Drummond," Rachel said. "What'd he do?"

"Not sure. The euphemism in the press was, he left to *spend more time with his family*. There were no charges. So I'm guessing drunken lechery rather than, say, taking bribes."

Rachel scoffed. "Drunken lechery—you'd get promoted round here. Bloody legend."

On the left, a line of vehicles was snarled at the McDonald's drive-through.

Rachel pointed. "Couple of kids burnt down the Macca's playground last year. Oh boy. That was bad."

"Sacred ground."

"Too right. You'll get away with a lot in Cessnock, but not that. They were nearly stoned to death."

"More folklore."

"That's it. You're getting all the hits."

She ignored the map and took a back route to a grid of suburban streets on the southern edge of town. The houses were all weatherboards, painted and maintained, on roomy blocks. Rachel pulled up. Drummond's lawn needed a mow. A driveway led to a garage at the back of the property.

"He's only expecting me," Bowman said. "You right to wait?"

Examining the house, she nodded.

The cottage was set back about fifteen meters from the street, with no front fence and no path. Bowman crossed the grass and went up one step to a timber porch. There was a window on either side of the door. He knocked.

After half a minute the door opened to a man, early forties, pudgy, pale gray, unshaven. He looked past Bowman. "Who's in the car?" he said.

"Pokolbin girl. My driver."

Drummond looked left and right down the street, and moved aside to wave Bowman in.

The hall was polished floorboards. They went down to a living room at the back, with a kitchen to the left. Drummond gestured at a chunky wooden dining table, and Bowman took a seat. It was a family home. He guessed Drummond had spent a moment tidying before his arrival, but there were still things lying around: a skateboard in a corner, a tennis ball on the floor, a school textbook on a couch, a guitar plugged into an amp.

Drummond stood behind the kitchen counter, rotund under a blue T-shirt. "I searched you up," he said.

Bowman nodded.

"You're here for the murder," Drummond said. "Why did you email me?"

"I was looking into Oakeshott, regarding the town house where the woman was killed. And the journalist Laura Nolan had caught my attention."

Drummond sniffed.

"You put those names together," Bowman said, "you get to Matthew Drummond."

He winced, red eyed, and scratched his jaw.

Bowman bent to pull his notepad from his bag. "Want to tell me what happened?"

"I fucked up royal, no doubt. But it was a setup, they lured me in."

"Who?"

"Neville Oakeshott. With drinks, a girl."

"Kompromat," Bowman said.

"Exactly. I was at a party—at a pub in Newcastle. It was seamless, they knew I was going to be there. My wife was away for the weekend—they knew that, too, I reckon. I got talking to a woman, you know, bit seedy but a glamour, late twenties. Went on for quite a while. I couldn't believe it—you know, her interest. We were having fun, or I was—pretty pissed. She said she had a room at the Novotel. I went back with her. Sex. We were doing coke. That was that. They had it all on film."

"Oakeshott approached you?"

"No. No one owned it, but it had to be Oakeshott. I was getting in my car at council one day, and a man came up—big bloke dressed in black, in a balaclava. He held a photo to the windscreen in front of my face. Me in the room at the Novotel with the girl. I went to get out, to confront him, but he raised his other hand and pointed a gun. He held the photo there for a long time, like twenty seconds, didn't say a word. Then he was gone. The next day, they came at me through the journo, Nolan. She wrote a bit of innuendo, then a little more. Then she paid a visit, here"—he gestured—"to my house. She made it clear that if I didn't get off council, they'd be publishing photos."

"That's blackmail," Bowman said. "You didn't think to report it?"

Drummond looked at Bowman's notepad. "Maybe that's what I'm doing now."

Bowman paused. It was grubby stuff, falling in his lap. Grubby people, everywhere. Including Drummond, who seemed a bit too keen to spill his failings.

He read Bowman's hesitation. "They're blackmailing me," he said, "but I still did what I did. I snorted coke and cheated on my wife with a hooker—they didn't make me do that. They facilitated, there was no coercion. I've got a wife—just barely—and two kids. That's why I rolled. I didn't want to expose my family to what I did."

"What changed?" Bowman said.

"You said it yourself. It's why you're here. The town house, Oakeshott, Nolan." He counted on his fingers. "You put it together, it spells 'dead girl.'"

"Can you prove it?" Bowman said.

Drummond studied Bowman's pen and paper. "I can get the ball rolling," he said.

23

Riley sat beside Patel in the parked Calais on Flood Street, Leichhardt, and stared at the tired block of brown flats. It was 160 kilometers from Red Creek into Sydney's inner-west, a ninety-minute trip. Riley had read the Adelaide file on Gina Watson while Patel drove.

Now Riley looked in her lap at the mug shot of John Watson, sallow and haunted.

Patel sipped from a bottle of water. Riley closed the laptop and scanned the flats, counting the balconies on the northeast wall. Three on each floor, fifteen all up. There were bits of junk on some, but no signs of life. It wasn't the sort of place where people sat out in the sun with a pot of Earl Grey. John Watson was Adelaide establishment, descended from a line of surgeons—he would never have seen himself ending up here.

Watson pulled beers in a live-sport and gaming pub, three hundred meters down the road. Uniforms from Glebe had walked through an hour ago and stopped for a casual chat. Watson was knocking off at four. Riley looked at her phone: 4:07.

"Anything I should know?" Patel said.

"Standard total fuckup. Both families are upper crust. Gina's uncle has political connections. The pressure was on, cops were in a hole—and kept digging."

"He's not going to like us," Patel said. "That's for sure."

"True. But let's see what shape he's in."

Patel exhaled and rubbed her forehead. Watson had had holes punched through him and taken heavy water. They'd need to refloat him. Riley thought Patel might manage it—if he wasn't drug fucked.

"If you get him talking," Riley said, "focus on their life in the year before she was killed. Where they went, where they stayed. Business or pleasure. The Hunter and Canberra. But anywhere—Queensland, Uluru."

Patel nodded at the windshield. "Here we go."

He came down the street, head bowed in a cap, moving slowly, a plastic bag in one hand. Riley got out and walked around the front of the car and crossed the road with Patel.

John Watson didn't look up. He reached for the gate to the flats.

They were beside him on the footpath. "Mr. Watson?" Riley said quietly.

His hand stopped on the latch. There was a takeaway container in his bag.

"We know you didn't kill Gina," Riley said. "We know you'd never hurt your wife."

Watson didn't move, his arm outstretched to the gate.

Riley kept her voice soft. "We're here to help you."

The cap peeked up, a hollow face. He opened the gate and went through.

Patel followed. "Mr. Watson—"

He spoke over his shoulder. "No cops."

Patel got a foot in the lobby door as he entered. "We just want to talk with you. About Gina. Can we come in?"

Riley came down the path and watched as he took the stairs. Patel stayed with him, and Riley followed. On the third floor his hand shook as he unlocked his flat and shuffled in, leaving the door open. Riley went first, down a grim hall. Not fetid, but stale and greasy. You learned a lot from the smell of a dwelling. She entered a room with a skew-whiff pine table and two chairs, a galley kitchen, a hairy couch that looked like it had been hauled up from the street.

Watson put his plastic bag on the sink and stood with his back to them. There was a door open to a second room with a bare mattress and a vinyl sleeping bag on the floor. Patel was beside Riley as he turned to them, eyes down. A black fleece with a pub logo on the breast, black jeans, Blundstones.

"No cops," he said.

Patel crossed to him and touched his upper arm, and he shied. She led him to a chair at the crooked table and took the other seat, adjacent. There was a milk crate in a corner, and Riley fetched it and sat on it in front of him, a meter from his knees.

"We're investigating two murders," Patel said. "Near Cessnock and in Canberra."

Riley watched his throat as he swallowed under a three-day growth. He was shaving sporadically, he didn't reek, his fingernails were bitten but clean.

"The murders, we think it's the same person," Patel said. "And we think he killed Gina."

Watson was following. "Who?"

"We don't know yet. We need to find him." Patel nodded at Watson. "That's why we're here. We know you're innocent. We need your help."

His eyes slunk to Riley. "Are you from Adelaide?"

"No," she said. "We don't know those officers. But we know what they did. And we know it was wrong."

He was steady, no jitters or tics. "How did you find me?"

"There was a shoe impression, at your house," Riley said. "Did they talk to you about that?"

He looked at his boots.

"We found a shoe impression too," Patel said. "At a scene in the Hunter Valley."

His lips tugged down.

Patel smiled. "You know the Hunter?"

His head wobbled: Yes.

"What about Canberra?" Patel said. "Have you been to Canberra?"

He dug at a palm. "Once or twice."

"Did Gina go with you?" Patel said.

Under the brim of his cap, he inclined his head: Yes.

"To Canberra—and the Hunter?" Patel said.

He thought for a moment and nodded.

The file said he had been an executive in the Coles supermarket group. "Your work at the time of those trips," Riley said. "What was it?"

"Wine," he said. "I worked in wine."

Bowman sat at Matthew Drummond's table, taking notes as the man talked.

"I stymied Oakeshott's plans in council for four years," Drummond was saying. "At first, he tried to glad-hand me with offers of lunch. I always said no. You can't accept that stuff, not as a councillor."

Bowman pinched an earlobe. The Oakeshott lunch scenario rang true.

"He'd set up meetings," Drummond said. "I'd hear him out, but I never budged. He was good with dropping hints—you know, if I needed anything, if I wanted something, it was clear he'd buy me off."

"What did he want?"

"Height, mainly, for the Pokolbin developments. More density. I was the vanguard, leading the fight to keep him low-rise. If he can't build a certain number of dwellings, he takes a bath. And he's committed, he's already started. So he's got his arse hanging out." In tracksuit pants and socks, Drummond came around the kitchen counter and sat across from Bowman at the chunky table. "That

Armytage town house is part of a parcel that runs down to the motel, the Quirk. But he couldn't get the Quirk people to sell. So he did a deal. He built the motel for them knowing he'd get the surrounding land rezoned. When they wouldn't budge, he brought them in on it. He'd make a killing with the rezoning, and so he'd give them a cut. The rezoning would boost the value of their property, and he agreed to buy them out at that. Classic Oakeshott play, to grease the wheels. But they still wouldn't sell. He doesn't like that."

"Why?"

"Because the motel's on a big block, stretching east. It eats into his development, crimps what he can do. And the Quirk people, the Cassidys, are landowners, neighbors, so if they raise an objection, it carries weight. It's a tough shot on the rezoning application."

"The Cassidys objected?" Bowman said.

"Not at first, but I talked them around."

There was a small pile of paperwork at Drummond's elbow, and he passed Bowman a couple of stapled A4 pages. Bowman scanned them: a letter from the Cassidys to the council, listing a series of issues with the proposal to develop a residential precinct of 333 dwellings on the site.

"That was a poke in the eye to Oakeshott," Drummond said. "Really got him riled."

Bowman turned the page on the letter. "He's a developer. Surely he gets this all the time?"

"No, see, this was personal. He built the Quirk for the Cassidys, and they backed him in. They'd bought the land for the motel, knowing Oakeshott's plan. They thought, *Great—he can build it and then we'll flog it to him*. But then they turned on him. All he had was a handshake, but they dishonored the deal."

"You dealt with Cassidy. What's he like?"

Drummond blew air. "Yeah, well, I mean *different*. But in the end, that was good, in that it worked in our favor."

"Different?"

"Hard to pin down. He'd just turn on a dime. And I mean, he'd lie—like, to your face, brazen. And then it was all smiles."

"If you can't trust him, how does it work in your favor?"

"I didn't need to trust him. I just needed him to stand up to Oakeshott. Cassidy knew what he was dealing with, so it's a big ask."

"Why?"

"Oakeshott's a pig—ruthless, dangerous, completely corrupt. Look at how he came at me."

"He came at you afterwards. Cassidy stood up before that."

"Of course. But I wasn't the first. Oakeshott buys people off everywhere. Unions, state politicians, journos, cops. Cassidy knows that."

"Maybe Cassidy objects on business grounds," Bowman said. "He gets the motel built and decides to keep it. His wife wants to run it. But now there's the threat of hundreds of apartments, Airbnbs at his front door."

"Yeah, but even in that scenario, he wanted that. It's why he bought the land, because it was on the edge of this mooted major development. He sees it as an opportunity. Lots of people coming into the region equals more visitors—more guests. And he's in on the ground floor."

"So why is he objecting?"

"I don't know. Like I said, he just turned. He never explained his thinking to me. He just said, *Let's go, let's make it hard for this bloke.* I think it's sport to him, giving Oakeshott a black eye. That's brave— or crazy. And I don't think it's bravery in that he's not upholding a principle. He doesn't object to the development on ecological or aesthetic grounds."

"Has Oakeshott threatened him?"

"I don't know. I hear whispers."

"Saying?"

"Cassidy's dodgy, he's got debts, he's got charges."

"Tax stuff?"

Drummond shrugged. "Word is, the motel's a front. That's why he doesn't care if it sits out there on its own. He just uses it to launder."

"Drugs?"

"Dunno. It's just rumor. But it makes sense in one way."

Bowman looked up. "He's a crim, so he's not fazed by Oakeshott?"

"Exactly. Look at how Oakeshott operates. He pays a sex worker to set me up, he pays stand-over muscle to deliver the message, he pays a journo to work me over in the press. And now you've got a young woman dead in the first row of his new development. Whichever way you slice it, it's dirty. And Cassidy crosses a man like this, why? For a laugh?"

"Cassidy's saying he saw the victim out jogging, just before she died."

Drummond threw his hands up. "I mean, who knows? Maybe he did. You'd have to say he did, because what's the alternative, he just says this shit for fun?"

"The talk you're picking up, on Cassidy," Bowman said. "Do you think that's Oakeshott? He's smearing Cassidy?"

"I don't know. But a whispering campaign is classic Oakeshott. That's how it starts. Watch for what Laura Nolan writes. If she zeroes in on Cassidy—that's Oakeshott."

"Oakeshott built the town houses to sell, right?" Bowman said. "That's the model. They weren't to lease or for him to hold on to and offload as a complete development . . . ?"

Drummond nodded. "Build and sell as he goes. To fund more building."

"Then why kill her? She's done what he wanted, bought a house. She's not in the way."

"I don't know that either. That's where you come in. I didn't call you—you called me. Why?"

Bowman waited.

"Because you joined the dots . . . Laura Nolan, Oakeshott, Penelope Armytage. There's a connection—you know it, because you made it."

"The connection leads to you."

"All right. Okay. I killed her? Is that what you want me to say?"

"No." Bowman shrugged. "Unless."

"Look, you're here through your research," Drummond said. "I mean, I haven't even heard from the cops. I've told you what happened to me and that you can write it."

"And why is that?"

Drummond angled his head. "Why?"

Bowman shrugged again. "What's in it for you?"

His face curdled, a look of sour disgust. "Jesus. You people. I thought, you know, you liked to expose this type of crap."

"Yeah. But he blackmails you, and you resign and stay quiet. Now I turn up, and you're talking. I'd like to know why."

"My motivation?" Drummond's eyes were wide. "Christ, he kills a woman and that isn't enough? I've been weak, sure. But fuck that. It's got to stop."

Bowman stared at his notebook. He was going to need more than he had.

"You're not from here," Drummond said, "so you're clean."

"I'll need evidence to prove the blackmail," Bowman said. "You could go to the cops?"

"Not likely. You're not listening."

Bowman caught on. Drummond was telling him what he'd already told Riley: Oakeshott had a cop in his pocket.

"When the journo, Nolan, came and knocked on my door," Drummond said, "there was a cop in a police car, parked where your driver pulled up just now. When Nolan left, she acknowledged him, and he drove away too."

"Highway Patrol?"

"No. But marked. Brazen. It was there to send a message."

"Did you get a look at him?"

"No. He sat in the car with the sun visor down, so I didn't see his face. But he was a big bloke, in uniform." Drummond patted his ribs. "All I saw was his chest."

24

There were a lot of complete deadshit detectives, and Paul Todd was one of them. Riley picked it before he opened his mouth, from the way he was slow to get up from his desk and then the slow strut across the room.

She'd known it before she'd even got to Adelaide, before she'd laid eyes on him. The Gina Watson file was like a biography: not of Gina or her husband, John, or their lives together, or even of Gina's murder in her own home at the age of twenty-six, but of Detective Sergeant Paul Todd. You didn't have to read between the lines of the briefing notes to see the mongrel fucker in all his glory. Criminally incompetent, nasty and lazy, a consummate office politician, he sucked up and punched down.

In the Homicide squad at Adelaide HQ, with Patel beside her, Riley held her nose and her tongue and got what she needed out of Todd: cooperation. She'd had her Super, Trevor Toohey, email the request to Todd's boss: a review of the physical evidence from the Watson case and a swing past the house. The email said, the Sydney detectives hope the strategies used in Adelaide might help them in a case they are running in regional NSW. It was ongoing training via routine overview, Toohey wrote, and my officers won't need to trouble Detective Sergeant Todd if Detective Constable Gordon Ross is available.

Beth Gatjens had spoken to the Adelaide analyst and come back with the name Gordon Ross. Riley had read Ross's reports in the file and agreed he was the sweet spot. They were right—even as Todd made the introductions, Ross greeted her with a look that said, *Welcome to Shitsville.*

Todd left them to it. Ross was mid-thirties, neat, and serious. He led them to a meeting room with eight cardboard boxes on a table and closed the door. "You matched the shoe impression," he said.

"How do you know that?" Riley said.

"Angela told me."

"The analyst?"

"Yeah." Ross looked at the door. "I know you told her to keep it quiet. She just told me. She's under duress."

"From Todd?"

"From the case. Todd doesn't give a shit." Ross looked like he'd trodden in something. "But we know we fucked it. For Todd, it's simple—Watson killed his wife and the court let him get away with it. Case closed."

"And for you?" Riley said.

"John Watson's innocent. The killer's at large. We carry that around."

Patel put her bag on a chair. "You and Angela?" she said.

He nodded. "Couple of others."

Riley pointed at the eight boxes. "Let's have a look."

Ross laid out pictures of the crime scene and exhibits. There were photos of nine pairs of men's shoes. "John Watson's," he said. "We never got a match."

"The shirt Gina was wearing?" Riley said.

Ross reached across the table for a folder of photographs and passed it to Riley.

She looked at the yellow T-shirt in the images. She had seen Gina lying in it in the crime scene photos. "Cut up the front?"

"Sheared," Ross said. "With scissors."

"You found scissors," Riley said. "Can I see them?"

He dug in a box and passed another folder of photos. "Two pairs. One in the study on a desk. One in a kitchen drawer. The lab said no to the pair in the study, but with the kitchen, it didn't rule them out—but it was nowhere near a definitive match."

Riley had read the report. The lab had said it was *possible* the scissors in the kitchen had been used to cut the yellow T-shirt. Todd had leveraged the finding to make the arrest. The magistrate had speared him with it at the committal.

Ross and Patel picked through the images, with Riley taking photos and notes. Then they went down to the car park and Ross's Mitsubishi. The police center was in the middle of town, and they headed south. Ross took a left, and the road ran straight for a while before turning. A bush city, wide streets on a grid. There were hills in the distance.

The Watson place was on a suburban road of gentrified cottages, a couple of streets parallel to Norwood Parade, just across parkland that bound the town center. The house had been leased to another young couple, both out at work, and Ross had arranged for the real estate agent to come and open it up. Ross went in with Patel, and Riley walked down a side path to a turfed backyard with a clothesline and a lemon tree. There was a shed in a corner and a tall back fence with a gate. It was unlocked, and she went through to a dunny lane—secluded, narrow, just access gates and the occasional garage door.

Back in the yard, she looked at the house. A modest bluestone with a tin roof. Through the rear glass doors, she could see Patel and Ross in the open-plan main room—a kitchen to one side and lounges around a TV on the other. Ross reached up to unbolt the glass doors, and Riley went in. It was clean and light, with pale-wood floors and white cabinetry. She followed Ross down terra-cotta tiles in the hall. Three bedrooms, one bathroom.

Ross stood on the front porch. "The impression was there." He pointed to the paved path. "We got lucky. Gina had a green thumb. She'd been feeding the lawn, repatching. There was some soil on the edge of the slate."

Riley went down the step and turned on the spot. "The techs think he was stationary, that he stopped here?" She'd read it in the file but looked at Ross for confirmation.

"He paused, at least," Ross said. "We don't know for how long."

Riley looked left and right and behind her. "Why? He's fully exposed."

Ross didn't answer. He must have sensed it was rhetorical—she was running through the file in her head. Her eyes roamed the streetscape, the yard, the house. John Watson had come home just after 8:00 p.m. The pathologist put time of death as early evening, between five and eight. In September, but it had been a warm day.

There was a screen door that didn't lock. "Front door was open," she said, "and Gina had the screen closed?"

Ross shook his head. "All we know is, John says the screen was closed and the front door was locked when he got home."

Patel had come out and was listening. "It's the same with our scene, and Canberra," she said to Ross. "How's he getting in?"

"We thought he might be impersonating someone—a deliveryman, meter reader, a God botherer." Ross nodded at the path. "He stops there for a moment, to compose himself. Then he knocks on the door."

"She invites him in?" Patel said. "And he attacks her?"

Ross frowned—he wasn't sure.

"It's stealthier than that," Patel said. "Our shoe impression in Red Creek—it's inside. In the hall."

"He's already in the house when she gets home?" Ross said.

"Correct," Patel said. "He's waiting inside. If she was inviting someone she didn't know in, that's when you'd see a struggle. A broken light, a chair knocked over. Three women killed—and none of them fight?"

Riley looked up at the house. "You check the roof?"

Ross followed her gaze. "There's no access. And he didn't cut in."

She had asked Dick Laver the same question at the Morrow house in Canberra and received the same reply.

Her eyes came down from the Colorbond roof, and she turned down the path to the red front gate. Something chimed. *Access. No access.*

Standing at the red gate, she had a flash of the Quirk—she saw Jayson Cassidy on the CCTV in the guest corridor of the motel. They had followed him. Patel in the storeroom. Behind the commercial fridge, the red door.

Riley reached out . . . Her hand rested on the red gate. The red door in the storeroom, it didn't lead outside. There were no windows in the end wall of the motel, and no doors.

No access.

Patel was watching her.

"Roof access," Riley said. "Jayson Cassidy was going into the roof."

25

Riley and Patel landed at Mascot from Adelaide in the late afternoon and headed north. Night fell, and with it came rain. After her visit to the farm with Bowman yesterday, Riley had asked Rodrigues to brief her on Dew. She'd just turned off the M1 for Cessnock when Rodrigues called.

"Okay, so Dewie boy," he said. "He's under supervision orders and got a job through the old man. He was shacked up in Sin City. No longer."

"Sin City?" Riley said.

"Housing commission—Cessnock."

"Lives in Broke," Riley said.

"That's it. Dew is Bradley John Lucas, thirty-eight. Raised on the family block, out at Rothbury. Went off the rails early, and we got a long list of priors—shoplifting, break and enter, vehicle theft, willful property damage, possession. You still listening?"

"Yep."

"Sheet stretches back to when he's thirteen. Arson, theft, truancy, possessing a drug of dependence. Time in juvie and then two stints in adult jail. Both for dealing. So you got form. But it's drugs," Rodrigues said. "It's all drugs with Dew."

Patel cleared her throat. "Don't s'pose he was locked up for either our Canberra or Adelaide date?"

"No, I checked that. Both times he's at large. You want him on the warrant?"

"Yeah," Riley said. "Bank records, plus phone."

"And I'll go see him," Rodrigues said, "get his movements for Monday."

"Good. Thanks. Bear in mind, the father says Dew was with him and the mother on Monday."

"Parent alibi," Rodrigues said. "Fits our theme. Everyone's weak."

Riley nodded at the Bluetooth. Karen and Jayson had a spouse alibi, so did Bob Bruce. It was the same with the retired neighbors in the town house at the end of the Armytage row, even the two couples running the café and the takeaway on the intersection. The dirty weekenders with the Volvo, who had been staying at the Quirk, were even less reliable—a cheating-lover alibi—but their movements around the vineyards on the Monday had been corroborated by third parties.

"Bob Bruce is a spouse alibi," Patel said. "I'll go see the wife."

"She works in ceramics," Rodrigues said. "You should take your author Bowman. They can talk arts and craft."

Riley guessed he was joking. His cynicism popped out when he got tired. But the idea of sending Bowman to Bruce's potter wife had merit. He might disarm her and get something real.

Patel was thinking the same way. "That's clever. Fresh perspective."

"Wait." Rodrigues had been joking. "Really?"

"Bowman's here with us," Patel said. "We've used him before. He's an asset, and should be deployed."

"What've you got on Jayson Cassidy?" Riley asked.

"Clean," Rodrigues said. "And there's nothing from the station. A patrol's never been called to the motel."

Riley went left on Broke Road.

"Jayson grew up in Singleton, went to school there," Rodrigues said. "Then TAFE in Newcastle."

"Is that where he met Karen?" Patel said.

"Yeah—or maybe even before. But that's where they set up. Married young, no kids. Twenty years in Newcastle, running a hotel. Then they bought the land in Red Creek, had the motel built, and moved out there . . ."

In the night rain, Riley drove through Pokolbin, the wipers squeaking a beat. Patel thanked Rodrigues and ended the call.

At the Quirk, reception was closed and there was no sign of life in the office. It was Tuesday, and the motel was nearly empty. Riley was beginning to get the rhythm of the place. Thursday through Sunday was busy, and Monday was turnover day, when the housekeeping women started on their rounds, working through Tuesday and then coming in for a day later in the week, depending on the load.

Riley's room had been straightened—clean sheets and fresh towels—and Patel's was the same. They dumped their bags, showered, went to the pantry, and warmed frozen pizzas in a communal oven. They'd slept in Sydney last night, after seeing John Watson in Leichhardt, and been down to Adelaide and back in a day. They sat at a table with a bottle of red and their backs to the CCTV. Patel ate a piece of pizza with a knife and fork.

Riley took a slice and studied it. "What actually is this?"

"Acciughe."

"What's that?"

"I think it means 'nice.'"

Riley took a bite. Patel was fucking with her, it was definitely anchovy.

In the pantry, the oven pinged, and Riley went over and extracted her pizza with a tea towel and dumped it on the table.

"What?" Patel's mouth fell open. "Ham and *pineapple*?"

Riley tore a slice and slid it onto her plate. "You eat rice with your hands and pizza with a knife and fork. Surely you can spoon in a bit of pineapple."

Patel held her piece aloft. "We balance the five elements, with the four fingers and the thumb. Nehru said eating biryani with fork and knife is like making love through an interpreter."

"Sweet." Riley's slice drooped. "What's next?"

Patel ate and typed on her phone. Riley's screen lit with the message and she read it. At the house, in Adelaide, your instinct said Cassidy.

Riley poured more wine and drank. She texted: And yours?

Patel's head was down, and she murmured, "We drove, Sydney and back, in your car."

Riley took a bite, molten cheese burning the top of her mouth.

Patel went back to her phone. The thing is, she texted, I left my keys—here, in the room.

Riley looked over her slice. They'd stayed in their own homes in Sydney last night. She spoke out the corner of her mouth. "What about the key to your flat?"

Patel typed. I hide a key with my brother, in his yard.

Riley read and took a bite. Patel lived around the corner from her brother.

Patel texted. My keys were here. I keep them in a particular pocket in my bag.

Riley had stopped chewing.

The bag had been moved, when they cleaned. They'd put it on a chair.

"And?" Riley said into her glass.

The keys are in a different pocket.

Riley turned away with her phone. They fell out when the cleaner moved the bag, she wrote. She put them back.

The pockets are zipped.

Riley swallowed.

Patel pushed away her phone, and they ate in silence. They finished the wine, put the rubbish in a bin, and walked down the corridor. Patel keyed into her room, and Riley followed and closed the door and they stood close.

Patel nudged her chin at her bag on a chair. "Someone went through it, emptied stuff, put it back wrong."

Riley folded her arms. She'd been wrong about hidden cameras— jumping at shadows. Projects had given the all clear.

"Your room, my room," Patel said. "Someone's snooping. Maybe that's all it is."

"But?"

"Access. Opportunity. Kind of narrows it down. Then, in Adelaide, your gut said Jayson."

"What do you want to do?"

"Get Cassidy on the warrant," Patel said. "Have a look behind his red door."

26

In the morning, the young woman from Broke, Belinda, was on the desk at reception. Riley, leaving for the incident room with Patel, changed course across the lobby and went to say hello.

Karen wasn't around. Belinda's smile was shy but her eyes were warm.

Riley smiled too. "Busy day?"

"Pretty quiet," Belinda said. "Check-in's not till two."

"How many rooms you got booked, aside from us?"

"Two tonight." She looked at her screen. "Along with you. Then it builds up Thursday, Friday . . . and on Saturday we're full."

Riley had her forearms on the raised desk and kept her head down. "You always work Wednesday?"

"Yeah." Belinda skittered a glance toward the office. "Lets them go out."

Riley talked into her arms. "They in there now?"

"No. At their house."

"But they're going out?"

"Yeah. Well, usually. About eleven."

"Usually, or always?"

"Always."

Riley straightened, tapped the desk in casual thanks, met Belinda's eye. "See you soon."

In the car park, Patel had the Camry running. The rain had stopped, the air was rinsed. Bowman was right: Spring had sprung. It was September 3.

Riley checked the time on the dash: 9:13 a.m. Rodrigues had fronted the magistrate first thing to request the warrant be expanded to include electronic surveillance and search powers on Jayson Cassidy's motel and home. The magistrate had signed.

Patel reversed. Riley called Rodrigues. "I think the Cassidys will leave the Quirk in about ninety minutes. For how long, I don't know. We need eyes on them—from when they leave, the whole time they're gone."

"I'll do it myself," Rodrigues said.

Patel went left toward Red Creek. The road sloped up, and at the top of the rise there was a turn onto a fire-access trail into grassy scrub. Rodrigues was still on the Bluetooth.

"There's a dirt road, along a fence, on the ridge before the Quirk," Riley said. "There's tree cover. If you sit in there, you'll see the house, the motel, their vehicle on the move."

"I know it," Rodrigues said.

Riley hung up and called Projects. "You any good with locks?"

"Yeah," the tech said. "Depends."

"We need to get through a door in the storeroom at the motel. Can you meet us at the room in Red Creek, pronto?"

Projects grunted assent. Patel went right at the crossroad. Riley hung up.

"Techs can pick locks?" Patel said.

"Old-school techs can," Riley said. "They're like Depression-era housewives."

◆　◆　◆

Projects arrived at the incident room a few minutes after 10:00 a.m. By 10:15, Rodrigues was tucked in on the dirt road above the Quirk in his

Passat. At 10:58 a.m., he called Riley. "Okay, they're on the move. Both of them. White Kia. Heading east."

Riley had her feet on her desk. "They at the crossroad?"

"One minute."

She stood and motioned at Patel and Projects.

"Coming up now," Rodrigues said. "Indicating left . . . and you're clear."

"Ta," Riley said, and Patel and Projects followed her out. Projects climbed into his gray iLoad, Riley rode with Patel in the Camry.

They pulled up in the car park at the Quirk, and Projects slid open his side door and slipped on a backpack. Belinda was at reception. Projects and Patel walked past, but Riley went over to the girl again and looked around the empty foyer and the pantry. "I might use the laundry," Riley said. "Is housekeeping around?"

Belinda looked apologetic. "Not today. Bec's in tomorrow. She could make up your rooms."

"No trouble. I just didn't want to be in their way." Riley lowered her voice. "Although I might grab a fresh towel. Are they in the room out back?"

Belinda opened a drawer and picked out a white card. She passed it to Riley. "Access all areas." She put a finger to her lips. "Grab what you need."

Riley took the card and pushed off the desk with a wink. Down the corridor, Patel's door was ajar. Projects was inside, perched on a chair, and Patel was standing with a plastic bag.

"Coast is clear," Riley said.

The reception desk was offset from the center of the foyer, so Belinda had no line of sight along the guest corridor. They walked down to the green door and into the Besser-block antechamber, and a light came on. Patel pulled booties and gloves from the plastic bag and handed them around. The room marked STORE was locked, and Riley keyed through with the card and clicked on the light. Projects followed, and she led him to the red door in the rear wall behind the fridge. It was shut tight, no give. It wasn't keyless entry, she could see the lock cylinder, but she tried the card anyway. Nothing.

"All yours," she said.

Projects tried the handle and then went down on one knee and shrugged off his backpack. He unzipped his bag all the way around and laid it out beside him on the floor. Riley looked at the rows of tools strapped in place. He picked out a wire and some dental tweezers and started in on the lock.

Riley backed off. Patel was standing in the room with the door shut. In the hum of the fridge, Projects worked silently—no cursing or muttering or the clanging of tools.

They stood looking at the dry goods on the shelves . . .

"Got it," Projects called. He was on a knee, zipping his bag, the door open. There was a broom in a corner, and he grasped it to prop the door ajar.

Riley went first. It was dark, but in the glow from the store, she found a light switch. The room was another rectangular Besser-block space—cool, dry, windowless. There was nothing, except a set of open steel stairs leading up to another red door.

Riley went up the flight to a small landing. There was no lock visible. She tried the handle. Open.

She peered into darkness. Projects was at her shoulder. "One sec," he said. She heard the zip of his bag, and then he was shining a flashlight. He stepped through and played the light around and reached for a switch by the door.

Muted wall lights lit a long void. Riley went in and stood with Patel beside her. It was a triangular roof space, four meters high in the center, at least forty meters long and fifteen meters wide. There was a walkway down the middle, battened over exposed beams and joists. In a corner, close to where they'd entered, flexible tubes of aluminum ducting were coiled, uninstalled.

"This is weird," Projects said.

Riley turned. He had swung the door shut, and he pointed. There was a horizontal bolt drilled onto the face below the handle. He didn't touch it.

"You can bolt the door closed," Patel said. "But only if you're inside."

His eyes swept the space. "There'd be only one reason to lock yourself *in*."

Riley followed his gaze. Privacy.

The central battened walkway was more than a meter wide and roughly laid with carpet. Projects knelt at the start and picked up an end. "Four layers," he said. "Felt, rubber underlay, carpet—over plywood."

Riley walked onto it, felt it spongy underfoot.

Projects followed. "Insulated," he said. "For sound." He looked down. "The walkway tracks along the guest corridor." He pointed to either side. "That's the ceilings of the rooms."

The walkway ran for thirty meters and ended in a horizontal wall of partition board. Riley guessed it was where the foyer started. The lit area encompassed the ceilings of all the guest rooms. She walked fifteen meters down the spongy aisle to where two carpeted branches forked off the central path at right angles, one on either side. The offshoots ran for several meters out over the ceilings, and each stopped at identical pieces of what looked like canvas mats, about a meter square.

Projects went past her and walked along the right branch. Riley could tell from the way he moved that he felt it too—strange air, stilted and furtive. He knelt and picked up a corner of the beige canvas, and Riley walked over. "It's a padded cover." He shined his flashlight. "For a vent."

"A vent for what?"

Projects put the flashlight down, removed the square of canvas, and placed it aside. "It must be in the ceiling of a room." He gripped the slats of the vent and tried to lift it but quickly gave up and pointed. "Screwed down."

Riley knelt and picked up the flashlight and slanted the beam. "Can you see through it?"

Projects dipped his head around to change his lines of sight. "Not really."

Patel was standing over them. "What about a camera?"

Projects ran his fingers around the slats and the sides, then knelt up straighter and raised the edge of the felt and foam and carpet. "Nope." He grunted and lay down flat to look again at the vent. Riley saw his body tense. "Oh fuck," he whispered. He pushed himself up and moved aside and gestured at Riley. "You go. Lie flat on your stomach and look through."

She lay down, her chin between the carpet and the vent. The angle allowed a clear view through the slats. She was staring into an empty guest room—she could see the entire space, but the focus, front and center, was the bed. She sat up and scanned the vaulted void, the padded paths, the bolted door. It was neatly laid out. Two covered vents: two viewing platforms. Cassidy had gone to a lot of trouble so he could creep up here and spy on guests in two rooms below.

27

Projects replaced the canvas cover on the vent, and Riley was going back to the central walkway when Rodrigues called. Jayson and Karen had been in Branxton but were on the road again, heading south.

"How long?" Riley said.

"Fifteen minutes," he said.

She stood for a moment with the phone to her ear. The partition wall at the end of the walkway cut across the width of the building and enclosed the space with the viewing vents. She walked back toward the door and looked at the surplus tubes of aluminum ducting. There was nothing else.

She said into the phone, "We're coming down," and hung up.

Back in the storeroom, Projects removed the prop from the red door and locked it behind them. In the guest corridor, Patel stepped out her rough measure from the aisle upstairs. She counted and stopped and looked at the room numbers on either side: 13 and 14. She knocked on 13 and when there was no answer, Riley tried her white card. The lock clicked and they went in. There was a vent in the ceiling.

They closed the room and knocked on 14 before letting themselves in and eyeing the vent. Riley and Patel were farther up: 7 and 8. Cassidy wasn't spying on them from his cavity.

The three of them removed their gloves and booties. "Call Nigel Armytage," Riley said. "When did they stay here?"

Patel took out her phone, and Riley went down the corridor and crossed to Belinda at reception. "I need a favor," she said. "On the quiet."

"Okay," Belinda said.

"We're re-creating a precise timeline of the Armytages' movements. It's standard, it helps us fill in little gaps. When they stayed here, I need to know, what was the room?"

Belinda's tongue darted. "Do you have the month?"

Patel was standing in the foyer, still on the phone. "September," she mouthed.

Riley watched, with Projects beside her, as Belinda tapped at her keyboard. It took a while, almost a minute.

"Here," Belinda said. "September twelfth. Armytage. For three nights. Room fourteen."

Time slowed . . . Riley blinked at Belinda. "Thanks. It would help us, um, if you could keep this to yourself."

Her eyes flicked to Projects and back. "Sure."

Patel had hung up and the three of them walked into the car park. They stood beside Projects's van, shielded from the CCTV.

"We need an electronic trail for Jayson Cassidy on the three dates," Riley said. "Phone, rego, credit cards. I want to bring him in."

Patel had her arms crossed. Now she tilted her head down and eyed Riley. "Breathe."

"If we charge him with spying on guests," Riley said, "what's he get?"

"Bail," Projects said.

"The whole setup"—Patel lifted a finger at the roof—"he could just claim it's for maintenance."

"How does he explain the vents?" Riley said.

"He's ducting the air-conditioning," Projects said. "He's got the tubing right there."

"So what?" Riley said. "We leave him in place?"

"Stay covert," Patel said. "Build the case. Put him in Canberra or Adelaide on the dates."

"We get a camera up there," Projects said. "Film him in the act. Then at least you've got him for peep and pry. It won't put him away long, but it's leverage."

"We can't arrest him for Penelope." Patel nodded at the roof. "Not with that. That's not even circumstantial."

"What about he comes home now and looks through the CCTV from the morning?" Riley said. "If he knows we've been in there, he goes to ground and we're fucked."

"That's the risk," Patel said.

Riley knew it: It had been the same with the room sweep. Her phone buzzed again, and she answered. "How long?"

"False alarm," Rodrigues said. "Drove straight past."

"To where?"

"Dunno. But you're clear. Looks like Cessnock."

Riley hung up and studied Projects. "We've got a warrant for the house. Can we sneak in without him knowing?"

"No idea." He shrugged. "We can try."

Patel took Riley in the Camry and Projects followed in his van. They went down the car park, onto the drive behind the motel. The bitumen gave way to gravel, and after seventy meters it ended at a single-story cottage surrounded by trees. It was a new build, with the same materials as the Quirk—and the Armytage development. Oakeshott had built the Cassidys a house.

Riley grabbed fresh gloves and booties from the car and handed them out. They picked their way, careful not to over-tread any shoeprints.

Projects examined the front door, peered in windows, disappeared down the side with his backpack. Alarms were rare in the country, but so, Riley guessed, were men like Jayson Cassidy. For all she knew, he'd been watching them all morning on a live feed on his phone. She texted Rodrigues a heads-up: We're at the house. He could bolt.

There was a chest to the left of the front door, and Patel bent to open the lid. "Shoes."

Riley looked in. A pair of old Redbacks, two pairs of trainers, gum boots. Patel pulled them out one at a time, and Riley photographed the soles with her phone.

The front door opened, and Projects's scruffy head popped out. "Window was ajar in the laundry." He turned and surveyed. "Looks clear. Well . . . no alarm."

They entered into a living area with a kitchen at the back. Everything was neutral, including the smell. Projects opened his backpack to sweep for cameras. Riley walked down the room. The carpet was the same as in the Quirk, and so were the soft-focus photographs of vineyards framed on the wall. So were the tea bags in a jar on the counter and the coffee pods and Nespresso machine. The breakfast crockery on a dish rack was the same as what was used in the motel pantry.

Riley went through a door to the right—a main bedroom. There was a big built-in wardrobe with sliding doors. She dug around in it and checked for false walls. Patel came in and they went through the shoe racks, photographing the soles. The clothes and accessories were stacked and hung tidily. Riley felt around in jacket pockets.

Patel moved to the bed, sifted the side drawers, and felt under the mattress. There was an ensuite that led through to a laundry with a casement window pinned open on a stay. Riley took pictures of the cleaning products. She did the same in the bathroom, photographing the medicines and toiletries in the cabinet. There was no foam, no gauze or crepe, no duct tape, no bandages.

In the kitchen, Patel was on her haunches, looking under the sink. A door on the other side led to a second bedroom, another bathroom, and an office.

Projects stood at the desk in the office, staring at a computer. "Password protected," he said.

He moved away and Riley looked at a bookshelf: accountancy and management textbooks and manuals. The whole place felt corporate, like a leased executive apartment.

The spare bed was made up with hotel linen, and in the bathrooms the soap, body wash, shampoo, and conditioner were all in the same miniatures used at the Quirk. Riley stared at the little tan bottles. Everything in the house came from the Quirk. So what? The Cassidys had paid for it. She heard Bowman again: *thrifty disposition.*

A thought struck her, and she searched on her phone for the crime scene images of the drawers from the Morrows' bathroom in Ngunnawal. She pinched to zoom in on the mini shampoos and soaps taken from hotels. They were in muted pinks and blues—not tan. Not from the Quirk, or at least not recently. She made a note to check the history of toiletry suppliers to the motel and to the Cassidys' hotel in Newcastle.

She took another photo and went out. Patel was in the main room.

"What do you see?" Riley said.

"Transactional." Patel turned in a circle. "Commercial. There's nothing that says 'family,' not even a picture on the fridge. There's no sign of siblings, or nieces or nephews, or parents. Not even friends."

Riley nodded. It felt like a business, not a home. "Partners," she said. "But financial. Not man and wife."

"They've been at it a long time," Patel said. "Refining the model. They run things on their own to keep costs down."

Karen's tight ship. "Low overheads."

"No one rostered on from six," Patel said. "The evenings are clear, no prying staff."

"To catch Jayson prying."

"Say they didn't build the motel around a business model," Patel said.

"Then?"

"They built it around a fetish. The whole operation is designed to allow them to perv on guests."

Riley caught up. *They.* "Karen," she said.

"Jayson doesn't work at reception. He's hardly seen. His roles are in the back rooms, inventory, ordering. And then consulting. He's developed this model for perving but thinks, *Fuck, we've got costs down, we're saving money*—so he pitches it. But that's not the point."

"If he's not front of house, he's not assigning guests to his viewing rooms."

"Exactly," Patel said. "So does he leave it to chance? Does he go into the roof and peer in and see what's turned up? Maybe. But I doubt it."

"Karen's directing traffic," Riley said.

Patel nodded. "She put the Armytages in room fourteen."

Riley's eyes roamed the barren house, came home to rest on Patel. Karen was selecting.

28

In the Camry, Patel and Riley retreated to the incident room. Projects followed in his van.

Pictures of the shoe and boot soles at the Cassidy house were sent out for the experts to examine, although Riley knew they didn't look promising—there were no crescents or swirls. But there were two other pairs she wanted to look at: the shoes Jayson and Karen Cassidy were wearing.

The flurry of activity around the Cassidys' footwear provoked a call from Beth Gatjens. "The shoeprint at the crime scene is a male size ten," she told Riley. "From what you've sent from her wardrobe, we put Karen at a female seven. Now, okay, that doesn't eliminate her. It's possible she was there in an oversized boot. But it's unlikely."

Riley hung up. The Cassidys had driven back to Red Creek and gone home. Rodrigues came in and sat at his desk while Riley briefed him. "One question before all the others," he said. "Should you still be at the motel? I think you should get out."

"For safety reasons?" Patel said.

"Well, yeah. These two look like our best suspects." He crossed a leg. "Which means you might be staying with a couple of sexual psychopaths."

"So we pull out," Patel said. "And what about the other guests? There'll be women in the viewing rooms this weekend, you can bet."

"Place is booked out Saturday," Riley said.

Rodrigues was running a thumbnail between his teeth.

Riley knew they couldn't pull out, not in good conscience, and they couldn't bring the couple in. "If we arrest now," she said, "we might not even get them on a perving charge."

"Shut them down," Rodrigues said. "Stage an accident. Kill the water, or the power."

Riley shook her head: They needed to gather evidence. The Cassidys had to be free to go about their business.

"We sit tight," Patel said. "We're right on top of them. We know about the roof, but we don't want to waste it. We give Projects time to get footage in the attic."

Projects, fidgeting at a desk, looked up. "You get me forty minutes, I'll put a camera in the rafters."

"The Cassidys go out Wednesdays," Patel said. "But that's another week."

"Fuck that." Rodrigues threw his pen on his desk. "No way. We need to expedite."

"Okay," Patel said. "How?"

"You've been at the motel for ten days, and you haven't clapped eyes on Jayson," Rodrigues said. "So, two birds. We want him out of the place for an hour, and we want a look at him."

"Yeah," Riley said.

"He's a witness, among the last to see Penelope alive," Rodrigues said. "What about we put the word out in the district that we're asking potentially helpful locals in for a chat? Then we ask people in as a screen—Bob Bruce, the café owner, the neighbors. Whoever. Couple of staff from the pub, get the word through there. Red and Dew. We ask Jayson in, Karen too. Keep it basic, routine questions, make it clear we're talking to everyone."

Riley liked it. They could get the Cassidys out of the Quirk and get a look at Jayson. "Let's set it up—for Friday," she said. That gave a day for the word to pass around.

Projects excused himself, saying he'd be back, and went out to his van while the three of them worked at their desks. Rodrigues rang the Quirk, and the girl on the desk put him through to Karen. He explained there was a callout to locals who might be able to help with the investigation, and he requested Jayson and Karen be at the Cessnock police station at 11:00 a.m. Friday.

"We're talking to numerous members of the public," he said into the phone. "I know your time is precious. We'll try and keep it brief." He stayed on the line, nodding. Riley watched him as he hung up. "Lock it in," he said. "We're good to go."

"Both of them?" Riley said.

"Yeah. Belinda will cover a few hours on reception."

Patel called the Armytages' neighbors in the row of town houses, the owners of the café, and the owners of the takeaway. Rodrigues called Sandra at the Packhorse, then Red Lucas and his son, Dew. Riley phoned the winemaker Bob Bruce and asked him to bring his wife.

Bruce assented and Riley hung up. Bob Bruce—he'd put it on the grapevine. She wanted chatter around the callout to locals, so the Cassidys would hear it and not think they were being targeted. She rang Police Media and asked them to monitor for any news about the police request for interviews.

Riley placed her phone on the desk. One detail stuck out: Rodrigues had omitted the name *Neville Oakeshott* from his list of people to bring in. She signaled Patel with a coded glance and locked eyes with Rodrigues. "What about Oakeshott?"

Rodrigues deflected with a twitch of a shoulder. "Sure. You want me to call?"

"Priya can do it," Riley said. "You got a number?"

His eyes moved between them. "I can get it."

Riley folded her arms as he picked up his phone. He made a call, spoke softly, hunched at his desk, and hung up. After thirty seconds, a text pinged and he read it, scrawled on a sticky note, and walked it over to Patel.

"Thanks," she said.

He gave her a look—*No trouble*—and went back to his desk.

"Who was that?" Riley said.

"That," Rodrigues said, "was my wife."

"Your wife knows Oakeshott?"

"No. But her best friend works in his office."

"What a coincidence," Riley said.

"Not really. Between here and Newcastle, Oakeshott employs maybe forty people. That's just white-collar staff, before you get to all the contractors."

"Have you ever met him?"

"No."

"Has your wife?"

"Once, maybe, at some lunch." He held up his phone. "Should I ask?"

"I'd like to meet your wife."

Wrong-footed, Rodrigues missed a beat. "She'd like to meet you too. And your journo, Bowman."

Riley raised her eyebrows.

"She's read his book about you." If there was innuendo, Rodrigues kept it out of his tone. "I've been meaning to ask you round."

"Sounds good, let's do it." Riley looked over as Projects reappeared, carrying two small objects in his hand.

He put one on Patel's desk and brought the other over to Riley. It was a wedge-shaped piece of wood. "It's a chock," he said. "Jam it under the door before you go to bed. Then no one's getting in. You'll sleep better."

Riley turned the piece in her fingers. She could smell the timber. God love him: an old-school tech. He must have just cut it from a block in the back of his van and planed it into shape. He probably had a lathe in there too. "Thanks," she said.

He smiled with solidarity and started to pack up. It was 6:00 p.m., and Riley was about to get food from the takeaway and eat at her desk when Bowman texted. Come to the pub. Got something for you.

◆ ◆ ◆

Projects and Rodrigues went out to their vehicles to head home, and Riley watched Patel lock the incident room with the single pink key Rodrigues had given her. She put it in her trouser pocket, took her usual bunch of keys from her fleece, and pressed the fob for the Camry.

In the car, Riley stared ahead as Patel backed out. "Tell me you've never left the key to the incident room in the motel," Riley said.

Patel's left hand patted her hip pocket. "No. Never."

"Even when we went to Adelaide?"

She stopped her reverse and went still. "No. I had it with me. I remember, I put it on the table at home. I can see it there. Pink."

"Good. As long as you're certain. Because if you're not, you need to say."

They sat, looking in silence at the old stone post office. What would someone see if they gained access to the incident room? Case files and briefing notes were mostly stored digitally. But there were images of the Canberra and Adelaide scenes, pictures of the victims, pinned on the wall.

Patel swallowed. "We're good. I'm certain."

Riley nodded. She'd seen it once before, a job in a small town where an incident room had been breached. "Let's go have a drink," she said.

Patel pulled away and drove through the crossroad and down to the Packhorse. In the car park, there were three utes, Bowman's Audi, and a city SUV.

The pub was quiet. Two men drinking at a raised table were locals Riley associated with Bob Bruce, although neither Bruce nor Red Lucas was there. There was a single male, in orange hi-vis, in a corner. Two older couples, tourists, were eating together at a table. The barman Michael was behind the counter, and Riley could see Rachel moving through the dining area. Bowman was alone in his booth to the right, and Patel went over to him. Riley crossed to the bar, and Michael, a sheen to his forehead, greeted her with a nod. She ordered three Stone & Woods.

In the booth, Bowman was beside Patel. Riley slid in on his other side and they sat in the same configuration as last time, ducks in a row, facing the room.

"What've you got?" Riley asked.

"This developer, Neville Oakeshott," Bowman said.

She scratched her neck. "I'm listening."

Patel and Riley sat sipping as Bowman told them about his visit to the former councillor Matthew Drummond. He saved the best till last: the idea of a dirty cop, a faceless male in uniform. Likely large, definitely broad across the chest, although Drummond had only seen him sitting in a car. It could be the Senior Sergeant Harris, Riley thought, but it could be countless others too. A Newcastle cop, or Muswellbrook, or Singleton . . . She took some solace: Rodrigues was never in uniform.

The facts were meager, Drummond had no evidence to tie Oakeshott to any blackmail.

"Can you write it?" she said.

"Not like I just laid it out to you," Bowman said. "Although I was thinking maybe Drummond could sign an affidavit." He put his glass down. "Or of course, I could write that police are pursuing certain avenues of inquiry."

Riley had an ulcer starting in her lower left gum. She bit her lip. They could strip Oakeshott down, go through everything—the purported sex worker at the Novotel, Laura Nolan's phone, email, and hard drive—but it would take some digging. Was it relevant? Was it even true?

Bowman squeezed out from the booth and went to get a round.

"Thoughts?" Patel said.

"Drummond's a corrupt grub," Riley said, "playing Bowman like a harpsichord . . . ?"

"You think Bowman's susceptible to being used, in relation to Oakeshott?"

"Yeah, Oakeshott's pissed him off. I mean he's sitting here with his driver's license suspended."

"Or take Drummond at face value," Patel said. "Oakeshott is corrupt, he's after the Quirk. If we were just looking at Penelope Armytage, I'd be liking him a lot. But that angle, a developer motive, is constrained to the Red Creek scene."

"A question, though," Riley said. "Does Oakeshott's company have any projects in Canberra or Adelaide?"

"If so, the motive needs to change from the scenario Drummond laid out. It's not a corrupt developer killing a woman because she's somehow blocking his interests."

"It's a stray tradesman affiliated with Oakeshott's company. Someone who's moving around."

Patel drank. "One thing that's interesting . . . Drummond talked of a whispering campaign against Jayson, this idea that he's got criminal charges. But he's clean, even with the ATO."

"Who benefits from whispers against Jayson?"

"There's a dead girl," Patel said. "She stayed at the Quirk—Karen's telling everyone. The whispers start, it might be Jayson Cassidy. Oakeshott sees an opportunity. If the Cassidys go down, the Quirk goes on the market." Patel paused. "But if it actually is the Cassidys, why's Karen blabbing?"

"She figured we'd find out anyway, and then that would raise our hackles—we'd be asking why she didn't tell us. And Belinda told me that Karen likes the drama."

Patel pushed away her glass. "Inserting."

Riley pinched at a beer mat. It was the same with Jayson—he'd inserted himself into the investigation as a witness, claiming to be among the last to see the victim alive. But then he'd melted away.

Bowman came back with a bottle of wine and three glasses and jostled Patel into the middle of the booth. Rachel brought menus, and they ordered food.

"So," Bowman said, "I think you owe me a story."

"For what?" Riley said.

"Oakeshott, the idea of a dirty cop. And Laura Nolan."

"What about her?"

"If she starts smearing Jayson Cassidy in the press, you'll know it's coming from Oakeshott—and you'll know what I'm telling you is true."

Riley poured wine. She had considered giving Bowman the angle that the police were calling back locals on Friday to provide additional statements, but she resisted, wanting to see if it surfaced elsewhere.

"You got anything to tell me?" he said.

Riley closed an eye. She probably did owe him a story. But it was dicey, engaging with him, especially with Canberra and Adelaide under wraps, because he was a talented bottom-feeder, expert at picking up nuance from detritus. She squinted at her glass . . . Maybe they could go on the record and clear Nigel Armytage, state categorically that they weren't looking at the husband. It was ethically correct, but she worried about unintended consequences—whether releasing the information might weaken the case.

She leaned into Patel. "Nigel?"

Patel understood, and agreed with a nudge of her shoulder: *Sure.*

Riley bent across her, toward Bowman. "We can clear Nigel," she said. "When will you publish?"

He pursed his lips. "I'll write it now. They'll put it straight up."

Patel wriggled past Bowman. "I'll call Nigel and let him know." She squeezed out from the booth.

Bowman pulled out his notebook and pen, and Riley drank as she briefed him. She kept it simple and gave no hint to Bowman, even off the record, about Adelaide or Canberra, or any mention of the Cassidys and their attic at the Quirk. The message was clear: The police had categorically ruled out Nigel Armytage as a suspect in the killing of his wife, and the media should respect his privacy and allow him to mourn.

Patel had found a secluded corner to speak to Nigel, and Riley watched as she hung up and wandered back. "He's very relieved—and a bit ropable." She slid in next to Riley. "He did ask me to pass on his thanks."

The meals came. Bowman ate quickly and went off to his room to file, and Patel and Riley took their time and finished the wine, then drove back to the Quirk.

Riley took a shower and got ready for bed. It was after ten when her phone lit up with a message from Bowman: a link to a story in *The Mirror*. The byline was Laura Nolan.

Police investigating the murder of Red Creek woman Penelope Armytage are pulling in for questioning local man Jayson Cassidy, the co-owner of the Quirk motel.

Her phone buzzed with a call, and she answered.

"Told you," Bowman said. "That's Oakeshott."

Riley poured a bourbon.

"Is it true?" Bowman said.

"Yes and no. It's a beat-up."

"Fuck that. Thanks for the scoop."

"You've got your angle. Write it."

"Do I incorporate this?"

She sipped and gave him a line: Police had called in a dozen local business owners to help with their inquiries. "Jayson Cassidy is coming in with Karen," she said. "They're two among many. Don't make a thing about them."

He swore again and hung up.

Riley put her phone on charge and finished the drink. Leaving a light on in the bathroom, she got into bed. Her Glock was beside her, on the night table. She lay still.

Her mind rolled, processing the day. After a minute, she sat up. Her shoulder bag was on a chair, and she went to it and dug in it until her fingers found the angular piece of timber she was looking for: Projects's wedge.

She crossed to the door and pushed it under the frame, kicking to jam it in tight.

29

Riley pecked at some breakfast at a table in the communal pantry of the motel and read a briefing note on her phone. The analysts were building electronic trails on Bradley John Lucas, also known as Dew, and Jayson and Karen Cassidy. There was nothing to put either of the men in Canberra or Adelaide on the dates. But there was nothing to put them anywhere else on those dates either. Both men's phones were often dormant, and Jayson rarely used his credit card. Bradley "Dew" Lucas had no credit facility with any financial institution. He had a debit card with an account at the Commonwealth Bank, but the only transactions in the past eighteen months were ATM withdrawals in the Hunter region, JobSeeker payments and, more recently, a semimonthly wage from Bob Bruce's company, Gully Breeze Estate. If Red Lucas was paying his son for work, it was probably in cash.

Karen Cassidy's digital record was different. There was a credit card transaction at Cessnock Woolworths on Friday, November 8, of last year, the date Jennifer Morrow had been killed in Canberra. There was nothing in Karen's electronic trail for Saturday, March 16, last year, when Gina Watson was killed in Adelaide. But the day before, Friday, March 15, Karen had paid for fuel on a credit card at a BP in Wallsend, Newcastle—1500 kilometers from the Watson crime scene.

The analysts had run the vehicle registrations and driving records of Bradley Lucas and the Cassidys: Their plates hadn't pinged in South Australia or the ACT, and none of them had been fined in either jurisdiction.

Riley closed the note. The analysts would dig deeper, through the daily and digital lives: health records, search histories, social media. They'd look for subsidiary email accounts and any hint of burner phones, details to harvest and layer, in the hope they'd hear the sound Riley and her colleagues all coveted: the chime that went *ping*.

It was 9:25 a.m. on Thursday. Karen was at reception, and guests were on the move in the lobby. Riley was at her usual spot, with her back to the CCTV, waiting for Patel. There were two males in their thirties at a table down from her, eating toast and cereal. A few minutes before, pausing in the corridor to lock her door, Riley had seen them emerging from Room 4. They were dressed in clean white sneakers, neat sweaters over T-shirts, casual trousers in muted tones.

Patel walked past, heading for caffeine.

It was the first time Riley had sat in the pantry with other guests, and she watched as it served its communal purpose. An older couple— man and wife, North Shore, retired—had finished eating and bickered as they stacked a dishwasher.

Patel put a cup of coffee on the table and went for another pass of the Quirk's "continental" offerings, returning with a single-portion box of Sultana Bran, a bowl, a spoon, a small ceramic jug with milk, and a green apple. "Sleep well?" she said.

Riley didn't answer. They had their patterns. Patel liked to talk in the morning. Riley didn't like talk, or Patel, in the morning.

"Me neither," Patel said, and looked around the foyer.

Riley sipped her second coffee and listened to Patel eat. The two men from Room 4 had finished and began to clear their plates—bumping up against the squabbling North Shore trendsetters, who smiled, surrendering the dishwasher. Niceties ensued, and Riley listened . . . both couples up from Sydney, both attending the same wedding this afternoon.

Patel had gone quiet. Riley looked over.

A man had come through the entrance and crossed behind reception. Average build, average height, light-brown shirt, tan windbreaker, fawn trousers. Riley couldn't see his shoes. Sandy hair, receding, brushed back.

He kept his eyes dead ahead. They watched him slide past Karen, pull a card from his pocket, and tap into the office.

Patel's spoon was suspended just below her lips. She put it down. "The brown whale."

"Careful," Riley said. "He'll be watching."

Toast popped on the counter, and Patel went to get it. Ten nights at the motel, and this was the first time they'd seen Jayson Cassidy physically. Riley wondered if he was sticking to his routines. If he was keeping to his patterns, it indicated he didn't know that his roof space and his house had been searched.

Patel buttered a piece of white toast and added a smear of Vegemite. Riley finished her coffee. "Let's get out of here."

They traded nods with Karen as they passed.

In the car park, guests were arriving to check in. Two young women in a racing-green Mini, another young couple in a silver Lexus. Patel bit into her toast and watched the guests unload.

In the Calais, Riley pressed the ignition, and Patel climbed in beside her.

The man from the Lexus carried a suit bag at shoulder height, and his female partner did the same with a frock in dry cleaner's plastic.

"It's a Thursday wedding," Riley said.

The women from the Mini went past, long, dark hair and short skirts in denim.

"I'm not liking this," Patel said.

Riley watched the women as they dragged their cases into reception. "I called Belinda," she said.

"And?"

"Karen does the room allocations. If Belinda takes a booking on the phone, she assigns a room provisionally, based on availability, and makes a note for Karen. Karen's always moving things around."

Patel waved her toast with an accompanying waft of Vegemite. "Rodrigues has a point. We can't just sit and watch people walking in there to be perved on."

Riley felt it, too, her umbrage rising—all these couples at the motel, the thought was repulsive. The Cassidys' voyeurism was criminal behavior. But she couldn't see a shortcut. The Cassidys were due at the Cessnock station tomorrow, to allow Projects forty minutes to access the roof and install a camera.

"If we get Jayson on peep and pry, catch him in the act," Riley said, "then what?"

"Then it would be good to talk to Farquhar."

Riley's tongue kept sliding to her ulcer. Wayne Farquhar was a forensic psychiatrist they'd used before—good with serial rapist killers. He was on sabbatical, in Europe, last Riley heard.

"Jayson Cassidy's a voyeur," Patel said. "Is that really a path to what we're looking for?"

"It's too timid," Riley agreed. "A voyeur's not a participant, just an observer."

"Exactly. It feels flaccid—like a critic, watching."

"Our boy's not that. Stalking, breaking and entering, raping, manual strangulation."

"Without the breaking," Patel said.

An idea rolled in Riley. She glimpsed the flash of its underside but couldn't catch it. "What?"

"He's not *breaking* and entering," Patel said. "But yes, he's gaining access. He's in the houses. So in that sense, he is watching. He's waiting. Then he acts."

An ambush. A participant.

Riley's phone rang on the Bluetooth. Rodrigues. "Might have something," he said.

"Cassidy?" Riley said.

"No. The winemaker—Bob Bruce?"

She indicated to turn left. "Yeah?"

"Something just went ping."

30

In the world of wine, Bob Bruce was a big cheese.

Riley, having grown up on the periphery of the vineyards, knew something about the cultural heft of the industry—that it was farming and production and not very glamorous, until, after bottling, it was sent off to market and the alchemy happened . . . the bouquet of wanker came alive in the glass. Lots of strivers sniffed and slurped: surgeons, solicitors, sommeliers, stockbrokers, sports stars, shock jocks, spivs in the press. These were Bob Bruce's fans and customers, and he'd tapped into them online, with an email newsletter and an Instagram account with about five thousand followers.

One of Rodrigues's young Cessnock detectives had seen the public account—not private, not anonymous—while scouring the socials for links to witnesses and persons of interest in the Armytage case. Rodrigues had told her to flag any reference to Adelaide or Canberra, although he hadn't explained why. The detective spent several hours collating dates and data from Bruce's Instagram feed and then sent Rodrigues a report.

In the incident room, Riley and Patel sat on either side of Rodrigues, and he took them through it.

"Five thousand two hundred and twelve followers," Riley said. "Is that a lot?"

"It's hardly Beyoncé," Rodrigues said. "But not bad for an old bloke."

"He told me he was a Luddite," Riley said.

"It's Instagram," Rodrigues said. "He's putting up pictures. We're not talking Julian Assange."

"Still," Patel said, "his version of events is, he's a hopeless dinosaur and Penelope Armytage was there to drive his digital marketing. Now it turns out he's got a vibrant social media presence."

"Has he posted since her death?" Riley said.

Rodrigues shook his head. "The last activity was four days before the killing."

"What did he post?" Patel asked.

"A picture of two bottles of wine and a couple of lines of commentary." Rodrigues read from his screen. *"Good or great Bordeaux still has a wow factor. 2000 Cos edged out the Las Cases."*

"And, what?" Riley turned her palms. "You think Penelope was helping with the account?"

"No. Sorry." Rodrigues held up a finger. "We're jumping ahead. Just listen."

Riley sat back.

"Okay, so." Rodrigues took a breath. "Bob Bruce's handle is Robert the Bruce. He's got a shtick. Every time he opens a bottle of wine—and he opens a lot of bottles of wine—he takes a picture and posts it with a comment about what he thinks. It's not only the wine he makes, it's all sorts of stuff. So it's not only about sales and marketing, it's also about sharing his expertise. He's knowledgeable, and he keeps it bright and breezy, and people find it interesting. He keeps the feed rolling, and he has a following."

Riley flipped through her notebook, back to her interview with Bruce in his shed. *Says I'm a Luddite.* Penelope had said that—he hadn't called himself a Luddite.

"I briefed my detective on our places of interest," Rodrigues said. "Each time you post on Instagram, you can insert a geographic marker under your handle, saying where you are. It's part of the brag factor. *Look at me, I'm in Rio.*"

"Mm," Patel said.

"Now, with Bruce, it's usually Pokolbin," Rodrigues said. "But he moves around a bit. Bondi, Newcastle, Palm Beach, the SCG . . ."

Riley looked up from her notebook.

"Canberra," Rodrigues said. "Adelaide."

"When?" Riley said.

Rodrigues pushed his chair back a bit so he could see Riley and Patel from either side. "He was in Canberra at the end of October, eleven days before Jennifer Morrow was murdered," he said. "Before that, with Adelaide, the timing blows out even further. He was there—but in January. Two months before Gina Watson was killed."

Riley grimaced. "You said he moves around a bit. Where else?"

Rodrigues leaned over the screen. "There are about one thousand six hundred posts. Seventy percent of them are Pokolbin or elsewhere in the Hunter. He goes to Newcastle regularly, then Sydney. The rest is more random, but he does travel. Thredbo, Italy, France, London. Perth."

Riley chewed her pen. Bruce's visits were something, but not much. "It's good work," she said. "Thanks."

Rodrigues crossed his arms. "He's a person of interest," he said. "His social media is data. So we crunched it."

"It feels like coincidence," Riley said. "We place him in Canberra and Adelaide in the weeks or months leading into each killing. Then what?"

"He sees the two women," Rodrigues said. "They're his marks. He heads back on the dates. But he goes dark—no Instagram, no electronic trail."

"On that"—Patel was reading the screen—"there's no activity on his Instagram account on the day of each killing, including Penny Armytage."

Riley turned to Rodrigues. "What do you want to do?"

"Keep digging. Where was Bruce on the dates? Phone, credit card, rego, diary. Can we put him in Canberra or Adelaide? How does he travel? Who books it? Check car hire, check the airlines."

Riley closed her eyes and stretched her neck. Adelaide, Canberra, Red Creek. The timing was way out, but they could put Bob Bruce in each.

"It's two better than the Cassidys," Patel said. "Or Dew."

Yes. Riley rubbed her cheeks.

"And Penny Armytage worked for Bruce," Patel said.

"But she stayed at the Quirk," Riley said. "Karen put her in room fourteen. And the Cassidys likely have form—premeditated voyeurism."

"It's not violent," Patel said. "It's not what we saw on the slab."

"It's sexual," Riley said. "It's a sex crime."

"We're looking for someone who's choosing," Rodrigues said. "Red Creek, Canberra, Adelaide. He *sees* them. Maybe months before—then he goes back. Bruce is a person of interest. Now we have evidence to put him in the three places."

"There's nothing in his background?" Riley said. "You said he was what, a bit handsy with women?"

"That's his reputation, but it's talk," Rodrigues said. "His record's clean."

"With the Cassidys, we've got apparent aberrant behavior," Riley said. "A pair of sick fucks."

"And a different class of offending," Rodrigues said. "Voyeurism to multiple manual strangulation—that's a leap."

Observer to participant: Rodrigues was making the same point she and Patel had just discussed in the car. "Escalation," Riley said. "Let's say Jayson started peeping early in life, and it's built. He meets Karen, she learns of his predilection but doesn't reject him, and they bond. Why? Because she's got predilections of her own. Wouldn't be the first time—think Rosemary West."

Patel stood and went to a large map of Australia that Rodrigues had pinned on the wall. "Adelaide, Canberra, Red Creek." She pointed. "They appear random. Two bush cities and a flyspeck. What's the common denominator?"

"Wine," Rodrigues said. "Adelaide's the wine capital of Australia, it's surrounded. Canberra has its district. Red Creek is basically a vineyard."

Riley stared at the map. Bob Bruce was a winemaker, and he moved around a lot. "Why bring it home?" she said. "Red Creek is Bruce's home."

"That goes for the Cassidys too," Patel said. "And Dew."

"Look at the alibis," Rodrigues said. "They're all shit."

"All right," Riley said. "Let's dig into Bruce. Priya can take Bowman, go see the wife." She made a face. "Talk arts and craft."

"You'll recall Bruce is on the warrant." Rodrigues smiled. "You wanted a peek in his first aid kit."

Bowman crossed the pub car park as Patel came down the drive, and he got in the Camry.

"Déjà vu," she said.

He pulled the door closed—all over again—reached for his belt, grunted, "Mm." He'd first met Patel during the homicide investigation at the school, when Riley had sent him out to interview a suspect and Patel had accompanied him, posing as his media colleague.

He watched through the windshield as she traversed the lot. She'd called an hour ago, asking him to come along while she talked with the wife of the winemaker Bob Bruce.

She rolled up to the yield sign.

"What's the story?" Bowman said.

"I'll introduce you as Adam." Patel looked left, across him. "She probably won't ask for more. If she does, I'll say you're freelance police media, or some such. If she really twigs, we'll deal with it."

"Bruce knows me, from the pub."

"He's not there. We checked."

"Why am I here?"

"We want her guard down, talking. She does pottery—like, ceramics. That's her job."

"And?"

"That's your field—arts and craft. You can show some interest, get her chatting."

Bowman's lips flapped as he blew air. This had Riley written all over it, the idea that potters and writers were all the same, peas in a pod, bonding over adverbs and glazing. "Fucking lunacy. What's her name?"

"Diana Bruce." Patel went right, toward the crossroad.

Bowman didn't mind, it got him out of the pub and into the case. And he relished time with Patel—she was smart and funny and glorious, one of his favorite people.

She noted him settling in. "It's like I've sprung Grandpa," she said. "Out for a day trip."

"I thought I was your uncle."

Her eyes widened, pale blue in the vivid white. "If I had kids, that's what they'd call you. Uncle Adam."

"How you going on that front?"

"Now you sound like my mother."

"So you're looking at Bruce?"

"Yeah. His version is, he was home with Diana on the Monday. Cooked her pasta. We want to test that."

They drove on back roads. Rosebushes had been planted at the end of the rows of vines. Rachel had explained it to him. The leaves of the rose were an early-warning system, a canary in the coal mine—a change in leaf color indicated mildew.

Patel raised a finger off the wheel. "No CCTV, no cameras. This is the route we think Penelope took when she drove to Bruce's place the day she died. We know she then left the winery and came home via Cessnock. But we've got no coverage of her out here, just at Woolies." She checked her mirrors. "So Bruce could have driven this way, to Penelope's place and back, unseen."

"Electronically," Bowman said.

Patel nodded.

"Penelope was seen physically, by witnesses, at the crossroad," he said. "It could be the same for Bruce. Did anyone see his vehicle?"

Patel slowed to turn into a gate marked GULLY BREEZE ESTATE.

"Has that question been asked?" Bowman said.

Patel rattled over a cattle grid in silence. The set of her jaw, in profile, gave Bowman his answer. "Specifically?" she said. "No."

"And, um, unspecifically?"

She drove up a manicured drive. "The witnesses were asked what else they saw, including vehicles and regos. No one saw Bruce or his Hilux."

"What's Diana drive?"

Patel followed a VISITOR PARKING sign. "There's a question. I'll ask."

"Maybe potters are like poets. They don't drive."

"What?" She unclipped her belt. "Now you tell me. Shakespeare didn't drive?"

"Shakespeare was a dramatist, primarily." Bowman followed her out and caught up as she strode across the macadam. "There *are* modern poets like, you know, working now. Riley wouldn't know that, but I expect more from you."

"Why don't they drive?"

"They do." Bowman imagined them, hunched at the wheel, grinding the gears of their Subarus. "It's just a literary joke."

"Hilarious." Patel opened a door marked TASTING ROOM. "Still, that's good. You're warming up."

"Eh?"

"Arts and craft." She tipped her head to usher him through. "That's why you're here."

Patel must have told Diana Bruce they were coming. Behind a tasting counter, in the cellar door, a young woman, early twenties, nodded when Patel introduced herself and led them into a whitewashed corridor. They followed her past ceramic bowls displayed on shelves and windowsills, out across an internal courtyard paved in terra-cotta, through more doors to a rear garden and along a path behind a big wine shed. They came to a separate, small square building with a domed roof, and the young woman knocked on a rusting metal door.

A raised female voice answered, "Come."

Their guide opened the door and slid away, back along the path.

Patel entered and Bowman followed, into a workshop warm with kiln air and baked mud. A tall woman in a black tank top under an apron was standing behind a trestle table, which stood itself on wheels. She raised her head and came around to greet them, chin up, back straight, like a soldier. A helmet of black hair, cropped and streaked with gray. She was in thick socks and clogs, and her apron was well-splattered with ecru sludge at the waist.

"Mrs. Bruce, thank you for seeing me." Patel introduced herself, shook hands, and made a dismissive gesture toward Bowman. "Adam, from police press. He was helping me with something else so came along for the ride."

Bowman hung near the door, and Diana Bruce took him in with a half glance—nondescript middle-aged white male, brave sweater—then went back to studying Patel, as though she might model the detective in clay.

There were sketches and a collection of small colored tiles on the trestle, and pictures tacked up behind: pots, Greek vessels, images torn from magazines. Sets of fired, unfinished objects were stacked on open shelving along the walls: mugs, goblets, plates, and saucers.

"Sorry to intrude," Patel said.

Diana wiped her hands on a ragged towel. "It's all right, I'm finished for the day."

There was a throwing wheel in a tub on a steel base, low to the ground, with a stool attached, and to the side, a chamois, slop bucket, sponges, a garroting wire.

"Is this the only place you work?" Patel asked.

The potter arced an eyebrow. "Yes. Every day."

"I meant, you don't have a separate office," Patel said, "or work in the winery buildings?"

"Nope, this is me"—she waved the towel—"just here."

"You sell your . . . pottery," Patel said, "with the wine?"

"Yep. There's a shop, off the cellar door. The girls run it. They take the pieces from here and do the displays. It's their show. I keep my distance."

"And Penelope Armytage . . ." Patel opened her notebook. "Did she play any role with your work or the shop?"

"No. Never. Nothing. In fact, I'm ashamed to say, as I said on the phone, I never actually met her."

"Ashamed?" Patel said.

"Well, she worked here, for Bob. I mean, it's a family business. So she worked for us. And yet, cooped up in here"—she flung the towel into a porcelain sink—"I never even bothered to greet her."

"Was she here often, on-site?"

"No. Hardly at all. I mean, how much, exactly, you have to ask Bob. But she hadn't been with us long. And, you know, these days—work from home."

Bowman had moved to a wall and was looking at a row of glazed coffee cups on a shelf. Not fine boned, but wonderfully controlled, all the same shape: squat, angular, generous, and earthy. Simple yet precise, and difficult, he guessed, to master. "Delightful," he said.

Over the wheel, the potter threw him a glance. "Thank you," she said.

"You do purely . . ." He ran his eye down the shelf in search of a word. "Functional?"

"Yes. Only tableware. Not fine art."

Craft . . . Bowman could respect that. There was no pretense to the woman, but she was serious about her trade, and the work was strong. She made useful things with her hands, daily objects suffused with joy—not many people could lay claim to that.

He fondled a mug. "To master your craft, did you find you needed a routine?"

"What, like throw my first dish at seven a.m.?"

"Yeah," he said. "Do you start work at the same time every day?"

She rubbed an eye. "Mm. Basically. I'm an early bird. But I'm not rigorous about start times."

"And do you need discipline?" he said. "Or are you drawn to it?"

Her hand went to her hip. "It's work," she said. "But it's never a question of will I do it today. I'll always turn up. So yes, I suppose you can say I'm drawn to it."

"I've read that, but with writers. 'Desk hunger,' the Irish call it."

"Okay. Well, for me, it's the wheel."

"And a blessing and"—Bowman plowed, gallantly, through the cliché—"a curse."

"Perhaps." She began to tidy pencil-size wooden tools on the counter.

"You have a calling. But you have no say in it, you have to turn up. So you must be guarded—selfish, even—with your time. It keeps you from other things."

"Maybe," she said. "Yes. Clichés are clichés because they're true."

"Right. So you shouldn't be hard on yourself, about not meeting Penelope." There was an intermittent clicking coming from the kiln down the room. "About being cooped up in here. You were working."

Diana met his eye in reappraisal, unsure if he was dissembling.

Bowman wasn't sure either. He just wanted her talking about timing, and how she spent her day. He picked his way to another shelf, past Patel.

"With that in mind," Patel said. "Your routine. Can you take me through what you were doing on the Monday before last?"

Diana stood studying the trestle counter. "I've recalled it, of course, in the light of what happened—but also because I was finishing a big commission that had given me trouble for weeks. And the Tuesday, I remember viscerally, because it's when I heard the news. I know exactly where I was."

"Where?" Patel said.

Diana gave a half laugh. "Here. Of course."

"Someone came and told you . . . ?"

"No." She pointed at a dusty black radio, silent on a shelf. "I heard it on the news. I turn on ABC Newcastle early, while I'm setting up. I like the presenters."

Bowman listened while Patel took Diana's version, working backward from that Tuesday morning. After hearing the news, Diana had stumbled out to find her husband, who was in his office, alone, at the back of the main building, across the apron from the wine shed. Bob Bruce hadn't heard the news and was shocked, dazed, confused. His phone had started ringing, locals who had heard. He had held Diana, and they'd gone to the kitchen and made cups of tea. People in the district had kept calling, and Diana had sat listening to her husband on the phone. She'd felt a harsh weight in her chest, it had come up her throat, and she'd walked to her bedroom and sobbed.

Patel let her talk. On the Monday, Diana had worked in the morning, as usual. After four she'd hung up her apron, headed into the house, and made herself a gin and tonic and put some olives and cheese out. Bob had emerged and opened a white wine, and they'd snacked and talked while he prepared dinner.

"What time was this?" Patel asked. "When you first saw Bob?"

"Five or just after. Cork-pulling time. He has a rule, on a normal day—no drinks until five."

"A normal day?" Patel said.

"A non-lunch day."

"What did he cook?"

"Zucchini pasta. That's one of my rules—no meat, twice a week."

"Does he always cook?"

"No, we share it. But he does a lot. For some reason, Monday's become pasta night. He always does that."

"Did he talk at all about Penelope?"

"On the Monday?"

"Yes."

"No."

"Did he ever talk about her or mention her?"

Diana frowned. "Yes. In that I knew the name. But only that he'd hired her, for marketing online. I sort of nod at that business talk, half listening. I get it, we all need a sounding board. And I'm Bob's."

Patel paused.

"Is Bob yours?" Bowman said.

Diana turned to him. "No. Not really, anymore." She spoke plainly, with no regret.

Bowman thought of Bob Bruce, the man he'd seen over the past two weeks in the pub. Bowman had never interviewed Bruce one-on-one—the grape grower Red or the other locals, Vat or Stalk or Bore Drain, were always around.

"When you started out," Bowman said, "you liked to talk to him about it, your day at the wheel. But now your work does the talking, it speaks for itself . . . ?"

"That's probably right, yes."

There was an extended click from down the room. Diana excused herself and crossed the studio and turned a dial. "Sorry." She came back. "Kilns are like husbands—temperamental. You need to nurse them."

Patel steered her to the Monday evening.

After Bruce had cooked dinner, the couple had eaten together. Then Bruce had gone to his office, along the hall from the kitchen.

"And you?" Patel said.

"I came in here." Diana rubbed the nape of her neck with a hand. "I'd finished glazing and had to pack the kiln for the second firing."

Bowman felt Patel's interest.

"You came in here?" She flattened her voice. "For how long?"

"Hard to say."

Patel peered up from her notebook.

"I was preoccupied, fully immersed." Diana's eyes flicked Bowman's. "The kiln was going, I'm cocooned. When I'm like that, time flies."

"Okay," Patel said. "Sorry. I just need to get this down, with the timing. Just the facts, so we're clear."

Diana propped herself at the sink, hands out gripping the counter on either side.

"Bob prepared dinner from five, and you ate," Bowman said. "So you returned here after six?"

She considered her clogs. "It was dark, on the path."

"Sunset was five thirty," Patel said. "On the night."

Diana lowered her chin to her chest. "Yeah, it was past twilight. So between six and six thirty. Thereabouts."

Patel made a note. "Okay, good. And?"

The potter sighed through her nose. "I went from here to get ready for bed. I like to sleep eight hours. I know the Tuesday, I was up at five thirty." She nudged her forehead at the kiln. "So sleep by nine thirty. I had a shower. So in the house by nine."

"And you saw Bob"—Patel smiled hopefully—"and said good night?"

Diana made an oval shape with her lips. "No . . . I don't think so. The telly was on. The kitchen was clean, from dinner—I took a glass of water to my room. He was in the office. I didn't see him."

"You know he was in the office, but you didn't see him?" Patel said.

She shrugged. "Yeah, that's often the way. He's in the office, I'm in the studio. We mightn't see each other before bed, but we know where we are."

"Do you share a bed?" Patel said.

"Yeah, unless he's had too much to drink and he snores. Then he sleeps in the spare room."

"And that night?" Patel said. "The Monday?"

"That night was fine. Not a lunch day. So no drinks till five."

"Do you remember him coming to bed?"

"No. Or I don't think so. He's quiet at night and keeps the lights off. I do the same, in the morning."

"You set an alarm," Patel said. "It doesn't wake him?"

"I set an alarm for eight hours, but it doesn't go off—or very rarely. I wake before it."

Patel let a silence build.

"You're investigating Bob," Diana said, "for the murder."

Bowman watched as the women stared at each other.

"Your husband is a person of interest," Patel said. "He knew Penelope, he employed her on contract. Penelope visited him here on the day she died. We have to eliminate him from the investigation."

Diana scrunched her nose, dismissive. "It won't be Bob—doesn't have it in him. He'd like to have fucked her, maybe he even tried. But as though she'd have been interested. It's pathetic, really. But there you go."

"From your statement, you didn't see your husband from six thirty p.m. on Monday until the next morning. That destroys his alibi. He told us he was here with you."

"Yeah, well, I was here, and I believe he was too. If you asked me to summarize, I'd say the same—I was home with my husband."

"But if he'd left in a vehicle at, say, seven p.m. and returned later that night, would you be aware of that in any way? Would you have heard it?"

"No. I'm insulated in here. And I was completely focused."

"And you say your husband was sexually attracted to Penelope Armytage and probably propositioned her?"

"I don't know that. But I say my husband has a fondness for boorish lechery. I'd have left him two decades ago, except for the kids. And he's dialed it down the last ten years. We seem to have reached some accommodation. We've become . . . companions. And I have my work." She cast Bowman a frown. "It makes me selfish, with my time. It steals hours from things I should be doing, like being with my husband. But he's forfeited the right to demand my time. So that suits me. I don't feel guilty pouring everything into this." She motioned at the room.

"But then, at five o'clock, we have a drink and a chat and dinner. And that's it. I wouldn't leave him now, because, well, I'm selfish. I've got my studio and my perfect routine. That's all that matters. And my kids. And Bob, well, I still like him. I'm happy to talk with him. And we have sex if I want. And that's it."

"You said, regarding the murder of Penelope, *It won't be Bob?*" Patel said.

"No. He's too lame. He likes his comforts—wine and beer and food and, once upon a time, a bit on the side. He might make a pass at a woman and get rejected, but he wouldn't kill for it. He's got no passion, he's just an . . . opportunist."

She drizzled the word with disdain, and it hung in the air.

Bowman knew enough Homicide basics to find the term hard to swallow. *Opportunity. Capability.*

"Does Bob travel much, out of state?" Patel said.

"Yeah, a bit."

"For work?"

"For work, for pleasure."

"Do you travel with him?"

"No."

"Does he have a diary or a schedule?"

"He's got Jenny, in the office. She knows everything."

Patel made another note.

"There is one odd thing," Diana said, "with the killing."

Patel paused with her pen.

"On that morning, Tuesday, when I heard . . . ?"

The kiln clicked.

"The pieces I was firing, they'd been giving me hell for weeks, all the way from the throw. I came in on the Tuesday, opened the kiln, and . . . oh God, something had exploded, the shelves collapsed, destroyed the whole load. The red glaze was blasted everywhere, baked on. It actually stopped me, physically—I flinched in, well, horror."

She took a breath.

"And then"—her voice coarse—"right then, I heard the news."

The studio went quiet.

Diana's gaze moved from the kiln and found Bowman. "It was like an omen," she said.

31

Friday morning, a sour tide of bleary guests washed through the pantry at the Quirk, survivors of the Thursday-evening wedding. It had obviously been a big night—they squinted through communal breakfast, with no banter traded at the dishwasher. Riley watched, just an observer. She'd been keeping an eye on rooms 13 and 14, hoping to see which revelers might have been selected by Karen, but no one had emerged from either door.

Belinda was on reception, covering for Karen so the Cassidys could be at the Cessnock police station. Leaving Patel to finish her breakfast, Riley got up and went over to the girl. "A colleague will be here around eleven," Riley said. "He'll be in my room, down the corridor, out the back."

Belinda had a cup of tea and gulped. "Okay."

"Call me if there's an issue. But can you pretend he's not here?"

"If Karen asks, I never saw him?" Belinda said.

"That's it." Riley winked. "But if Karen says anything, can you let me know? Like, straightaway?"

Belinda nodded.

Patel cleared her plate and walked with Riley to the Calais. There was traffic on the road, and at the Red Creek intersection, the café was busy and tourist cars clogged the verge. Riley went left for Cessnock. Patel had her notebook open on her lap and thought aloud as they drove. The focus was the Cassidy interview, but there were crosscurrents running. Laura Nolan's piece in *The Mirror* late on Wednesday enhanced Bowman's theory that Neville Oakeshott was targeting Jayson Cassidy. If so, who else was in on it? Nolan's story contained no detail that could only have come from a source within the investigation. But Bowman, encouraged by the former councillor Drummond, went further: Oakeshott had bought off a cop.

Riley parked on the street down from the Catholic church.

"So be aware"—Patel nodded at the police station—"in there."

Someone was talking to Nolan. Riley caught the inference and looked at the blue-tiled entrance: The call came from inside the house.

The senior sergeant, Harris, met them at the desk and took them through to the interconnected suite they'd used to interview Nigel Armytage.

Rodrigues was at his laptop and nodded to a screen on the wall. There was an aerial image of a streetscape. "This is a bird's-eye of the cop shop." He drew on his touchpad and a circle appeared. "We've told the Cassidys to park here, an empty lot next to the church." He traced a road parallel to the station. "We'll have a uniform directing traffic. We'll put them here." He marked a spot in a corner of the lot. "There's been a bit of rain. We'll have a wide strip of damp sand down on the ground here." He traced an arc. "They'll have to walk over it. We'll have Shoe and Tire in a van—they'll get the sole impressions as soon as the Cassidys are inside."

Riley studied it. "We'll do the same with all of the interviewees?"

"Yeah." Rodrigues brought up dots on the image. "Bob Bruce and Diana here, the Armytage neighbors here. Red and Dew Lucas. And so on. We'll get all the shoeprints."

"Neville Oakeshott?" Patel said.

Rodrigues blinked. Harris kept his eyes on the floor.

Rodrigues traced a shape on his laptop. "He'll be here." A circle appeared on the screen on the wall.

Harris put his thumbs in his belt. "I'll make sure everyone sees each other," he said. "We can hold people at the desk, make sure some are waiting in the foyer when the Cassidys enter and again when they leave."

He turned and headed out. Patel and Riley sat at the central table with a view through the glass to the interview room.

"Do you want to drill into Bob Bruce today?" Rodrigues said.

Riley deferred to Patel.

"No, go gentle," she said. "The wife will have told him we dropped by, and I think she'll have told him what transpired."

"That she killed his alibi." Rodrigues scowled. "That it's dead and buried *and* cremated. In her kiln."

"She'll tell him she told the truth," Patel said. "He did, too, if you read what he told Rose. He was home with his wife. She says the same, just with more detail."

"And now we play dumb?" Rodrigues said.

"We were there yesterday, so they'll feel pressure." Patel looked to Riley. "Just have them reiterate their versions."

Riley agreed. "Put them in the room together. No questions about travel, or going out of state. The wife's probably told him we asked about that yesterday. Let's see if he nibbles around it, looking for info."

"And if he does?" Rodrigues said.

"Run with it," Riley said. "But be docile. Let him lead. Give him nothing."

Harris came back. "Cassidys are on the road."

Riley nodded. A surveillance team in a requisitioned Telstra wagon were watching the Quirk, and an unmarked car would follow the Cassidys to town. Projects was waiting in his van at the incident room in Red Creek. He had the motel access card that Belinda had passed to Riley.

"They're clear of the crossroad," Harris read from his phone.

Rodrigues did the same. "Projects is heading in."

Riley had the case file open in front of her. Patel was doodling. They would only observe. The statements would be taken by Cessnock officers. None of the people asked in to the station would see the Homicide detectives at all. Riley wanted the interaction with the police to feel routine, even amateur. Everything was designed to make the visits feel like an exercise in box-ticking—and to get shoeprints and buy time for Projects to install the camera.

"Ten minutes," Harris said.

Rodrigues and one of his junior detectives would interview the Cassidys and then the Bruces. The local cop was nowhere near fully briefed on the Homicide investigation, but she'd studied the version of events the husbands and wives had given and knew to probe for discrepancies. Rodrigues had passed on Riley's advice to his detective: *Take your time, play a bit slow, try to lull them. We want them to think we're talking to everyone again because we've got nothing.*

Riley leafed through the crime scene photos: Penelope Armytage, Jennifer Morrow, Gina Watson. Time passed. Rodrigues went out.

"Here we go," Harris said.

Through the window, the door to the interview room opened and the local detective walked in. Karen entered next. Riley stared as Jayson appeared, took some blithe steps, and halted, his hands in the pockets of his tan windbreaker. His eyes moved around the space—the walls, the ceiling, the one-way glass. His shoes were a chunky sneaker, in brown canvas or leather, that Riley hadn't seen at the Cassidys' house. Rodrigues came in and took a seat beside the detective at the table. Across from them, Karen sat too. There was a delay as they waited on Jayson. He considered the seating arrangements with a smirk, dragged out his chair, and sat.

The local detective went through the preliminaries for the tape: names, date, time. Karen nodded and blinked along. Jayson crossed his legs, ankle onto knee. A thin scar on a thin lip, sun-blasted face, thin sandy hair.

"Umm." The detective ran her pen down a list in a spiral-bound notebook. "You run a hospitality business at the crossroad," she said. "Is that the pub?"

Jayson gave a snort and shook his head. "Oh boy."

"No," Karen said. "The motel. The Quirk."

"Beg your pardon." The detective turned pages. "Yes. Your home address is listed as the Quirk?"

"That's us. You got us." Jayson held up his hands. "Guilty."

The detective ignored him, still wrestling with her notebook.

Karen explained: They lived on-site, but in a cottage detached from the main building. "It's part of our inventory," she said.

"Is it?" the detective said. "Your what?"

"Our available rooms," Karen said. "The cottage has been built to be incorporated into the motel, to be rented to guests, if we expand."

Rodrigues twirled his pen. "Are you expanding?"

"It's an opt—"

"We might"—Jayson cut his wife off—"if we want to."

"You've got approval for that?" Rodrigues asked.

"Yeah. Pretty well." Jayson grinned. "Need a new builder."

"What happened to the old one?" Rodrigues said.

"Cracked the shits," Jayson said. "You know what they're like."

Rodrigues shook his head.

"Neville Oakeshott." Jayson looked at the female detective's notepad. "Owns half the valley but always wants more. He tried to buy us out, we said no. So he went on a go-slow, never finished the job."

"He built the Armytage girl's place," Karen said. "That's his land."

"Finished that one quick," Jayson said. "She got the full treatment, I'll bet."

"The full treatment?" Rodrigues said.

"Nifty Neville. Wining and dining—likes to put on a show."

"You're saying Neville Oakeshott entertained Penelope Armytage?" Rodrigues said.

"Yeah. My oath."

"With her husband, mind," Karen said.

Jayson scoffed at his wife. "He'd drop in on you when I wasn't around."

"That was only the once." Her throat bobbed. "But yes, that's true."
The detectives waited for more, but the couple went quiet.

"Sorry," Rodrigues said. "Maybe if you could just explain what happened, with Mr. Oakeshott . . . ?"

"Tell them about the decanter," Jayson said.

Karen touched her hair. "It's really that Neville was trying very hard to woo us—into selling. He had us up to the restaurant. Several times."

"All fancy," Jayson said. "Karen went along with it."

She sniffed.

"Then one day, I'm away on business—and he turns up at her door." Jayson notched his head at his wife. "With this present, eh?"

"It was two wineglasses, all boxed up with a decanter," Karen said. "The brand I liked. From the restaurant."

"Riedel," Jayson said.

Karen nodded.

"That's a six-hundred-dollar pack," Jayson said. "I looked online."

"Did Mr. Oakeshott come in the house?" Rodrigues said.

"Yes." Karen's eyes skipped sideways. "Only for a moment."

Jayson smiled.

"Was there something else?" Rodrigues said. "Regarding Mr. Oakeshott?"

"No." Karen shook her head. "Except, well, things became . . . unpleasant—when we wouldn't sell."

"The point is, that's how he operates." Jayson's mouth went lopsided, a mean line. "He would have done the same with the dead lady. He came round to my wife, when I wasn't home—he'll have done the same with her. Ask her husband. Ask her neighbors, the older couple in the row." He turned a thumb at the door. "I saw they're in the hall."

Rodrigues sat back. The local detective cleared her throat and took the Cassidys through the account of the night of Penelope's murder that they had provided to the canvass. They'd been home alone by 7:00 p.m., with no one else to vouch for them.

"We had dinner," Karen said. "Lasagna."

The detective raised her eyebrows. "You cooked lasagna?"

"No. From the pantry—the motel. There are preprepared meals. We use up stock if the date's running out."

The detective kept them talking, taking Jayson back through his witness statement, his sighting of Penelope Armytage out jogging. He had a certainty to his tone, a curl to his lip, that said he would tolerate the questions but was three streets ahead. Riley had seen it before. Not aggressive, necessarily, but dogmatic. A mask for male inadequacy, worn by dickheads with something to prove.

Riley's phone pinged with a text. Projects had installed the camera in the roof and would be clear in minutes.

Through the glass, Karen was reiterating that there had been only one guest room occupied at the Quirk on the night of the murder—the philandering couple up from Sydney. The pair had been spoken to in the canvass, and their movements had been verified by third parties.

Riley's phone was on the table. She picked it up and dialed Belinda on reception at the Quirk.

"Monday, August twenty-fifth," Riley said when the girl answered. "There was a couple booked in at the motel. Which room, and how many nights?"

"One sec." Keys clacked, and the girl came back.

Riley wrote the answers in her notebook, thanked her, and hung up.

Across the table, Patel was waiting.

"Room fourteen," Riley said.

Patel's index finger went to her lip. "Penelope Armytage's murder was premeditated," she said. "If Jayson killed her, he planned it in advance."

Riley tapped at her book. If Jayson had been out killing Penelope, would he really have needed a couple to spy on in a viewing room on the same night?

"But Jayson doesn't select the couples or the rooms," Patel said. "Karen put the couple in, not knowing he had other plans."

"Maybe." Riley's widened eyes led Patel to the next point—if the guests had also been at the Quirk for the weekend prior, Karen might have booked them in for Jayson's viewing pleasure as a prelude to Monday's murder.

"How many nights were they booked?" Patel said.

"Monday." Riley shook her head. "One night only."

Patel stared through the glass. "So, on the Monday night, there was one room booked at the Quirk, a couple having an affair. Of the eighteen rooms available, Karen booked them in number fourteen, one of only two rooms where they could be spied on. Same night, Penelope Armytage is strangled in an organized, meticulously planned killing. Therefore, we say Karen didn't know what her husband was up to and that Jayson acted alone."

"Or, the room selection means nothing," Riley said. "Other rooms needed cleaning from the weekend. Or Karen favors fourteen, it's her habit."

"Or dumb luck. Room fourteen is pure chance. We're extrapolating from coincidence."

A phrase looped in Riley's head: *Like an omen.* Another coincidence. Nigel Armytage had said it in the interview room and then, yesterday, Diana Bruce had repeated it to Patel and Bowman.

Things were winding up next door. Karen stood and tucked in her chair. Riley watched. She didn't like coincidence.

32

They came into Cessnock on a back road from the west with the sun in their eyes, Bowman beside Riley in the Calais. They passed a high school, empty on Saturday morning. The town seemed quiet after the weekend bustle of the vineyards, where tourists were on the move, *doing* brunch, sniffing cheese, preparing for weddings. Bowman watched the retail chains slide by: Supercheap Auto, Best & Less, Priceline, BWS. They passed a café where, after interviewing the ex-councillor Matthew Drummond, Bowman had bought neenish tarts for himself and Rachel. He'd known they were homemade because they overspilled their foil cases and looked like they'd been dropped on the floor.

"Where are we going?" he said.

"Cop's house," Riley said. "A local detective, Christian Rodrigues. His wife wants to meet you. And I want to meet his wife."

"Why?"

"She read your book." Riley glanced over to explain. "She's a teacher."

In Riley's worldview, only teachers read books—and maybe librarians. "Why do you want to meet her?" he asked.

"I dunno. Be polite. Show some interest."

"Bullshit," Bowman said.

"What?"

Riley didn't do Saturday-morning coffee with colleagues—or friends—and she most certainly didn't do brunch, unless she spied a

Macca's drive-through at elevenses. If she was taking him to a cop's house, there was a strategic reason for the visit.

"He your leak, this Rodrigues?" Bowman said.

"Don't think so. Don't know. He's plainclothes, never in uniform."

Bowman nodded: This Rodrigues wasn't the cop Drummond had seen sitting on his street. "So why do you want to meet his wife?"

Riley was following the GPS on the dash. She went left. "At the interviews yesterday, Rodrigues was in the room with the Cassidys. Oakeshott's name came up. There was a suggestion—just body language, really—that Oakeshott might have put the hard word on Karen when Jayson was away. It chimed with what you told me."

"That Oakeshott's sleazy."

"Right."

"And what, this Rodrigues didn't pursue it?"

"Yeah. But maybe because he didn't pick up on the nuance. Or even that I'm overthinking it and it wasn't there."

"What does Priya think?"

"She thinks it was there."

"Then it was there," Bowman said.

Riley wobbled her head. "It was microgestures, between man and wife. I'm not married, neither's Priya. Rodrigues is."

"Maybe he's good at ignoring his wife. I'd go with female intuition, every time."

She didn't answer, and Bowman stretched and rolled his neck to steal a glance. She was always in dialogue with herself, testing assumptions. Intelligence and talent were separate things, and Riley had both—and her talent for policing warned her that intelligence was not enough, that rational thought and logic often led cops to the shaded uplands of false dawns. When she explained this to Bowman, Riley liked to quote her mentor, O'Neil. Homicide left logic dying in the gutter. Logic and the extremes of human behavior did not go hand in hand. A true detective had to be able to accommodate that and think past it.

"Have you got an ulcer starting?" Bowman said.

Her tongue rippled her cheek. "Thanks for reminding me."

"It's that stage in the case?"

"Maybe."

"And now you want to meet this wife."

"Mm."

"Because if Oakeshott's corrupting cops, part of it might be supplying sex."

"Given what Drummond told you."

"And if this Rodrigues is knee deep in sex workers, then his wife will know and you'll pick it up via osmosis."

"Something like that."

"And what am I, a second opinion?"

"No, you're the celebrity author."

"So, a diversion?"

"Yeah . . . and a bit of a sheila. You've got your own intuition."

"What does Priya think?"

"Of Rodrigues? Good cop. She likes him. Solid."

"So that is why you brought me, see? You're second-guessing."

She slowed and went left. They were on the western edge of the town, a street of cottages on well-maintained blocks. Riley cruised down and pulled up across the road from the address, a white weatherboard. Next door was a construction site, with bunting strung around the block and three utes parked. On the footpath, in front of the builders' tape, a man with a spatula was cooking over a gas barbecue, and three younger workers were standing in a line, each holding a stubby of beer. It was not quite 11:00 a.m.

"Get a load of it," Bowman said.

Riley sat watching the fry-up.

Elevenses. "They're doing brunch," Bowman said.

Next door, a man appeared from down the side of the weatherboard in a blue shearer's undershirt, black shorts, football socks, and work boots. "That's Rodrigues," Riley said.

He'd been mowing the lawn. He saw the Calais and waved. Riley got out and crossed the road, and Bowman followed.

Rodrigues met them at his front gate. "Jesus." He shook his head at the scene on the footpath. "Give me a sec."

Bowman loitered as Rodrigues walked along to the barbecue, and the three beer drinkers looked him over. They were young, early twenties, dressed as laborers. "Fuckin' what's up your arse?" one of them said.

Riley had taken a few steps but hung back. There was a plastic table with a loaf of sliced Tip Top, a tub of Meadow Lea, and a brown bottle of sauce. The cook was frying pink sausages, bacon, and eggs. He was older than the others, fortyish, in a blue KingGee shirt with a thick, flat pencil in the pocket at his chest. There was a cooler on the ground, empty ice bags, a crushed carton of Great Northern.

"Fuck's sake, Wilso," Rodrigues said. "What are you doing?"

The cook half turned and waved his spatula over the construction zone. "Building a fuckin' house."

"You're drinking on a worksite," Rodrigues said. "On a footpath. At morning tea."

One of the young laborers put his beer down and adjusted his cap. "What are you, eh, fuckin' council?"

Rodrigues looked along the row at the three of them. One in an undershirt had a black eye. "What happened to your face, Zac?" Rodrigues said. "New tattoo?"

"Fuckin' you're a funny prick," Zac said.

Next to him, his mate in the cap lit a cigarette and pointed it at Riley. "Youse should show her your new tat but."

"Fuckin' a." Zac lifted his shirt and thrust his waist at Riley.

Bowman read the ink etched in a crescent across his torso: *No Fat Chick's.*

"Nice," Riley said. "Except you can't spell."

Zac let his shirt drop and leered at her. "Works heaps but, eh."

The man on the barbie was laying eggs and bacon on slices of bread and handing them out down the line. When each of the three younger blokes had a sandwich, he shooed them away. "Come back in five for a sausage," he said. "Now fuck off down the back and eat."

"Righto, fuckin' ease up, yeah?" said the one in the cap, reaching into the cooler for a six-pack. "We're goin', eh."

They trooped off and set up on milk crates on a corner of a concrete slab.

The cook went back to the grill and looked from Rodrigues to Riley. His spatula was a paint scraper. "You want a sanger?"

They shook their heads.

"So what, you're here to bust me for beer on a worksite? It's the only way I can get the mongrels to work."

"Pack it up." Rodrigues started to move away and pointed at the utes. "And make sure they don't drink and drive."

"Midstrength." The man toed the cooler. "Bricklayers drink that shit all day."

Rodrigues walked with Riley to his front gate, and she introduced Bowman. They shook hands. There was the smell of cut grass, and lawn clippings lay on the paving of the central front path.

In the yard next door, on the other side to the building site, an old woman in a yellow housedress stood at the low fence. She waved at Riley, then pointed behind her and spoke.

Riley stepped on the grass toward the woman. "Pardon?"

"I was saying he mows my lawn every time"—the woman pointed again—"and I don't even have to ask." Riley nodded and the old woman stared past her to Bowman. "Looks like two visitors."

"Looks like it," Rodrigues said. "Thanks, Nancy."

She stood her ground to watch.

Rodrigues corralled them down the path. The front door to his house opened, and a woman came out and stood at the porch rail.

"Bun in the oven, mind," Nancy said from the fence.

"Hi." The woman waved. "Come in."

Rodrigues nodded at Riley and Bowman. "Give me a tick. I'll get cleaned up."

Bowman followed Riley up the stairs to the porch, and the woman introduced herself as Fiona. They went into a hall strung with framed photographs and through a door, left, to a kitchen. There was a dining table down the room and a fireplace with charred logs, unlit, in a low grate.

"Sorry to barge in," Riley said.

"Not at all. I've been wanting to meet you. And the author." Fiona welcomed Bowman with a glance. "Have a seat."

They sat on either side of the table, and Fiona opened the fridge, poured milk into a pottery jug, and brought it over with four mismatching ceramic mugs. They didn't look like Diana Bruce's work. Fiona was slight and moved fast in an orange woolen cardigan and green cotton pants. She must have felt Riley's eyes on her, because she stopped and smoothed herself down. "Scuse the UGG boots."

"I'm jealous." Riley smiled.

There was a plunger of coffee on the counter. Fiona pushed the press, brought it across, then poured two mugs and placed the milk jug before Riley. "Sugar?"

"Two, thanks," she said, and Bowman declined. Riley poured milk for them both.

"See you met Nancy," Fiona said. "And the boys next door."

"You're surrounded," Riley said.

Fiona shook her head. "Christ knows how anything gets built. All they seem to do is drink beer and screech at each other about drugs. 'Baggie' this, 'baggie' that. 'You get your baggie? I got to get a baggie.'"

"You're a teacher?" Riley said.

"Yep." She poured herself a mug. "Kindy, thank God."

"No teenagers," Bowman said.

"That's it. Well, except the mums—half the mums are still kids."

They sipped.

Fiona's eyes danced, dark brown in her glowing face. "This little girl in the library yesterday, she says to me, *You look nice, you look like my nana*. I'm thinking, *Oh great, that's just wonderful*. Then it dawned on me."

"Nana's about twenty-nine," Riley said.

"Exactly."

"You're not from Cessnock?" Riley said.

"Nah. Brissie. Been here three years."

Bowman put his mug down. "How is it?"

"Insular." Fiona's bottom lip came out. "They're proud. Extremely territorial. They've always had the coalfields, I guess, to provide. They stay put, they get a trade, they marry their best friend's sister. That's the cycle. I prefer it, in a way."

"To what?" Riley said.

Fiona retied her dark hair. "To the wine crowd. I mean, not the producers—they're down to earth. But after that, wine—it attracts certain . . . types."

Riley notched her chin at Bowman. "Like him?"

Fiona chortled. "No. Not at all." She gave him a grin. "I loved your book, by the way. Being married to a cop, I mean, I found it, well . . . forceful yet ambiguous."

"Thank you." He raised his mug at Riley. "I didn't have much to work with."

Fiona laughed again. Rodrigues had come in and was listening. "I'm trying to get him to read it," she said.

"Feels a bit like work," he said. "No offense."

"Pfff." She looked at Riley. "You must be proud."

Riley blinked. "Of the book?"

"No. Well, yes. But of what you did."

She shrugged. "That's just the job." She nodded at Rodrigues. "Your husband does the same."

Fiona accepted this with a frown.

Rodrigues took a seat and poured himself coffee.

"Christian said you're expecting?" Riley said.

Fiona's hand went to her belly. "Fourteen weeks."

"Congratulations," Riley said.

"No kids for you?" Fiona's eyes flashed at Bowman. "From what I read."

"No," Riley said. "No kids."

A moment's silence.

Rodrigues shifted in his chair.

"Christian says you know Neville Oakeshott?" Riley said.

"Oh." Fiona's forehead creased. "Not really. My friend works for him."

Rodrigues had found something interesting in his fingernail.

"Awful man," Fiona said. "I know that."

"In what way?" Riley asked.

"Greedy, slimy, rude. Brought up in a house with no morals—that's what my friend says."

"Have you met him?" Riley said.

"Sort of, once. I went to a property launch at his restaurant. I was the plus-one for my friend."

"And you spoke with him?"

"He worked the whole room. We had a chat."

"And?"

Fiona scratched her scalp. "And nothing. My friend had worded me up. I was polite. He was oily. That was that."

"Did he know you're married to a cop?"

Fiona looked blank. "I doubt it. He didn't ask. I can ask my friend. Why?"

"What's your friend's name?"

"Helen Musgrave."

"Can I get her number?"

"Of course."

Riley had her notebook. Fiona reached for her phone. Rodrigues sipped his coffee while his wife read a number out and Riley wrote it down.

Fiona glanced between them. "Are you looking at Oakeshott, for this girl?"

"I haven't really discussed the case with Fiona," Rodrigues said.

"Of course," Riley said. "Oakeshott's not a suspect, but his name does come up. He's a person of interest. I knew you had some connection, that you'd been able to give Christian his number . . . so I thought I'd ask."

"Okay," Fiona said. "That's fine."

More silence. Riley sat back.

"I had lunch with Oakeshott too," Bowman said to Fiona. "In that restaurant."

"That didn't end well," Rodrigues said.

Fiona raised her eyebrows. "What happened?"

"I had a few glasses, got in the car. Cops pulled me over, DUI."

"Oh." She winced. "But see, that's what I mean with the wine types. Stupid big glasses, tiny white plates. Give me a break."

They talked for a few minutes more. Riley was ready to go, Bowman saw. Rodrigues got up and reached for the mugs and took them to the sink. Riley put her hands on the table, thanked Fiona, and stood. Bowman did the same, and Fiona shook his hand. "It was nice to meet you," she said.

They left her in the kitchen and went out and down the path with Rodrigues, and he crossed with them to the Calais. In the driver's seat, Riley lowered her window.

Rodrigues had his hand on the roof. "That was weird," he said, "but I'll cop it."

"Good," she said. "We'll talk."

The window went up and Riley pulled out. Rodrigues watched them drive off.

"By 'weird,' he meant . . . ?" Bowman said.

"That I came over for coffee and questioned his wife."

Bowman tugged at his seat belt.

She had her phone out, and he read a name on the display on the dash as she dialed. *Beth Gatjens.* "You're not here," Riley said to him as it rang on the Bluetooth.

"Rose," a woman answered.

"Beth, the wineglass you bagged on the Armytage counter—you got a brand?"

"One sec."

Bowman's pen was in his hand and his notebook in his lap. Riley idled at the end of the street. There was the sound of typing over the Bluetooth.

"One of those big diamond-shaped beakers," Gatjens said. "Wide bowl, tapered brim."

Bowman could see it—on white linen on the table at Oakeshott's restaurant.

"The shape is supposedly to enhance aroma," Gatjens said. "It never sat right with me."

"It's pretentious," Riley said. "But Penelope was in the industry."

"Yeah. Not that."

"Then?" Riley said.

"Not a print on it—completely clean."

"Out of the dishwasher?"

"Do you unload a dishwasher wearing gloves?"

Riley stared out the windshield.

"There was no other glass matching it in the house," Gatjens said. "It wasn't even a pair."

"Patel can call Nigel," Riley said. "Ask where it came from."

Gatjens didn't answer.

"What else?" Riley said.

"Nothing. Well—have a look at the scene photos, the glass on the counter before we bagged it . . ."

"You're saying it was staged?"

"I'm saying it niggled me, on the night."

Riley nibbled her lip. Bowman held his pen to an open page.

Keys were clacking on the Bluetooth. "Here we go," Gatjens said. "Brand stamped on the base."

"Mm," Riley said.

"Riedel."

33

Riley deposited Bowman at the pub, briefed Patel from the car on the Riedel glass, and called Gatjens back. The Crime Scene sergeant had more to discuss, and Riley didn't need Bowman listening. She was happy to feed him stuff, but at her pace—and not unfiltered.

"All right," Gatjens said. "Let's talk shoes."

Riley drove to the incident room as Gatjens went through the preliminary findings on the shoe impressions the Cassidys, the Bruces, Oakeshott, Red and Brad Lucas, and others had left in the sand at the Cessnock station. None of the soles matched the impression found in the Armytage hall. Gatjens made a further point: The shoe impressions from the Cassidys at the station were not from any of the pairs Riley and Patel had photographed at the couple's house.

"You're saying that with the Cassidys, I'm running out of shoes?" Riley said.

"Yes," Gatjens said, "and no. When you tossed the house, the Cassidys were out and wearing shoes. We've *probably* now printed those shoes, when we brought them to the station. Because the station shoes were separate to the pairs you saw at the house."

"Yeah, but?"

"It's not definitive. If Jayson's our guy, we know he's bringing things in."

Scissors, foam, crepe. "Backpack," Riley said.

"Exactly," Gatjens said. "Penelope is his third, that we know of. He's hyperorganized. There's a way to mirror that, to get in his head, even just a little. What's the most organized profession?"

"Surgeon?"

"No. But good guess. Aviator. There's a book I can give you, lays it all out. It's actually *written* by a surgeon."

"Mm."

"So, our boy, call him Jayson. He thinks like a pilot, he's running checklists. He'll have his uniform—practical, comfortable. It's camouflage, he can hide in plain sight. It might be a dark tracksuit, it might be hi-vis—but he's tested it, it works, it's not left to chance."

"Shoes are part of it," Riley said.

"Right. And afterwards, he packs it away. Uniform—check. Shoes—check. Tool kit—check."

"He keeps it together, like a grab bag."

"Exactly. He's bringing things in, so his tool kit is portable. Like you say, a backpack. And yes, his shoes might be in it."

"We flipped his house on the fly," Riley said. "We could have missed that."

"Sure, the house, the motel," Gatjens said. "Or the boot of his car."

Riley hung up and parked at the incident room as Rodrigues was arriving. They locked their cars, eyes averted.

"Thanks for coming by—and for bringing the writer," Rodrigues said. "Fiona got a real kick out of that."

"Pleasure."

They walked up the path, and he held the door. Riley saw he was going to let sleeping dogs lie and not raise her prodding of his wife, or mention Oakeshott.

Patel did it for him. "Nigel Armytage has never met Neville Oakeshott, and he never heard Penny mention him," she said while Riley and Rodrigues were still pulling out their chairs. "Nigel never dined at Oakeshott's winery, and he says he doesn't believe Penny did, either, in that she never mentioned it. They bought the town house through a sales manager at Oakeshott Construction. There was a gift hamper in the kitchen the day they moved in—it contained bottles of wine, condiments, all sorts of shit, but no glasses. That's the only gift associated with Oakeshott that Nigel is aware of."

"And?" Riley said.

"I sent him a picture of the wineglass forensics bagged in the house," she said. "He's never seen it before. But it didn't surprise him."

"Why?"

"Wine people fetishize glassware, it's a tool of the trade. Penny was into it, and she'd often mention names, including Riedel. There was another brand she preferred . . ." Patel looked at her notes. "Zalto. Nigel bought her six last year, for her birthday. Cost him four hundred bucks."

"If the Riedel glass doesn't surprise him," Riley said, "where does he think it came from?"

"He thinks Bob Bruce, or some industry type, gave it to Penny to trial. It's normal to have multiple large glasses around. They have different sizes and shapes for every different type of wine."

Riley counted on her fingers. "There's only red and white and . . . fizzy?"

"Mix them together," Rodrigues said, "you get rosé."

"And fizzy rosé," Patel said. "But Rose drinks that through a straw."

Riley left one finger up and gave it to Patel. "So we know—or Karen claims—that Oakeshott gave her a present of two Riedel glasses. And now we have a lone Riedel, on the counter, not a print on it, at the Armytage scene. And Nigel's never seen it in the house before."

"With Karen"—Rodrigues crossed his legs, as though to hide discomfort at his segue—"I was thinking about your point that on the Monday, the night Penelope is killed, there's one room booked at the Quirk, and Karen puts them in fourteen."

"The Volvo philanderers," Patel said.

"Right," he said. "And Karen picks that they're up for sex. So she puts them in that room to watch. But we're suggesting Jayson is too busy for that, he's out strangling Penny."

"Which suggests Karen is not part of it," Patel said. "She's unaware of Jayson's killing spree."

"Okay," Rodrigues said. "But there's a viewing platform in the roof—you saw Jayson access it one evening. He went into it, through the red door. There was nowhere else he could be going."

"In that, he knows about it. It's not something Karen has built on her own," Riley said.

"Correct," Rodrigues said. "It's shared. They both know about it. We say Karen is aware of it, in that she's booking the guests."

"She facilitates," Patel said.

"Correct," Rodrigues said. "Why?"

"She's getting off on it too," Patel said.

"Or?" he said.

Riley chewed on her pen. If Jayson Cassidy had killed three women, where did Karen fit?

"She's keeping the peace," Rodrigues said. "She knows of Jayson's predilection, she's lived with it for years."

"She knows it's not going to stop," Patel said.

"Exactly," Rodrigues said. "So, as you've thought, they build the Quirk around it. This keeps him contained, in house. He's not out at night, driving around the suburbs, perving in bedroom windows."

"And then, look at Karen at work," Patel said. "Her bearing, her manner. Efficient, organized."

"Corporate," Rodrigues said.

"You think she's done a deal?" Riley said. "With Jayson?"

"Could be," Patel said. "Why else would she put up with this lame shit from this creepy husband, help him spy on guests?"

"All right," Riley said. "So she knows about it, his dirty secret. She has this knowledge about Jayson. It gives her power."

"Bargaining power," Patel said.

"She clues in to Jayson's peeping and plays along," Rodrigues said. "What's the deal? What does she want for it?"

"Well, first—remember, she has a role in Jayson's transgressing," Patel said. "Choosing the guests."

Selecting. An idea crept up on Riley. How was access gained? Maybe Penelope Armytage hadn't answered the door to a man—and so she'd let her guard down.

"No forced entry, no sign of a struggle," Riley said. "What if Penelope answered the door to a woman?"

Patel was already there. "Karen makes the approach."

"Penelope knows her, asks her in," Rodrigues said.

"Here, yes," Riley said. "In Canberra and Adelaide, it's unlikely they knew Karen."

"She talks her way in," Rodrigues said.

"She assumes a role," Patel said. "Distressed female, perhaps. Jennifer Morrow and Gina Watson are good people. There's a woman on their doorstep. They offer to help."

"Okay," Riley said. "She herds them into the kitchen. Leaves the door open for Jayson."

"He attacks from behind, trusses them up," Rodrigues said.

"That's the deal," Patel said. "For all three, Karen's in control. It's her thing. She's lived with Jayson's peeping, and she's called in her debt."

Riley stared at her desk. Maybe it was true. Maybe Karen was the strangler. Jayson got to watch.

34

The rings of pineapple on Riley's Hawaiian parmigiana glowed canary yellow.

"Looks nice," Patel said.

The fruit was in perfect processed circles—straight from the can. Bowman peered at Riley's plate. "The cook's gone bananas on that pineapple," he said. "Wonder where he sourced it?"

Rodrigues had gone home. Patel and Bowman were eating a mixed grill with gravy—an off-menu special he'd charmed out of Sandra. After twelve days in her pub, he had won her over, and now he was wallowing in the spoils. There was a bottle of Robert the Bruce Shiraz at his elbow, deposited by the barman, Michael.

Bowman refilled the three of them. "On the phone, in the car, your colleague said the glass on the Armytage counter was a Riedel," he said to Riley. "I looked at the Oakeshott restaurant website. It talks a lot of shit, but it doesn't mention glassware."

"You didn't call and ask, I hope?" Patel said.

"No."

"At your lunch, they were using big glasses?" Riley said.

"Yeah. Like drinking out of a bucket."

She took out her phone and pulled up the crime scene photo of the lone glass on the Armytage counter. "Like that?"

Bowman studied it. "Similar, if not the same. You're on the right shelf."

Riley had her notebook open beside her. Fork in hand, she wrote, *Oakeshott Restaurant Glass Brand.* She stared at the page and thought about Rodrigues. In the incident room earlier, Patel had brought up Oakeshott, and Rodrigues had steered the conversation away, into theorizing about Karen.

The pub was busy with Saturday-evening trade, mainly tourists tipsy from rounds of cellar doors. Sandra had put Bowman and the detectives on a table in a quiet corner of the dining area, out of the way. Rachel and two other young servers in white Packhorse polos were working the floor, back and forth through the kitchen swing door. Riley counted eleven tables of diners, and small groups of drinkers were clustered through the saloon. The grower Red Lucas was in with two other locals, the three of them standing at their favored raised round table near the bar. But no Bob Bruce . . . Of the winemaker, there was no sign.

Bowman swigged, following her gaze. "That's Vat and Bore Drain with Red," he said. "In that order."

Riley watched them. All nicknames. Local knowledge. She thought about how much she didn't know. "Why Bore Drain?" she said.

"Hate to think." Bowman frowned. "But it gets shortened."

"To Bore?" Patel said.

"No, actually. To Drain."

"How's it goin', Drain?" Patel said.

"That's it. Good, eh? Vernacular Australian poetics."

Patel spooned more gravy from its boat.

Riley was looking at Red, who now owned her family farm. "You ever see Dew in here?" she said to Bowman.

"Nup. He's banned."

"Why?"

"Came in pissed on a meth binge and tore the place up, screaming about his father. Not pretty."

"They call the cops?"

"Apparently not. Michael was on. He shut it down."

Riley cut into her chicken. A drunk male on meth was a nightmare to contain. "How'd he do that?"

"Calm and fast with a baseball bat, is what I hear. Took Dew out at the knees, trussed him up, and threw him out the door with his hands still tied to his ankles. Told him if he came back, it was the cops."

"Did Michael tell you that?"

"No. Rachel told me, then old mate Drain filled me in. When Red wasn't around to hear it."

Sandra was behind the bar. Michael was out swooping tables, collecting empty glasses in a tower. He glided on his heavy frame, carrying his weight with ease, eyes hooded in his meaty face. Riley watched him. As he moved, a slight tension stiffened his gait—he knew she was observing him.

"You know Drain's punch line about the Dew imbroglio?" Bowman said. "Michael brings him down, throws him out, and . . ."

Michael circled a table, light catching the perspiration on his brow.

"He doesn't crack a sweat," Riley said.

"Correct."

They finished eating, and Bowman pushed his plate away and headed to the toilets. Patel stood, too, and followed.

Riley sat with her back against the wall. She could see the whole room: Two couples were splitting their bill, another group of four was leaving. The swing door to the kitchen was flapping, the servers on the move.

She took her pen and thought about Gatjens' organized aviator and ran through checklists in her head. The analysts weren't helping Riley's ulcer. They were coming up short: There was no whisper of the Cassidys in Adelaide or Canberra, and no evidence to put Bob Bruce back in either city on the dates. Rodrigues was applying for a Supreme Court warrant requesting the Cassidys' and Bob Bruce's phone records going back four years. Flicking through her notebook, Riley stopped on a page labeled BOB BRUCE and scanned it. Under a subheading, FORENSICS, she had written: *First Aid Kit: Substrates.*

Her pen hovered. They could execute their existing Bruce warrant on the quiet and have a look at the first aid kit in his wine shed. If there were bandages or foam, the lab could try to match them with the sheared fibers found at the Armytage and Morrow scenes.

On the page, her hand went still. There was a presence to her right, and she looked up from her jottings. Michael stood at her shoulder. His eyes were on her notebook, and she flipped it closed.

He'd brought the laminated wine list and held it out to her.

Riley's heart rate had pumped up, and she was holding her breath. She hadn't sensed his approach—he'd come in hugging the wall to her side. Strange. The radar around her physical space was ultra-fine-tuned and always spinning: Had the big man fluked his way under it, or was he able to move with stealth?

He bent to put the laminated list on the table. His forehead glistened in the light. "Did you, um, want some wine?"

Riley blinked, breathing. Bowman emerged from the toilets and was headed to the bar.

"He can order." Riley pointed Michael to Bowman. "Put it on my tab."

Patel returned. Michael acknowledged her and left the wine list on the table. It was after eight, and the room was thinning out.

"What do you make of him?" Riley said.

Patel sat and studied Michael's departing back. "Quiet, but self-assured. Capable."

"He just snuck up on me."

"Bowman said ex-army. Grew up in Singleton. With Jayson Cassidy."

Riley nodded. "Military families."

"Michael followed his father," Patel said. "Jayson deviated."

Rachel was dumping dirty glasses on the bar. Michael swung in close and said something, and she made a face for him as he passed.

Bowman came back with a fresh bottle and poured for the three of them.

Rachel had slipped behind the counter and was racking glasses. Michael worked beside her, bumping shoulders.

Riley motioned toward the bar with her wine. "He pesters the girl?"

Bowman sipped, watching, and spoke into his glass. "You could say that."

"She's been driving you around," Riley said. "Has she said anything?"

"No. She's a good kid. Fun, credulous. She treats him well. But that's how she treats everyone."

"And he misconstrues the dynamic?" Patel said.

Bowman swayed. "Maybe."

Michael was drying glasses. Riley pictured him at the bar a few days back, in conference with Bob Bruce, their heads almost touching, moistly, as they whispered.

"You said Michael did some work for Jayson Cassidy, down at the Quirk?" Riley said.

"Yeah, some Oakeshott building fuckup. In the roof. The air-conditioning. Michael had to run the ducting."

35

In her room at the Quirk, Riley took off her Glock and emptied her pockets. She poured a bourbon and picked up Projects's door chock from among the minibar bottles where she'd stowed it. The wood was furry where it had been cut against the grain, and she held it to her nose and breathed deep. Spliced timber.

The smell summoned a memory. She was maybe six years old, on the swing out back behind the farmhouse, trying to keep time with the rhythm of her father at the woodpile with the axe. The white swing rope rough in her hand, her father had gone still, and then the warning tone under his vowels as he called for her mother without taking his eyes off the ground. Her mother heard it too. She was out of the kitchen without the screen door banging and her arms under Riley from behind, grabbing her up and off the swing. Riley held on to the rope with one hand, her mother's no-nonsense fingers broke the grip, warm breath in her ear. Riley's eyes didn't move off her father's shoulders as she was pulled away in her mother's arms. That was all she remembered. The rest she knew as a family story, recounted later—an eastern brown in the woodpile, her mother had taken the shotgun and gone back out to end the standoff with one blast.

Riley took a sip of bourbon and swilled the spirit around the ulcer on her lower gum. Bowman was right—it was that time in the case, too long on the road and her body protesting her diet. His knowledge of her was molecular, gleaned from listening and watching. She recalled him at the pub just now, in a dark-chocolate heavy-cotton quarter zip, demure for his current wardrobe standards. The sweater suited him, she thought, its embossed Longhorn logo also reminiscent of her father.

She sipped again. Across the room, the doors to the deck were locked and bolted from inside. There was no key and no access from outside if the doors were secured. Riley pushed the sofa up against them anyway and scanned the ceiling. There were no vents, no trapdoors, no hint of any incision. She walked to the main door and jammed Projects's wedge back into the gap above the sill. Across the corridor, she knew Patel would do the same. It wasn't perfect, but it would buy them time if anyone came calling.

In bed, she drifted for hours and then fell into deep sleep. In a dream she saw a brown snake slither in the rafters with the Cassidys in their secret chamber. She saw her father, by the woodpile with Bowman, and then other faces—Red Lucas and Dew at the farm. Red was remonstrating, and Dew came forward to whisper in his ear and quieten him.

She woke, overheated under the quilt, and checked the time, 6:41 a.m., as she propped on an elbow to gulp water.

The dream was gone, but the image of Dew Lucas was still with her. Rodrigues's voice on the Bluetooth: *Dew is Bradley John Lucas, thirty-eight.*

Brad Lucas.

Raised at Rothbury . . .

Riley knew him. She'd seen him in Bob Bruce's wine shed and then on the farm with Red. But she knew him from before. He'd had the life sucked out of him, but she saw it now, in his jaw and his nose.

Sheet stretches back to when he's thirteen. Arson, theft, truancy, possessing a drug of dependence.

She knew him from before all that. Brad Lucas. She put the water down.

Riley had gone to school with Brad Lucas, from Kindy to Year 4. Brad Lucas was her friend.

He'd seen it too. He'd known her when he saw her in the shed, and on the farm, he'd whispered it in his father's ear to calm the bastard down. She could guess now what must have been said: *She's a Riley. That's my little friend, Rose Riley. This used to be her land.*

Riley could see his face, his knees, the way he moved, his silhouette—as a little boy, he'd burned so bright.

She kicked off the quilt and went into the bathroom. She sat on the loo for a while, thinking, then flushed and stripped and turned on the shower. Under the hot jet, she squinted to read the labels on the small bottles. She squirted out body wash and rubbed it all over and then wet her hair and found the shampoo. She rubbed it in, then rinsed and reached for the conditioner, squeezing and shaking the mini bottle to dispense the thick liquid.

Riley rinsed again and stepped out and dried herself, wrapping a second towel in her hair. She caught a glimpse of herself in the steamed mirror, swathed in white, and her mind jumped back—to the Armytage scene . . . forensic investigators clad in white Tyvek in the town house. Her brain didn't quite click, dissatisfied with the recollection, there was something more . . . She looked from the mirror to the crumpled tan bottle of conditioner on the shelf in the shower.

The Armytage's bathroom cabinet, the drawers.

Riley went to the Nespresso and slotted in a pod. Bowman had been there with her a few days later, at the Armytage scene . . . *Thrifty disposition* . . . She opened her laptop on the counter and pulled up the Red Creek file, scrolling to find the pictures she'd taken in Penelope Armytage's bathroom, zooming in on the contents of a vanity drawer. Bulk buys of supermarket toiletries: razor blades, shaving cream, toothpaste, shampoo, conditioner, deodorant.

That wasn't it.

She reached for the coffee, drank it black. Fuck Karen and her long-life milk.

Low overheads, fewer staff . . .

Thrifty.

Karen's house? Riley went back to her laptop and looked at the pictures she'd taken in the spare bathroom in the Cassidy place: the soap, body wash, shampoo, and conditioner were all in the same bottles Riley had just used in the shower. She stared at the picture of the little tan bottles. Everything in the house came from the Quirk.

So what?

Her mind was telling her something was there, ready to click. She retraced her steps to the bathroom, still in her towel turban, peered in the mirror, looked around. Mini bottles, a surplus soap, wrapped in tan, on the sink.

Back at the Nespresso, she ejected the pod and slotted in another. She bent for the fridge and took out a mini box of UHT. She pressed the button for a second coffee, Bowman in her mind again . . . sitting with Fiona Rodrigues in her kitchen. Fiona speaking to Riley: *No kids for you? From what I read.*

Bowman's book had made that clear: No kids for Riley.

She speared the straw in the box and squirted the milk . . . Another kitchen. A mother nursing her infant. Baby paraphernalia drying in a rack by the sink. Bottles, nipples, pacifiers.

Another book. *Baby Love.*

Dick Laver in the Morrow house in Ngunnawal.

At the laptop, she pulled up the crime scene images of the drawers from the Morrow bathroom. She pinched in on the mini shampoos and soaps taken from hotels. There they were in muted pinks and blues. Not tan, not the Quirk.

So what?

Drawers. Bathroom drawers. The Watson house in Adelaide, Gordon Ross had shown them the crime scene photos. Riley pulled up the pictures she had taken of those photos. Ross had focused on the scissors in a kitchen drawer . . . Riley looked at that image and kept scrolling. Bathroom drawers.

The Watson vanity. She peered at the pictures. She'd noted them at the time, the contents of the cabinets and the drawers—noted that they were different from the rest: no stockpiling of toiletries.

Her hand stilled on the laptop, and then her fingers pinched out on the pad to zoom.

There it was: a mini square bottle in dull green.

In her mind, the click was physical.

Riley toggled between the two images on the MacBook. There were five of the mini bottles in the Morrow house, two pink and three blue. There was only one at the Watson scene—the sage green. The colors were in a uniform faded palette. And each bottle was the same square shape. Not similar: identical.

She pinched to read the brand. Apple Blossom Apothecary.

It was made in Australia, she could make out an address in Marrickville. It was enough—from the manufacturer, they could find the suppliers to track where the product was stocked.

She sat back, her scalp prickling, tingling down her neck to her shoulders. It was the link, the one thing that connected the victims.

Riley pulled the wedge from under the door and went out into the corridor and knocked at Patel's room. After twenty seconds she knocked again, and, hair tangled, Patel opened up.

"It's a hotel," Riley said. "Where they're being chosen. I think we can find it."

36

Patel gathered her laptop and phone and crossed into Riley's room. She was groggy with sleep and sluggish grasping details.

Riley started dressing, and explaining. "Gina Watson and Jennifer Morrow had the same brand of mini toiletries in their bathroom drawers. They stayed at the same hotel—I don't know, months apart? They each took shampoo or some lotion with them."

Patel pulled back her hair.

"It can't be the Quirk, because it wasn't built yet," Riley said, and turned her screen to show Patel the image of a mini square blue bottle in Jennifer Morrow's drawer. "But both women have stayed somewhere stocking this brand."

"The Cassidy hotel in Newcastle?" Patel said.

Riley had thought the same. Patel was waking up.

"Or"—Patel padded to the bathroom sink and washed her face—"could be an airline. An amenity kit from a plane."

True. There were options. So, start with the manufacturer and work out.

Riley made Patel a coffee from the Nespresso, and the two of them sat at the built-in counter in the room. They called Gatjens, Rodrigues, Laver in Canberra, Ross in Adelaide, the three analysts working the case.

The website for Apple Blossom Apothecary listed the office hours as nine till four, Monday to Friday. It was 7:47 a.m., Sunday, and the contact number from the page was ringing out. Riley hung up. She still had the towel wrapped around her hair.

Patel was in striped flannel pajamas. She hung up her own phone. "Marrickville cops are sending a car round. They know the building, it's an old factory. They'll see if there's any movement, or if they can get an after-hours number from the neighbors."

At 8:49 a.m. Riley's phone rang: Dick Laver in Canberra, calling from his car. "Okay, this apothecary," he said. "We got a hit."

Riley put him on speaker.

"My analyst got one of their suppliers through Instagram," Laver said. "The supplier gave her a mobile for the main sales rep at Apple Blossom. I just spoke to the rep. They're small, mainly retail. They sell through niche shops, day spas—and twenty-three hotels."

"Anything in Newcastle?" Riley said. "Going back three years."

"Negative. As in, never. Nothing in Newcastle. And the name *Cassidy* doesn't register."

"Twenty-three hotels?" Riley said.

"Yeah, I just emailed you the list."

She saw it in her inbox and opened it. She read it with Patel at her shoulder. Nothing in Pokolbin or the Hunter. Nothing in Adelaide or Canberra.

Nothing jumping out. Patel exhaled and straightened.

"One thing sticks out—for me," Laver said.

Riley was forwarding the list to everyone. "Yeah?"

"There's a group on the list, three motels," Laver said. "Right at the top. Aurora."

Riley saw it.

"They're a loose little franchise chain. Each property runs their own race, but there's a silent partner who owns it overall. I just spoke to him."

"Aurora?" Riley said.

"Aurora Katoomba, Aurora Daylesford." Laver paused. "Aurora Murrumbateman."

Riley's eyes met Patel's. "Murrumbateman?"

"Thirty-five kays north of me here," he said. "It's the heart of the Canberra wine district. I'm en route."

Riley stood at the counter. "Booking records for the victims?"

"The Murrumbateman manager is coming in from home. I'll meet him on-site."

"Staff lists?"

"He'll collate employment records, plus all guest bookings. Going back three years."

"We'll disseminate to Adelaide," Riley said.

"I'll call Andrew Morrow," Laver said.

Riley hung up. Patel went out to shower. Riley finished dressing, packed her laptop and her notebook, clipped on her Glock.

Patel was ready fast. Karen was at reception, guests were checking out. Patel rode with Riley in the Calais. They parked and were entering the incident room when Laver called back. She put it on speaker.

"Aurora Murrumbateman's got booking records under both names," he said. "Watson and Morrow."

Riley stopped, stared without seeing, her hand went to her scalp. *Sweet Holy Jesus Christ.* She swallowed, made it to her desk, dropped her bag.

"Jennifer Morrow stayed in June last year," Laver said. "The Watsons, the October before that."

"Staff?" Riley said. "Employed at both dates?"

"I've got an employment list going back four years. There are twenty-eight names—casuals, dishwashers, gardeners, the whole show. The manager thinks it's definitive, from the payroll. There are eleven names in bold, staff who were employed last June back to the previous October."

Riley sat.

"The names—nothing pings for me here," Laver said. "I've sent the lists through." He hung up.

Riley hadn't noted Rodrigues at his desk, but he stood now and joined Patel at Riley's shoulder as she opened her laptop and clicked on the email. The three of them bent toward the screen and looked down at the names in bold. Nothing jagged. Riley scrolled up and went down it again. "Anyone?" she asked.

"No," Patel said.

Riley half turned to Rodrigues.

He was biting his lip. "No."

She went to the top of the complete list and slowly scrolled down. It was alphabetical. Rodrigues and Patel were on either side of her, both very close, cheeks almost touching.

Patel's breath caught, and Riley saw it.

The third name from the end. Not in bold.

Michael Sharp.

37

Michael Sharp's record was clean. He had a vehicle registered to a street address in Singleton.

"It's his mother's house," Rodrigues said. "He uses it for documents, when he needs to list an address."

"You don't think he's living there?" Riley said.

Rodrigues's head wobbled. "We know he's moved around. *Maybe* he went home to Mum. But I doubt it."

"Can we see his army file?" Patel asked.

"I can have a warrant in an hour," Rodrigues said. "But rousing the ADF on a Sunday—that'll take time."

"He could be living back in Singleton," Patel said. "What's the commute?"

"To the Packhorse?" Rodrigues shrugged. "Half an hour."

"Sandra will know where he resides," Riley said.

Rodrigues pointed at his phone. "You want me to call?"

She clicked her tongue. It would be better to come at him very quietly. Sandra might be standing next to him right now. "I don't want him getting wind of us," she said.

Patel tapped at her keyboard. "Packhorse opens at midday on Sunday. Or so it says."

Riley looked at the time. It had just gone 10:00 a.m. She called Bowman.

"Morning," he said.

"Where are you?"

"Confined to barracks. Having, um—brunch."

"In the pub?"

"Yeah."

"Is anyone with you?"

"No."

"Can you talk with no one listening or seeing you? Including staff?"

There was a pause. "One sec. Yeah."

"Which staff are there?"

"Rachel. And a chef?"

"The barman, Michael?"

"Not yet."

"Is he on today?"

"Probably. Sundays are busy. I can ask Rachel?"

She thought about it, one eye closed. "No."

"I know he has Mondays off—'cos, you know, that's a night Rachel locks up."

Riley nodded. Michael hadn't worked the Monday Penelope was killed.

"I first arrived on Tuesday," Bowman was saying, "and he was behind the bar . . . so Wednesday, I reckon—"

"What time would he clock on, if he's working?"

"Not sure." She felt his shrug down the line. "I can check."

"No." She put her hand out. "Listen, just act normal. I know, that's an ask. This call never happened. Don't say a word. Maybe go sit in your room."

"You could knock on *his* room."

Her hand gripped her hair. "What?"

"Christ, sometimes, with you, I swear—it's like dealing with an imbecile." Bowman was eating something, having brunch in her ear. "He lives here. Michael. Out back."

In the Calais, Riley came down the Packhorse driveway with Patel beside her and Rodrigues in the rear. She pulled up on the driver's side of Bowman's car, and Rachel opened the window of the Audi. Bowman was in the front passenger seat. As instructed, Rachel had the engine running.

Riley nodded at the girl. "No word from Sandra?"

Rachel shook her head. Riley had asked her to call and text her boss, but Sandra hadn't picked up or returned the message.

"Typically, when you text, is she quick to respond?"

"Depends." The girl puckered her nose. "She might be in the shower?"

Riley tried to see in the rear of the Audi. "Who you got there, just the chef?"

"Yes. Just Kenny."

"And there's no one in the saloon?" Riley said.

"No. The overnight guests checked out at nine. Sandra's around, in her flat, I guess. And Michael."

Riley had instructed Rachel not to go looking for Sandra through the building. Michael Sharp had military training, he was big and light on his feet, good with a baseball bat. He wasn't a registered gun owner, but that didn't mean shit.

"Have you ever heard Michael talk about guns?" Riley said.

Rachel's bottom lip pushed out as she frowned. "No. Never."

Riley scanned the pub facade through the windshield for CCTV. At least one camera on the door.

If Sharp was keeping watch, he would be used to seeing Riley and Patel turn up in their vehicles in the morning to meet Bowman—they'd done it at least three times in the past week. If he had been paying attention, he would have seen Rachel in Bowman's car over the past few days. But not the chef. If Sharp was watching now, he'd know something was up.

Fifteen minutes ago, in the incident room, Rodrigues had called Tactical in Cessnock. Riley looked at him in her rearview mirror.

"Seven minutes out," he said.

She stared ahead, adrenaline coursing.

"I say we wait," Rodrigues said.

"Tactical pull up here, we lose surprise," Riley said. She didn't want Sharp cornered, taking Sandra hostage, deciding to shoot his way out.

"They'll bring one vehicle down the drive," Rodrigues said. "Five men, slide in quiet."

Riley looked across to Rachel. "The building layout, Michael's room—can you describe it?"

Patel and Rodrigues leaned in and listened as the girl described the pub. Directly across the saloon from the entrance was a door into an internal passage that led through the original stone inn and out to a rear foyer with a staircase up to the guest rooms. "Don't take the stairs," Rachel said. "There's a door on the left that leads out to an extension. It's single story. There's a hallway. Michael is second door on the left."

"And Sandra?" Patel said.

"She's in a separate outbuilding. In the hall, you take the first door to the right to a courtyard. Diagonally across, there's a black door in a sandstone wall. That's her, in the stables."

Bowman bent forward to speak around Rachel. "If Michael's not in his room, he might be in the cellar. He's often down there."

Rachel nodded. "The door is third right off the inner passage, from the saloon."

"And"—Bowman pointed—"there's a cellar hatch beside the building, along the side. Trucks unload kegs straight down. It's an exit."

"All right," Riley said. "You head up to the main road. There's gonna be cops there in five. You stay behind them." She waved them off and edged the Calais up to the pub wall, into a blind spot from the CCTV. They were already in ballistic vests.

Rodrigues called the Tactical sergeant and briefed him on the pub layout. He hung up and reached for his door handle. "Here we go."

Riley adjusted her mirror and watched an unmarked black Land Cruiser turn into the car park and pull up beside them. She got out with Patel and Rodrigues as a sergeant and four constables unloaded in full kit and headed straight to the pub door. Rachel had unlocked it, and Michael hadn't been down to secure it. The sergeant pushed it open, and the constables went in and fanned out, called, "Clear," and the sergeant waved the detectives in and they crossed the saloon and waited as the sergeant sent his constables through the door into the stone passage.

Riley followed last, blinking in the gloom. It was damp and cold, and a phrase looped in her brain. *He's tall, he's fast, he's strong.* Dick Laver had said it, in Canberra. She kept her back to the passage wall in a sideways stance, her rear always visible. There were nooks off the passage as they moved along—a scullery, Riley guessed, a coal closet.

At a third door, access to the cellar, the sergeant stopped and raised a fist, and a constable edged over, tried the handle, and went through with a second constable, followed by Rodrigues with both hands on his Glock.

The sergeant and two remaining constables kept moving, and Patel followed. At the rear, Riley thought of Michael Sharp standing over her at the table yesterday. He'd come from nowhere. Her notebook had been open, and he'd seen them, the dot points: *Adelaide, Canberra.* Riley had spread it out for him, shown him they'd connected the series.

She was worried about Sandra. If Michael knew he was done, he'd be capable of anything.

They came out of the passage to a landing and went around the foot of a staircase and through a door into a long timber hall. The sergeant moved to the second door on the right, and the constables took up position. Riley noted their hardware: a Colt M4, a Heckler & Koch. The sergeant was old-school, with a tactical shotgun.

Patel and Riley hung back as the sergeant tried the handle. It gave and the constables fanned in with the sergeant close behind, his shotgun at high ready.

"Police." The sergeant's voice boomed in the small space. "Stay down."

Riley entered.

Michael Sharp was sitting on a single bed in a white undershirt and gray tracksuit pants, bare feet on the floor. His face was calm as he took in the raid, his eyes tracking over the assault rifles trained on him and coming to rest on Riley.

The sergeant jerked his shotgun. "On the floor, slowly. Face down. Hands where I can see them."

Sharp was still, only his eyes moved—from Riley to Patel. His arms were by his sides, fists balled on the bed.

The sergeant spoke again. "Now. On the floor."

His Adam's apple bobbed. He pushed off the bed, raising his hands as he knelt on the floor. There was a funk off him. Riley breathed through her teeth.

"Hands behind your head," the sergeant said, "and lie down."

Sharp complied and a constable moved on him, the sergeant repeating instructions along the snub barrel of his shotgun. "Easy . . . Stay down . . . Don't move . . ."

The constable went in with a knee to the back, dragging the wrists down and cuffing them. He rolled Sharp onto his side, patting him down. Nothing on his person. The constable stood.

Silence. Sordid air. Sharp lay trussed, his hairy, pale belly exposed. An eye on Riley.

Sexual homicide: Yes, there were patterns—it was always the same when you caught them, stunted men in stained tracksuits.

"Get him up," she said.

38

The car park was flashing red and blue when they brought Sharp out. Patrol cars, a Crime Scene Sprinter van, unmarked Kias, an emergency ambulance. No press that Riley could see, no Laura Nolan—yet. Bowman's Audi was in the middle of the melee, and he lounged on the hood, arms and ankles crossed, notebook drooping at his rib cage, pincered by a forefinger and thumb.

A Tactical constable handed Sharp off to two local detectives, and one pushed his head down to get him in the back seat of a Sorrento and slammed the door.

Bowman's limbs untangled to jot a note.

Patel was in the saloon, talking with Sandra. The licensee had been in her flat, just out of the shower, when they knocked.

Gatjens was directing her section from the back of the Sprinter. Crime Scene would go through Sharp's room, the cellar, his Nissan, parked in a lean-to around the back of the pub. A forensic investigator came out of the main entrance carrying Sharp's laptop in a bag. Rodrigues had secured a warrant to upend every corner of the barman's life.

He was arrested on suspicion of murdering Jennifer Morrow, Gina Watson, and Penelope Armytage, but had not yet been charged. He wore a size 11 shoe. The magistrate had granted an extension on the time they could detain him—with the usual tricks and tactics, Riley could hold him fifteen hours without charge.

She looked at her watch: 11:33 a.m.

A patrol car cruised in and stopped, and Harris got out and came over. "Having fun yet?"

"Maybe," Riley said.

He twitched his chin toward Bowman. "You want me to move him back?"

"Nah. He gave us a hand earlier. He knows the rules."

Harris scowled. "Must be Sydney rules. He comes up here, goes DUI. No respect. Mate of yours, too, I'm told."

"Who told you that?" Riley said. "Neville Oakeshott?"

Surprise flicked his face.

A white Mitsubishi had pulled up, and Nolan was steaming over with a snapper in tow. They'd driven straight in—there was no perimeter in place.

Harris saw Nolan but was slow to react, leaving it to Riley to raise her hand. Nolan kept coming. "No comment," Riley said.

Nolan was up close, with her phone in Riley's face. "You've arrested a Packhorse employee. On what charges?"

"Back up," Harris said.

"Don't fucking touch me." Nolan lashed him with a look.

Patel emerged through the saloon door and approached. The photographer had stopped and was shooting.

"C'mon." The journo was back in Riley's face. "Just a line."

"I'm not doing this now," Riley said.

Nolan's nostrils flared. "We've got pics, so I'm filing. You give me facts, or I speculate."

Riley ignored her, half turned to go.

"Penelope Armytage," Nolan said. "I hear she was a tease."

Riley swung back, stung by the word. Bob Bruce had used it to describe Penny. *She was teasing.* "Off the record, be careful," she said. "You fuck my case, I'll come after you. And so will the judge."

Nolan showed her teeth. "It's not before a court."

Patel was beside Riley and touched her arm: *Easy.*

Nolan looked them up and down, and called to her photographer, "Get 'em both."

He pointed his big lens at the detectives and the camera whirred.

Nolan fluttered sad eyes at Patel. "That'll look good. Homicide, on the beat."

Harris seemed cowed by Nolan's bristle. Riley jerked her head. "Can you move them back? And tape it off."

He herded Nolan and the photographer, pushing them across the car park.

"She's milking Bruce," Riley said. "Got him talking."

Patel nodded. "Something going with Harris too."

At the Mitsubishi, Nolan was remonstrating with Harris while gesticulating toward Bowman—still leaning, arms crossed, on his Audi, enjoying the show.

Rodrigues had come over to stand between Riley and Patel. "You know yesterday, after you came to my house with the journo and questioned my wife?"

Riley faced him.

"I'd been meaning to tell you, but then this took off." He hoisted a thumb at the pub.

Riley's head angled.

"The Bowman DUI," he said. "And Oakeshott. I had a look."

"And?"

"The arrest was standard—radio dispatch, Highway Patrol, RBT. The only query was around the original tip-off. It's not on the log. My question to the supervisor was, *Did Neville Oakeshott call it in?*"

"And?"

"No," Rodrigues said. "The call was internal."

Riley's eyes went to Nolan and the senior sergeant at the Mitsubishi.

"Harris," Rodrigues said.

Michael Sharp didn't have a lawyer and declined the offer of Legal Aid. At the Cessnock station, they put him in the interview room they'd used for the Cassidys and Nigel Armytage. The clock was ticking with Sharp, and Riley felt it. No lawyer meant she could play a little loose with time . . . but she had fourteen hours to crack him, give or take.

At the pub, Gatjens had unearthed no portable tool kit, no shoes to match the sole impression, no gauze or foam. No trophies. No lawyer? Riley wondered what that meant. She watched him through the one-way glass. He sat still, eyes on the table.

Gatjens had bagged a pair of scissors from Sandra's alcove office behind the bar. But they'd looked at home among the pens and sticky tape and paper clips, and Sandra had never noticed them go missing. Gatjens had sent them to the lab, priority one.

Rodrigues was down the hall, in the detective's room, chasing Sharp's military records.

Next to Riley, Patel stood and slid a selection of crime scene pictures into a manila folder, and they went out and into the interview room. Sharp watched in silence as they entered. Patel put the manila folder on the desk under her notepad and went through the preliminaries for the tape: names, time, date. "Mr. Sharp," she said, "is there anything you want to tell us?"

"'Bout what?"

"About why you've been arrested. These are very serious crimes."

"On suspicion of."

"Yes," Patel said. "Did you commit those crimes?"

His head tilted with surprise. "'Course not. You said three names. I only ever heard one."

"Which one was that?" Patel said.

His hands opened. "The . . . Penelope Armytage," he said.

He was too calm. Patel sat back for Riley.

"Mr. Sharp," Riley said. "Michael. Why do you think you're here?"

He splayed his hands again. "You're pulling people in for a chat. Red and that—and Sandra."

Riley put an elbow on the table. The back of her fingers rubbed her lips. After a moment, she dropped her hand. "We asked some people to come in, yes. You think that's what this is, your turn?"

His frown deepened into perplexion. "What else?"

Silence. He was good, but he had to be playing dumb.

He waited for them, expectant.

Riley felt a twinge. The notion that they were asking locals in by arresting them with tactical-unit heavy weaponry was so absurd, you couldn't make it up. But maybe he believed it.

"We didn't *arrest* Sandra and tape the pub closed when we asked her in," Riley said.

Sharp nodded.

"We called Sandra on the phone, and she drove into town," Riley said. "With you, this is very different. You know that."

He sniffed.

More silence. Riley let it brew.

Sharp shifted slightly . . . "You saw my discharge."

"What did I see on your discharge?"

"He didn't press charges, the corporal. 'Cos he knew, like, he deserved it."

"What did he deserve?" Riley said.

"What he got. He started it. Well, so—I finished it."

Riley took her phone and texted Rodrigues. **Any luck?**

"Mr. Sharp," Patel said, "how long have you lived in that room—at the pub?"

"Few months."

"And you knew Penelope Armytage?" Patel said.

"Only to look at."

She paused for Riley, who said, "Did you like looking at her?"

His eyes skidded between them. "Not like that."

"Like what?" Riley said.

"Like"—lines crinkled his damp brow—"staring."

"You were her neighbor," Riley said. "Have you ever been in her house?"

His head went back, slowly. "No." He drew the word out in disbelief.

"On the Monday, August twenty-fifth, when Penelope Armytage died," Riley said, "where were you that evening, from, say, four p.m.?"

"In my room."

"In your room at the Packhorse?" Patel said. "You weren't working?"

"No. Monday's off."

"Was anybody with you?" Patel said.

"No."

"Did anybody see you?"

"No."

"Are you sure?" Patel said. "You seem certain. No one can vouch for you . . . ?"

He shrugged. "I remember it. It wasn't a normal night—like after, the next day. The night was normal, for me. Me night's off, if I stay in, I don't see no one, normally."

"What did you eat?" Riley said.

"Bacon 'n' eggs. 'N' toast."

"From the pub kitchen?" Riley said. "The chef?"

"No. There's like a galley. In the staff lodgings."

Riley had seen a kitchenette at the end of the hall from Sharp's room. There were showers down there, too, and toilets. "Do other staff live on-site?" she said.

"Nah. Well . . . Sandra. But she's got her flat."

Riley's phone pinged. A text from Rodrigues. **Come out.**

In a rec room in a barracks at Puckapunyal, Lance Corporal Michael Sharp had taken to another corporal with a pool cue, ruining his mouth, removing three teeth, and fracturing his cheek in five places.

Other soldiers had seen the fight develop and claimed Sharp had been goaded, and in the washup, the bashed corporal had declined to press charges. There was no tribunal, no court martial, no resort to the criminal justice system—but it wasn't Sharp's first offense, and he was forced out of the army on an "administrative discharge" for "inappropriate conduct" that was "not in the interests of the Defence Force."

"Too violent for the soldiers," Rodrigues said. "Thing is, the way they got him, his dismissal, he loses his service rights."

"No veteran's pension," Riley said.

"Correct. And one more year in, he was eligible. He could have appealed and won, there was no due process. But again . . ."

"No lawyer," Riley said.

"Correct."

She looked at Sharp through the glass. He was capable of inflicting grievous bodily harm on a fellow soldier, and he'd subdued a raging Dew Lucas with a bat, but he didn't brag about his exploits. He'd been railroaded by the army, forfeiting his right to a lifelong pension, and he had walked away, accepting punishment without fuss.

"Is he stupid, or stoic?" Riley said.

Patel watched him. "A stoic would be rare, in our prancing zeitgeist."

"Look at his alibi," Rodrigues said. "I mean, c'mon. He's not even trying."

"That's what worries me," Patel said.

Riley took a breath, worried too. The killer was hyperorganized, the murder meticulously planned. If Sharp had done it, why not organize himself an alibi—have a drink at the bar, ask the chef for a staff meal?

"Pub CCTV?" Patel said.

"Nothing with Sharp on Monday afternoon or evening," Rodrigues said. "But the cameras are in the saloon, the entrance, and the car park. He can easily skirt them. His vehicle's out back."

"He could have been on foot," Patel said.

"Shoe and Tire are examining if he exited from the rear of the pub and walked," Rodrigues said. "But there's been rain."

Next door, Sharp was in police-issue slides after his barefoot arrest. "Let's go back in," Riley said, gesturing at Patel's manila folder. "Hit him with Murrumbateman."

39

Bowman sat in his Audi in the pub car park and typed out the story of Homicide detectives using the Tactical Operations Group to arrest a barman at the Packhorse Inn at Red Creek on suspicion of involvement in the murder of Penelope Armytage. No charges had been laid, sources said. Bowman filed and *The National* broke it, leaving Laura Nolan and *The Mirror* eating dust. Scoops always felt good, but shredding Nolan was extra sweet.

Folding his laptop, Bowman unfolded himself from the car and stretched. Nolan's Mitsubishi had departed. He crossed to Sandra near the main entrance, standing with Rachel and Kenny the chef. The pub would be closed for two days, according to police, and Sandra told Bowman he would need to vacate until probably Wednesday. There would be no staff on-site—even Sandra was going up to Branxton to stay with a nephew. The police allowed her and Bowman access to pack their bags, and Rachel and Sandra offered to drop Bowman and his car down at the Quirk. Kenny the chef bid them adieu—"See yers later but, eh."—and went his way on a motorbike.

Sandra drove the Audi, with Bowman beside her, and Rachel tailed in her Subaru to take Sandra back to her own car at the Packhorse. The pub drive was taped off at the main road, and Sandra waited while a uniformed officer lifted it to let them pass. "Dear oh dear," she said. Sandra was tough, a bush publican—but shock was descending. She had employed Michael, worked by his side, lived under the same roof, often alone with him in the building overnight.

"It's . . . a lot," Bowman said.

She drove, stared ahead. "I mean, really. I can't believe it."

He had his notebook on his lap.

Sandra turned into the Quirk and parked. "They'll have a room here, for sure," she said. "But we'll wait while you check."

There was movement around the motel, guests packing cars, checking out. Sunday. "I'll be right," he said.

She unclipped her belt.

He cleared his throat. "I'm going to need to work up a picture—of Michael," he said. "Can I ask you some questions?"

"Now?" Sandra asked.

"Yes."

The seat belt ran through her hand at her shoulder.

"I don't need to quote you," Bowman said. "And I'll talk to others too."

"Which others?"

He nudged his head toward the waiting Subaru. "Rachel. Some of the locals. Bob Bruce. It's all on background—I'll keep your names out of it. Unless there's something specific you want to say."

Her phone rang and she took it from her fleece pocket.

Bowman watched her hesitate. "Who is it?" he said.

"Unknown number."

"Guest booking?"

"Can't be. We've got a dedicated line. This is my private phone."

He put his hand out, touched the phone. "Don't answer. It'll be media."

"How would they get this number?"

Bowman tried not to scoff. "From a friend of a friend. Your locals. People in the district."

She worked her jaw, biting down. "Of course."

"Bob Bruce, for a start."

The phone had stopped ringing. "Why Bob?"

"He gave Penelope Armytage work. The press will have talked with him about that. Then this happens. The same press ring him back."

She turned the screen over in her lap.

Bowman pointed, swept his finger through an arc. "Every phone in a radius of twenty kays is now ringing—about the Packhorse and Michael. About you. That's just the grapevine. Every few minutes, the circle grows. Newcastle. Sydney media will send crews. Can I ask a favor?"

She swallowed.

"Can you just talk to me, no other press? You know me. I can show you what I'm doing, explain how things will work. Because right now, you're in the eye of a storm." He pointed up. "That's why it's so quiet." He made eyes at her phone. "Any minute, it's going to start flying. And it's gonna piss down for about a week."

"What about the police?"

"You talk to the police, obviously. But through Riley or Patel. You do everything they say—and nothing else. If some local cop tracks you down, uh-uh. You call Riley or Patel. If they don't answer, you call me."

"I don't have their numbers."

"I'll talk to them." Bowman dug out his phone and unlocked it. "What's yours?"

She said it, and he pecked it in and dialed, and the phone rang in her lap. They saved contacts as Rachel appeared at his window.

He lowered it. "All good?"

"Yeah." Rachel peered in. "Are we going?"

He jerked his head. "Get in."

The girl slid into the back and closed the door.

Bowman reiterated his lecture about the press and the cops, wanting to secure Rachel as another exclusive source.

She listened, shrugged a shoulder, and said, "Of course."

He drummed his pen. Nolan would be digging dirt. Michael was from Singleton, maybe Nolan was there, door-knocking his rellies.

Bowman was too flat-footed to follow—he needed a different angle. "You worked closely with Michael," he said, twisting to face Rachel. "Did you ever feel anything off him—coldness or cruelty? Did you feel threatened or unsafe?"

"No. Sort of the opposite." Rachel frowned. "He was, like, a bit stilted. You know, socially, he didn't flow. But he wasn't, like, creepy. Or even that awkward. He just wasn't smooth. He didn't try to charm you."

Sandra was nodding. "That's what I feel too. I *liked* having him around. He was never even moody. Never any sense of threat. But I knew if there was trouble, he could deal with it. Because I'd seen it with my own eyes."

"Dew?" Bowman said.

"Yeah. That was once. There were others. Drunk miners wanting a fight."

"And Michael, what . . . ?"

"He just put them down," Sandra said. "Calm as you like."

"Do you know why the army kicked him out?"

"No. Only rumors. He never talked about it."

"You didn't ask when you employed him?" Bowman said. "Criminal record? Background checks?"

"No," Sandra said. "He had a reference. A hotel near Canberra."

"Do you remember the name?"

"No. But I'll have it on file." A click of the tongue. "Or ask here." Her head bobbed at the Quirk. "They set it up."

Motel guests crossed the car park. Bowman flicked back through his notes. "Michael said Jayson Cassidy had found him work in the past. You're saying Jayson fixed up a job for Michael with you?"

"Yeah. Well, Jayson vouched for him. Michael mightn't know that. Jayson called me up and said there was a bloke he knew, from Singleton. He'd been away but was home, looking for work. I told him to send him in."

"Why didn't Jayson give him a job?"

"Doesn't need him." Sandra peered out at the Quirk. "No bar in there, no kitchen. They set up some system, so the place runs itself. Jayson hawks it around motels, like a road show. They sell it as an IT package—integrate your bookings, orders, wages, roster, keyless entry, CCTV. If you sign on, they'll install and bed it down. If there's a problem, Jayson's on call. For a fee."

"Singleton," Bowman said. "Michael have parents there, or siblings?"

"Dunno." Sandra shook her head, and so did Rachel.

"Any talk of a partner?"

"No." They shook their heads again.

Bowman stuffed his pen in the ring binds of his notebook and opened his door. The three of them got out.

Sandra handed him his car key and he thanked them, told them he'd call when they were in Branxton, then watched them get into the Subaru. He popped the trunk for his bag and headed for reception. He suspected Jayson Cassidy wouldn't speak to Laura Nolan—not after she'd gone after him in her story on Wednesday night. Still, Bowman wanted to get to Cassidy first and lock him down, another exclusive source.

40

Michael Sharp's eyes stayed on the table. Patel pulled the manila folder out from under her notepad and pushed a glossy A4 photograph of Jennifer and Andrew Morrow into his view. He placed a finger on the edge of the picture to pull it toward him. He stared at it for a time and then turned his palm away.

"Have you ever seen either of these people before?" Patel said.

"Maybe—the woman," he said. "Not sure."

"Have you ever been to Canberra?" Patel said.

"Yeah. Sure."

Riley had her arms crossed. "Ever been to Adelaide?"

The corners of his mouth hung down. "Been to Edinburgh. Yeah."

RAAF base. "When?" Riley said.

He blinked. "Few times. Coupla years now."

"When did you go to Canberra?" Patel said.

"Worked down there," he said. "Before I came up here."

"Where did you work?" Patel said.

"Motel. Bit out of Canberra. Murrumbateman."

"What was the motel called?"

"Aurora."

Patel paused. Chin down, eyes up, he watched them. She slid another A4 photograph toward him. Gina and John Watson.

Michael stared at the image for a long time.

"Ring a bell?" Riley said.

"Like, I dunno. Am I supposed to know them?"

"Do you recognize them?" Patel said. "Have you ever seen them?"

"No. I'd say never."

"You'd say?" Riley said.

"I seen a lot of people, eh. Working behind a bar."

Patel reached over for the photograph of the Morrows and held it up. "This woman's name is Jennifer Morrow. She lived in Canberra. You said you recognize her?"

"Maybe, is what I said."

Patel kept the picture up. "Jennifer Morrow stayed at the Aurora Murrumbateman for two nights last year, June twelfth and June thirteenth. You worked at the Aurora Motel from January last year until March this year. Is that correct?"

"Yeah." He sniffed. "Sounds right."

"Does the name Greg Gammage ring a bell?" Patel said.

"Yeah. Gammy."

"Who is that?" she said.

"He was the manager down there. Not a bad bloke"—he finished under his breath—"for a tool."

"He's still there, at the Aurora. We spoke with him. He sent through the staff roster for last June. You worked on June twelfth and you worked on June thirteenth."

"Prob'ly. Worked me like a dog, Gammy. He was lazy, but . . . That's why, you know, he bought what Jayson was selling."

The name detonated from nowhere, sucked the air out of Riley.

Patel went blank, stunned by the blast.

They sat there, mouths a little open. Patel recovered first. "Jayson?" she managed.

Michael sniffed again. "Yeah. That's why I was there. Jayson had been down a few times, setting up the system. Got me the job."

Riley, staring at the wall, tried to sound offhand. "You saw Jayson at the Aurora?"

"Yeah." He thought for a moment. "Once."

"Do you know the date?" Riley said.

His face scrunched: *Not likely.* He pointed at Patel's notebook. "Gammy'd know." His wrist turned. "Or Jayson."

Riley texted Rodrigues, who was watching through the glass.

"Mr. Sharp"—Patel was writing—"I'm going to give you three dates. I need you to think carefully. I need to know where you were on each of these days." She printed them in neat, large font, tore out the page, and laid it in front of him.

He studied it for a while, rubbed his chin. "Cor."

"Do you have a diary?" Patel said.

He looked confused, as though she'd asked him if he had a handbag. "Nah."

"What about the calendar on your phone?"

"Nah."

"If we bring your phone, will it help?"

He thought about that, eyes up to his left. "Yeah. Maybe."

"Social media, texts, emails? You may have taken photos"—Patel nodded at the list—"on those dates?"

"Maybe," he said. "Photos."

She stood. "What's the password for your phone?"

His gaze shifted to Riley, then back to Patel. The tip of his tongue touched his lips. "Zero-zero-seven-one," he said.

Patel went out. The door clicked closed.

Silence. Sharp studied his hands in his lap. Riley looked at the string of dates, upside down. Two, both from last year, marked the killings of Jennifer Morrow and Gina Watson: Friday, November 8, and Saturday, March 16. The third date, from two years back, was the night the Watsons had been checked in at the Aurora Murrumbateman: Wednesday, October 11. Twenty-three months ago.

"You said Jayson had been down at the Aurora a few times," Riley said. "But you only saw him there once?"

Sharp rubbed a finger, hard, under his lower lip.

"How's that work?" Riley said.

"They called him, I s'pose, to come install his system. He does that—then, you know, they're asking maybe if he knows any staff to come work there. So he lines me up for the job."

"I thought the point of Jayson's system was to automate things. Self-service, fewer staff. Like a caravan park."

Michael barked a laugh. "Wouldn't call it that to his face. He sells it as, like, integrated. But yeah."

"So if the system is installed, why are you hired?"

"'Cos Gammy sacked about nine others. He'd been runnin' breakfast, plus dinner and a bar, seven days. He shut it all down, got rid of the lot. He wanted one person to do ordering, stocking, maintenance, stripping beds, filling in on the front desk. That was me. Then there was a woman, part-time, did the laundry, made up the rooms. Gammy done the rest, and his missus."

"You were employed after Jayson put in the system. But you saw him there?"

"Yeah, later—down the track. I'm workin' there, and there's some problem with the IT." He scratched an ear. "Jayson came back. I saw him. We had tea."

"In the motel?"

"No. There's a pub. Bit down the road."

"But Jayson stayed the night in the Aurora?"

"Yeah."

Patel entered with Sharp's phone. She placed it between them on the table and sat.

"When you came up here, to the Packhorse," Riley said, "you did some work for Jayson, too, at the Quirk?"

"Bit, yeah."

"What did you do?"

"Just finished off with running the aircon. They hadn't done the ducting down one side."

"One side?"

"On the back row. You're staying there, yeah?"

Riley nodded.

"So, the two rows of rooms." He drew in a breath. "The front, on the car park, that was all sweet. But in the back row, the units were installed, yeah, when the builder walked off the job—didn't hook 'em up."

The motel's roof space had been empty except for a coil of unused ducting. In her mind, Riley retraced her steps around the exterior of the building. There were no utilities, no compressors or condensers, mounted on the walls. "Where were the units installed?"

"Up." He tipped his head back. "In the roof."

"Where in the roof?"

His eyes narrowed on her, appraising.

"We've been through the motel, including the roof. I don't recall any air-conditioning units."

He nodded. "You come up them back stairs and there's a big space?"

She was conscious of her breathing.

"There's a partition, further down." He waved ahead, two fingers. "Particleboard. Cuts across the room." He traced a finger sideways.

Her head tilted, she saw the partition wall.

He cocked an eyebrow. "You look behind there?"

They hadn't. The day they'd searched the motel's roof space, Rodrigues had called, warning that Jayson and Karen were heading home, telling them to get out. "Not sure," she said.

His frown weighed her response . . . found it unconvincing. "I reckon you'd remember if you looked."

Her pulse had picked up. "Why's that?"

He drew it out, sensing he had the initiative. "Units are there"—he held his hands up, pointing at ten and two o'clock—"in the corners."

"What else?"

"Man cave. Counters. Tools. Shelving. Old timber dresser. Keeps it real neat."

It went still. Patel didn't move, but Riley felt tendrils. A whisper. *Hyperorganized. Tool kit. He packs it away.*

41

A red-haired woman sat at the Quirk reception desk. A badge at her breast said KAREN—the name of Jayson Cassidy's wife, Bowman recalled. Dressed in tones of camel, lips puckering, she looked him over. "You press?"

"Yes, but I've been at the Packhorse for two weeks," he said, as though he'd been living down the road all his life.

It worked. Her mouth unwound. "Oh. You're that one."

He gave a humble smile.

"I saw the story." She saw his suitcase. "Pub kick you out?"

"Yeah, well—police shut it down. So here I am."

"We're filling up." She nodded at her screen. "Journos. But I'll fit you in. How long?"

"Two nights?"

"No problem. Poor Sandra."

Bowman rested his notebook on the joinery above the desk.

Karen pecked at her keyboard. "I always said it. He's a chameleon, that one. Could turn his hand to anything. Too quiet."

"How well did you know him?"

"Bit. But you best talk to Jayson—he knew him as a kid."

"How's he a chameleon?"

She stopped typing and exhaled. "I've been in hotels, motels all my working life. I've got a theory about certain types."

"What theory?"

"You're a certain type, working in a hotel," Karen said. "You spy a woman you like, a guest. She doesn't notice you, because—chameleon, you're good at blending into backgrounds. But you know her name, her home address." Karen waved at her screen. "It's all at the front desk."

Bowman had watched Michael at the Packhorse, his almost childlike fascination with Rachel. Riley had seen much less of the barman but had noted his behavior last night, the way he pestered the girl.

"What type?" Bowman said.

"Patient, observant, a loner." Karen looked over his shoulder and he turned: Guests were coming to check out. She handed him a room card. "Number three. Second on the left."

Bowman closed his book.

"You ask Jayson," she said. "He smelt it too."

Bowman looked at the door marked OFFICE behind her. "Where will I find him?"

Her eyes skimmed the ceiling. "Don't know where he's at. I'll tell him to come find you."

Michael Sharp's phone sat in the middle of the table, beside the piece of foolscap Patel had written the dates on. Riley pushed the phone toward Sharp. "Start with that third date." She pushed the paper at him too. "Friday, November eighth, last year. About ten months ago. Where were you?"

He held the phone flat, just off the table, visibly swiping at photos. "Not much round then," he said.

"Social media?" Patel said.

He glanced up, a shake of his head. "None of that."

"Were you in Murrumbateman?" Patel said. "Working at the Aurora?"

"Yeah. I did through Christmas. Left in like March, April."

"When you worked there," Riley said, "where did you live?"

"Canberra. In a flat. Right north."

"Address?"

Sharp gave a street name and number. "In Casey, it was called."

Riley took her phone and searched. She found the street and the block and zoomed out. The suburb Casey was on the boundary of Ngunnawal. She mapped the route from Sharp's place to the Morrow house. Six streets, 1.2 kays, a four-minute drive. You could walk it in fourteen. She held it out to Patel.

Sharp was tapping at his phone.

"Try the middle date," Riley said. "Saturday, March sixteenth. Last year."

He grunted.

Gina Watson had been strangled in Adelaide, five months after her stay at the Aurora.

Riley pushed her chair out and found herself standing, looking down at Sharp's fingers crawling over his phone. It wasn't adding up. They needed to move. "Were you working at the Aurora that March?"

"Think so, yeah, reckon just."

She heard her own voice, the grind of impatience. "When did you start?"

"Bit after New Year's." He held up the phone with an image. "That's me in Torquay. So, drove Geelong, round the bay, up the coast." With his free hand, he counted with his fingers. "Took me time, but I remember Jase called me 'bout the job. I was in Bairnsdale. That's mid-Jan." He went to scrolling and held up another picture: him, on his own, at a beach. "Early Feb., I reckon. That's when I started."

Riley stared at the one-way glass. Sharp hadn't seen Gina at the Aurora. He hadn't been employed at the motel when the Watsons had stayed there the previous October.

Patel leaned toward him. "Anything for March sixteenth?"

"N'yeah . . . actually." His tone changed. "Bloody bingo—that's it." He squinted at the screen and gave a whistle. "March fifteenth."

Riley's mouth was dry as she swallowed.

"That's me friend Joan, from Pucka." Sharp held out the phone. "She came through on her way up to Townsville. Stayed for three days in me flat."

There was a selfie of Sharp with a woman, mid-thirties.

Patel looked. "That's March fifteenth," she said.

"Yeah. But she was there the weekend, 'cos Sunday, we went to see Raiders versus Cowboys at Bruce—like, down the road." A smile. "Joanie's a massive Cowboys fan." He kept scrolling. "Here's us at the footy. On the Sunday—so March seventeenth."

Riley had crossed to the door. She went out.

Rodrigues was in the corridor with two uniformed constables. "Wait." He put a hand up. "We're not just riding off and letting him walk."

Patel joined them and closed the door.

"We need to hold him," Rodrigues said. "Get this Joan. Test the alibi."

"Sure." Riley watched, hands on hips, as Rodrigues spoke with the constables. They went in to retrieve Sharp.

"We've had a camera in the roof of the Quirk for forty-eight hours," Rodrigues said.

"And?" Riley said.

Rodrigues waited while the constables brought Sharp out, cuffed, and led him away. "We've got footage," he said. "We should review it."

Patel watched as Sharp disappeared around a corner. "You think he's playing us?"

"He's been in the attic," Rodrigues said. "He knows the whole layout . . ."

Muscles tensed in Patel's throat as Riley's stomach rolled.

"You see?" Rodrigues said. "Sharp's in Jayson's perv space."

"They're working together," Patel said.

42

Bowman went into Room 3 and kept the door open to the corridor while he stowed his suitcase and set up his laptop on a counter that ran along the wall. There was a desk chair and he sat, checking through the news.

The Mirror had the Sharp arrest, under Laura Nolan's byline and with a picture of Riley and Patel at the scene. He read it through. In the last paragraph, Nolan had taken a gratuitous swerve. Mr. Sharp is known to have worked at the Quirk motel in Red Creek, where he did maintenance for the owner Jayson Cassidy. Bizarre. It had to be Oakeshott gunning for Cassidy. Bowman didn't mind—he could use it to his advantage, show it to the Cassidys, and they'd freeze out Nolan and *The Mirror*.

He heard a voice in the hall and looked up to see Jayson Cassidy march past, talking on his phone. Bowman grabbed his notebook and crossed the room to peer into the hall. Cassidy walked down the guest corridor, and Bowman followed, jogging to catch up as the man came to the end, transferring his phone to his other ear to open a green door.

He went through. Bowman tailed him into an atrium, catching snatches of phrases—"roster . . . go back . . . June"—as Cassidy went into a room marked Store. Bowman got a foot in the door and waited, thinking the man would grab whatever he had come for and emerge. But . . . nothing.

Bowman ducked his head in: a storeroom, racks on the walls . . . no sign of Cassidy. He heard a key in a lock, then a metallic click and squeak. He went through and, behind a fridge, saw Cassidy's back exiting through a red door. Bowman scurried, got a foot in, glimpsed through: a bare Besser-block chamber, Cassidy breathing hard on the phone, going up a set of steel stairs.

Bowman stayed hidden. At the top, Cassidy came to a landing, spat into the phone—"Wait . . . Morrow?"—pulled open an unlocked door, and disappeared.

Bowman tried the outer handle of the red door. No give, it would lock closed. If he went up the stairs, he couldn't come back out this way.

He looked around the storeroom. There was a mop within reach, and he grabbed it and laid the handle along the ground through the doorway to keep it from closing. He took the stairs two at a time and cracked open the landing door.

A roof space, cavernous, dimly lit. Not a sound. Cassidy had either traversed through and was elsewhere, or he was off the phone. Or both.

Bowman slipped in, tested the handle to make sure it wouldn't lock, and let the door close quietly. He went to call out but held his breath instead. The air was heavy, not to be disturbed.

He stayed still, fearing he had come too far. He needed to speak to Jayson before other reporters found him, but standing there, Bowman felt soiled, as though he'd raised a veil on a hidden place.

A noise now, down the room, straight ahead. The thud of something dropped to the floor, then an indignant curse. There was a central walkway laid over rafters, and twenty meters down, branches left and right. The middle path led on to a walled cross-section of particleboard. The sounds came from behind the partition.

Riley drove with Patel beside her and Rodrigues in the back. No siren, but her lights were flashing as she passed Sunday traffic and squealed left onto Broke Road.

Rodrigues's phone pinged. "Jayson Cassidy sold his management program to the Aurora Murrumbateman two years ago," he read. "He went down there for three days from Tuesday, October tenth, stayed two nights—October tenth and eleventh. Coincides with the Watsons on the Wednesday, October eleventh."

"Fuck me," Patel said.

"Then, eight months in," Rodrigues said, "there's a glitch with the system. They call him back. He heads down in June—again, midweek. Wednesday, June twelfth. He stays two nights. Coincides exactly with Jennifer Morrow."

They were passing cars parked on the verge, and lines of tents and stalls in a paddock, and a sign that said HANDMADE MARKETS. Riley slowed into the middle of the road so as not to clean up any basket weavers, then corrected left and hit gravel to undertake a big Porsche that had drooled out from a fudge factory.

"Cassidy's there, he marks them," Patel said. "He's all over the front desk, installing or fixing the system. So now he's got their names, addresses. But still, at their actual houses, how's he getting in?"

"With Sharp," Rodrigues said. "He's practical. Picking locks."

Riley didn't think so. At first, they had thought Karen was involved, talking her way past the victims. Now they had Sharp, picking locks. It was neater than all that. Riley came up to the wide Pokolbin roundabouts and blasted through. "This system Jayson's selling," she said. "It runs everything, right?"

"That's the idea," Rodrigues said. "Full integration, lower costs."

Full access. Riley still had the all-access card Belinda had given her at reception. "He's going into rooms," she said.

"At the Aurora?" Rodrigues said.

"At the Aurora, at the Quirk. All the guest rooms are on cards. He can go where he likes."

"Your room," Patel said. "Then mine."

"Right," Riley said. "It's like a habit. He does it all the time."

"Priya's keys," Rodrigues said.

Patel looked around at him, then across at Riley.

"He marks a guest," Riley said. "When she's out, he goes into her room, looking for house keys. If he gets lucky, he takes them, gets them cut, puts them back. In Red Creek, that's a round trip of less than an hour. In Murrumbateman, the same. He tells the manager, *Sorry, I need to buy a digital cable.* He can pop to Canberra, gets Gina's key cut. Next time, to mix it up, he does the Morrow key in Yass. Now he's got name, address, key to the house."

"Bit hit-and-miss," Rodrigues said. "How many people leave their keys in the room?"

"Sure, it doesn't always work," Riley said. "But if someone's away from home and not driving, or if their partner drives, sometimes they will. I mean, why carry things you don't need? All *he* needs is patience."

Patel swayed as they went left. Leaving the station, Rodrigues had called Tactical, but they would still be ten minutes out. Riley kept her foot down, thinking Cassidy would have seen news of the Sharp arrest. No details or links to Canberra or Adelaide had been released, so the reporting only named Penelope Armytage. But Cassidy would be jittery, sweating on how the cops had connected Sharp to Penelope Armytage—and where the arrest might lead.

Another thought worried Riley: Jayson had recommended Michael Sharp to Greg Gammage, the manager in Murrumbateman. After today's police inquiries, Gammage might well have called Jayson and laid out the whole show: *The cops have been asking about your mate Michael Sharp, guests named Watson and Morrow, these particular dates.* If that was the case, Jayson would be destroying evidence and preparing to bolt, or already on the move.

From the back, Rodrigues made a noise, and Riley adjusted her mirror to look at him. He was reading on his phone.

"What?" she said.

"*The Mirror,*" he said. "Nolan's report. It says Michael Sharp was arrested in connection to the murder of Penelope Armytage, but then, at the end, it jumps to Jayson Cassidy. It links Michael to Jayson."

"How?"

"Says Sharp did maintenance work for Cassidy at the Quirk."

"So that's the aircon," Patel said. "The roof."

"Might just be Oakeshott feeding Nolan scraps," Riley said. "Oakeshott knows the aircon was unfinished, because he pulled the plug on the job. Word gets around that Cassidy got Sharp in to finish it."

"Still, we'd just brought Sharp in, thinking he was it. But these fuckers"—Rodrigues held up the *Mirror* story—"were already thinking about Cassidy."

The Aurora, the victims, the dates: It all pointed to Jayson Cassidy and clicked into place. Riley couldn't see Neville Oakeshott in the main frame—he was a bit player, a corrupt opportunist blowing smoke.

The Red Creek intersection was snarled with vehicles. Riley wove through and went right. They passed the town houses, the Packhorse Inn sign, the pub driveway strung with tape.

The *Mirror* story stoked her fear that Gammage would contact Cassidy. "We've been drilling Gammage," she said. "He'll be searching the news. He knows Cassidy—and he knows Cassidy knows Sharp. Even if he doesn't see the link in *The Mirror*, he'll probably call Jayson."

"So we assume Cassidy knows we're all over him," Patel said.

Riley nodded: *How to proceed?*

"If he's still here"—Patel looked out—"he's in a corner."

"Tactical goes in, takes him down," Rodrigues said.

Riley topped the rise, went down the dip, and turned into the Quirk. Pulling up, she felt her heart stop.

The Audi.

"Bowman," Patel whispered.

43

From where he'd been standing at the door, Bowman pushed into the attic.

Of course there were no dark currents in the room, he was overreacting. Moments of physical cowardice dotted his past, and they reared up as he trod onto the boardwalk. It was spongy underfoot. Cowardice stayed with you as shame. Bowman had written about that, when he'd written about Riley. Riley was human, so shame-wounded— but not by cowardice. Cowardice was not among Riley's sins. She would never say that, of course, but Bowman knew. For his book, she'd talked to him about fear, about what it did to her body when she was confronted with it, and about how she called on her training to try to overcome it.

He padded along the walkway. He had no training, so he summoned Riley. *Keep moving, be brave.* He tried swallowing to dismiss his unease. He was trespassing, that was all, a journalist with his foot in the door. All he risked was Jayson Cassidy's displeasure at the intrusion.

He came to the partition and saw it was not a single unbroken wall, but two sections coming from either side that didn't quite meet in the middle. They overlapped, creating a short gap to pass through. He slid in and along, sticking his neck out to look.

It was a storage area, with shelving, cupboards, chests of drawers. Jayson Cassidy was standing a couple of meters away, his back to Bowman. At shoulder height to Cassidy's left, a cabinet door was swung open, and rows of keys hung on hooks on a pegboard. Three rows of three, Bowman counted—nine keys on the board. They must be spares for the guest rooms. Cassidy was wearing blue nitrile gloves, and there was a black sports bag on the floor to his right. He yanked open a drawer, pulled out an A4 folder, and reached up, took a key off a peg, and dropped it in a clear plastic pocket in the file. Bowman watched as Cassidy removed all the keys, one at a time, placing each in a separate plastic sleeve.

"Knock, knock," Bowman said.

Cassidy spun around fast in a crouch, his eyes flashing, vicious, his face a wild mask.

"Whoa." Bowman shied back, rocked by the sheer hate.

A hiss, Cassidy scuttling to his right like a spider. The man's hand went out to a shelf, pale fingers wrapping on a handle. Hissing again as he closed in on Bowman with a knife.

Time stretched, Jayson crept up slow. Bowman, immobilized, saw his dead brother, Chick, with Riley on her farm, and heard a murmur: *Be brave.*

◆　◆　◆

Riley got out of the Calais and called to Rodrigues in the back, "Paramedics."

Fear roiled as she crossed the car park and went through the entry doors. Karen at reception.

Riley walked straight up and leveled her Glock at the pale face. "Hands where I can see them." Karen's hands went up. Riley twitched the gun left. "This way." Karen edged from behind the desk into the space of the lobby. "On your knees," Riley said. "Now face down on the floor." Karen lowered herself. Patel was beside Riley, and Rodrigues was coming through the door.

"Cuff her," Riley said to Rodrigues and, nodding for Patel, moved to the office door behind reception. Patel went to the handle, locked eyes with Riley, and pulled it open. Riley went in, sweeping her Glock top right to left across the room. No one. No one behind the door.

She moved down the side of the room, checking the aisles and under the rows of desks. She stood at the CCTV monitors and looked, breathing. No movement on the screens.

"Clear," she said, and came back out and past Patel.

Rodrigues had Karen cuffed and sitting on the floor.

"Where's Jayson?" Riley said.

Karen tried to swallow and gawped. Riley crouched and got in her face. Karen made a noise, trying to speak. Her eyes, up the walls, touched the ceiling.

Riley looked at the roof. "He up there?" she said. "In his perv space?"

Karen was gray under her red speckled hair.

Riley straightened.

"Tactical in seven," Rodrigues said.

"There's a journalist here." Riley looked down at Karen. "Adam Bowman?"

Karen managed to get words out. "Number three."

Riley headed down the guest corridor with Patel at her shoulder. The door to Bowman's room was open, and Riley went in. His laptop on the counter, his suitcase in a corner.

Patel stuck her head in the bathroom. "No," she said.

They went back into the hall and down through the green door. The store was open, and there was a mop handle lying as a chock in the doorway behind the fridge. Riley felt panic wedge in her throat as she and Patel went through and up the stairs. On the landing Patel opened the door, and Riley went in and swept the attic in a crouch.

She spoke low. "Clear."

Patel came in, and Riley silenced her with her eyes and strained to hear. There'd been something. They stood. There it was again, a low moan.

Riley was moving fast down the central walkway. As she got close, she saw that the partition wall came in from left and right and overlapped, creating a gap in the middle. She halted, Patel with her. The opening was two meters long by half a meter wide, a funnel to a space behind. More noises—thuds and scrapes of someone packing. The whiz of a zipper. *Tool kit.* Riley went first.

Shoulder to the partition, elbows bent with the Glock, she rolled her neck to glance in. She took in Cassidy, his back to her, three meters away, a hunting knife to his right on some shelving. Her eyes went down and to the left.

Rage pulled her training away in a wave. Bowman fetal on a sheet of plastic, red hands to torso, bleeding out.

She made no noise, but Jayson seemed to sense her. His hand reached for the knife as he turned, fingers gripping, arm bending to throw.

Riley shot him between the eyes, killing his momentum. A long moment held him in suspension. He sagged, began to drop. Riley put two in his chest—for the hell of it, for the victims.

Shrugging out of her fleece, she was at Bowman, trying to stanch the flow. Patel was on her knees beside her, on the phone.

His face was clammy, but he swallowed. "I saw my brother," he said.

"Chick." Riley leaned in and kissed his forehead. He was cold. "What'd he say?"

"That you were coming. That I should be brave."

CODA

Before his shower, Bowman had laid his clothes out on the bed, and he peered at them now. A moment earlier, in his bathroom mirror, he'd been examining his scar. He was scared of heights, but when a builder had erected scaffolding on the house and dragged him up to look at something on the roof, he'd found his fear had gradually abated. He'd stared it down, his fear of heights. He was trying to do the same with his scar—locking eyes, playing chicken, seeing if it might blink first. The scar was patient, and was winning.

He started to dress, swathing his abdomen in the sheen of a new shirt. The surgeons were happy—physically his recovery would be full and complete. The blade had nicked his spleen and missed all else that mattered. Except his psyche. He notched his belt and chose his favorite socks. He'd been in sarongs and T-shirts for days because he hadn't left the house.

Riley had him seeing a psychologist, a woman who treated police post-trauma. Bowman went along, he talked, he did his sessions—they might be helping, he wasn't sure. Trauma, he believed, was subjective, and thus, difficult to treat. To each their own.

In his thinking, he tried to put the attack in perspective: Worse things were happening to people every day. In the clogged carnage of history, his stabbing really was just a flesh wound. This was true, but Bowman feared his perspective had changed, or that he might have lost it. He couldn't rationalize his attack away and found himself flinching at shadows on the street—or in bed, in dreams.

One thing had helped, and Riley had organized that too. She'd sat Bowman down with the husbands of Jayson Cassidy's three known victims. Patel and Rodrigues had been there, too, with Riley. They'd all had lunch, the seven of them, at the Dry Dock in Balmain. Toward the end of the meal, others had arrived—Nigel Armytage's parents and John Watson's sister. Bowman found perspective, looking in their eyes.

Afterward, on the footpath, the sister had given Bowman a gentle hug.

"What will you do now?" he had asked.

"I'm taking John back to Adelaide tomorrow." She'd nodded toward her brother. "I came up to bring him home."

In his bedroom, Bowman smiled. He finished dressing and went through the cottage and out his door. It was January, a humid morning, as he walked up the lane to meet Riley in the Calais. She had a day trip planned. They were driving to Red Creek.

Bowman was still fragile, Riley could tell from the way he sat in the car. She had never been cut, but she'd seen it with colleagues, and she knew the road back was winding and narrow.

The psychologist was concerned about Bowman living alone. Riley did her best to check in all the time, and so did Patel. *His* colleagues, not so much. A couple of them had been good to begin with but soon dropped off. Riley understood. Bowman had media people he got on with, but he didn't have journalist friends. And, having gone freelance, he'd written himself out of the newsroom—he had no exposure to the office and worked from home, alone. O'Neil had stood up, visiting Bowman through his convalescence, and had even taken him to the pub for a beer. The forensic psychiatrist Wayne Farquhar, returned from a

European sabbatical, had shown up, too, dropping in on Bowman and talking with him on the phone.

There was no family, no kids or spouse or partner, no nieces or nephews. Bowman's parents and only sibling were dead. Riley knew it was Chick, the little brother, whom Bowman missed most. He spoke about it, sometimes, the knowledge that as you got older, your infant attachments returned home. Life is a circle, and it ends in yearning for those you loved as a child.

Farquhar had called Riley last week. "Keep with him, it's going to take time," the psychiatrist had said. "What worries me is, home alone he retreats in on himself, stops even leaving the house."

Hence the drive.

She went left off Darling onto the back streets, glimpses of the harbor and the top decks of a cruise ship very close, tied up at White Bay. They left the peninsula and crossed the bridges.

"Rodrigues call?" she said.

"Yeah."

"And?"

"Another week."

She nodded. Two anti-corruption agencies had opened covert investigations into Neville Oakeshott, on the back of allegations made by the former Cessnock councillor Matthew Drummond. Rodrigues was in the loop, but the case was being run out of Newcastle and kept very dark. Oakeshott, Laura Nolan, and the bent cop Harris were all going down. When the raids came, Rodrigues would give Bowman the drop.

They drove north.

"Saw the Quirk's on the market," Bowman said.

Riley hadn't heard that, but she knew Karen Cassidy would have to sell. Karen had pleaded guilty to complicity in her husband's voyeurism and had her license to operate a venue permanently revoked. That was all. She denied any role in or knowledge of Jayson's murder spree, and there was incontrovertible evidence to prove she'd been in Newcastle on the dates of the Morrow and Watson murders. Riley believed Jayson Cassidy had acted alone.

But he'd had nine keys in his folder, including one to Penelope Armytage's front door. A second had opened the Watson cottage in Adelaide. Another, it was believed, was to the Morrow house in Ngunnawal, but the locks had been changed, and so no one could be sure.

That left six keys. One, horribly, had slipped into the lock and opened the front door at Patel's unit in Harris Park.

That left five. Riley didn't know whether they represented potential victims, or Jayson Cassidy had used them to access and kill others in the past. Databases were being scoured—missing women, unsolved strangulations—and run against guest lists of the former Cassidy hotel in Newcastle, the Quirk, the Murrumbateman Aurora, and seven more motels contracted with Jayson. So far, nothing.

The fact that Jayson had copied Patel's key had rocked Riley and dispelled the notion that killing Penelope Armytage on his doorstep was a departure for Jayson. They knew his MO, but they didn't know his patterns. He'd lifted a key from a Homicide cop at his motel, and he might have planned to pay her a visit next year, when things had blown over. If he was operating like that—reckless, arrogant—anything was possible. All they knew was that he'd killed in other states and close to home—he was comfortable anywhere, he didn't have a zone. This fed Riley's instinct that there were more victims out there.

Bowman was pensive beside her as they drove through Cessnock into the vineyards and stopped at the Packhorse for lunch. Sandra was there, and Michael was serving. Rodrigues had dug into Michael and come up with nothing, not one piece of hard evidence to support the theory he was involved with any of Jayson's crimes. Indeed, Michael's friend Joan had reinforced his alibi, proving beyond doubt that he had been in Canberra at the time Gina Watson was murdered in Adelaide. Michael had been freed without charge, and his response to his arrest had been stoic: He'd gone back to work.

At the pub, there was no sign of Rachel—she was in Bali for a week before heading to uni in Bathurst. Rachel had visited Bowman on the ward in Royal North Shore in September. The girl had seen him again a week before Christmas, calling on him at home in Balmain with her mother and father and a case of the family Shiraz. Riley understood that, too, the way bonds were forged.

They sat up at the counter to eat. Michael put a big wineglass before Bowman and tipped in a healthy dose of red. Riley was driving, and stuck to water.

Bowman raised the glass to her. "Riedel?" he said.

She made a face. That had been another erratic play from Jayson. The Riedel glass in Penelope Armytage's kitchen had been matched to a single glass found on a shelf in Jayson's attic.

"They're the glasses Oakeshott gave to Karen?" Bowman said.

"No. They were still in the house. Jayson must have bought an identical pair and taken one when he killed Penelope, leaving it at the scene. He'd stowed the other one in his roof."

"He thought it through," Bowman said.

"Sure." Karen, prompted by Jayson, had told the police Oakeshott gave Riedel glasses as presents, while Jayson had pushed it further, claiming Oakeshott would have given Riedel glasses to Penelope as part of a campaign to sell her the town house.

"He plants a glass," Bowman said. "It's like a gimmick. That's heedless."

To Riley, it was more of the same. The Cassidys and Oakeshott had fallen out, and Jayson had been impervious to pressure from the developer. To Jayson, it was a game, taunting and toying with Oakeshott over the sale of the Quirk. The glass was a manipulation to throw shade and frame Oakeshott, planned *and* impetuous.

After lunch, they drove past the Quirk, still shuttered, and Riley picked up the road to Broke. The state forest was dried thin by summer, khaki and yellow. At the edge of the village, she slowed and turned right, into the grid of streets, and followed her nose to the house, the green Navara ute in the drive.

As she got out, she heard the bang of a screen door and looked up to see him on the porch. He'd been waiting, keeping an eye. He knew she was coming, because he'd asked her, and she'd said yes and given him a date and a time.

Today, 3:00 p.m. Now.

He came down the path through the gate to where she was propped on the hood.

Brad Lucas, her first friend, whom she'd loved like a brother when she was five.

He stopped, kept a little distance, greeted her with a nod.

It was sad to look at him. She tried to keep it from showing on her face.

"You remember, we'd get the bus?" he said.

From the first day of Kindy, they'd walked together to the school bus. Until maybe Year 4. His eyes had blazed so clear and bright.

"The land," he said. "Thought you might want it back."

"The land?" she said.

"Your place."

She blinked, unsure what the offer was. "You want to sell me the farm?"

"Yeah, but cheap. Like how we picked it up, after you left."

She looked away. "What's your dad say?"

"Don't care. It's in me name, like a tax dodge. Anyway, he's taken enough."

Riley didn't want a farm. "What would I do with it?" she said.

"Nothin'." He shrugged. "I'll do the grapes. You never even need come up. But then, down the track—it's yours."

"Down the track?"

"One day. You'll see."

Bowman had got out and was beside her.

Brad nodded in recollection. The three of them had stood like this once before.

Riley knew where, and smiled at the symmetry. She'd taken Bowman to the farm, on instinct, led by her mother's reading of his book and pulled by Chick, his dead brother.

Life was a circle.

Maybe Brad was right. One day she'd want to come home.

ACKNOWLEDGMENTS

I'm indebted to Dr. Allan Cala, Gary Jubelin, and Detective Sergeant Jenny Chrystal for their generosity (and patience) in explaining to me aspects of their work in forensic pathology, homicide investigation, and technical evidence. In the Hunter Valley, the winemakers Iain Riggs and Andrew Margan shared their knowledge and wisdom. And heartfelt thanks to my friend Richard Parker from Long Rail Gully Wines at Murrumbateman. My geologist mate John Howard guided me along Triassic cliffs down into coal measures. Curly Collins led me around a potter's wheel.

The reference to the joke that "Poets don't drive" is from *The Information* by Martin Amis. The idea for the viewing platform in the Cassidys' attic stems from "The Voyeur's Motel" by Gay Talese, *The New Yorker*, April 11, 2016.

THANKS/LOVE

Gracie Doyle. Cate Paterson. Catherine Drayton.
Kate Goldsworthy. Angela Handley.
Rachel Norfleet. Kellie Osborne. Jill Schoenhaut. Emma Reh.
Jarrod Taylor.
Steve Waterson. Malcolm Knox.
Meredith Rose. Tom Gilliatt. Christine Farmer.
Kelly Morton. Kate Mumford.
Scott Hedge. Daniel Hanna.
John Wilson. John Ferguson.
Keith Johnson.
Mark Sundquist—niche legal advice.
Luke McCormack—hotter than a solar flare.
Rob Carlton. Misha Hammond.
Mick Wines. Andrew Crocker.

And, as always, Sachin, Shivani, Sanjay.
Last and foremost—Ritu Gupta.

About the Author

Photo © 2022 John Feder

Matthew Spencer was a journalist at *The Australian* for twenty years, with long stints running the Foreign News desk and as opinion editor. He has written for newspapers and magazines in Uganda and Kenya and been published in *The Australian Financial Review* and *The Sydney Morning Herald*. He has an honors degree in English literature from the University of Sydney. *Black River*, his debut and the first novel in the Rose Riley series, won the 2023 Inaugural Danger Award for Debut Crime Fiction. Spencer lives in Sydney with his wife and their three children.